VIOLENT BLUE YONDER

VIOLENT BLUE YONDER

AERIAL ALTERNATIVE HISTORY

Edited by

JAMES YOUNG

DEDICATION

To the men of No. 303 Squadron, Royal Air Force. May your tenacity in the face of adversity and defiance against overwhelming odds continue to serve as an example to further generations.

THE WAR GOD'S WORDS (AS RELAYED TO YOUR EDITOR...)

Violence. A simple word encompasses all the horror, madness, and chaos that is the universal language between you foolish mortals. Given how easy you slip into worshipping me by your thoughts and actions, it is unsurprising that eventually you would take your conflicts to the heavens. Indeed, after watching that idiot Icarus ignore the warnings and incur my brethren Apollo's ire, I quite hoped that you would be clashing in the skies far sooner than you did. I waited for millennia to hear that sweet, sweet sound of a human being brought crashing to earth to earth in flames. Although tempted to speed the process along (my sister, Athena, is not the only one who can give foresight), we all know what happened with the last god who brought you an incendiary gift.

So instead I watched and waited as you took your first tentative, faltering steps into the heavens. Laughed as you tried to match Hermes' speed, cackled when you failed to mirror Nike's agility and, ultimately, smiled in anticipation as you finally reliably reached out to touch Aether's face. Even as you prepared to make millions of sacrifices to me in the traditional ways of bleeding in the mud and feeding Poseidon's denizens, I earnestly awaited your first attempts to murder each other in the realm you called the "blue yonder," for as the god of war it is *my* purview to who lives, who dies, who suffers once you have set upon this path. Thus when you released the forces of nationalism, it was I that set the paths that you trod upon.

But even as I decided the fates of nations, the end of empires and, most amusingly, the deaths of rulers, I often wondered "What if..?" For while I do not have the gift of Chronos to change time, I can certainly see for a short distance what the Fates would have wrought had I or you mortals made different choices. As it is my understanding that some of you even find such tales of "alternate history" to be entertaining, I have brought you a dozen tales of what might have been. From the time of your canvas falcons, there are stories of your most prominent warrior ("Perchance to Dream"), pilots who tried to avert disaster at high cost ("In Darkening Storms"), and those from a wholly different timeline of alliances ("Friends in High Places"). Although I had hoped for more flaming comets that were formerly primitive machines held together by flammable glue, there is something to be said for channeling dear Athena than myself.

Thankfully Athena's calming influence is swiftly lost as we move into aviation's golden age. Although I found the Romans to be a particularly annoying people with their divine theft (what kind of name is *Mars*?!, Philip Wohlrab's portrayal of them in "Eagles of Dacia" has me both rethinking their martial abilities and the lost potential of what you called the "interwar" period. I am sure that feeling will only grow within you as well after reading Lee Allred's "Airacuda." Oh what might have been with hostile Canadians and Americans dueling over the vast emptiness of the Great Lakes.

Please, pardon my wistful sighing as we slip from what might have been to different versions of the blood letting that actually was. I understand why you called World War II "The Big One," and the possibilities of different fates could fill a volume of their own.* Alas, space constraints exist even for the divine, so this volume has an alternate Battle of Britain ("Londonfall"), a modern day samurai's survival ("Sword of the Sun"), and what happens when you mix atomic weapons with submarine search and rescue ("Morning Suns"). I am partial to how your species' greatest ceremony in my name actually turned out, but fiddling with these what ifs brought me more pleasure than watching Achilles in a Trojan temple.

I'd have even more fun than that if Zeus would just let me have

* Editor's note: Amusingly enough, there's an entire World War II alternate history anthology entitled *The Big Ones* that this crazy Greek god apparently doesn't know about. Further proof that if these yahoos actually had foresight, Hera would've had Zeus... nevermind. Anyway, feel free to go check that out.

Humanity to go whole hog with splitting the atom, but alas father has strictly forbidden *that*. Instead, I am only left to dream about what chaos would arise while reading Eric Swedin's "Foolish Games." For those who want a little less dying in a rain of plutonium hellfire, "Per ardua ad astra" and "Zero Dark Thirty" provide two more instances where *I* would have let things spiral out of control, but *someone* (*cough* Eleos *cough*) decided to snitch. Finally, if you want something that sets the traditional Cold War on its head, I suggest "Red Tailed Tigers." Odds are it's why you're currently reading this introduction, seeing as how Robin Olds' P-80 gunning down a Me-262 on the cover. Don't worry, toying with the unholy love child of the Tuskegee Airman and American Volunteer Group squaring off with exiled Frenchmen flying Nazi castoffs was as fun as it sounds. Put a smile on my face the rest of the day, and I hope this anthology does the same for you – Ares

CONTENTS

IN DARK'NING STORMS

Rob Howell

IN DARK'NING STORMS

31 March 1915

The band started playing the moment they could see the famous mustache rise above the deck.

The normally bright eyes over that mustache were hard and black. They flicked from the officer at attention in front of him to a group of men clustered at the bow of the ship. He turned to the officer. "Permission to come aboard?"

Captain Washington Irving Chambers of the USS *Langley* saluted. "Yes, Mr. President."

"Thank you, Captain Chambers." Teddy Roosevelt returned the captain's salute. "And I'll thank you for dismissing this band. We have too much to discuss for all the normal formalities."

"Of course." He glanced at his executive officer. "Dismiss the welcome party."

Commander Pope Washington saluted, turned to the band, and commanded, "Welcome party, dismissed!"

The band and honor guard saluted and left.

President Roosevelt gestured at the men who had followed him aboard the *Langley*. "Have you met Admiral Fletcher?"

"No, sir." Chambers saluted the Commander-in-Chief of the United States Navy's Atlantic Fleet.

"I apologize, Captain," said Admiral Frank F. Fletcher. "These aren't the circumstances in which I had hoped we'd meet."

"I understand, sir. I appreciate you coming to see us personally."

"President Roosevelt has convinced me that your project has great potential. I have, of course, seen all the reports that suggest the *Langley* is a waste of money. However, I remember my time with the Bureau of Ordnance, and I wanted to see what you're doing here before we make any decisions."

"Thank you, sir."

Chambers turned to the other admiral and saluted. "Welcome aboard again, Admiral Mayo."

Admiral Henry T. Mayo returned the salute. "Captain Chambers, you look like hell. When did you last get some sleep?"

"Last night."

"How many hours?"

Chambers looked embarrassed. "Two, sir."

"And the night before?"

"Even less."

Roosevelt shook his head. "I appreciate your dedication, but we're going to need you to have a clear head."

"Yes, Mr. President."

Roosevelt gestured at the last person behind him, a civilian. "In any case, you've met Mr. Curtiss, I'm sure."

"Yes, sir. Welcome aboard." Chambers held out his hand.

"Thank you, Captain," replied the spare man with deepset eyes.

The President tugged down his vest. "Now that the introductions are over, let's get to it."

"Yes," agreed Fletcher. "I read the report from the yard, but I wanted to come see the damage myself."

"If you'll follow me." Captain Chambers gestured, and they walked to the bow.

Several men in cheap suits and loose ties pointed at various things. A number of workmen bustled around. The bulk of the damage had been to the forward starboard strut holding up the flight deck. A temporary replacement had been fitted to hold up the undamaged wood planks of the deck and sheets of plywood had been laid to cover the scorched, damaged portions.

"I'd like to hear your description of what happened."

"Yes, sir. We were trying out the new bomb racks for our BE.2.cs.

When Lieutenant Bronson started to pull up to fly, the left-hand bomb fell off the rack and landed on its fuse. It exploded, as you can see, and flipped the plane over the bow. We assume both Bronson and Lieutenant Welsh, riding in the front seat, were killed instantly."

"We can hope for that small favor, Captain."

"Yes, Mr. President."

"What engine did you have on her?" asked Curtiss.

"A Liberty L-8. We've needed the extra power-to-weight ratio for increased payloads. With those, the BE.2.cs can even carry the short Bliss-Leavitt Mark Sevens. Without an observer, of course."

Curtiss sighed and ran his fingers through his hair. "I worry about those."

"What do you mean, Mr. Curtiss?" asked Roosevelt.

"Well, Mr. President, thanks to your efforts getting appropriations for aviation in general, we've managed incredible advances. The Aircraft Production Board has done great work these past five years. Those Liberty engines wouldn't have been available so quickly without it, nor, for that matter, the aerial torpedoes. However, I wonder if we're going too fast."

"With all that's happening in Europe, I don't think that's unwarranted," said Admiral Mayo.

"I don't disagree, Admiral. However, my first guess at what happened here is the power of the L-8 and the acceleration these pilots must use to lift off from the *Langley* torqued or twisted the airplane's wing, which was originally designed for an engine with a third of the horsepower. That twisted wing then caused the rack prototype to release the bomb. I'll bet anything that the engineers designing the new racks didn't take that into account."

"Makes sense, Mr. Curtiss," agreed Chambers. "We've been adding and upgrading these birds since we got them, and they bear little resemblance to the original ones we bought in 1913."

"We're pushing the mechanics, as well," mused Mayo. "We keep accelerating their training, but we're expanding naval aviation so fast they almost have to learn on the go."

"Then we should slow down the program," stated Fletcher.

"With respect, sir, I disagree," blurted Washington. He looked as startled as anyone at his presumption in this assemblage.

"Continue, Commander Washington," directed Roosevelt.

"Well, Mr. President..." he hesitated.

"Too late now, Pope," said Chambers with a smile. "But I have an idea what you're about to say, since you've said it to me often enough during these past months. They'll want to hear it."

"Yes, sir." The commander straightened. "Mr. President, I was on the *Maine* at Santiago de Cuba."

"You were?"

"Yes, sir. I was sent by Captain Crenshaw to lead the lifeboat party to safety." His eyes dropped. "I was the highest-ranking survivor."

"But only because Crenshaw ordered you off the *Maine?*" asked Fletcher.

"Yes, sir."

The admiral's mouth tightened. "And how does that inform you in this instance?"

"Sir. I'd have gladly followed Crenshaw into that, even knowing it was to our deaths. We knew at that moment the rest of the squadron needed time to reform against the second Spanish squadron."

"Yes. Fighting Bob's report made that clear."

"Well, Admiral, if the *Langley* had been there with these aircraft, the *Maine* would have survived."

Fletcher glanced at the President and then back at Washington. "And why is that, Commander?"

"At any given moment, we have over twenty BE.2.cs fit to fly. We have over a hundred of the Mark Seven torpedoes in our magazines."

"Are you saying they would have sunk the ships in that squadron, Commander? Yes, they were Spanish, but there were two battleships and two armored cruisers in that group."

"Probably not, sir, but they didn't have to *sink* them. All they'd have had to do was slow them until the rest of the squadron could reform. *That*, Admiral Fletcher, *that* we can do. Right now. With the training Lieutenant Commander Ellyson has pounded into them."

"Those that have survived, at least," said the President.

"Yes, sir." Washington paused. "Sir, we've all heard the nickname. The *Langley* is 'Teddy's Toy' to every newspaperman."

"And Congressman."

"Yes, sir. But it's the 'Covered Wagon' to us. It's not been that long since people went west to the frontier in covered wagons, and many of *them* died along the way. We're taking the navy to a new frontier on this ship. They might scoff at 'Teddy's Toy,' but didn't they scoff at Jefferson for the Louisiana Purchase?"

"Out of the mouths of babes," murmured Roosevelt. "They did, Mr. Washington."

Fletcher stared at Washington with narrowed eyes. "Are you willing to risk your career saying that to Congressmen, Commander?"

"I've never forgiven Captain Crenshaw for sending me away, admiral."

The commander of the Atlantic Fleet considered that for a long moment. "Very well, Mr. Washington, I'll take your words into account."

The group glanced at the damage.

"Shall we continue this in my briefing room?" suggested Captain Chambers after a bit.

"I don't need to see any more," said Roosevelt. "Do you, Admiral Fletcher?"

"No, sir. This confirms what I expected to see."

Once in the briefing room, an orderly provided coffee for all the visitors as they settled in.

Afterward, Roosevelt continued, "This is becoming one hell of a mess, especially if Mr. Washington here is actually prescient."

"Sir, the *Langley* suffered only superficial damage." Chambers leaned forward. "You saw the initial repairs. We made those before reaching port. If we were in a battle, we could have still launched and landed our aircraft. Now that we're here at Newport News, the shipwrights say they'll have her repaired in just a couple of weeks."

"That's not the damn point and you know it."

Mayo leaned forward. "Sir, we've had far fewer casualties in 1915 than we had in 1914. This was the first fatality since January and that was caused by ice."

"I know, I know, but your little mishap here happened the day after the *F-4* sank and every Congressman is girding up their loins to correct mistakes in previous appropriations bills to 'protect our valiant young men.'" Roosevelt snorted. "There's only about two of them that know anything, but they're about to cut your funding to the bone unless we can do something to prevent it."

"What do you have in mind, Mr. President?"

Roosevelt leaned back. "I hate to say it, Admiral Mayo, but I don't have any good ideas. I wish we could have used the *Langley* during the Tampico incident."

"That was barely a month after you first visited us. We weren't ready. It would've been worse publicity than you have now," interjected Chambers. "Far worse."

"I know, Captain," said Roosevelt in a clipped, testy voice. "I was merely thinking that had she been available at that time, you could have proved the *Langley*'s usefulness once and for all. Non-believers like Admiral Fletcher here might have even been convinced."

"Don't be too sure, Mr. President," snorted Fletcher. "Many other admirals own positions far more entrenched than mine. I'm much more likely to look favorably on something like this, given my time with Ordnance. I often think every officer should spend some time there."

"Be that as it may, Admiral, I can't think of anything we can do now to prove just how valuable the *Langley* and those who follow her will be." Roosevelt sighed. "But we have to do something."

Mayo considered. "All we've done is sail her around Pensacola and up the East Coast to Virginia. We've never sent her anywhere else."

"Where do you propose to send her?"

"Mexican Coast?"

Roosevelt shook his head. "The Mexicans are still angry about the Tampico Affair. I'd rather not press them."

"Fair enough," agreed Mayo. "However, I'd rather not send her into the Mediterranean right now. Not with the battle happening at Gallipoli."

"The Philippines?" suggested Chambers.

"That'd be a possibility." Mayo's face turned grim. "However, thanks to General Wood, we don't have a big enough base in Subic Bay to properly support her."

"I doubt Admiral Howard would thank you for sending the *Langley* to the Pacific Fleet, anyway," said Fletcher.

"Also, I'm not prepared to send the *Langley* all the way there without at least a torpedo boat squadron to escort her."

"I think we can agree we'd want her to have some escorts, wherever we send her." Fletcher smiled. "But that, at least, is no real problem. The *North Carolina* was scheduled for a training mission, anyway, and there are three squadrons in Hampton Roads waiting for an assignment." The commander of the Atlantic Fleet thought for a moment. "And if I remember correctly, the *Nereus*, a collier which would have been a sister of the *Langley*, and the *Culgoa* are currently unassigned. That's sufficient escorts and supplies for a decent cruise."

"That's an idea." Roosevelt mused. "And I think I can make it better."

"What do you have in mind?" asked Mayo.

"You've all heard of Frederick Palmer?"

"The correspondent who's been just about everywhere? What, the

Boer War, Boxer Rebellion, Greece, Philippines, even the Russo-Japanese War?"

"That's the one. He sent me a letter after the Mexicans released him from jail. He's looking for a good story. We could send him with the *Langley*."

"Hmmm. And if he writes about the challenges facing the crew and the pilots, maybe he can sway public opinion."

"Exactly," said Roosevelt. "He won't sugarcoat any mistakes, but he's seen enough to know what's what."

"A good, honest reporter would be better, anyway," Fletcher agreed. "That leaves only one question. Where do we send her?"

"The only option left is the Atlantic, Mr. President," said Mayo.

"The Germans have been more aggressive with their submarines. I'm not sure that's a good idea." Fletcher shook his head.

"Sir, we've been practicing with our subs in the Caribbean. Ellyson and his pilots have scored their fair share of successes, and he thinks aircraft might be extremely valuable fighting submarines. Again, it's something we have much to learn about, but the possibility is there. Wouldn't it be better to learn that now, when we're still neutral?"

"That makes sense, Captain," agreed Fletcher.

"Gentlemen, we are *not* sending the *Langley* out to fight German submarines," growled Roosevelt. "I do not want American young men to get anywhere close to that madness on the Western Front. My time as president is short, I don't want to run again, and I certainly don't want to leave my successor involved over there." His face twisted. "Especially if *Wilson* runs again."

"No, sir, that wasn't my thought," responded Chambers. "I meant if a submarine did approach us, our planes and a squadron of torpedo boats wouldn't be their easiest target. Besides, we're still painted white and are clearly neutral. I assume the *North Carolina* and the other escorts are also still white."

"They are, Captain," agreed Fletcher. "If you stay out of the Kaiser's new exclusion zone, there should be no reason for the Germans to threaten you."

"Agreed. That would risk 'Teddy's Toy' unnecessarily."

The President grimaced. "Getting the *Langley* sunk would essentially eliminate all money for naval aviation."

"I understand, sir. However, having the *Langley* perform flight operations on that side of the Atlantic would be a major step forward."

"Mr. Palmer's reporting certainly would influence Congress." Roosevelt's mustache bristled in his anger. "Those shortsighted fools."

"Yes, Mr. President," agreed Fletcher.

"Very well. Captain Chambers, do you completely understand what you have to do?"

"Yes, Mr. President. I am to push the limits of the *Langley* as much as possible without involving myself in naval skirmishes between the Germans and English. I'm not to risk the *Langley* overmuch, though I am to make sure Mr. Palmer is impressed."

"I don't envy you, Captain Chambers," said Admiral Fletcher.

"Admiral, in the officer's mess just two decks down is a wall with over forty names after adding Bronson and Welsh. Every man on this ship understands the risks. We all know what we're doing is difficult and we all know we could be the next name painted on that wall. Yet, every single man on this ship chooses to remain. They believe in what we're doing." Chambers shook his head. "I won't deny this will be a tough mission, but I'd rather try to complete it with these men than any other job you could give me."

Roosevelt suddenly grinned. "Far better to dare, is what you're telling us."

"Yes, Mr. President. Jones, Farragut, Crenshaw, and all the other great heroes of our navy's past deserve no less."

"Well, Captain Chambers, with you and Commander Washington here —" the President nodded toward the executive officer, "—I'll admit to much more optimism than when I boarded my 'toy.'"

---

28 April 1915

"The plan was to harmonize sailors, officers, aeroplane mechanics, and pilots into a force so homogeneous that flesh and blood became machinery, with every crewman aboard the USS *Langley* working together with that sort of efficiency; but human elements older than the United States Navy, which had given warriors cheer on the march and fire in battle from the days of the spear to the days of the quick-firer, hampered the practical application of the cold professional idea worked out in conscientious logic in the academic cloister.

"In more traditional branches of the navy, there is a sentiment and association among the sailors. Their tradition is based upon memories of Old Ironsides, Mobile Bay, and yes, the *Maine*. If they were not proud of it they would be unnatural fighters.

"The members on the *Langley* are not immune to that sentiment and association, of course. Indeed, the second-ranking officer aboard the *Langley* was on the *Maine* at Santiago de Cuba. However, the machinery they are trying to learn and embrace is so foreign to many of these boys as to be much like the very top of the unconquerable Mt. Everest. And yet, like that soaring peak, they are seeking to lift our eyes to the heavens.

"If you, dear reader, often peruse pages such as this across the country, then you are likely to have learned of their defiant efforts to reach the sky from the sea. What sentiment and tradition these men have is often of death, as can be seen by the somber mural in their officer's mess. Upon that wall are listed those who have perished to achieve this dream, and we have all too often mourned the fate of these heroes.

"It is the sad duty of your correspondent to inform you that yesterday, these crewmen had to emblazon that mural with yet another memory. Lieutenant, j.g. Richard Caswell Saufley, while attempting to land his Royal Aircraft BE.2.c upon this selfsame *Langley* suffered an engine failure and his aeroplane fell as a stone into the cold, gray waters of the Atlantic Ocean. Despite speedy reactions by Captain Washington Irving Chambers and his doughty crew, the plane sank with Saufley's body before anyone could reach it."

—Frederick Palmer*

Early Morning, 1 May 1915

Chambers stepped onto the bridge.

"Captain on the bridge!"

"As you were," replied Chambers. He glanced around. His command might not have been necessary. The bridge crew had barely responded to the announcement. He had never seen them so lethargic.

"What's our position?" he asked the navigator. Upon the response, he replied, "That should put us about one hundred miles south of Brest? About ten miles from the exclusion zone?"

* Palmer, Frederick. *Our Greatest Battle* (New York: Dodd, Mead and Co., 1919), 42-3.

"Yes, sir."

"Have you the course laid out when we are forced to skirt the zone?"

"Yes, sir." The navigator rolled out the map. "When we get to this point in approximately an hour, we'll change course to 350 to skirt the zone."

"Good." He turned to the bosun's mate at the voice tubes. "Please call for Commanders Ellyson and Washington join me in my briefing room."

"Gentlemen, we have a problem," Chambers announced when they had gathered.

"Yes, sir," replied Ellyson. "Saufley's death seems like the end."

"True, and while I understand, we will correct it. We're not going back to Norfolk with our tails between our legs."

"Agreed, sir," replied Washington, straightening a touch. "What did you have in mind?"

"We have little to lose at this point. Therefore, we are, as of this morning, going to commence full aeroplane operations. We're going to push the sailors and air crews on the *Langley*. We're going to log flights everywhere we can. We're close enough to France we can fly over their coastline. We'll do the same to Cornwall and Ireland when we get there. Then we'll loop back and surprise the Danish in Reykjavik."

"Is that legal?"

"I'll radio ahead and warn them we're performing maneuvers. And then, once we've done all that, we'll make a visit to Halifax. Mr. Washington, when we get there, arrange for as much shore leave as possible. Their little funk notwithstanding, the men have performed admirably, and I doubt we'll have the opportunity reward them once we return home."

"Yes, sir."

"Once we leave Halifax, we'll sail along the coast, making surprise bombing runs over every American base we can."

"That'll get you cashiered!"

"Likely so, Mr. Washington, but we both know my career is over once this jaunt is completed. Might as well earn my way out of the Navy."

The two commanders glanced at each other.

"Very well, sir," said Washington, his eyes filled with doubt.

"Make sure Mr. Palmer has complete access to everything. I want him watching us refuel those planes, and I want you ensuring that refueling process is fast and smooth. Just like we would have to launch for an imminent battle."

"Yes, sir."

"And you, Mr. Ellyson, will tell your pilots they're in for the hardest time of their lives. They're going to fly every day. Some will likely die. We've danced around this issue too much to doubt it, but those who survive will be the best pilots in the world anywhere."

"Aye, air, sir!" snapped Spuds, his eyes bright. "And we're flying over the exclusion zone?"

"Yes, Mr. Ellyson. I want you to find and play tag with every ship in the area, be they English, French, German, or Japanese, for that matter. I want everyone to know we can cover something like 300 square miles at a time. The U-boat commanders are welcome to try and shoot you down. At least then you'd have an excuse to fly bombing runs at them."

"With live bombs?"

Chambers shook his head. "I think not, Mr. Ellyson. It's not worth getting into the war, but it is worth putting the fear of God's angels into those commanders. And, for that matter, any English and French captains that get upset."

The two commanders laughed.

"I'll get right on that," agreed Ellyson.

"Do that. I'll want a formation flight over Brest when we get to our closest point. At least ten aircraft, including one of the radio aeroplanes. Arrange for Mr. Palmer to be in an observer seat for that flight. Come to think of it, get him up as often as possible."

"Yes, sir!"

"Get to it, gentlemen. I want this crew so angry at me that they forget they're about to get tossed away by Congress."

The two commanders saluted and left the room, almost bouncing in their excitement.

Now all I have to do is forget I'm *about to get tossed away by Congress.*

Early Morning, 7 May 1915

"Damn this fog!" growled Ellyson. He stood on the bridge of the *Langley*. "We're not doing anything until this lifts."

"Agreed, Commander." Chambers gestured ahead of his ship. "You can't see her, but the *Terry* is about ten thousand yards ahead of us, making sure we don't run into anything."

"Hope her captain knows what he's doing."

"Admiral Mayo has high hopes for Commander King. He'll probably claim him for his staff as soon as he's reassigned from the *Terry*."

"Good." Ellyson snorted. "Guess I'll just gather all my pilots and observers and we'll go through the list of ships that are supposed to be in the area. If this pea soup ever leaves, maybe we can find them all."

"That's a good idea. I know the *Partridge*, a boarding vessel, should be around here. Also, the radio telegraph picked up messages from the *Juno*, a British cruiser, saying she was heading back to Queenstown."

"We'll find those, no problem."

"Check with the navigator and radio telegraph men, they'll know more."

"Aye, aye."

Ellyson went to both, scribbling down the list, and then assembled his pilots to show it to them.

"Gentlemen, we're going to find all of these ships, especially that one." He pointed at one name. "I want all of you to review the silhouette books."

The aviators gathered around a table and began swapping the silhouette books back and forth. Ellyson stared at boarding vessel silhouettes for about ten minutes, but he was too restless to properly focus.

"Spuds, get the hell out of here," Lieutenant Melvin Stolz, his observer, finally snapped.

"I need to memorize this."

"Why? That's what you have me for. And frankly, you're driving us all mad right now."

The other aviators laughed and nodded.

Ellyson shook his head. "Fine, I'll go up and yell at the fog to clear off."

"Excellent decision, sir. Glad you thought of it."

With a bark of laughter, Ellyson left the room and went onto the flight deck. He glared up a time or two, but mostly stared forward and watched the gray waves roll towards him.

Suddenly, he realized he could see more ships. He glanced up. The sun had definitely started to burn away the clouds.

"Enough waiting, by God!" He stormed down to the hangar deck. "Get every plane ready to go. The weather's clearing and we'll launch as soon as we can."

The hangar burst into activity, and Spuds almost ran down the steps to the other aviators.

"Get ready, gentlemen. The weather's clearing, and we've got flying to do."

"Heaven be praised," snapped Stolz. "I thought my eyes were about to become permanently crossed."

Half an hour later, the fog had completely cleared off. The Atlantic was as smooth as it ever got and was the blue that caught the soul of every romantic nautical poet. Ellyson climbed into his BE.2.c with Stolz in front of him. Two more BE.2.cs waited behind him to follow.

Spuds accelerated, and with a pleasant sigh of relief, he felt air catch under his wings. He pulled back on the stick and brought his plane into an ascending spiral. He waited until the others formed up on him and then headed them all northeast at an easy fifty knots some eight hundred feet over the water.

He yelled to Stolz. "If we're right, the one we want should be about thirty miles that way."

"I'll keep my eyes open. If she's there, she's the biggest thing around, so we should see her easily enough."

"Four stacks."

"I know, I know."

Spuds grinned. "At least I remembered that silhouette."

Stolz laughed, but kept his head swiveling back and forth from either side of the twin-bladed propeller, periodically staring through a pair of binoculars.

"Spuds!" Stolz pointed. "Is that smoke over there?"

Ellyson squinted through his goggles. "I can't tell, but we can certainly check it out. Send the signal for course change."

"Aye, aye." Stolz raised the appropriate signs and waited for confirmation. "Got it."

Spuds did not say anything, but banked the BE.2.c slightly to the west.

"It's definitely smoke, sir."

"Agreed." Spuds thought about accelerating, but they'd be to that pillar of smoke soon enough, and while this might be the prize, she wasn't the only ship out here.

"That's a lotta smoke, Spuds."

"Might be our fish, Melvin."

"Yes, sir."

As they approached, Stolz muttered, "One, two, three... Four! Four stacks. It's gotta be our baby."

"Yes!" agreed Ellyson when he got closer to the four-stacked ship sailing east. "It's definitely her."

"If only the 'Covered Wagon' were that big," Stolz said with a laugh. "The book said she was almost eight hundred feet long. I'd sure like to land on a deck that long."

"It'd make it easier, wouldn't it?" Ellyson banked the B.E.2c around. "Shall we give the passengers a thrill?"

"Absolutely."

Spuds zoomed across the liner, with the other two following closely. He then banked around and approached from the stern. The planes flew at about two hundred feet along the starboard side of her, waggling their wings. Passengers lined the rail, waved their handkerchiefs, and lifted their drinks at the aeroplanes.

Laughing, Ellyson continued east toward Ireland.

"That took a goodly amount of our fuel, sir. We should think about heading back to our five hundred feet of deck in about thirty minutes."

"That'll still give us time to get to Queenstown. The *Juno* is supposed to be there. Send the signals to the others."

They soared over Queenstown, then zoomed over the *Juno*, berthed at Haulbowline Island. They continued south into the Irish Sea.

About fifteen miles southwest of Queenstown, Stolz yelled, "Spuds! To our left—is that a submarine?"

"I don't see it, but signal the others we're going to check it out." Moments later, he banked the BE.2.c over the spot Stolz pointed out to give his observer a clear look.

"It's definitely a submarine, sir. And it's submerging. I think it's German."

Ellyson's eyes sharpened. "It's right on the shipping lane to Queenstown and all the ports in the Irish Sea."

"What about the liner? They wouldn't sink her, would they?"

"They shouldn't, but the Germans have been talking tough about this exclusion zone. We've to get back to the *Langley*, anyway, and Captain Chambers will want to know as fast as we can get there."

Ellyson pushed his throttle ahead as fast as he dared, given his fuel level.

Fifteen minutes later, his seat harness yanked him back as the arresting gear caught. The deck crew began pulling his B.E.2c into place.

"Stolz, get everything organized down here. I'm going to Chambers." Ellyson jumped down and ran up to the bridge. Breathlessly, he saluted the captain. "Sir, I believe we have a potential issue."

Chambers eyebrows went up. "What is it, Commander?"

"There's a ship about thirty miles away, bearing about 030. I think it's our big prize."

"Well done, Commander."

"However, about forty miles ahead of her, ten or fifteen miles south of Queenstown, is a submarine. I think it's German."

Chambers' eyes widened. He pulled out a map. "You're saying there's a U-boat in the path of the *Lusitania*?"

"Yes, sir."

Chambers stepped over to the radio telegraph station. "Mr. Howell, please send: 'Attention RMS *Lusitania*. This is Captain Chambers of the USS *Langley*. Submarine activity detected ahead of you. Please take appropriate action.'"

Startled, the communications officer complied. After a moment, he turned back. "Sir, Captain Turner asks our location."

"Send it back."

Howell complied. Then he leaned back with a wild look on his face.

"What did he say?"

"Uh, sir, he said, 'If you are where you say, you cannot possibly see a submarine in any position along my path. If you can see a submarine, you apparently have no proper understanding of navigation and therefore are more hindrance than help. Please refrain from bothering me in the future.'"

"Save me from arrogant old men who haven't discovered we're in a century of many wonders!" snapped the captain.

The bridge crew stared at Chambers.

Chambers continued, growling, "Please inform Captain Turner that we are an aeroplane carrier and that we do, indeed, possess the ability to see things along his path. I should not have to remind him that he is responsible for approximately two thousand people. Even should we not possess that capability, it behooves him to pay attention to the warning."

"He says he believes has things well in hand. He says his ship was designed to be too fast for any submarine to catch."

"Captain Turner, this is not a drill. Please take evasive action and prepare for a torpedo attack."

"He replied, 'Doing such would disturb those chattering monkeys unduly.

I am unwilling to listen to that chattering on the word of some bloody colonial who is at best a poor sailor and at worst a danger to his crew.'"

Chambers took a deep breath. "Very well, Captain Turner. Understand that I will hold you personally responsible if any of your passengers are harmed from your inaction. Should, of course, you yourself survive." He shook his head. "Mr. Howell, record any future messages from him, but don't bother me with them unless they are relevant."

"Understood, sir."

The captain turned to the bosun at the speaking tubes. "Please inform Commander Washington I need him in my briefing room immediately." He turned to Ellyson. "Come with me."

When Washington entered the room, Chambers said, "Commander Ellyson, please explain the situation to Mr. Washington."

"Aye, aye, sir." He complied.

"Mr. Ellyson, what do you suggest we do?" asked Washington.

"I take my BE.2.c with three other birds out, all with full bomb loads."

"And do what? The United States is still neutral. Are you suggesting we attack the U-boat in contravention of the President's desire to stay out of the war?"

"As we were reading up on the ships in the area, the references said the *Lusitania* carried something like two thousand people. If the U-boat does decide to attack her, it could be worse than the *Titanic*."

Chambers looked troubled. "Commander, I have to think about this."

"With all due respect, sir, we don't have any time."

The captain shook his head. "Yes, we do." He led them out of the briefing room. "Mr. Howell, please inform the rest of the squadron and all other vessels in range that we have spotted submarine activity in the area." He turned back. "Mr. Washington, where's the wind coming from?"

"Wind out of the northwest, heading 330."

Turning back, "Mr. Howell, you will then signal, not radio, to all the other ships of the squadron that we will be turning into the wind imminently."

"Aye, aye, sir." The lieutenant at the communications station turned to his equipment.

"Pope, have the navigator plot a course to where Ellyson saw the *Lusitania*. Then would you be so good as to order four planes, including Commander Ellyson's, fueled and armed with live munitions? Also, make sure Lieutenant Chevalier's radio-equipped plane is ready to join them."

Now it was Commander Washington's turn to raise his eyebrows. "As you command, sir." He snapped the orders across the bridge.

"Thank you, sir," said Ellyson, and he turned to leave.

"Not so fast, Spuds. We have about ten minutes before the planes are ready to launch. That gives us a bit of time to determine our course of action. Mr. Washington, what do you think?"

The executive officer pondered for a moment. "Sir, I think we have to seriously consider sending a flight to assist the *Lusitania*."

"If we attack the U-boat, we may very well have committed this country to this Godforsaken war. Given the casualty reports from the Western Front, if we attack that boat, we might be putting the lives of hundreds of thousands of American boys on the line."

"That's true." Washington grimaced. "However, didn't we get sent out here in order to show we could operate away from the American coast? To tell the world what we could do? What better way to do that than to dissuade the U-boat from attacking the *Lusitania*?"

"Yes, sir!" Ellyson turned to the captain. "I don't have to attack the U-boat directly. Between the four armed birds in the flight, we'll have twelve bombs. We can simply use those to herd the U-boat away from the *Lusitania*. We needn't attack the Germans, just drive them off."

Chambers tapped his fingers together. Eventually, he replied, "Thank you, gentlemen, for your words. Go make the preparations, and I will give you a decision when you are ready."

The two commanders left, and Chambers went back to his quarters. There, he took out his Bible, pulled out a folded piece of paper, set it to the side, and turned to Psalm 104. Then to Psalm 107. Then he unfolded the piece of paper carefully. It had yellowed, which was not surprising, since his mother had sent it to him nearly forty years before. In her delicate script, the first words were, "Eternal Father, strong to save."

Someone knocked at his door.

"Come," commanded Chambers.

Commander Washington leaned in. "Sir, Ellyson's flight is ready."

"Lieutenant Chevalier?"

"Ready to go as well."

I can't not act.

"Please inform Mr. Ellyson he has my permission to continue. He is to do all he can to prevent the U-boat from attacking the *Lusitania* up to and including attacking her directly if no other attempts succeed. He is to keep us apprised of all that happens via the radio. And may God have mercy on our soul."

"Aye aye, sir. For what it's worth, I concur."

"Thank you, Commander Washington."

Washington saluted and left.

Chambers stared at the page. A single tear dropped on it, blurring "brethren's shield."

Ellyson barely waited for the other planes in the flight to launch. He yelled back to his observer, "Relay a heading of 040, height 600. Tell them not to worry about formation, but to extend our line. Two go to my left. Two to my right. Make sure Chevalier is next to us. They're to go as far as they can and still see signals from the next plane over. We want to cover as much sea as we can."

The signals went out. "You're going to owe them some beers, Spuds. They're not exactly happy with you."

The pilot laughed harshly. "They'll get over it, especially if we get the *Lusitania* to safety. Now keep your eyes peeled."

"Will do, Spuds."

The five BE.2.cs flew at about six hundred feet over the ocean. The line stretched about a mile in length.

"Sir, I see smoke, bearing 350."

Spuds looked where his observer was pointing. "Good eyes, Melvin. Relay that down the line."

"Aye, aye."

"I'm going to wheel around the ship, then start zigzagging across its path."

"Relayed."

Spuds turned slightly. Presently, he saw the tips of the stacks. Given the wake behind her, the *Lusitania* had just turned.

The gaggle of passengers welcomed him again. This time, their revelry seems hideous and horrible.

"Have Chevalier explain who we are and remind Captain Turner of the submarine activity."

"Aye, aye." Wryly, Stolz added, "Probably just as well we can't receive radio telegraph signals ourselves." Then he lifted the complex series of signals.

Presently, a sailor on the *Lusitania* came out on the foredeck of the liner and waved.

"Tell the others, I'm going to swing over the ship and then we'll begin our search pattern." After a moment to allow the message to get to the other planes, Spuds guided them over the *Lusitania*. They swung back and forth several times before the far right plane started flashing signals.

"Sir! Lee's spotted a submarine on the surface approximately eleven thousand yards away."

"Heading?"

"110."

"Are they in range of their torpedoes?"

"I don't know, sir. We never got briefed on that."

"Yeah. Was just hoping you had an encyclopedia handy."

The observer laughed grimly. "If their torpedoes are anything like ours, he can't be too far out of range if he launches at the lower speed."

"If he does that, the German torpedoes can't be that much faster than the *Lusitania*, right?"

"Probably not. Ours wouldn't be."

Ellyson sighed. "That's probably why Captain Turner was so sanguine about the possibility. The submarine commander will have to get closer. Ours have a maximum range of about three thousand yards at high speed. We'll just try and keep the sub about five thousand yards away. Order the flight to close in. Tell Chevalier to report the location of the sub to both the *Lusitania* and the *Langley*."

"Done, sir."

"Tell the others we're going to circle between the U-boat and the *Lusitania* at about two hundred feet. Let's make sure the sub sees us. Maybe they won't want to tangle with us."

"Won't she just submerge?"

"Probably, but hopefully we can still see her shadow. It's a bright, clear day, after all."

"We could just go bomb her now. She hasn't reacted to us at all, yet."

Spuds stayed quiet for a long moment. "We can't, Melvin. We don't even know if it's German or not. We have to wait for it to attack before we can do anything."

"Yeah, that's what I thought you'd say."

"Make sure everyone knows to keep watching that sub."

"Signals sent, sir. Chevalier reports radio messages sent, as well."

The commander didn't respond, but put his plane in a slow fuel-conserving circle between the *Lusitania* and the submarine.

"They see us, sir. Looks like they're preparing to dive."

"I'll keep us banked as much as possible. Tell the other pilots to provide observers the best sight lines possible."

"Yes, sir."

"When she's submerged, tell me if you can or cannot see her shadow."

After a few minutes, Stolz responded, "She's completely under, but on a day like today, I can probably see her shadow fifty feet or more below the surface."

"Good. Has she changed course?"

"Yes, sir. Looks like she's slowed and is creeping to an intercept route ahead of us."

"I'm going to spiral over ahead. Tell the others to go ahead of us. We'll try and keep a line between the *Lusitania* and her."

"Aye, aye, sir."

After about five minutes, Ellyson asked, "Has she moved away?"

"No, sir. I don't think the sub believes we can see her, or maybe doesn't care."

"Blast! Have Chevalier send to the *Langley* we need a relief flight. We can stay out here for another half hour or more, but we're going to need help if he doesn't go away."

After a moment, "Signal sent and confirmed."

"Let's get her attention. Send to Lieutenant Mustin to do a bombing run. He is to drop one bomb at about four hundred yards ahead of the sub."

Ahead of him, one of the BE.2.cs curved around gracefully to fly ahead of the sub.

"Bomb released, sir!" announced Stolz.

A moment later, they heard the sharp crack of the bomb exploding on the surface of the ocean.

"Any change, Melvin?"

"No, sir."

"Damn his soul." Ellyson looked to the west. "The *Lusitania* is just coming straight this way. Send to Chevalier to warn that idiot of a captain we're over a submarine, maybe he'll do something smart."

"Radio telegraph message sent, sir."

Spuds stared at the liner, willing her to shift course or do something, anything.

Nothing happened.

"Stolz, tell Mustin to do another run."

Afterward, the submarine and liner still headed for each other.

"By Christ! Hang on." Spuds twisted his controls and the BE.2.c dived towards the shadow beneath the water. At the very last moment he pulled up, yelling at Stolz to release two bombs.

Behind him he heard them explode and he twisted around.

"Still no change, sir."

"Tell Bellinger and McIlvain to drop two of their bombs each right on top of the shadow. Then they are to circle above it."

The shadow continued to settle into what would be a perfect shot if the liner did not adjust.

Spuds thought for a moment, circling over the shadow of death beneath him. Finally, he yelled to Stolz, "Signal Mustin and Chevalier to keep on my tail."

"Confirmed."

Ellyson pulled the stick around and aimed his aeroplane at the *Lusitania*. A few minutes later, he dove right at her. If the earlier pass to cheer the passengers had seemed close, this one was insane. The three planes went across the liner's bow right in front of the bridge windows.

"That got their attention, sir, but..."

"But what?"

"They seem angrier at us than worried about anything else."

"Tell Chevalier to keep sending the warning."

"He is."

Spuds kept flying around the *Lusitania*, but Stolz's assessment proved correct. A number of officers appeared on her deck, waving them away. One even had a revolver, though Ellyson never saw him fire it.

He looked over. The planes over the sub seemed far too close. Not even a mile away.

The sub is well within range.

"Signal to all planes, we'll drop our last bombs right on top of the sub. Follow me."

After a moment the flight regained its formation and Spuds led them down. Whatever inexperience these pilots might have had when they left the Newport News shipyard had long since been trained out of them. Each put their bomb directly on top of the black shadow.

But nothing changed.

And then something did.

"Sir, I have a track in the water!"

"What?"

Ellyson banked his plane over and there, to his horror, he saw a line on the water heading directly for the *Lusitania*.

Six hundred yards away.

Five hundred.

"Melvin. I wish you weren't here."

---

8 May 1915

"It has always been the great heart of our men, beating as the one heart of a great country—simple, vigorous, young, trying out its strength—on the background of old Europe, which appealed to me. It is the spontaneous incidents of emotion breaking out of routine which revealed character.

"Yesterday, a flight of aeroplanes landed on the *Langley*. The aviators of that flight stepped down from their amazing examples of human ingenuity and technology. They did not move quickly off the deck, as they usually did. Instead, they simply stood and stared at each other. I cannot tell you for how long, for I, too, was mesmerized. I do not know if a single word was said among them, but the fellows, at some length, went below decks. It was also their wont, as they left the deck, to laugh, shout, and show with their hands the incredible aerial maneuvers they could achieve, and indeed inflicted upon myself. This, too, they did not do on this day.

"It is but ten days since it was my sorrowful duty to report the death of Lieutenant Richard C. Saufley. It was yet another in what seemed to be an endless string of deaths for little gain in the field of naval aeronautics. The very recent addition to the Navy Hymn by the poet Mary C. D. Hamilton that asked, 'Lord, guard and guide the men who fly through the great spaces in the sky,' seemed in that ancient time, but ten days ago, a desperate plea for clemency as they lifted their way to assured death.

"Today, I have learned more of the great heart of our men for there was to be one more aeroplane in that flight. In peril in the air, these aviators certainly are and will be, yet this they offer, and willingly, that others may live. That plane, piloted by Lieutenant Commander Theodore G. 'Spuds' Ellyson accompanied by Lieutenant Melvin Lewis Stolz, through great skill and bravery, prevented an attack by a German submarine on the RMS *Lusitania* by intercepting its torpedo with the incredible feat of diving their plane into the torpedo headed for the liner, knowing they would die, and saving perhaps as many as two thousand souls. It is possible, as I think of it, the more than two score deaths accrued by these, the bravest and best of our great country, is but the price to pay that we become greater than old Europe has ever been."

—Frederick Palmer *

* Ibid., 478-9.

ABOUT ROB HOWELL

Rob is the publisher of New Mythology Press, creator of the Firehall Sagas, a writer and editor in Luke Gygax's World of Okkorim, a reformed medieval academic, and a retired soda jerk.

Without books, it's unlikely he or his parents would have both survived.

Find him here:

- Website: robhowell.org
- His Blog: robhowell.org/blog.
- Firehall Sagas: firehallsagas.com
- Amazon: amazon.com/-/e/B00X95LBB0
- Twitter: @Rhodri2112
- Rob's Riddles: patreon.com/rhodri2112

FRIENDS IN HIGH PLACES

Joelle Presby and Patrick Doyle

FRIENDS IN HIGH PLACES

"Do thank that very charming Rear Admiral Fiske for his encouraging words. It shall greatly reassure my dear sister-in-law to know the Aide for Operations has made me the promise that my nephew shall not go on one of those dreadful escort ships. He's to do something with aeroplanes instead.

"Did you know that a Russian princess has taken up flying? It must be a much safer occupation."

— *EXCERPT OF A LETTER FROM THE DESK OF THE SECOND LADY OF THE UNITED STATES, MRS. LOIS IRENE MARSHALL*

January 1915,
Port of Hamburg, Germany

"Chief Hays!" The surprise of hearing a familiar accent so soon after disembarking in Germany startled me.

Europe might be in the midst of their Great War, but an American abroad had time to speak for a few moments with a fellow countryman—as long as it was truly only a few moments.

My young officer charges had multiplied from the nephew of Vice President Marshall to now include a half-dozen sons of successful businessmen and even one senator's son. I personally had suspected half of the men's families of terminal ignorance on the subject of aeroplane safety, and the other half of a more cold-blooded calculation. The political value of a war hero weighed against the risk of losing a family member shouldn't come out ahead, but if they were valuing a dead war hero against a reckless young pilot just as likely to crash into some Stateside barn on a dare if left at home...

The well-dressed and older gentleman with a pile of his own luggage waved me down, and with a reluctance that I hoped didn't show too clearly on my face, I stopped.

My charges were halted, too, so I wouldn't lose track of them if I also paused. Lieutenant Marshall and Lieutenant Thompson stood outside a dockside bar waving energetically up at an aircraft fitted with pontoons now soaring overhead, bound, according to pier side gossip, to embark with a German cruiser and serve to extend a squadron's observation range.

The rest of the Americans in our group would be inside the bar.

The gentleman abandoned his baggage to his escort and waved delightedly at me.

"Sir, I don't believe—" I started to form my regrets.

I tried for politeness in acknowledgement of the bespoke tailoring of his clothing but also firmness because this man, for all his upper-class Boston accent, was not my responsibility. *And darn it all,* I reminded myself, *as a United States Navy Chief Petty Officer, it was high time I herded my new band of officers past the dockside bars and got everyone to work.*

The gentleman stood a few inches under six feet, boasted a well-groomed beard, and favored me with an expression of absolute delight. Behind him trailed an underling who earned a second look from me and a salute.

A U.S. Navy commander in a crisp uniform with a look of much exhaustion on his face made the tracings of a salute back at me, and I dropped my salute as neatly as I could manage. The top three medals the officer bothered to wear indicated he'd served well and been amply recognized for it by senior naval leadership.

"Tell the ship to wait for us, Edmunds." The older man waggled a hand in the general direction of the busy dockside and not towards any specific vessel.

"Yes, Ambassador," Commander Edmunds replied.

Any sailor could see the already outgoing tide and mark the emptying piers, though. *No ship's captain worth the title, whether military or commercial, would be pleased to waste the ocean's gift of easy sailing,* I thought. *But maybe for a senior enough passenger, he'd wait an extra dozen hours or so for the next tide.*

Edmunds gave the ambassador a blank look, with the skepticism of his expression only showing through a slight wrinkling around the eyes, and did not scamper off to deliver any such message to the, presumably, waiting vessel. But he did incline his head politely.

"Ambassador," he said, "I see you've already recognized Chief Hays, whom you'll remember was present with the Marshall boy during that Kamerun incident." And I noticed that the gentleman was immediately distracted from remembering to repeat the foolish order and instead allowed the officer to direct the conversation. "Chief, this is Mr. Belmont, who has been serving as our ambassador to Germany for these last few years."

"Sir," Edmunds said to Belmont, "we really should be making our way to the ship."

"In just a moment," the ambassador said. "I really must have a chat with the chief."

The commander quite obviously did not sigh. He turned and whistled to catch the attention of a pair of roughs wandering the docks and gestured for them to take charge of the gentleman's luggage. Some German spoken faster than I could follow resulted in the men hefting trunks between them and hauling them off.

The aircraft with the pontoons had vanished from view, but Thompson and Marshall continued their discussion. From the way Thompson's hands moved this way and that, I was certain aviation was still the subject of their discussion.

Lieutenant Marshall, tall, of neat dark hair, and a striking physical similarity to Vice President Thomas R. Marshall, leaned in to listen with rapt attention to Lieutenant Thompson's tales. Thompson came from a southern family and had flown on dirigibles, and was eager to study the workings of aeroplanes with their impressive speed and, perhaps, military utility as observer units.

I dragged my attention back to the man in front of me.

"My pleasure, uh, Mr. Ambassador," I said. I had no idea what the proper mode of address was. Now twice assigned as part-aide-de-camp and part-keeper to the Vice President's nephew, I wished there'd been some sort of instruction manual on handling these people who'd never speak to me in the normal course of events.

Commander Edmunds gave me a sympathetic smile.

"We really should be making our way to the ship, sir." He gestured beyond, to where the porters now carried Mr. Belmont's trunks across a gangway.

He had my sympathy.

A returning overhead engine's eager roar drew matching hoots of delight from nearly everyone around us. The seaplane buzzed overhead, and even Mr. Belmont grinned up at it.

"Those the ones they were considering embarking on the armored cruisers?" I asked, not willing to let a source of information go.

Commander Edmunds nodded. "So the Germans say."

Mr. Belmont squinted at it. "Is that what they intend to do with those? I wouldn't know. German military secrets, I suppose."

"An extended observer, I understand. Just the one pilot instead of a whole zeppelin aircrew, so it's easier to make accommodations for them onboard," Edmunds replied. "They haven't, at least yet, attached any rig for bombs aboard the aeroplanes, either. So a tradeoff, to be sure, for the military utility of it all."

"Bombs?" Mr. Belmont snorted. "What a ridiculous notion. Good thing you're escorting me back, Edmunds, or you might give these Germans far too many ideas."

"I suspect they'll have plenty of ideas on their own, sir," I said with as much mildness as I could infuse in the words. People swirled all about us on the busy waterfront, and most, if not all, were Germans. This was Germany, after all, and some would surely have proficiency in English. Likely, no one would repeat what I said and make my officers' lives more difficult for it, but I saw no reason to risk offensive words against the host nation.

"But, Mr. Belmont, your ship does seem quite ready to depart," I reminded him.

I could see the fine passenger liner was ready to pull away from the pier with tug boats and line handlers all standing about, waiting on a last few elite or perhaps even a single, final important passenger to get onboard so they could go before the tide turned, and they'd have to waste coal powering out against the currents instead of with them.

Commander Edmunds favored me with a grateful smile, and gestured

Mr. Belmont again to the ship, as if another handwave would be enough to shift him.

"It'll wait," Mr. Belmont said with complete confidence. "I could hardly go without stopping to congratulate the very fine sergeant here."

"Chief," Commander Edmunds corrected while I tried to keep up.

"Congratulate, sir?" I was baffled. Certainly, my lieutenant had survived his Africa assignment, but I'd been honest in my report back to higher authority about what exactly we'd done during the defense of Port Doula.

"Yes, of course congratulate!" Mr. Belmont patted my shoulder. "The whole Marshall family is delighted with you! Well, our esteemed vice president didn't say as much directly, of course. You know how he is, always hoping for Mr. Wilson's recovery. As we all do, naturally.

"But a young war hero relative will be ever so useful for the next presidential campaign. I do hope you enjoy going to all the fine Berlin parties. The Kaiser, bless him, doesn't throw many these days, but the younger set can have quite a good time."

"Uh, thank you sir." I didn't expect the lieutenant would attend all that many parties. The orders had said, "Make a close study of German military aviation."

Over Mr. Belmont's shoulder, the bar's door opened, and Lieutenant Junior Grade Roberts popped his ruddy blonde head out long enough to call out something that drew the other two lieutenants in after him.

If Marshall, Thompson, and the rest were settled in at the bar for a while, I would've liked to head on down past the commercial shipping docks to see if I could get a good look at the other piers which might hold some of the German naval fleet.

The ambassador looked at me expectantly.

"I, um, don't expect to attend parties," I said.

Mr. Belmont laughed. "You sound just like those admirals!"

Commander Edmunds gave his charge a concerned glance, which only amused the ambassador more.

"Sir?"

"My understanding is the young lieutenant requested sea duty following your tour in Africa, and certain esteemed persons felt he was too important to risk of assignment onboard a naval escort," Commander Edmunds explained.

"It would've been an absolute waste." Mr. Belmont shook his head. "I heard those Navy boys were almost going to give him that assignment, too. Ridiculous, the level of pressure required to make them see sense. And after that masterful piece of work in Africa, too!"

"I'm afraid I don't understand, sir." I remembered quite clearly that Lieutenant Marshall had telegrammed asking for a follow-on assignment instead of resigning his commission. Yes, there had been a mention of sea duty, but he'd been more than a little intrigued with aviation, and I was almost certain he'd mentioned that, as well, in the message.

"You didn't tell me he was so modest, Edmunds." Mr. Belmont continued to beam at me.

"I'm sure Chief Hays does all he can to help his officers, sir," Commander Edmunds said.

"Help? This far beyond that." He turned to me. "You are a master!" He clapped me on the back. "I heard it directly from Lois Marshall herself, who had it from the young lieutenant's own mother. Excellent job keeping the Marshall boy close enough to get a bit of the glory from that nasty business in the African colonies. Be a different story if he'd been in that madcap boat loaded up with explosives, of course!" He chortled at his own joke, and I firmly kept my face as blank as I could manage.

Commander Edmunds's face matched mine.

The boat in question had in fact included both myself and Lieutenant Marshall in the crew.

"I can't imagine the guts of those natives getting on the thing. But I suppose their lives are wretched enough that it doesn't take so much bravery to risk them."

I supposed quite the opposite, but it wasn't my place to say. I made a polite listening noise and said, "Sir, what was it you needed? Your ship needs to depart soon, I believe?"

Commander Edmunds gave a small shrug to indicate that it didn't much matter how long it took to shift the senior man.

The ambassador in turn looked at the ship with a sense of glum, and I guessed from his gulp that I was facing a man prone to seasickness who'd like to delay his departure as much as he could.

Mr. Belmont finally squared his shoulders, looking resolutely at his luxurious passenger liner.

"Well, I must be off." He patted my shoulder one more time. "You keep it up. You get the slightest hint that there's a change on the front, and any vessel flying American colors will load you both up for the next trip to the States."

"And the others?" I inquired. I'd been led to believe they were all fairly well-connected young men.

"Ah, if you can." Mr. Belmont shrugged. "Some boys'll run wild on any continent they find themselves on. Others matter quite a bit more. The president's own nephew." He smiled. "Gotta keep that boy of ours safe. Bright futures ahead for that one!"

"Vice president's nephew," I corrected automatically.

"Maybe, maybe. There's an election coming, you know. Reason I've got to endure the sea voyage, after all. People to speak with. Caucusing to do." He waggled a hand to indicate a great deal of other items too long to bother with listing.

"Then let us not miss the tide, sir," Commander Edmunds said. "It would prolong the trip," he added, which had the desired effect of causing Mr. Belmont to pale, gulp, and turn resolutely towards the vessel.

The ambassador waved over his shoulder a farewell to me, and off he went.

"Just what assignment did the Navy give our Lieutenant Marshall?" Commander Edmunds asked.

"Flight duty," I said.

"Ah." The commander murmured, "In dirigibles?"

"Aeroplanes," I corrected. "Experimental aeroplanes."

"Hmm. Very safe."

"Sir." It was as noncommittal an agreement I dared make. "I believe someone told his family that only the zeppelins held bombs, and someone might have thought that meant an aeroplane was safe. And possibly there'd been some concern regarding mines and submarine attacks if he'd taken the positions being bandied about."

"Good luck with that." The commander gave me a nod and hurried after his ambassador. His chuckles did not fill me with a great deal of confidence.

At least the naval service had not, this time, sent me with any instructions implying that they thought aviation was safe and easy. Perhaps it was less important to them than shipbuilding or the training exercises the fleets of the Atlantic and Pacific were engaged in. They had to prepare in the event we, one day, were sent to join in the great war and support our allies. But with our German allies fighting our French and British allies, it was anyone's guess who the United States ought to be fighting, anyway. My best guess remained that our nation would stay out a while longer, at least, though it was clear my little group thought it inevitable that we'd come in on the German side soon.

The mess in the African colonies certainly implied a level of duplicitousness on the part of the French and British colonial administrators, but our politicians back home had accepted the apologetic responses to that. And at least for now, Germany still held her territories on the southern continent. But those distant wrongdoings had little immediate impact on the war on the European continent. They did, of course, impact what the locals of that continent thought of the colonizer governments and a certain former colony over in the Americas had begun to notice, as well.

Lieutenant Thompson waved me down from the bar's open window.

"Hays! I say, Chief Hays! Come have a tankard of beer with us." A brimming second mug appeared in his hand before he finished calling out.

I entered the bar, and Lieutenant Marshall lifted up his own mug in a cheerful toast to our safe voyage.

"Roberts can go get us the train tickets," Marshall was saying. "There's a three-week flight observer course we all probably ought to enroll in, which'll let us get up in the sky before the war is all over. The pilot course is three months, so." He waggled a hand, indicating it might extend beyond the timeframe of the conflict.

"Some ought to take the pilot training," Thompson said. "We should learn what they do differently. I'll do it if no one else wants to."

"Oh, I want to, too. We both should." Marshall said, "Not much value in learning how to take notes in German about whatever the infantry is doing when we could be flying an *Albatros* instead."

"Or one of those scout monoplanes." Thompson clinked his mug against Marshall's in agreement.

Roberts looked back and forth between the two lieutenants. He was most junior and least confident. His blinking blue eyes reminded me of a pet bunny trying very hard to become a hound.

"I'll do the observer training," Roberts volunteered. "Somebody else can do the flying. Really, I don't mind." He patted his pockets to locate the group's travel funds. "I'll be right back with our train tickets."

I could be Lieutenant Marshall's observer, I supposed. *I couldn't lose track of him if I were in the same aircraft all the time.*

"Do you suppose he knows that the monoplanes, *Eindeckers*, I think I heard them called, don't have an observer seat at all?" Thompson said.

"He can join in with the ground crews and stay with Chief Hays,"

Marshall said. "Tell me again what you've heard about the new *Eindeckers*. One set of wings instead of two, of course I know. But also a bit faster and more maneuverable than even an *Albatros*?"

Lieutenant Thompson, who couldn't have actually seen either German aircraft type himself yet, drew in a breath to share his rumors.

But what had Marshall just suggested? No way would be I staying behind.

"I'll be entering pilot training, too," I said.

"The man's a commissioned officer, for God's sake. Did you expect the Navy to give him orders to sit at home and knit? Most of the boys begged off and took orders home after seeing a few Germans crash. How was I to know he wouldn't be one of the quitters?

"And if you do 'take a ship over to speak to the boy yourself,' you might indicate to him that we'd appreciate a bit more specificity in the technical details of his reports. 'Dashingly beautiful machines' is all well and good, but helps develop our own aviation industry not at all."

— –EXCERPT OF A LETTER FROM THE DESK OF REAR ADMIRAL BRADLEY A. FISKE, AIDE FOR OPERATIONS TO THE SECRETARY OF THE NAVY

April 1915,
The Skies Above Germany
to the East of France

Despite my misgivings, I had to concede that flying these crates around had grown on me...a bit. That said, I didn't have any illusions about my longevity in the flying business.

The warmth of Spring at ground level chilled to a fine frost at altitude, and my wool gloves could stand to have a few holes darned shut. The *Albatros's* engine growled in a constant thrum my ears had grown nearly deaf to over the last three months. The wind tore at my face, and I pulled my hat down more firmly and tucked in an edge of scarf threatening to pull free.

Poor Roberts, seated behind me, didn't need the shock of my scarf striking him in the face while he was trying to see to make notes and practice his navigation.

The shimmer of little streams embroidering the patchwork farm country below rolled on in a comfortably familiar landscape we'd flown over countless times now. But Roberts had a devil of a time recognizing any of it.

It probably didn't help that we were flying with a loaded rifle strapped in next to him. I had no gun as pilot, so it'd be up to him to shoot anything that needed shooting.

And good luck to him, because he'd need it.

Marksmanship in the sky might quite reasonably include prayer as much as practice. Our speed gave him eighty knots of wind to struggle against while attempting to hold a rifle steady. An enemy would not be flying alongside like a kite being towed for target practice, but instead would be maneuvering or possibly even diving towards us and shooting back. Roberts might get a few seconds in which a target was close enough for him to reasonably hit anything, and he'd need nerves of steel, too, and buckets full of luck to actually hit something.

I put higher chances on the German observers, Shultz and Hoffmann, riding with Lieutenant Marshall and Lieutenant Thompson just ahead. But they'd probably miss anything, too. The German Leutnant Boelcke leading our little air convoy had more experience in the air than anyone else we'd met, and much of it was much, much closer to the front than we were now. The French had taken to arming their observers with pistols, and Boelcke had been having his own observer fire back with a rifle. But today he was flying an *Eindecker*, which of course had no observer to use a handgun or anything else.

Our *Albatros* aeroplanes soared over the countryside quite as powerfully as the good luck bird they took their name from. Canvas stretched tight across a set of wings below my cockpit and another above. The engine rumbled below my feet, drowning any noise the propeller whirring in front made. Lieutenant Junior Grade Roberts huddled in the seat just behind me. The edges of his maps sometimes tickled the back of my neck as the wind tore at their edges. The implied warning that shooting at an *Albatros* would rain misery down on the enemy struck me as quite appropriate.

Ahead, Lieutenant Marshall drove his plane up to spear through a wisp of cloud off to my left. Shultz gesticulated from the backseat, and wiped one-handed with dramatic motions at his goggles.

Leutnant Boelcke flew in the *Eindecker* at the very front of our group. He shot bolt straight towards Douai, with none of the darting here and there of my American lieutenants. The greater power of his engines opened the space between him and us, but he'd glanced back from time to time and would angle up and down to slow enough for our slower aircraft to catch up whenever he judged the distance too great.

Lieutenant Thompson, in the fourth aircraft with another steady German, Leutnant Hoffmann, angled his plane off to my right, as if he was going to go through a much larger cloud bank well out of our way. Hoffmann reached forward and thumped Thompson on the head. The aeroplane returned to proper course.

Marshall threw back his head in laughter, inaudible over the sounds of our engines and the roar of the wind.

We'd seen aeroplanes crash during pilot training. An important strut could break. An engine could quit. The propeller could sheer off—especially on those aeroplanes with a pilot-operated machine gun. None of our current aircraft (thank heaven!) had one of those.

We already learned a few useful things to take back home with us. *If only I could convince Lieutenant Marshall to go before our luck ran out*, I wished.

On second thought, though, *Perhaps I shouldn't hope just for luck. The flight instructors had frequently drummed on the tables and declared: "The cemetery is filled with lucky pilots. Don't be lucky; be* good."

Tattered map edges slapped against my head. I twisted to look behind, in case my observer needed to signal something, and got my goggles knocked crooked by the wind for my trouble. I straightened them.

Roberts's hands shook more than could be explained away by the chill of altitude, and I could see his lips moving in a half-chant. He wasn't paying me any attention, and from his stricken expression, I knew what he was saying to himself. It was the flying instructions being repeated over and over.

One. You must focus your attention, all of it.
Two. You must always have a landing spot in mind that you can glide to if your engine quits.
Three. You must keep track of the time so you don't run out of fuel.
And finally, most of all, you must know where you are so you don't accidentally come down on the wrong side of the lines.

The chief instructor did tend to go on like that, but who am I to argue with someone with nearly 60 hours flying these machines?

I suppressed a quiet laugh at what that handful of hours' experience meant when spent in the sky. There were ten-year-olds aplenty who had 60 hours at sea, and it meant nothing. But flights came in short bursts, with days or weeks of preparation before and after, in an attempt to make the lightweight craft less dangerous to fly. But still there were crashes, so much so that perhaps the man who hadn't broken himself and hadn't broken his plane was more than lucky. Perhaps he was good.

The wind filled my lungs with a crisp air somehow more exhilarating than breathing was on the ground. We flew northwest, the sun flashing off the clouds, but not blinding us too much. We were to deliver our aeroplanes to an aerodrome near the town of Douai. Boelcke had arranged an early takeoff, exactly so we'd not be flying blind into a setting sun, a fact for which I was grateful. Our four machines, an unusually large group of aeroplanes, were haphazardly strewn about the sky in a rough diamond, with Boelcke in front, Thompson to the right, Marshall to the left, and me in the rear.

I flew a bit higher than the rest while the cloud cover remained sparse enough for me to see everyone. I liked the idea of more time to set up for a glide if some part of my aeroplane failed me.

Thompson pulled his cap off and waved it in the air, only to get thumped again by his observer. The energetic young man and his serious backseater made me laugh. They'd be buying each other rounds at the little tavern closest to the Douai airfield after we landed and joking about whatever this newest in-flight argument was about.

The other aeroplanes had shrunk with distance. I'd been gradually climbing without noticing it. I pressed the stick forward gently to level out.

Reminded to focus on my own flying, I checked the gauges. Rotations per minute for the engine hovered about where they should be. Nice oil pressure. The time on my watch told me we were about halfway to Douai. I double-checked the fuel level: eh, it matched well enough. I tapped the glass, and the needle wiggled up to where it ought to be. *We should make it, but there wouldn't be a whole lot extra.*

Boelcke dropped altitude to clear a few clouds and banked to the left and then to the right, examining the countryside for landmarks. He adjusted our course a few points to port, or rather to the left.

Fencing and scattered tree lines broke up much of the deceptively friendly countryside into plots too small to land on. The furrows and ditches between the new plantings would challenge the *Albatros's* wheels and struts. I kept track of the larger fields and pastures spreading out here and there beneath us. A nice fallow one would pass beneath us in another minute and would slip away out of gliding range not too long after. I scanned for another.

A glint in the distance flashed. I wiped at my goggles with the end of my scarf. The sun did tricky things with church steeples and farmhouse roofs, but I peered hard. The flash shone above the horizon in a patch of sky clear of all clouds.

I waved my left hand without turning and pointed at the spot where I'd seen it. My observer neither tapped my shoulder in acknowledgement nor thumped my head. I batted awkwardly at the edge of the maps and still got none of the responses I needed.

Thompson and Hoffmann's aeroplane flew almost directly in line with the odd flash. *Neither showed signs of having seen anything. Maybe there was nothing to see?*

I turned in my seat, and Roberts finally looked up. He glanced at tiny scattered farmhouses far beneath us, turned gray, and tried to bury his head in the maps again.

"That way," I yelled, gesturing back towards the flash.

Roberts, wide-eyed, gave me a thumbs-up and pointed not beyond Thompson's aeroplane, but beyond Boelcke's towards Douai. Then he looked at the ground again, his clenched hands shaking hard.

I faced forward and pulled hard on the stick to climb. Sunlight on the wings could make such a flash. I cursed. I'd looked away. Now I had no idea where to find that aircraft again. Marshall, Thompson, and Boelcke all flew straight, seeing nothing.

Maybe there was nothing to see?

A tiny black speck appeared just above the horizon in front and slightly right of our formation. A little bug framed by the wide blue sky. The front was that way, but so was the airfield at our destination.

Except there'd be no reason for a friendly pilot to be streaking directly at us. The dark thing—a flying aircraft, I was almost certain—didn't seem to be maneuvering and was moving roughly in the opposite direction of us. The dot hung in the sky, growing larger and rising higher above the horizon now; I assumed that meant an aeroplane at a higher altitude, though I couldn't tell by how much.

I pointed and yelled. I couldn't go any faster. The *Albatros* engine went the speed it went, or it was off. I could make slow left and right turns to reduce my forward movement, but that'd be pure cowardice. It would leave the three other aircraft flying on ahead, still unaware of the coming interceptor.

I couldn't help myself—I looked back again and waved to Roberts to point out the intruding aircraft. He attempted a smile and waved back as if I were trying to have a pleasant chat midflight. I turned again to Boelcke, Marshall, and even Thompson: none of them saw it.

No one pointed. Not one of the observers attempted to signal anything. No one made any attempt to communicate the presence of another aeroplane, and not a one of them was looking back at me. I had no wireless to signal them with and shouting into an 80-knot wind over the drone of the engine was futile. I couldn't hear Roberts from my own backseat, let alone someone in another aeroplane a hundred yards or more in the distance.

I looked back to the right to find the black dot, but saw only a vast empty sky.

I suppressed a surge of panic.

I shouldn't've looked away, except of course it would've been very nice if someone else in our little formation could've looked around and paid attention to my waving arms to all be alert to the danger.

Scanning the horizon, I saw nothing above or below. *It shouldn't have been possible to disappear.* Then I realized it: *my own wings could blind me!*

I pushed the stick to the left which raised my right wing slightly to reveal the sky behind it. *There it was!* I felt momentary relief, but I would not look away again. I would not make the same mistake three times in a row. Though even while I promised myself that, I realized it no longer mattered.

The spot had grown into a French single-winged *Morane* too large at its closing range to be lost even in the wide expanse of the sky.

Its engines must've been shrieking down on us, but it dove, utterly silent under the sound of our own racket.

It grew giant. Propellers and nose angled straight on. *All the whole sky, and did he mean to ram me?*

But no, I could see a bit of the *Morane's* tail. The Frenchman had a different target. It fell on the closest *Albatros* from above, with Thompson blinded by his own upper right wing.

Hoffman threw his hands up, seeing it at last. A split second later, the German was reaching for his rifle.

The front of the *Morane* flashed with bright sparking.

If it were burning, shouldn't there be smoke? And the propeller would be visible instead of that blur if the engine had given out...

God help us, that was machine gun fire! And on a single-seater aeroplane! How the devil had the French done it?

Then everything happened at once, and I didn't even have time to swear.

The *Morane*'s dive dropped it underneath Thompson, streaking by far too close for either aeroplane's safety.

Hoffmann fired his rifle, tracking the French plane as it fought to pull up.

Thompson jerked my way and slumped over the stick, pitching the *Albatros* up as it began the slowly increasing left turn of a propeller-driven aeroplane with no living hand on the controls.

Hoffmann sighted his rifle and returned fire as the passing French plane buzzed under their aircraft.

The *Albatros* turned and turned. In the moment when it faced back to Douai again, I thought maybe Thompson might yet manage to land it, but the downward spiral continued, and the pilot didn't move.

The French plane shot up away from Thompson's erratic circling. The floundering *Albatros* threw the German observer this way and that, and still he tried to find the French aircraft for another shot.

And I saw what Hoffmann could not see: the aircraft dropped.

Dodging Lieutenant Thompson's plane seemed to have the spoiled the Frenchman's interest in taking a shot at the rest of us. The *Morane* hung in the air for a moment as it banked towards a heading to France.

Marshall's *Albatros* streaked across the sky with Shultz twisting to fire at the fleeing Frenchman.

In the silent skies, I could only imagine Shultz's rifle fire.

Crack! Crack!

I jerked in my own seat to see that Roberts, face white with fear, had his gun up and was shooting as best he could even with the poor angle I'd given him on the target.

Crack-crack-crack! I dove forward. I had more altitude that either Marshall or the Frenchman. I could close and give my terrified gunner a chance to hit something, too.

Roberts swung the barrel of his rifle over my head and down following the *Morane*, now passing under our plane. It banked into a left turn and fled to the southwest.

The Frenchman lifted his face to stare directly into my eyes in the split second our planes passed each other. He gave the smallest shrug as though acknowledging the insanity of war as my observer shot at him. The distance opened, and Roberts would need a miracle to hit the now zig-zagging Frenchman.

Lieutenant Marshall's aeroplane roared beneath us. I threw my body against the stick to roll right, straining against the guide wires. He buzzed past, wingtips mere feet away. Oblivious to the near collision, he leaned forward against the biting cold wind, focused entirely on catching the *Morane.*

Shultz gave an exaggerated shrug at the foolishness of pilots and touched his temple in an ironic salute.

Marshall's *Albatros* and the *Morane* shrank into toy planes in the distant sky.

Boelcke's *Eindecker* circled well clear, and I could imagine his exasperation at being the only unarmed aeroplane in the fight. I half-expected him to produce a brace of pistols from under his jacket and bring down the *Morane* all on his own. Instead, his aeroplane tracked over the spot where Thompson's *Albatros* met the earth.

The Frenchman realized too late that his zigzags had let Lieutenant Marshall close to nearly on top of him. And worse for the *Morane*, we had the advantage of altitude.

At the last moment, Marshall pulled out from his dive and slalomed over the Frenchman, letting Shultz rain bullets down on the enemy aeroplane while its own machine gun pointed uselessly at open sky. The *Morane's* nose began to lift and turn that deadly barrel.

Roberts and I were closing, but still too far to be of any help.

The French plane slowed.

It hung in midair for a fraction of a second and began to drop.

We closed fast, but it was over. The Frenchman hadn't begun an engine-powered dive to regain speed and circle around to strafe us. This was a mere glide. A motionless propeller betrayed his complete loss of engine power. The *Morane* drifted with gentle corrections down towards a long fallow strip of farmland.

One lucky shot in that hailstorm of bullets had actually struck the Frenchman's engine!

Lieutenant Marshall followed alongside and above the stricken enemy plane and I trailed him. Boelcke settled in behind us. My nerves kept me scanning the sky, but no other aircraft appeared.

Shultz secured his rifle. Marshall kept his *Albatros* over the *Morane* and pointed with increasing agitation at it.

The wounded French plane maneuvered with lethargic slowness, angling only towards the open farmland with no power left for skilled evasion. It glided heavy and slow, now an easy target for Marshall's observer. Shultz shook his head and finished doing up the straps to secure the rifle for landing.

Boelcke behind us might not be able to read those jerky movements well enough to know Marshall was furious, but I knew my lieutenant.

The French plane maneuvered gently to angle towards the flattest-looking field. A railroad cut a neat line through the friendly German countryside, and the growing toy-sized buildings nestled beside the tracks suggested a train station.

People spilled out of the buildings ogling up at us.

The *Morane* touched down with expert lightness, bumped along the rutted earth, and rolled to a stop.

Lieutenant Marshall and then I made safe, if less skilled, landings. I coasted to a stop and unstrapped from the airplane. Boelcke followed, shutting off the *Eindecker's* engine, and climbing out.

Soldiers from the train station ran toward the French plane, while curious onlookers gathered around all of us.

Boelcke stripped off his scarf and gloves while assuring them all that we were German allies and only the *Morane's* pilot was a Frenchman. I pulled off my own helmet and let the warm air restore feeling to my frozen skin.

The French pilot, first to land, stayed in his aeroplane fussing with the controls. My eyebrows went up. *His wood and canvas contraption might have broken speed records before the war, but he was grounded now and stopped. What did he hope to do?* I wondered.

Oh. The man hefted a wooden strut broken from his own aircraft and battered at the cockpit gauges with it.

Boelcke yelled a command to the soldiers in the crowd, and the man was wrestled from his airplane before he could do more than crack the glass on his oil pressure gauge.

I climbed from my plane, setting my boots down on soft warm earth.

Lieutenant Marshall pressed through the crowd, and I hurried to follow.

Two soldiers held the Frenchman, and the rest kept back the curious farmer's family and examined the *Morane* with Leutnant Boelcke.

Marshall strode forward, sweeping off his helmet and goggles to hang by their straps, and unbuttoned his coat to reach his revolver.

"Sir! Lieutenant Marshall!" I shouted into the commotion, but if he heard me, he didn't look up.

The German soldiers holding the still-struggling Frenchman saw, but looked back and forth to Boelcke and their own senior officer, uncertain whether to restrain their captive for Marshall or to defend the man against an obviously enraged American pilot.

"*Achtung*, Leutnant!" Boelcke yelled. "Leutnant Marshall!" The crowd hushed, and the senior German pilot's ringing command voice broke through.

Marshall's rising hand froze, and Boelcke waded briskly through the crowd and soldiers. In mixed German and English, he said, "*Das pistole*: put. It. Away!"

Lieutenant Marshall looked at Boelcke, then me and then at the revolver in his hand, as if he'd just woken up. He holstered the weapon and stood perfectly still in a pose I'd seen on more than one naval officer expecting to be publicly harangued by a superior for an infraction he hadn't been entirely convinced was wrong.

But Boelcke brushed straight past.

"Mr. Hays," he called over his shoulder to me. I could never convince these Germans to call me "Chief" or just "Hays" as a mere enlisted man. "The propeller." He pointed. "Most interesting. It is, how do you say?"

"Armored," I said.

I marveled at the construction. Creases on the metal plates lining the backs of the prop blades left shiny divots where bullets had stuck. I spun it by hand. The sluggish movement would reduce the aeroplane speed, but also, oh, the pings had deformed one of the blades. "He was lucky to be able to land."

"Maybe. Maybe," Boelcke acknowledged.

And the machine gun: I examined it, and did my best not to let color flood my cheeks. The French *Morane* mounted a 7.9mm Hotchkiss. The American gunsmith did live in France and had set up his factory outside Paris decades ago, but that hardly made it less embarrassing, since it had been built for suppling the frogs during the Franco-Prussian war.

"Normal gun," Boelcke said.

"Nothing special," I agreed.

"*Suffisamment speciale,*" the French pilot said, and clapped his mouth shut tight again when not just Marshall, but Shultz, too, glared at him with red-rimmed eyes.

A German officer consulted with Boelcke and took control of the situation, detailing a few men to guard the French plane, others to take the French pilot away toward the station and to disperse the crowd. The *Morane* was to be studied, with detailed reports to be sent to several of our own German gunsmiths trying out machine gun mounting techniques. The pilot was to go stay with some landed gentry relatives, if he would give his parole.

I walked to Lieutenant Marshall, who sagged in his overly thick flying gear. I shrugged off my own heavy jacket and encouraged him to do the same.

"My American friends," Leutnant Shultz said. "If you please, keep watch on our aeroplanes." The German's English had started quite fine and only improved on being paired with Marshall as his observer.

Shultz made a slight nod in the direction of the farmhouse barn's hayloft, where two boys stared in open fascination at our aircraft, and one seemed to be measuring the distance to jump on the upper wing of my *Albatros*. The soldiers assigned to the *Morane* were little better, turning the propeller this way and that as they'd seen me do.

Shultz gave a small shrug, as though apologizing for his countrymen's fascination.

"Mr. Boelcke and I must go to the telegraph office in the train station to send in reports and make arrangements for all the aeroplanes to be collected."

"Of course, sir," I said, locking eyes with the boy in the hayloft, who abruptly found a need to retreat into the shadows of the barn.

We obeyed Leutnant Shultz's request.

Or I did. Marshall turned his back to stare at the point on the horizon where Lieutenant Thompson and Leutnant Hoffmann had gone down.

Lieutenant Junior Grade Roberts followed Marshall's gaze and gulped.

"Chief, I, uh, I should make a report, too," he said, and hurried after Shultz towards the train station. I was pretty sure Roberts would be on a nice safe boat to America as soon as his family could get his telegram and answer it, and I was glad to see the brave little rabbit go.

Walking ahead with the soldiers and Leutnant Boelcke, the downed enemy pilot was waving his hands energetically, trying to explain something. His German was even worse than mine, but I gathered that the Frenchman was as shocked as the rest of us that rifle fire had succeeded in bringing an aeroplane down.

Roberts's quick strides had him at the back of the crowd, and he blended in out of sight in moments.

"You saw this coming," Marshall said to me.

I hurried to salute, having forgotten my manners, and my officer batted my hand down.

"Never mind all that. Tell me about the beginning of the engagement. When did you spot him? And how the Devil did he manage to shoot down Thompson and Hoffmann without destroying his propeller? Could he have done it again? Or could anyone, do you think?"

The French pilot was being peppered with much the same questions in German. I replied with much less hesitancy than they did.

I hadn't seen this coming, not really, but I wondered if maybe an admiral had at least suspected it could happen.

"Absolutely! We must have a full series on America's First Flying Ace in the papers immediately. If the other side can claim the munitions ship Lusitania *is an innocent commercial liner because some fools took passage on it, we can call our favorite war hero an ace.*

"Oh, and see if Rear Admiral Fiske will make some sort of arrangement with the Germans about a medal. It's the least he can do after causing Lois Irene such distress."

— –EXCERPT OF A LETTER FROM THE DESK OF THE CHAIRMAN OF THE DEMOCRATIC NATIONAL COMMITTEE, MR. WILLIAM F. MCCOMBS

AUGUST 1915,
DOUAI AERODROME AT THE
FRENCH-GERMAN FRONT

The engineers who examined the *Morane* found a frozen fuel line and bullet holes. Officially, the credit for the capture went to no one. Unofficially, Leutnant Shultz and Lieutenant Marshall had yet to buy their own beer even months later. And even better, the weaponry on the French plane had proven inspirational for arming the remarkable single-seater *Eindecker* aeroplanes.

Marshall and I soared, each in our own *Eindecker*, on our second flight in the new machines.

The wonders of better and better gear made flying almost comfortable. My face had frozen again, with my wool scarf not quite wrapped thickly enough on the warm morning before takeoff. Engine oil splattered at me in searing droplets, whipped over the small windshield, but my goggles and scarf saved me from the worst of it and icy wind chilled any burn instantly. A length of silk around my neck protected my skin from chafing against the cold-stiffened collar of my flight jacket.

Lieutenant Marshall and I had flown for about an hour already. The controls felt light, turning so easily compared to an *Albatros* with half as many guide wires to throw my strength against, and the whole sky opened up with no upper set of wings to block my view.

The openness brought back a sense of how truly fragile we were in the sky, and I'd convinced a harness maker to construct some straps to secure us to the aeroplane seats. Most of the pilots rolled their eyes, but when Boelcke accepted them, everyone else did, too.

Even better, we each had one of the new machine guns installed. Much like the Maschinengewehr 08s, which of course I remembered from the Port of Doula in Kamerun, these were Spandau LMG 08s—air-cooled in the chill of altitude instead of water-cooled. And Fokker's clever timing belt made the gun fire in bursts between the propellers.

We hadn't used the guns on each other, of course, but we'd taken practice targeting dives and done every other tag-teaming maneuver we could think of. Leutnant Boelcke planned to go hunting in the twilight this evening, and Marshall and I were going with him.

We turned now, low on fuel and tired, towards Labrayelle airfield just outside Douai.

Where smoke rose in the distance.

I stared, rubbed the surface of my goggles to clear them, and looked again. Black streaks smeared ugly lines in the bright blue sky.

The heavily trenched front could not move so fast in just an hour for Douai to be shelled by artillery. The infantry, poor souls, would do well to move ten feet forward and take another trench without it being wrested back immediately in that time. To have moved over ten miles and now have field guns in position was impossible. And yet something, multiple somethings, burned.

Lieutenant Marshall hand signaled that he'd also seen it.

I nodded in an exaggerated motion to say, "Yes, I see it, too, and understand."

We dove for speed, with Marshall leading. First, the Douai cathedral spire and then the buildings of the town emerged, undamaged but eerie in the emptiness of their streets. My sense of dread grew as the smoke wisps darkened into arrows narrowing at the horizon just southwest of Douai, pointing at Labrayelle, at our own airfield.

Tiny flashes peppered the ground, followed by dirty puffs sometimes spreading into fires if a grounded aircraft or a cache of fuel caught flame. The smoke over the airfield fogged the sky.

Marshall waved for my attention and pointed upward with urgent jerks of his arm. A moment later, his machine began to gain altitude. I dragged the stick back to follow him up and held pressure on the rudder to counteract the *Eindecker's* natural inclination to twist left and follow the spin of its propeller.

The desperate struggle for altitude ate at our previous speed. Our engines rattled on in ear-splitting growls, but the pressing rush of the wind weakened.

Specks above the horizon swirled through the billows of smoke.

We climbed with increased desperation into the thinning air and blazing daylight. Marshall leveled out and pointed down.

A half-dozen aeroplanes circled below us. A few alternated taking a dive to release tiny specks and then climb again. Less brave ones scattered their bombs from altitude with no effort to aim.

Not one looked up at the blinding noon sun to notice us.

Marshall picked a target, pushed his nose over, and began a shallow dive. I followed.

The leather straps pushed against my shoulders, keeping me with my machine rather than floating out of the cockpit. I fervently hoped these suddenly very important straps did their part and held me in.

Staying with Marshall required me to focus every ounce of attention I had on his craft. His wing bent, and I must bend mine immediately, too.

But this did no good, I realized. I was too close to watch for danger without becoming a collision danger myself.

I climbed and added gradual s-turns to slow my forward progress until his machine was another hundred feet ahead. Continuous stick and rudder adjustments kept me in position behind him.

I stole a look out ahead of the lieutenant's machine now that I had a little more room to maneuver. A fine mist of engine oil covered the little windscreen at the top of my cockpit, but better covering the windscreen than my goggles. I leaned out to get a better view.

The enemy aircraft continued their bombing runs, oblivious to us still.

Marshall angled towards one of the non-diving aeroplanes. It circled, unaware of any danger. The double wings weren't right for a *Morane*. And the paint...oh, these were the British *B.E.2c* biplanes! Two-seaters, but the one in front of us held only a pilot.

The British pilot reached down, paying no attention to the sky above his upper wings, and lifted up a bomb.

I realized why the observer and his seat were gone. They'd made room for the weight of the bombs and the fuel needed for a long flight by doing without a second crewmember.

The British pilot lobbed the bomb over the side, in the direction of our maintenance crew's tents.

Marshall's hand came up to prime his Spandau machine gun.

I itched to do the same, but my barrel pointed far too close to his *Eindecker*.

The rat-a-tat of his attack was a long vicious growl, louder even than our engines.

The *B.E.2c* banked to lift his wings even as Marshall's *Eindecker* raked at him with machine gun fire. The pilot brandished a pistol and fired it, not at the lieutenant, but at me!

I released my hold on the stick in shock and my *Eindecker* turned immediately to the left. Even that reaction was more than a second too slow to matter.

Shaking, I took hold of myself. No one had ever looked me square in the eye while trying to kill me before. At once terrified and furious, I longed for a target of my own and cursed the orders keeping me glued to the lieutenant's side.

My arms ached from an hour of forcing the guide wires this way and that in close maneuvers, but I'd let them ache ten times worse and be happy for it if I could shoot at someone bombing our home.

People boiled out of the tents below. One lone *Eindecker* rolled around burning aircraft onto the airfield and launched into the sky.

I pointed my nose ahead of the Lieutenant Marshall's aeroplane so I could catch up to him. He aimed for another Brit heading to the southwest toward Arras. This bomber flew in a straight line and seemed unaware of the lieutenant stalking him.

Another rat-a-tat announced Marshall's next attack. Realizing I was catching up a little too quickly, I pulled back on my stick to get above them both and slow down.

The pilot of this second biplane must have seen the lieutenant fire from hundreds of feet away. It would've taken a miracle to hit anything from that distance. All that Marshall had accomplished was to alert his target.

The lieutenant flew closer and fired again.

The British pilot jerked his bomber left and right in a desperate erratic zigzag that made my back ache in sympathy, and my eyebrows lift in slow understanding.

Marshall didn't fire. He closed.

The enemy's wild evasion had slowed him so much he became almost still.

Marshall released a single burst dead into the British machine. The biplane propeller stuttered and stopped as smoke wafted off the engine.

Lieutenant Marshall, still moving faster, came alongside his victim to hold position next to him.

The smoke grew thicker, and flickers of flame emerged. The fire crawled towards the cockpit.

Marshall waved his arm at the man, pointing downward. He needn't risk a field or sheep pasture landing. A mowed, well-graded airfield waited beneath him. And he must land immediately!

The man stared out at nothing.

"Land, for God's sake!" I shouted uselessly into the wind.

Marshall fired his machine gun at nothing, and at last, the British pilot looked up and saw the urgent gesturing down towards the airfield.

Too slowly, he started to descend. Lieutenant Marshall followed him down.

The flames licked over the biplane more quickly now, and I knew there would be no escape for this British airman. The fire engulfed the fabric and frame of the two-seater, burning its way to the cockpit. I looked on in horror as the engine fell away, the wings folded upward, and the flaming fuselage plummeted earthward.

Marshall broke off even as Leutnant Boelcke joined us in the sky, dodging around the falling wreckage of aeroplane.

A deadly dance ensued as other German pilots found the remaining unburned machines and launched after us. The former attackers became the attacked, and Fokker's guns proved every bit as deadly as the British bombs.

"I do believe Rear Admiral Fiske is quite as stunned as the rest of us. As for 'Our Boy,' I say if the man wants to fight, let him fight. And for the United States, I see no reason to overturn President Wilson's past decisions. He kept us out of the war, and if America would like to continue that, they shall be free to say so in the coming election."

—Excerpt of a letter from the desk of the Vice President of the United States, Mr. Thomas R. Marshall

ABOUT JOELLE PRESBY

Joelle Presby is a veteran U.S. Navy nuclear engineer who grew up in West Africa. She hunts cross genre writing opportunities and has snared gigs for everything from urban fantasy and high fantasy to alternate history and humorous science fiction. She wrote THE DABARE SNAKE LAUNCHER and co-writes in the Multiverse series with David Weber.

Where you can find Joelle Presby:

LinkTree:
https://linktr.ee/joellepresby

Author Website
Joellepresby.com

ABOUT PATRICK DOYLE

Patrick Doyle is a pilot for a major airline and a retired U.S. Naval officer. He has been an airline simulator instructor and check pilot. He graduated college with a degree in history and is an avid sci-fi fan and wargamer who also dabbles in writing projects from time to time.

He co-wrote 2 alternate history short stories in the Phases of Mars series with Joelle Presby. He has worked with BuNine, a group that advised David Weber on his Honor Harrington novel series, and co-hosted Starfleet Tactical on YouTube.

As a gamer, he wrote the "Federation Commander Tactics Manual" (available from the Amarillo Design Bureau) and won several national championships. He is the lead game designer for Mariner Games, focusing on StarForce Commander, a tactical starship combat game. (available at https://www.mariner.games and Wargame Vault).

PERCHANCE TO DREAM

Sarah A. Hoyt

PERCHANCE TO DREAM

Near the destroyed village of Cappy by the bank of the Somme, where the river flowed due west, a muscular young blond man turned on his camp bed inside a stone hut.

Despite the rain falling outside, sending tendrils of dampness through every crack in the old walls, the hut was almost too warm, thanks to the blaze in the fireplace. The blaze itself was a sign of the occupant's importance, since wood in the French countryside—long martyred by the marche and countre-march of armies in the conflict the world called the Great War—had grown scarce.

Manfred von Richthofen, youthful leader of Jagdgeschwader One, flung the woolen blanket from him and turned again, this time lifting his arm above his head, as though to ward off some threat. The scar on the side of his head, imperfectly hidden by the short blond hair, seemed to pulse, livid.

"No," he whispered.

He was not speaking of the distant thrumming of artillery that served as the devil's lullaby to a countryside devoid of innocent sleepers. He'd heard it too much over the last three years for this, the Kaiser's latest and desperate push to victory, to disturb his sleep. And the flapping of the tent-hangars, like housing for prehistoric beasts, was a true lullaby. For beneath those hid the planes of the Jagdgeschwader One, his very own flying circus, the source of his glory and, more importantly, a source of comradery, of hope.

And yet Richtofen's sleep was agitated, perturbed by dreams that marched beneath his eyelids. In the morning, sitting on the side of his bed, rubbing the place on his head where an old and never perfectly healed injury sometimes spit up fragments of bone, he couldn't remember anything of the dream.

No, that wasn't true. As he pulled his coveralls over his monogrammed gray silk pajamas, a single memory came back, sharp-edged like a fragment of ice on the surface of a deep frozen lake, like a fragment of bone emerging from the flesh.

It was a pamphlet, white and crudely printed. It showed a picture of a flower-covered grave, and beneath it read in English:

To the German Flying Corps.
Rittmeister Baron Manfred von Richthofen was killed in aerial combat, on April 21st, 1918. He was buried with full military honors.

The memory was so sharp that Richthofen stood, fastening the coveralls, staring ahead, as though the pamphlet hung there in midair, in front of him.

It's just a dream, the Red Baron thought. *A strange one, but still a dream.*

"No, Moritz." Menzke's voice sounded, with just an edge of exasperation, as he tried to prevent the Deer Hound-Great Dane cross from rushing the Rittmeister and bowling Manfred over with exuberance.

The orderly carried an ewer Manfred would know was filled with cold water. Manfred woke enough from his thoughts to brace against the dog putting his paws on Manfred's shoulders. Managing, just barely, to stop his face from being licked, Manfred managed a half-laugh. "No, Moritz," he said, then scratching at the dog's ears as the animal fell to all four paws and squirmed in happiness. "How is my little lap dog this morning?"

Even Moritz couldn't distract him from the nightmare.

Moritz was dry. And Richthofen, looking out his window, could see that the pervading rain that had dogged them for days had finally lifted to reveal a hazy sky. Great wisps of fog drifted across the airfield, like fingers searching out something.

Chances were that later on the fog would burn out, and the sky would clear, revealing good hunting weather, which they'd had rarely enough in this wretched place. He should be eager to climb the sky in his red plane, but something felt wrong.

Where had that damnable note come from to invade his dream? Why now? What dormant thing in his life had kicked up that shard of fear to put horror in his night and confusion in his morning?

It wasn't that he thought himself invincible. Oh, once, perhaps, long ago, when he watched the enemy flyers go down in flames and thought that he was too good, too lucky for such a fate to befall him. But since the crash that had left the scar on his head, it had become far too personal, far too possible. Richtofen knew that like the many men he'd shot down, he was mortal. He knew very well that not all crashes ended in an awkward landing and being taken prisoner. He paused again, absently petting Moritz, where, in his mind, the flames that had almost consumed him before he could land and escape were felt anew.

For a time, he got ill every time he shot someone down, and only the greatest of will powers could keep him flying and serving his country in the air.

Menzke poured his water in the basin, and Manfred splashed it on his face, welcoming the cold as a reviving shock.

I should shave, Manfred thought. Before his wound, it would not have been a question, as he was a fastidious man. When his thought was in disorder, it was doubly important that he present himself as ordered and in full control. Catapulted into command at the age of twenty-five, he maintained the respect of his men by behaving as though he were someone apart. That included appearing impeccably dressed and shaved, whenever humanly possible.

No, instead I will have breakfast, he thought. *I can shave after the mission.* He knew lately—since his wound in October of the year before—he'd relaxed a little, and might sometimes be seen to drink a little too much, or stay up too late, with his companions. He no longer had the courage some of his men had, who decided to forego breakfast in order to fly as early as possible. They'd return from the hunting, ravenous as hawks.

The ones who returned.

Manfred had never understood how anyone could cheerfully face death on an empty stomach. Facing death, surely. He did it every time he flew. But not on an empty stomach.

The thought of death brought the image of that damnable note again. The problem wasn't even being aware of his own mortality, but being aware of his people's mortality. So many of those he commanded had died.

He thought of his friend Werner Voss, now gone. He'd promised Werner's father he'd come over and hunt during his upcoming leave. Normally, the prospect would cheer him up, except he felt as though it would never happen—as though it were a dim and distant prospect, something he could not quite reach. And it brought thoughts of Werner, and the other youths who had been his friends and crashed down in fire and blood.

Manfred shook his head to the inner voice, wiped his face and gave Menzke, standing by anxiously, the slight head shake that meant he wouldn't be require warm water for shaving. The orderly silently retreated, stepping outside of Richtofen's quarters. There was a single, precise knock on the door, as if the next visitor had been waiting for this precise opportunity.

"Come," Manfred said. He knew it who it was, as his adjutant, Karl Bodenschatz, was his customary morning visitor, usually with a cup of warm chicory to replace the coffee which had lately been in short supply. In fact, Manfred had not tasted coffee since he'd been home, recovering from his wound. And even that, procured at who knew what expense by his mother, had had more than its normal proportion of chicory embittering its taste.

Bodenschatz looked immaculate as he usually did, but his face was unusually grave. He handed Manfred one of the cups he carried, and absently used his free hand to pet Moritz, who'd come nosing around him for his morning greeting. "Rittmeister," he said. Just the one word on handing the cup over.

The formality while in quarters was preserved between them, even if Bodenschatz was one of Manfred's remaining friends and the one scheduled to go hunting with him in the coming leave.

Manfred's acceptance was as perfunctory. "Danke," but his eyes searched his subordinate. "Out with it, Bodenschatz. What troubles you?"

There was a half-embarrassed chuckle and a click of the tongue. "Nothing troubles me, Rittmeister. The air should clear, and the weather should be fine for hunting a Lord or two."

Since the Royal Flying Corps had initially been composed mostly of noblemen, the Germans had referred to them jocularly as "Lords." The phrase "hunting a Lord" was often used by Manfred himself, but the joke rang hollow today. In fact, every flyer he'd downed alive and taken prisoner had been a splendid fellow, the kind that might have become friends with Manfred, had Manfred met the man during his visit to England before the war.

It seemed to him the scar itched, and he rubbed at it. There was something to that. A scrap of dream, reaching for him like the fingers of fog outside. He made a sound, not quite a snort, expelling air through his nostrils. He was not usually given to foreboding and second thoughts. *You are becoming an old woman, Manfred von Richthofen,* he told himself severely. *Lothar would laugh at you.*

He knew this was true, too. Though Lothar, himself becoming an ace of some renown—though a hunter of rage, not of brain like his older brother—at the moment laid in a hospital bed, recovering from injury. He shook himself.

"And yet you are troubled," Manfred persisted.

"Nothing to speak of, Rittmeister. Only..." Bodenschatz took a sip from his cup, as though to hide his expression. "Only I saw a fresh column heading towards the front this morning."

And Manfred understood. Bodenschatz had been infantry himself. While Manfred's own time on the ground had been limited, Bodenschatz had had experience of the front in a more prolonged and fraught way. He felt for those going forth into the mud, the barbed wire, and the ubiquitous stench of death.

"I know," Manfred said. "I know."

He didn't say what else he knew, because he couldn't say where the certainty came from. He'd started the war sure that they'd be in Paris in no time, and in fact had burned with fear Lothar would be ahead of him in both honors and glorious moments. The certainty they'd lose, and that the Kaiser's last effort was just that, and utterly doomed, had come from nowhere. He'd tried to dismiss it as the result of his head wound, but he didn't think that was it. He thought it was rather the things he saw from the air, the comparative strength of the forces, the churned and desolate ground between, covered in the unrecovered remains of dead men.

Bodenschatz gave a half-hearted laugh, as though recovering himself. As though he, too, understood the words that Manfred hadn't said, and must distract himself from them, lest they come out and raise despondency and fear. Both of them were too loyal to do that. "Well, at any rate, they somehow knew who we were, and they asked about you and told me to tell you they'd be looking to you for protection."

Manfred smiled.

"They always ask," Bodenschatz said. "They always ask for you, and seem comforted you'll be flying above, protecting them."

"Well, it is certainly better than what they used to say, when I was doing my milk and eggs delivery," Manfred said, referring irreverently—as always—to his time as a courier. "Which was, *God punish the Englishmen, their artillery and our flyers.*"

"I'm not sure they don't still say it, Rittmeister. Except, of course, for you."

Manfred opened his mouth to protest that he was just a flyer, like other flyers, but that note from his dream rose before his waking eyes again:

To the German Flying Corps.
Rittmeister Baron Manfred von Richthofen was killed in aerial combat, on April 21st, 1918. He was buried with full military honors.

In the dream, that note and the grainy, black-and-white picture of a flower-covered grave had been dropped over the airfield. Would they bother doing that for any other flyer? No. Obviously not.

Manfred didn't know how, or when it had come about, though he knew the Kaiser had used him for propaganda—oh, with Manfred's full consent and the aid of Manfred's slim autobiographical volume—but there was more to it than that.

In this war of slow attrition, flyers stood out. They got to survey things from above. They were free of the mud—though not of the death and blood—the ground fighters endured. And most of them lived charmed and all-too-short lives.

It was the daring and the risk that had attracted Manfred, but he'd stayed alive despite the risk. Most flyers died with maybe ten kills to their count. He had over 80 kills. Most flyers, before he'd first painted his plane red, had tried to be as inconspicuous as possible, hiding against the sky, so they could take the enemy by surprise.

His style, his flamboyance, the touch of old-fashioned, unapologetic knighthood—the tradition of fighting in the open and boldly, laughing in the face of danger—that clung to him; the way he treated downed enemy flyers like equals temporarily on the other side; the way he looked for his fledglings and young flyers—all of it had made him a legend, not just to his own side, but the other side, as well.

The double-edged quality of being used for propaganda was that you became a pivotal point of the war effort.

In his own case, and for himself, he'd done very little. Surely, yes, the

English airmen were a danger to those in the trenches, both because of aerial bombardment and being the English artillery's eyes in the sky.

Yet, Manfred was a single man, and his death would not win or lose the war for his side.

The scar itched again, and some other thought, a memory from the dream, perhaps, tried to rise. It didn't manage to reach his consciousness, no matter how much he frowned, attempting to retrieve it. It was like trying to recall where one had left something, and thus it retreated further and further the more he tried. Something about his importance to Germany. He was sure they'd lose the war, yes. He'd been for some time. Staying alive would make no difference, but he still felt there was something, something to his life and death that—

No, it was gone.

He gave an uneasy shrug and put his now-empty cup down. "As well I have some breakfast," he said. "While waiting for the weather to clear."

Bodenschatz nodded, though he looked troubled.

Probably only because I'm having strange reactions this morning, Manfred thought.

"I had a nightmare," he said finally.

"Oh?" his adjustant asked.

"I can't remember it," Manfred hedged. "It just left behind an uneasy feeling."

"Ah," Bodenschatz said, but he didn't sound reassured.

They crossed the muddied field side by side, Moritz gamboling beside them, splashing water from puddles as he jumped them like a cat.

The mess hall, another long tent, was loud with young voices, alive with the smell of coffee—or yet more chicory, but close enough—eggs and marmalade.

Silence fell as Richthofen entered, and all eyes turned to him.

"Good morning, gentlemen," he said in way of greeting. He didn't require formality here, and there was no more than a moment of silence before the loud discussions returned. The Red Baron took his place at the table, asked for tea instead of coffee, and was grateful at the warm bread. So often, it was coarse and made with who knew what, but this morning it felt and tasted like real bread.

I'll have to compliment the cooks, he thought, looking over his flyers. His cousin Wolfram was waiting eagerly for Manfred's permission to fly the hunt for the first time. With an air of dread he hoped did not cross his face, Manfred nodded at the young man, an indication he'd be allowed to join the dawn patrol. Just as he did, there was an uneasy prickle behind his eyes, the memory of Wolfram getting in trouble, of having to rescue—

And just like that, it was gone.

This is getting ridiculous, Manfred thought angrily. It would not be unusual, of course, for the young pup to get in trouble. They often did, despite all the rules Manfred laid down, the rules that had come to him from Oswald Boelcke. And often the trouble the young pups got into was fatal. But—

Yes, Lothar would be laughing at me a great deal by this point, Manfred thought. He ate his breakfast, smiling at the young men's jests, then thanked the cooks for the meal. Leaving the mess tent, he then strode out into the field to inspect his plane. The scarlet *Fokker Dr. I* had been wheeled forth from the tent-hangar.

Please don't fail me today, he thought, looking over the plane. It still looked new, being the replacement for the one in which he'd crashed, proud and red. He knew the young men in the trenches would be looking for that red dot above them, and he would not fail them. It was for them that Manfred had ignored the pointed "suggestions" that he take a safer post at the rear. With his aircraft being so visible and well-known, that route would be the same as his being killed, his disappearing.

The men need to know I am alive, flying above them and protecting them. He looked at the clearing sky, then towards his quarters. Menzke would be gathering his flying gear there, waiting to help him dress—with the unobtrusive ease of long practice—in coveralls, jacket and boots.

I need to shake off this dread and lead my men, Manfred thought as the orderly set to his task. He continued trying to rally as he walked back toward the flight line. On his way to his plane, he found that Leutenant Richard Wenzl had lain on a stretcher while the squadron waited him. Seeing their leader coming, several of the younger pilots tipped Wenzl out, with a sly smile, as Manfred passed by. The men laughed, and as Wenzl climbed back on the stretcher, Manfred stopped to tip him out. His men's laughter and shouted jeers rising behind him, Manfred went and stood by his plane, looking back at the gathered pilots with an air of, "What, did something happen?"

At least they are all in good spirits, he thought, the laughter reaching a crescendo. As sunlight began to fall on the gathered assembly, Manfred looked up and realized the cloud cover was rapidly burning off. There had been reports of the Englishmen being more aggressive about trying to attack German fighters on the ground.

We must climb soon, Manfred thought. As always, the familiar need to be aloft, to be above, to be flying started to course through him. Utterly irrational though it was, he felt safer in the skies than down here, where they were sitting ducks for any English bombardment.

Perhaps not irrational. The skies, after all, had been mostly safe for him, save for one incident.

I am not going to let this funk come back! He turned to speak to his flyers, but heard Moritz whine and turned. The poor dog was struggling towards him with a heavy plane chock tied to his tail.

Ah, Wenzl's revenge, he thought. *Or perhaps Wenzl and some of his friends' retribution*. He grinned. This was good, as it was obvious they were in great spirits, and great spirits increased their probability of survival.

"Come here, you silly hound," Manfred muttered. He knelt to free Moritz and petted the animal, this time receiving a couple of unavoidable, grateful licks to the face. He stood, looking over his men, and felt suddenly grave. It was if, for a moment, he saw the passing shade of Oswald Boelcke standing in the back row, gazing at him sadly.

That...that was odd, Manfred thought. *Surely a trick of the wound.* Shaking his head, he suddenly felt as if whatever dark thing was reaching from his dream, the Dicta Boelcke was the way to avoid it.

"It is a beautiful day to fly patrol," he said, informally, to scattered chuckles. "You're all anxious to fly and sure of victory, as indeed am I. But it's been awhile due to this abominable weather, so please indulge me in a quick review of the Dicta Boelcke."

The chuckles died down. All eyes turned to him, and he stood, petting Moritz, whose panting seemed suddenly very loud.

"So, to begin," Manfred said. "Always try to secure?"

"An advantageous position before attacking," the men answered, initially with some hesitance, then with a strong common recitation. "Climb before and during the approach in order to surprise the enemy from above, and dive on him swiftly from the rear when the moment to attack is at hand."

"Very good," Manfred said. "And try to place yourself between the sun and...?"

"The enemy," the men finished, and added, with well-schooled harmony, "this puts the glare of the sun in the enemy's eyes and makes it difficult to see you and impossible for him to shoot with any accuracy."

"Do not fire the machine guns," Manfred prompted.

"Until the enemy is within range, and you have him squarely within your sights."

"Attack when the enemy least—"

"Expects it or when he is preoccupied with other duties such as observation, photography, or bombing," the men continued, the recitation almost resembling a chant.

"Never turn your back—"

"And try to run away from an enemy fighter. If you are surprised by an attack on your tail, turn and face the enemy with your guns."

"Keep your eye on the enemy and do not allow him to—" Manfred started, realizing he was grinning like a proud father.

"Deceive you with tricks. If your opponent seems damaged, follow him down until he crashes to be sure he is not faking."

"Foolish acts of bravery only bring death!" Manfred shouted.

"The *Jasta* must fight as a unit with close teamwork between all pilots," his men replied. "The signals of its leaders must be obeyed."

"Attack in principle in groups of four—"

"Or six. When the fight breaks up into a series of single combats, take care that several do not go for one opponent."

Manfred nodded. There was a feeling something in the rules was very important, but he couldn't think what. He always tried to follow them, at any rate.

"Very good," he said. "Let's keep it in mind as we bag our lords."

The last line was delivered with a sense of feline anticipation, a feeling which only grew as Manfred saw the telephone operator running from the communications shack. The Baron knew what the man was going to say before he gasped out his report.

"There are several English planes at the front."

Like that, the levity and laughter, the boisterous good humor of the flyers vanished, replaced by determination. The men rushed to their planes.

"Wolfram," Manfred said, treating the young man with the informality of family. The simple name arrested his cousin's headlong rush. Manfred knew the dream had involved Wolfram, and though he didn't believe in dreams, at least not as harbingers of fate, he thought perhaps his mind was trying to warn him of something. "Wolfram, obey the dicta, and stay clear of engagements, please."

"Yes, Rittmeister," Wolfram answered, seemingly obedient before plunging headlong towards his plane.

I hope that he's not giving me a child's simple promise to a parent before engaging in dangerous games, Manfred thought, frowning, before he climbed his own plane.

Shortly thereafter, his kette of five planes took to the skies, followed quickly by the rest of the Flying Circus.

It was a quick journey to the front. Adjusting his goggles as he closed with the trenches, Manfred scanned the surrounding sky. The men on the ground counted on him to keep the English off their backs as they massed for the Kaiser's great push. He would do just that.

These clouds haven't all burned off, he thought. The wisps of white were gradually thickening, breaking up lines of sight. Looking, he saw a passing flight from Jasta Five. Counting, he saw that there were only three of the aircraft from their fellow unit.

That won't do, he thought. Gaining Wenzl's attention, he signaled for the man to join up on Jasta Five's small formation. Waggling his wings, Wenzl lead Weiss in a reversal to turn and join up with the trio of aircraft. Looking back, Manfred quickly took stock of the four other pilots still with him on his patrol: Wolfram, Scholz, Karjus, and Wolff.

Pups are always the most likely to get in trouble, Manfred thought, justifying why he kept a close eye on Wolfram. In reality, something about the young man bothered him, something irrational and probably rooted in the unremembered nightmare.

The quintet followed the Somme, climbing to 10,000 feet before the trenches became visible. Putting his fighter into a shallow bank just on the German side of the lines, Manfred began to search their assigned sector.

Just past Cerisy, a hamlet on the banks of the Somme, Manfred spotted the enemy. Or, at least, a gaggle so large he was fairly certain they were British.

At least my eyesight has not failed me, even if my nerves are trying to, he thought. A great part of his exceptional fighting prowess was not his ability as a pilot—he'd never been more than adequate, and knew it—but the vision which let him distinguish in a vague glimmer against a bank of clouds the presence of aircraft. That same vision now told him that the gaggle was British, apparently eight of their Sopwith *Camels*, lazily circling just on the English side of No Man's Land.

Let us begin, Manfred thought, then signaled his subordinates. From below Manfred, there echoed the shellbursts from a battery of anti-aircraft guns. He ignored it. Unless you flew straight at them, the anti-aircraft were like an act of God: unavoidable, unlikely to be directed particularly at you, and a sign of bad luck if they struck you down. The best a pilot could do was hope it missed. Far more pressing were the enemy aircraft right here, up in the sky with them, while you kept your eye on your enemy right here, in the sky, close up to you.

As if they'd been conjured from his thoughts, sudden movement and sound attracted Manfred's attention.

Damn these clouds! He realized poor visibility had caused him to miss two Camels attacking Weiss's all-white triplane. Cursing softly at the loss of time, he wheeled his formation in a wide left turn, climbing, and prepared to single out a Camel on the edge of the melee for an attack. Out of the corner of his eye, he saw the original eight enemy turning suddenly towards his flight.

Well, this is about to get interesting, he thought. *But we will have an altitu... What is Wolfram doing?*

The pup had separated from the rest of Jasta Eleven, chasing some target that Manfred could not yet see. Then there was close-in jostling and shooting as his four remaining craft merged with the two, then eight more *Camel*s. Fire passed close by, well too close to him, and Manfred jerked reflexively.

I cannot tell if that was the English or someone shooting at the English, Manfred thought, growing concerned at the chaos. Then he was too busy dodging and turning, the numbers preventing him from going over to the offensive. Despite their numerical advantage, the English were too clumsy to draw blood, while the Germans were too worried about getting possibly swamped to do so, either. Two more *Camels* joined the fray, but ironically, the increased numbers worked against the English as Manfred's Jasta began working like a team versus the Englishmen flying as a dozen individuals.

That was, until the Jasta Five flight joined the fray. Even as he was starting to gain an advantage on an Englishman, the five additional *Fokkers* disrupted Manfred's command of the situation. The sky was suddenly filled with tracers once more, the Englishmen's rounds creating thin white threads that crisscrossed in every direction. Still, the Fokkers outnumbered the *Camels*, and he watched as the advantage grew with a *Camel* falling out of the sky with an obviously dead pilot at the controls.

Manfred looked around to select a target, simultaneously proud of his men for not breaking the dicta by rushing at the same plane and frustrated none of the Englishman would cooperatively separate away. Then, with a sudden rush of nausea, he realized Wolfram was in danger. Above his cousin's gaily decorated plane, with its purple wings and silver fuselage, a *Camel* hovered, diving on Wolfram as the latter stooped on a pair of Englishmen.

No, Manfred thought as he saw the *Camel* plunge, guns blazing. He only remembered to breathe again as the Englishman's initial burst missed behind the *Fokker*, the man having failed to lead Woflram. Wolfram, suddenly aware of his danger, plunged into a dive with the *Camel* in hot pursuit.

"Never try to run away from an enemy fighter. If you are surprised by an attack on your tail, turn and face the enemy with your guns," Manfred whispered, whipping his fighter around. The pup had forgotten.

He saw Wolfram level off and head towards Cappy, but the *Camel* was in pursuit, spraying bullets in all directions. Then it was suddenly not spraying bullets at all, but following a determined course away.

He has run himself out of ammo or jammed his guns, Manfred thought, following almost instinctively. He had selected his prey. He'd take this daring *Camel* who had attacked Wolfram.

The Englishman, unlike Wolfram, had kept looking around. Therefore, he saw the scarlet triplane diving on him and doubled his efforts to escape. Firing an initial burst that the *Camel* just barely evaded, Manfred cursed and continued to close in.

I will not waste any more ammunition firing at long range, he thought angrily, closing. He knew the *Camel* was disarmed. Or at least, it wasn't turning around to face him. Instead, it was attempting to zigzag in escape, which meant that Manfred would slowly gain on him.

Manfred was prey to excitement he hadn't felt in a long time.

Forgetting caution and misgivings, he stayed on the plane's tail. He forgot the ground flitting by behind him, forgot danger, forgot the very real possibility of death. This was the glory of fighting in the air: the chase, the heady flight, the air rushing past, the feeling that one was above it all.

The enemy was obviously trying to decide whether to land behind German lines or stick with his kite long enough to cross back over English lines. Manfred fired again, and once more the man ahead of him seemed to have a preternatural sense of when to zigzag. Even though it caused the Red Baron to miss, the maneuver also killed some of the *Camel*'s speed, leading to Manfred closing the distance some more.

The trench system flashed by under them, barbed wire and ugly jagged cuts in the landscape. And suddenly Manfred became aware of another memory from the dream. A voice in his mind, not his own, one with a distinct English accent saying something about chasing an enemy behind the English lines and getting cut down by anti-aircraft fire.

Almost imperceptibly, he became aware of his surroundings again. He realized he was about to cross the lines. He heard anti-aircraft fire up below, still too far to inflict damage. But not too far. Another two seconds and he'd be upon them.

He ceased firing and started climbing, watching the *Camel* fly on, lower and lower.

Better the Lord escape to fly another day than for Manfred to be brought down in flames, riddled with fire, or whatever other dark fate hung upon his half-remembered dream.

A sudden burst of fire behind him made him aware he had now become a target of pursuit. And that he'd become completely isolated, far from his own flight.

Foolish acts of bravery only bring death.

Well, at least he wasn't going to run. He turned around, facing the enemy and letting out a burst of machine gun fire, which was returned. There was a brief impression of some strikes on the enemy craft, and he heard canvas ripping on his own craft before the two craft were past each other. Manfred reversed course, seeing the *Camel* follow suit.

So, you accept my duel, then, Manfred thought with a haughty smile. The planes circled, two hawks in a deadly fight. He was so close he could see the other man's pose, hunched intent over control and machine gun.

You're a brave one, Manfred thought as he tried to circle behind for advantage. The *Camel* somehow managed to hold the turn long enough for his own triplane to shudder in warning of an impending stall. Manfred side-slipped out of the turn, lowering his nose to regain some airspeed while risking a quick glance for his original prey possibly circling back in. His quick glance told him that it was merely him and the single Englishman, now less than a thousand feet over No Man's Land.

Once more the duel was rejoined. Manfred quickly realized that the two men and their aircraft were evenly matched, and neither was going to turn for home. While the stiff breeze blowing out of the west gave Manfred some advantage if he turned to ran, he quickly realized that this *Camel*'s pilot was able to eke enough speed out of his aircraft to make that a difficult proposition. Likewise, Manfred was able to use his triplane's slim maneuverability advantage to keep the *Camel* from gaining a decisive upper hand.

As the sweat poured from his body and his arms began to burn with the onset of fatigue, the vision of that cursed pamphlet with the image of a grave and the announcement of his death floated before his eyes. And suddenly, as though broken forth by the burst of battle, he saw what would follow, or at least what had followed in his dream: the defeat of the Kaiser's push.

That part was no wonder. Manfred had thought this last, desperate, crazed attack would fail. Not that he could put in words why, but in his stroke of clairvoyance, Manfred realized it would be scarcity of supplies, ammunition, and men that would doom the Kaiser's last gamble. The best of Germany's youth would die at the front, leaving the nation with the dregs, the boys and the oldsters.

In the end, the trenches would consume the new advance as they had consumed others. With the Americans looming, the war would become one of attrition. Germany, surrounded by hostile countries and consumed by blockade, would almost certainly lose.

The dream showed me the future, he thought, even as he fired a snap burst that just missed his adversary. *It will be a nightmare. The French and Englishmen will be vengeful.*

The *Camel* somehow whipped its nose around, the pilot nearly stalling it to bring the twin guns to bear. It was only Manfred's own catlike reflexes and the *Fokker*'s maneuverability that allowed him to twist mostly out of the tracer's path. Still, he heard several impacts and looked back to see a brief bit of smoke back near his tail as the canvas tried to ignite.

Germany will perish, he thought. The country would despoiled, made to pay for a war that was only partly its fault. It would be doubtful that the Kaiser could keep his current amount of power, or indeed the throne, after such a spectacular defeat.

Once more the *Camel* was briefly in his sights, the Englishman having made a narrow mistake. Manfred fired, seeing bits flying off the Sopwith's top wing and more canvas rips down the fuselage. Then the two fighters were past one another, Manfred immediately whipping into a climb to separate from his foe to the north. The *Camel* followed suit. Dimly, Manfred heard cheers from the German trenches.

We are a proud people, he thought. Sure, they'd be defeated and broken, but they wouldn't lie still very long. He had the awful presentiment—the dream had made it a certainty—that as soon as another generation grew up, they would again engage in battle. That fire and blood would once again consume Europe.

Just as certainly as I will die here if I continue this fight, he thought in a sudden realization of his own fatigue, *so Germany will if she rises again*. His own lands, pressed close by the eastern enemies, would be destroyed. More than that, an entire way of life would be cast into doubt, destroyed.

Just as the men on the trenches cursed their own flyers, who were, in their minds, above them both socially and physically, and cared not for their plight, so would the people who'd fought and died and suffered from this defeat come to view the war. It would be seen as having been a game of Lords, an unjust and heedless fight between battle-mad barons heedless of what it did to those on the ground, the lower classes who had paid in blood, treasure and humiliation for what the nobility thought a grand fight.

"Nothing good comes from the peasantry feeling like they've had enough." His history tutor's words echoed in his ears. The last century, from the madness that had begun in France to his nation's own aborted revolution in the 1840s, had been a constant reinforcement of such lessons. Even now, the Russians were in the middle of such a convulsion.

What if that happens in Germany? he thought. Then again, his reflexes saved him, as a different *Camel* came slashing into the duel. Manfred whipped around on the interloper, firing a burst that saw a torrent of strikes into the enemy's machine guns and cockpit. The Englishman never recovered from his attack, slamming into the ground just before the German trenches.

Where is the... Oh no, he thought, seeing his long-term duelist having positioned himself between Manfred and the German lines.

Never turn your back and try to run away from an enemy fighter.

Sure. He never had. And he wouldn't again. But behind the Englishman, he could see three more *Camel*s attempting to move towards blocking his escape. Thinking back to his duel with Hawker, Manfred realized this was how the English ace had died.

My men can criticize my decision only if I'm alive, he thought. Sometimes the best option was to disengage. This close to the English lines, the odds against him would only get worse. For the first time in many fights, Manfred felt a sense of being in eminent, immediate danger. Dodging his original opponent's attack, Manfred circled upward, then made for the German lines as fast as he could. The *Camel* pilot belatedly reversed, attempting to catch Manfred before he got away.

Dammit, he thought, as his engine suddenly began running rougher. There was a sudden burst of fire, and his seat splintered. Manfred kicked his rudder, and the *Camel* turned away before overshooting, given the *Fokker*'s sudden loss of speed. Looking forward, Manfred only then realized that some fire must have holed his engine, as there was a horrible streak of oil along the *Fokker*'s nose.

I have to get away, he thought, suddenly feeling faint. He reached to where bullets had torn into his seat, touched his flightsuit, and had it come away with a shade of crimson that matched his fuselage. He didn't as yet feel pain, but he knew he'd been hit.

I cannot afford to die of this! his mind protested. There was a sense he was very important for Germany, very important to avert the future his dream had shown.

That future of more fire and blood. The future in which Europe plunged into a fight again and again, till all the things that had made it great, the things that had made it the primary world civilization were destroyed, and his own lands fell under the same sort of madness now consuming Russia.

With a rush, he realized they were passing over the German trench system. He was now behind his own lines, and his own anti-aerials were firing at the *Camel*. Manfred felt as though a haze was upon his thoughts, as a haze descended on his vision. The engine was now certainly in its death throes, and he had maybe 150 feet of altitude. Flames began shooting out of the nose in front of him, and Manfred had visions of crashing down in fire.

I have to bring the aircraft down, safely, he thought. It flashed into his mind that at least the dream couldn't be right. He might die, but it wouldn't be the English burying him. It wouldn't be the English sending that damnable pamphlet to his people.

Not important, he thought, sighting one of the many supply routes that ran towards the front line. Carefully, he controlled his descent into a road cutting through a muddy field. He was aware of the *Camel* still on his tail, as he made an awkward landing. At least the *Camel* wasn't landing. Just following him down, Manfred guessed, to make sure he wasn't faking it. Or perhaps the pilot of the *Camel* had also been hit by the anti-aircraft machine guns.

Manfred didn't care. His blood thundered past his ears with a sound like a rushing train, and he knew his heart was straining, which told him he was fast losing blood. The thud of his wheels was a welcome relief as his vision went cloudy. The plane bumped on as he instinctively shut off his engine, flung off his goggles, then pulled on the brake lever to try and bring the *Fokker* to a stop. With a roar, the *Camel* flashed close by overhead, then slammed into the ground ahead of him.

Is the Englishman mad? Manfred thought, as his conscious tried to fade. Through the enveloping darkness, afraid that the enemy would approach and—against all rules of gentlemen—put a bullet in his head, Manfred reached for his sidearm. Then there was a man climbing into his cockpit, a voice speaking in German.

"Easy, Rittmeister. Easy. You're among friends."

He was aware of being helped—pulled, to tell the truth—from the plane. Opening his eyes brought him confused glimpses of many men, of uniforms. He asked only, "The *Camel?*"

"Captain Roy Brown has been taken prisoner, Rittmeister."

It wasn't till days later, fully conscious in a hospital, that Manfred's brother informed him either one of his defensive bursts or one of the German anti-aerials had so damaged the *Camel* that it had no chance but to land.

"I would have liked a chance to meet the man," Manfred observed, his arm in a sling.

"Well, if hadn't been so fixated on trying to bag The Red Baron, the man probably would have had a chance to meet you again once you recover," Lothar observed. "That is, if you ever got over the embarrassment of trying to run from him."

Manfred fixed his brother with a silent glare. Lothar, after a few moments, broke away from the gaze while mumbling an apology.

"It occurred to me," Manfred said, candidly, "that being so famous, partly because the Kaiser made me so, I was needed. For...for the war."

If I tell him what I was really thinking, they'll lock me in an asylum, Manfred thought. The grave covered in flowers in his dream had been so jarring that its significance had eluded him—until he laid in a hospital bed, able to think. It was then he had realized that he was as famous—and respected—on the other side as on his own. He knew that, from his encounters with the men he'd taken prisoner.

The newspapers they've shared with me only confirms it, he thought. Several of the English papers were trumpeting his wounding and shooting down. Of course, they were far less triumphant in discussing the fact that he'd managed to, counting Roy Brown, take two of their pilots with him.

Lothar looked at him, dumbfounded.

Lothar has never been a thinker or a planner, Manfred thought. *That is fine. I will do the planning for both of us. For German and for Europe itself.*

"Now you won't be able to avoid taking a backseat in the war," Lothar said, scoffing. "They'll put you in as an inspector, at the rear, what with the shattered shoulder to recover from."

It was the sort of scoffing and teasing they'd engaged in as boys, each striving to be stronger and more visibly brave than the other.

Manfred was no longer a boy.

"Yes," he said. "That is likely."

He closed his eyes on Lothar's expression of incomprehension, of not knowing what had changed. Manfred didn't, either, except that whatever warning his mind had tried to send him in that nightmare had hit home.

He'd be alive after this war and try to make it the last great war to ravage Europe.

Before worse happened.

ABOUT SARAH A. HOYT

Sarah A. Hoyt was born (and raised) in Portugal and now lives in Colorado with her husband, two sons, and a variable number of cats, depending on how many show up to beg on the door step. She has over 40 -- the number keeps changing -- published novels, in science fiction, fantasy, mystery, historical mystery, historical fantasy and historical biography. Her short stories have been published in Analog, Asimov's, Amazing Stories (under a previous management), Weird tales, and a number of anthologies from DAW and Baen.

To learn more about Sarah A. Hoyt and read samples of her work, visit http://sarahahoyt.com

EAGLES OVER DACIA

Philip Wohlrab

EAGLES OVER DACIA

Campus Martius, Rome
July 25th, 2661 Ab Urbe Condita

"Now, Marcus, tell me what the significance of the Kalends of August 936 AUC is."

Marcus looked up at the stern visage of the Magister Titus Malleus Memno with equal measures of anxiety as well as a touch of not-quite consternation.

"Why, Magister, everyone knows that date! That is the day when the Senate and People of Rome restored the balance of power with the Imperial Crown, and achieved the government that we have today," Marcus beamed.

"Very good, Marcus. And can you tell me what the significance of the year 1364 AUC is?"

Marcus screwed up his face, then looked around the classroom at his fellow pupils. Mostly blank eyes met his until he caught the gaze of Caeso Elvorix. Elvorix made a crescent shape with his finger, but below his desk so the Magister couldn't see it. Marcus lit up as he turned back to the patrician teacher.

"It is the year that Muhammed founded the Abbasid Caliphate," he blurted out.

"Not quite, Marcus. You are correct in that Muhammed laid the foundation that would become the Abbasid Caliphate, but that would come after his death. Instead, 1364 is the year that Muhammed is widely recognized to have had his revelations and began the path to founding what would become the Abbasid Caliphate. Now the last one: what is the significance of the Ides of February 2012 AUC?"

"That is when Al-Mustasim the Great destroyed Hulagu Khan's forces at the last battle of Baghdad, thus ending the Mongol incursion in the East. It is also the start of the Billah Jihad, which ultimately led the Abbasids to conquer all the way to the Indus, and as far north to the edge of Dacia."

"Good, Marcus Junius Maltinus. I see you have paid at least some attention to my lectures."

Marcus was a bit shocked to receive even faint praise from Magister Memno, for it was widely rumored that the man held no such capacity. He started to respond to the Magister when a commotion broke out on the side of the classroom nearest the windows. The boys there were no longer paying attention to the Magister, and instead were excitedly pointing out of the windows toward the broad boulevard across the parade field of the Campus Martius Military Academy. Marcus moved from his seat and hurried over to where his friend Caeso was standing at the window, following his friend's gaze. Across the way, rank after rank of men marched in their dress uniforms of scarlet and gold.

"That's the 10th Legion marching out, but look behind them," gestured Caeso.

Behind the last rank of the men of the 10th was a second formation, these men swathed in black and purple. Unlike the silver loricas worn by the 10th Legion, these men wore black loricas over black tunics, with purple epaulets. Each man shouldered his bolt action rifle, while belted at their waist was a spatha.

"Look at them," exclaimed Marcus, awe on his face.

"Yes, boys, that is the Emperor's Praetorian Guard. Fifth Legion, if my old eyes don't deceive me."

Marcus and Caeso were startled at the almost longing tone in Magister Memno's voice.

"I was with them in the Central Atlantis campaign, against the Azteca. That is where I got this." He lifted the stump of his left arm.

The boys had never heard this side of their Magister's story, and though the Magister, like the others, wore his uniform, it wasn't the black of the Praetorian and instead the blood red of the Legions.

"Magister?" Marcus said in a tone that registered shock, and some disbelief.

The old teacher chuckled.

"Yes, boys, I was with the Praetorian Guard then, oh, some twenty-five years ago. I didn't transfer back to the 28th Legion until after the Central Atlantis campaign. After I was wounded, they decided that I was no longer fit to be in the Praetorians and that is how I ended up here, trying to inculcate your young skulls full of mush with the history needed to be good soldiers."

Through the windows could be heard the martial music of the bands accompanying the soldiers. Crowds had gathered along the boulevard, and the class could see other students rushing from the surrounding buildings to see the soldiers.

"Magister, may we be released to the sendoff?" asked one of the boys.

Seeing that he wasn't going to get any more from the boys, the old teacher pointed an imperious stump towards the door.

"Go, boys, go and see the soldiers," he said aloud.

I pray to Mithras that they won't need you anytime soon, the Magister finished internally.

Aerodrome 434, Dacia
Roman Lines
October 1st, 2676 AUC

Marcus looked at the newest pilots to join the ala with something akin to scorn.

So eager are these boys and yet no real idea of why they fight. Old Magister Memno wouldn't approve. Has it really been fifteen years since school?

The air in Dacia had yet to turn cold, but Marcus knew from long experience that it would in the coming weeks. Beside him, Caeso also examined the incoming crop of pilots with a somewhat more blasé attitude.

"At least they look the part," quipped Caeso.

Marcus harrumphed at that.

"What? You know what we looked like when we arrived. Tell me we weren't all that different from this lot?"

Marcus sighed before replying. "I don't like to think we were ever that young."

Caeso chuckled. The two officers were standing enough of a distance away that the new pilots couldn't overhear them, and that was making the recent trainees increasingly nervous. For their part, six fresh-faced recent graduates of the Ariminum Flight School stood around in a ragged though protective cluster.

"Well, enough of this. Let's get them about their business and then you and I can go find a drink," said Marcus.

"I live to serve Decurion!"

Marcus snorted at that as he and Caeso sauntered over to where the juniors were standing around.

"Group, ATTENTION!" barked Caeso.

The junior pilots snapped into a ragged formation and stood at the position of attention.

"*What in the seven hells do you call that?*" roared Caeso. "*Do you call yourselves pilots or are you instead schoolboys who don't know anything about soldiering?*"

The junior pilots all popped into exaggerated positions of attention, straining to please this sudden apparition of fury. Caeso Lentinius Elvorix was not a small man, and his voice carried across the entirety of the aerodrome. Once he was satisfied that the junior pilots were paying close attention, he stepped back from them and fell into the position of parade rest. Marcus smiled at the display and stepped forward to pace up and down the line of juniors.

"My name is Marcus Junius Maltinus, and I am your new Decurion," he said as he walked.

"What that means is that I have the misfortune of commanding you sorry lot for what time you have remaining here before you pass on to Elysium or Hell."

He stopped at the end of the line and surveyed the gathered group.

"I and Centurion Elvorix are veterans of the Dacian Front, and have been here for going on four years now. This war has been going on for sixteen years, and all of you don't look old enough to have been born before the war."

Marcus knew this was an exaggeration, but not by much. He started pacing the line again.

"The Abbasid are excellent pilots, and they will sure as shit shoot you down if you don't respect that. Get any silly notions out of your head that you are the next Gaius Gracchus or Anthelm Dresslerg. Though they were great aviators, and true knights of the air, they are now both dead legends."

Marcus stopped in front of one of the quivering new pilots. He looked the boy up and down before he continued pacing the line.

"Which is what you will be if you try to take on the Abbasid Flying Corps individually. Do you understand me?"

Marcus never raised his voice, and in fact, most of the junior pilots had to strain to hear him over the noise of the aerodrome in the background.

"The Decurion asked if you fine lot understood him?" quipped Caeso.

There was a desultory response.

"*WHAT?*" roared Marcus for the first time.

"WE GET YOU, SIR!"

"Good," Marcus replied.

"As I call you up, you will get your plane assignment. I expect you all to get checked out with your chief mechanic. I know you lot probably don't have a lot of hours in the *Eagle*...what are they training you all on these days? *PT-1s* or *2s*?"

"Sir, they are training us on *PT-6s*," replied one of the junior pilots.

"I see. Are these new birds monoplanes or biplanes?"

"Monoplanes, Decurion," answered another.

"So you won't need much time to transition to the *Eagle,* then. Monoplanes handle differently than biplanes, but you should know that already. How many hours do you all have on average?"

The pilots looked at each other before the one that had spoken first volunteered, "On average, we have 50 hours, sir."

"Mithras! Well, Centurion Elvorix, looks like we have our work cut out for us. Like I said, after I give you your assignments, link up with your crew chiefs and then find your bunks. We will be taking off tomorrow at 0600 for the early patrol."

Marcus read off the roster, and as each pilot was called, they stepped forward to receive their assignment. Receiving their chits, they then hustled off in the direction of the hangars. After the last of them had gone, Marcus wordlessly collected up Caeso, and the two of them went in search of a drink.

Tissus River Line, Dacia
October 1st, 2676 AUC

Naqeeb Faisal el-Kabir soared his *Sahir* parasol monoplane high into a cloud bank. The aircraft was sleek, with its wings mounted over the engine cowling and just forward of the cockpit. This particular machine was painted an olive green on top, with a sky-blue underside. Faisal had had a Green Crescent and a scimitar painted on the sides and on his wings to identify his personal aircraft. He was proud, and an Ace, a concept that the Abbasid Caliphate had borrowed from the Roman aviators.

I just wish that I had better forward visibility in the Sahir*; while it is a far better performing aircraft than the old* Saqr*, it doesn't have nearly the same view. Oh, well, the* Sahir *is still a better aircraft in every other respect.*

Faisal saw a flash of color to his right, and looking over, he saw his wingman, Molazim Sharaf el-Fares, pull into formation with his aircraft. The two Abbasid pilots motioned to each other rather than communicate via the new wireless sets. They had learned from hard experience that to transmit was to risk detection by Roman ground stations, and with it the possibility of a Roman patrol coming up and take a whack at them.

Faisal scanned the earth below them as they flew close to the river Tissus, which made up the front between the advancing Abbasid forces and the Roman fortified lines on the other side. The war had stalled on this front for years, but Faisal knew that a new offensive was being planned, one that was set to kick off in five days. The High Command had high hopes of catching the Romans unawares. All of this was in the back of his mind as he scanned for enemy fighters, or more importantly, the ever-watchful Roman observation planes.

Faisal's scanning was interrupted when Molazim Mukhtar al-Sayed's voice came across the wireless set.

"Naqeeb, I have spotted a Roman formation to the east!"

Faisal looked off in that direction, and sure enough, flying low and towards one of the main supply dumps for the forces attacking the Tissus Line, were three of the Roman *B-7* bombers. They were distinctive in that like his *Sahir*, they, too, were parasol-style monoplanes, but whereas his craft were sleek speedy machines, these twin-engine aircraft were blunt and slow-looking. Faisal scanned around looking for escorts, but didn't immediately see any.

"Jinn flight, *DIVE!*"

Faisal and his wingmen stooped on the Roman bombers. Lining up on one of the aircraft, he waited until it filled his aiming reticle to fire. A stream of .30 caliber rounds erupted from his twin guns. Unlike his last plane, these guns were mounted semi-recessed in the fuselage to either side of his cockpit. Every fifth round was a tracer, and the bright streaks first leapt ahead of the Roman craft. Faisal quickly corrected and walked his tracers into the starboard wing. Chunks were torn from the bomber, but it didn't fold up. Instead, a gunner on the topside of the aircraft shot back at him until Faisal flashed past. He pulled his aircraft out of its dive to nose back around so that he could see his prey. To his astonishment, the bomber was still flying along as if nothing had happened.

"Naqeeb, I..."

Identifying Molazim al Sayed's voice over the radio, Faisal searched for the other pilot's aircraft in the sky. Al Sayed was number four in the flight, but he was out of position. Finding al Sayed's aircraft, Faisal saw wispy black smoke trailing from it, but at first, he couldn't tell where the fire was. Then, to his horror, he saw the cockpit erupt in flames. Faisal saw al-Sayed beating at himself, trying desperately to put out the flames. Faisal said a quick prayer to Allah to deliver Mukhtar from his suffering, and to his relief, the plane exploded.

The Roman bombers closed formation with each other. Their forward and rear gunners trained their machine guns out to provide layered protection from both top and bottom of their aircraft while trying to cover each other's blind spots to the bottom rear.

"Sharaf, we can't approach them from the topside. We can come up from behind and under them. Attack them there."

"Understood, Naqeeb."

Faisal dropped his aircraft down to treetop level, weaving between the largest trees. His *Sahir* was faster than the Roman aircraft and far more maneuverable. He trusted that the topside camouflage would help to break up the outline of his craft and confuse the Roman gunners.

The bombers were not idle, either; the pilots of the three-ship formation had brought their craft back around and were heading for all their worth back towards the Roman lines on the other side of the Tissus. Faisal pulled up on his stick, getting behind one of the lumbering bombers, lifted his nose and brought his gun sight in line with it. He nudged the nose a little more to develop a lead, and then depressed his thumb trigger. A burst of fire staggered the *B-7*, causing it to shed more parts. Faisal walked his fire back along the craft until there was a giant explosion. His rounds had caused one of the bombs to detonate, and that caused the others to cook off, as well. The resultant explosion caught the *B-7* to its left, and it, too, exploded.

"Whoa, that got him and then some," exclaimed Sharaf.

Faisal scanned the area before responding.

"Do you have any ammo left?"

"Yes, Naqeeb, I will prosecute the third aircraft."

"Good, I am out."

Despite being out of ammunition, Faisal stuck with Sharaf as the other approached the last bomber from its stern. Sharaf was just about lined up when tracers spat past both him and Faisal. He looked up in alarm, but at first, he couldn't see what was shooting at him. The sun was in his eyes. Faisal threw up his left hand to shade his eyes, allowing him to just make out three stooping shapes coming directly out of the bright light.

"Sharaf, break right, stay low and get back over our lines!"

Sharaf didn't bother to answer verbally, instead waggling his wings before breaking right and away from the approaching Roman fighters. For his part, Faisal zagged first left and then brought his craft up on its left wing. This gave him a better look at the three new Romans, and he counted his blessings, for these were not the new Roman *Eagles*, but instead their older *Falcons*.

They may be fast for biplanes, but they aren't as fast as my fighter, Faisal thought.

The teardrop-shaped Roman craft were the first all-metal biplanes that Rome had fielded, but Faisal's *Sahir* had been developed from a racing aircraft and was faster. The Romans fired a few more bursts at him and Sharaf before giving up and returning to the lone bomber now winging its way back toward its home.

Soon, Romans, soon it is we who will be doing the chasing and not you!

AERODROME 434, DACIA
ROMAN LINES
OCTOBER 6TH, 2676 AUC

Marcus felt far too old for twenty-six years to be his actual age. He kicked his boots up onto his desk and just sat back in his chair. He was tired beyond his years, doubly more so now that he had already had to bury three of the new pilots that had arrived just five days earlier.

The longer this war goes on, the more it is going to chew us all up and spit us out.

A knock sounded at his door, and Marcus swung his feet down before indicating for whoever it was to come in. As the door opened, he was at first annoyed that his instructions to be left alone were ignored, but soon he was standing at the position of attention. In walked Legatus Legionus 12th Air Legion Julius Servius Cato.

"Legatus, I wasn't aware you were here, sir!"

"At ease, Decurion Maltinus. Indeed. Have a seat—we have much to discuss."

"Aye, sir."

Marcus looked over the commanding officer of the 12th Air Legion, who appeared every inch the tall patrician Roman and sounded like it, as well. Marcus wasn't surprised, though, for the Air Legatus was of old nobility, even by Roman standards. His snowy white hair was trimmed short, while a full mustache still had hints of the redhead that Julius Cato had once been.

"Now listen up, Maltinus: we have a bit of a problem, and we need to sort it out. We are getting nasty rumors from some of our Sarmatian Scouts that the 'Sids are up to something." The Legate used the shortened name for the Abbasid Caliphate that had come into fashion in the Empire.

"Up to something, sir?"

Legatus Cato pulled a pipe from his breast pocket. He took time to fill the bowl of the pipe with aromatic tobacco, and then he lit it. Once it was drawing, he took it from his mouth and used the pipe stem to punctuate his comments.

"There are disturbing rumors that the 'Sids are massing men and equipment for a major offensive in this sector. That would be bad for several reasons, least of which they are pushing very hard at present in Numidia. We have lost far too much of our territory to the 'Sids over the last couple of centuries to lose even further in our African provinces."

"Yes, sir," nodded Marcus.

"As you know, we diverted much of our proper Roman forces out of this region and have left it to the German Limitanei Legions. While these troops are very good, they don't have the latest tanks or artillery that are being sent to the other fronts. The recompense is that we of the 12th Air Legion are here."

The Legatus leaned back in his chair and put his pipe back in his mouth.

"Does that mean that we will be getting replacement *Eagles* for our losses, sir?"

Cato leaned forward; smoke billowed from his nostrils as he breathed out.

"Yes, the *P-26s* will be replaced, but more importantly, we will be fielding the new *B-10s.* This is a new type of heavy bomber, better than anything we have previously had on this front. They are better armed, carry a heavier bomb load, and more importantly, have a longer range than the *B-7s* and *8s* we currently have."

"Sir, one of the problems we are finding is that our guns don't do enough damage to the new 'Sid fighters or bombers. Like us, they have moved to all-metal fuselages, and the .30-caliber guns take too many rounds to do enough damage to make a difference. Fortunately, they seem to have the same problem, though some of their *Sahirs* are starting to show up with heavier guns."

The Legatus nodded.

"Yes, the boffins have been thinking about that, which is another reason I am here. While your *Eagles* are getting replacements, we have some updates that we want to field, as well."

Marcus's eyebrows drew down and together as an apprehensive look came over his face.

"Sir?"

"Your aircraft will have their nose-mounted machine guns replaced with a new type of heavier gun."

"Not to sound rude here, sir, but those slots are awfully small already. Will we have to sacrifice ammo to fit them in?"

"I understand, Marcus. I once had a very similar reaction when they tinkered with the guns on my old *D7*. However, that is why I have brought along several engineers with the replacement aircraft. They will assist your Immunes with retrofitting your existing aircraft with the new guns."

"Understood, sir."

The Air Legatus drew on his pipe for a few moments and then went on.

"Yes, these new guns are a larger caliber and fire a heavier round. They should do more damage, as we have also sorted the ammo to be a mix of tracer, armor-piercing, and incendiary. That should come as a rude shock to the 'Sids."

Marcus leaned back in his chair, taking in the implications of what the Air Legatus had said. He whistled softly when he thought of what incendiary rounds would do to high-octane gasoline.

"Yes, sir, I think you are quite correct."

"Once the planes are ready, we are going to need you and your squadron to scout out the area around Popesti. We think that may be a major hub for whatever is going on behind the 'Sid lines."

"Yes, sir."

"Good, man!"

The Air Legatus stood up from the chair he had been seated in and glanced out the window before he tugged down on the hem of his tunic.

"Yes, Marcus Maltinus, we are going to see the 'Sids off here in Dacia, if I can help it."

AL-TAMIMI DIVISION HQ, DACIA
ABBASID LINES
OCTOBER 9TH, 2676 AUC

Faisal curiously looked around the headquarters of the Al-Tamimi Division, for he had not spent much time around the "ground pounders," as the pilots had decided to call all of those bound to the land, and therefore were not pilots. This was recognized to be a lesser form of being that Allah had not blessed with the intelligence to join the Aerial Corps.

Surely, had the Prophet, Peace Be Upon Him, not ascended, as all pilots ascend daily?

Faisal snorted at his wry thought.

Seeing his amusement, Sharaf looked over to him.

"Naqeeb, something amuses you?"

"Aye, Sharaf, I was just pitying our landbound brethren."

Sharaf smiled at that, for he, too, held proper disdain for all non-pilots.

"You two, come with me," said a stern-faced Moqaddam.

The two pilots quickly glanced at each other, for they had not expected that this summons had come from a senior officer, but had instead thought they were here to coordinate with their ground counterparts.

"The Liwa has a mission for you lot, but it is a closely guarded secret, and so he wishes to meet you in person rather than send this via a courier," went on the Moqaddam.

"Yes, sir," replied the two pilots.

The three men walked through a long tunnel, and even though it was buried under six feet of earth and made of reinforced timber, they could still feel the pounding of the artillery regiments that were not far away. Noticing the two pilots' looks, the Moqaddam snorted.

"Oh, don't worry, that is just harassment fire to keep the Germans in place."

"Germans, sir?" asked Faisal.

The Moqaddam gestured in the direction of the front.

"The Roman forces sitting across from us are in fact troops from their German legions, though whether they are from Germania Major or Germania Minor, we haven't figured out yet."

"Is there a difference?" asked Sharaf.

"Oh, yes. Germania Major is the older of the settled provinces, and is basically Roman in all respects save names and some customs. Germania Minor, on the other hand, is wilder, but there is little difference in the fight from either. Both are just as bad as if we faced one of their Praetorian Legions, save the equipment they use. That tends to be older, thanks be to Allah."

"His ways are wise," replied Faisal absently.

They reached the end of the tunnel and came to a door. Outside of it stood two soldiers; their rifles were grounded, but both men looked ready to spring into action should something threaten their general. The Moqaddam rapped on the door with the butt of his swagger stick, which wasn't an affectation of his alone, but instead a holdover from the days when the Caliphate fought from horse or camelback. It was now a badge of office for senior officers. The door opened, and the three men were ushered in by one of the Liwa's aides.

"Good afternoon, gentlemen, I will be with you shortly. In the meantime, Muhammad has coffee ready—please have a seat and have some," said Liwa Sakeen al-Rasheed.

The two pilots sat down at a low table on some cushions that were arranged around it, and each took one of the small brass coffee cups. The aide dutifully poured the sweet coffee that was favored across the Abbasid Caliphate. Each pilot took sips and made appreciative noises, careful to follow both tradition and protocol.

The Liwa finished what he was working on, and then he, too, joined them at the small table. The aide moved in and filled the Liwa's cup, and the three exchanged pleasantries, again ensuring that protocol was met.

But after twenty minutes of polite conversation, the Liwa came to the point.

"Gentlemen, I don't know how, but the Romans know we are up to something. They haven't brought up any more ground troops that we can tell..."

The Liwa broke off as a shell crashed down close enough to rattle the office. The overhead lanterns swayed, and dust fell from the ceiling timbers.

"Damn those German gunners. They don't have very many long-range guns, but the ones they do have are maddeningly able to range this headquarters. And that is why you two are here today. Prior to the kickoff of the offensive, we want you to take out this gun here."

The Liwa passed over a map with markings indicating where the Roman gun position was thought to be located.

"We have tried to range it with our artillery, but even our *Saladin* gun has been unable to reach it. Naqeeb Kabir, you will lead your squadron on an attack on this so-called *'Fritz Gun.'* It must be destroyed so that it cannot interfere with our offensive."

"As you will it, Liwa," replied Faisal.

"Choose only the finest pilots. This mission is of vital importance."

Faisal and Sharaf bowed.

"You men are dismissed. I would offer more coffee, but unfortunately, I have to figure out how that idiot al-Saud managed to foul up one of my tank battalions."

No Man's Land, Dacia
October 10th, 2676 AUC

The early morning rollout of the 212th Pursuit Squadron, 12th Air Legion was completed before the sun was up. Their *Eagles*, bodies painted dark blue, while the wings were painted yellow, were barely noticeable at first in the predawn light, but as the sun rose, that quickly changed. There was a lively debate back and forth as to whether aircraft should be camouflaged, but so far, the old school had won out. The traditional paint scheme of the Roman Air Legions had remained. At the end of each wing was an oval roundel that displayed a stylized Roman eagle in gold against a red background.

Marcus had carefully chosen the pilots for this mission, and in addition to himself and Elvorix, he had chosen two other veterans, Caius Flavius Sissena and Decius Sertorius Erasinus, as well as two of the new pilots, Cassius Sennius Bubo and Titus Maelius Verinus. The two junior Centurions had proven themselves to be the best of the new pilots and had survived their first eight missions. It had been found by Marcus and the other veterans that if a pilot survived their first eight, they tended to live long enough to finish their tour and be rotated back to a training slot.

Of course, I am on my sixth tour at this point, and they have stretched out how long a tour lasts again. We must be getting short on pilots.

The six planes were flying high and passing in and out of cloud banks, each pilot constantly scanning for an early morning 'Sid patrol. Seeing the skies were clear for the nonce, Marcus concentrated on the landscape below to get a better picture of the land. He had a map displayed on a kneeboard so that he could sketch out their route, and he scanned for landmarks now that they had crossed over Roman lines. Popesti lay southeast on a bearing that would eventually take them toward the old Roman city of Constantinople, which had long ago been seized by the Abbasids.

Hell, half the reason this front was so important in the beginning of the war was the hope that we would recapture that great city, Marcus thought.

Marcus ceased his musings as he saw a shape flutter close to the ground. He brought up a pair of field glasses, and through them could see an older 'Sid pusher plane scout. That it wasn't diving away from them meant that the other pilot hadn't seen them yet.

Marcus pushed his plane over and dived on the unfortunate craft—he couldn't risk it getting off a message if it saw them. Fortunately, they were far enough from either line that there was little risk of the fight being observed, but that wouldn't be true much longer. He could feel the difference in his *Eagle* since the replacement of his nose guns, and the new cowling made the nose a tad bit heavier.

The *Eagle* was both sleek but also an ugly design. Its squat teardrop-shaped body was topped by an open cockpit that sat just behind the massive engine which gave the craft its speed. Stubby wings were attached low to the body, and were held in place by guidewires, while it had chunky fixed landing gear. Despite the *Eagle's* awkward appearance, it was fast, and the pilot had a good amount of visibility from where he sat, except directly behind him. Most *Eagle* pilots compensated for this by placing a mirror at the top of their windscreen so that they could see behind them.

The scout plane continued to fly a straight path towards Roman lines, and Marcus assumed it was an artillery spotter, looking to map the lines for they daily desultory bombardment. The spotter on the plane was focused to his front, but it seemed to Marcus that the man must have sensed something. Just before Marcus was going to fire, the spotter looked up and back at him.

"Almost there, you bastard," Marcus gritted out.

Marcus only held his fire a moment, just long enough for the spotter to realize what he was looking at. Marcus's forefinger squeezed down on the trigger, and rounds slashed down and into the spotter plane. Its pusher engine exploded into flames, but the pilot and spotter were both long since past caring, for they had both been torn apart by the machine gun fire. The plane nosed over and straight into the ground, throwing up a great shower of mud that extinguished the small engine fire. Caeso and Cassius both waggled their wings at Marcus, indicating that both had seen his kill.

Marcus turned his craft back toward his compatriots and advanced his throttle until he caught back up with the formation. They continued their way flying at 10,000 feet, managing to stay in cloud cover.

"If we can stay in this cloud cover, perhaps it will conceal us all the way in," said Marcus to himself.

This seemed to work until they drew closer to Popesti, where their luck ran out. The cloud cover that had concealed them seemed to be thinning out, and worse, the early morning fog had mostly dissipated. Marcus and the others could clearly make out the ground below them. Worse, the 'Sids looking up could clearly see that the aircraft above them were not theirs.

Black puffs began to explode in the sky, mostly behind the formation, at first, but then the gunners seemed to get their bearings and the flak started coming up among them. Marcus and the others zigged this way and zagged that way to try and throw off the aim of the gunners below. It seemed to work, as none of the shells got close.

Soon, the six planes were over Popesti proper, and the sight below took Marcus's breath away. Row after row after row of tanks, neatly parked. Behind them were artillery pieces, and worse, large groupings of tents.

Mithras, there is a whole separate army group down there.

Caeso's plane came close to Marcus's, and the other pilot waggled his wings to get Marcus's attention. Caeso pointed to a position at their one o'clock and then upwards at an angle. Marcus followed Caeso's arm up and saw that descending were four other airplanes.

Caliphate planes.

Damn, they almost got the jump on us!

Marcus elevated his nose and kicked his rudder to bring the lead 'Sid aircraft in line with his guns. Once there, Marcus squeezed the trigger, and a stream of .50-caliber rounds spat defiantly at the 'Sid *Sahir*. The other airplane shuddered as the rounds impacted, and then exploded as incendiary rounds found the plane's fuel tank.

He didn't have long to celebrate his victory as the other Caliphate fighters spat back their fury. Marcus could hear rounds impacting on his fuselage, and he jinked his aircraft out of the fire. Centurion Erasinus shot past Marcus, firing his guns into one of the remaining Abbasid fighters, and it exploded. He rolled up and on his right wing to avoid the burning wreckage. The other two 'Sid fighters decided that discretion was the better part of valor and dove for the safety of their own anti-aircraft batteries. Marcus signaled his flight to form up, and he turned his craft for home. They had seen what they came here to see.

The question is whether we can do anything about it?

Airfield 237, Dacia
Abbasid Lines
October 11th, 2676 AUC

Faisal was annoyed. He had been getting his squadron ready to depart for their mission against the "Fritz Gun" the day before when he had been pulled off the flight line and instructed to head back to the airfield headquarters. Arriving, he found the stern-faced Moqaddam and several Ra'eds hunched over maps.

"Naqeeb Kabir, please come in," motioned the Moqaddam, whose name Faisal still did not know.

"We have alarming news which has moved the timetable up for the offensive. The Liwa and his staff have been killed by an artillery strike on their headquarters."

Faisal was shocked by the news and took a moment to process it.

"Sir, how can I be of help?"

"The Romans have found our largest staging area for the armor assault that we intend to throw across the Tissus. We must protect the staging area at all costs from any large air attacks. As such, we are moving your squadron along with several others to Popesti, to take up patrols there to keep the Romans away."

The Moqaddam tapped the symbol for an airfield on the map near the town of Popesti.

"We know that their 12th Air Legion is across the Tissus from us, and it appears that they have brought up a new type of bomber. We have various reports of large aircraft dropping an inordinately large number of bombs, more than we have seen before. We also suspect they may be bringing up some of the airships to attack us."

"Sir, my squadron was never issued the special ammo for attacking airships."

"I was afraid of that. You will have to do the best you can, as we aren't likely going to get that ammo here in time to be of any use. We haven't seen airships in this sector in some time. In fact, I don't think anyone has seen them except in Atlantis, attacking those cursed Azteca."

Faisal wrinkled his brow at the mention of the pagans across the great eastern ocean. While it was true that they were no friends of the Romans, the savages had rebuffed every Abbasid attempt at alliance during the long war. He was no fan of the quasi-civilized Azteca or the Incan Empire that ruled South Atlantis, but at least the Incans had come to terms with the Caliphate and made their intelligence assets available to them.

"Do we know if these are some of their newer airships, sir?"

The Moqaddam looked Faisal in the eye and sighed before responding.

"We aren't entirely sure, Naqeeb. We think they may be second-line equipment, so I doubt you will see any of their parasite fighters."

"Thank Allah for small mercies."

"Indeed, Naqeeb, indeed."

The senior officer glanced back down at the map before looking back up at Faisal, again sighing.

"You have your orders. We cannot afford failure here—we have scrapped up these resources to try and punch through this line. If we are successful here, we will achieve breakout behind their lines, and there is nothing between us and the Alps. This offensive could end the war, with great concessions being made by Rome if it wishes to survive. We have to break through their lines first, and we can't do that if they destroy the depots at Popesti."

"I won't fail you, sir." Faisal popped to attention and saluted the senior officer. The stern-faced Moqaddam returned the salute, and Faisal left the office behind to get his squadron ready to move.

Aerodrome 434, Dacia
Roman Lines
October 18th, 2676 AUC

The men had been up for hours already, and the sun had yet to crest the horizon. Marcus and his fellow pilots had entered a large hangar to find the Air Legatus and his staff standing on a makeshift stage. Behind the Legatus was a large display board that had been covered over with a tarp to obscure what laid beneath. Marcus looked around to see that all the squadron commanders were here, as well as most of the pilots. All in all, some one hundred and fifty men were gathered under the bright hangar lights.

"I don't think we have ever seen all the squadrons this plussed up," said Caeso.

"You're right—I have never seen all of us at full strength, and with our three new replacements, it looks like everyone else got them, as well."

"Hey, sir, we saw some guys landing in older *F-3F Falcons*. You don't suppose they are going to send them against Popesti, do you?" This came from Centurion Decius Erasinus.

Marcus scratched his nose, in the process shewing away a fly.

"They might be biplanes, but at least they aren't too old, not like our old *Crows* from the midpoint in the war. They can carry five hundred pounds worth more in bombs than our *Eagles* can, so perhaps they are optimizing them for ground attack."

"I guess, sir, but I wouldn't want to be those guys if a bunch of *Sahirs* show up."

"Neither would I."

Any further conversation was interrupted when the lights suddenly dimmed and then came back to full intensity. The staffers on the stage had finished whatever it was that they had been doing, and now all but two moved off the stage, leaving the Legatus standing by himself. He tugged down on the hem of his crimson tunic and adjusted his web belt before stepping to the front of the stage. An aide called the hangar to attention, and the Legatus motioned them all to first be at ease and then to take their seats. There was a rustle of chairs as the flyers found their seats in their assigned squadron areas.

"Gentlemen, we face a very grave danger. Thanks to the efforts of the 212th Pursuit Squadron, we now know that there is a very large attack force being assembled in the enemy rear, near the city of Popesti. I do not have to tell you that if Caliphate forces break through the Tissus Line, they can do an end run around our entire line in either direction."

The Legatus paused to clear his throat, then continued.

"Or if they so choose, they could drive all the way up the Danubius River and on to Upper Pannonia. We would have to attempt to stop them there, and that would be catastrophic, even war-ending. The German Legions are stretched thin in this sector, and they do not have enough forces on their own to stop a concentrated armor attack from the newer 'Sid tanks."

The Legatus had been pacing back and forth while indicating places on the map, but now came back to the center of the stage. Theatrically, he placed his hands on his hips, allowing the map to frame him.

"This is it, gentlemen. We are all that stands between the interior of the Empire, and the forces of the Caliphate. As such, we will be launching the largest air offensive to date in this war. The entire 12th Air Legion, along with the Second and Third Bombardment Cohorts, will launch an all-out attack on Popesti."

A hand rose from one of the more senior squadron commanders, and Marcus couldn't see who it was, though he recognized him when he spoke.

"Legatus, if we have just found out this information, how are we going to launch the entire legion against this city?" asked Tribune Gerwig Reingard.

"It is true that we have not had a lot of time to put forces together on this, so we will not be as coordinated as we like. However, we have been fortunate that the Bombardment Cohorts were already on their way to join this Front. Additionally, the Navy has been able to dispatch four of their newest airships and another five of their older designs."

There was a stir at this news. Airships were powerful weapons, but they had the weakness of being slow, and were vulnerable to flak as well as incendiary rounds. Still, each of them could lift as many bombs as ten heavy bombers, and that wasn't counting the aerial artillery pieces that could rain precise fire onto enemy positions. The newest ones had the advantage of carrying four parasite fighters each for self-defense. While the *Gulls* might be biplane fighters, they were good enough in the defense role.

"I believe this addresses your concern, Tribune?"

Tribune Reingard would have been an oddity in one of the ground legions, but the air legions did not form along geographical lines like their ground-pounder counterparts did. The German Tribune nodded his assent, and the briefing continued.

"All right, squadron commanders, listen up for your assignments..."

Marcus and the rest of the 212th Pursuit Squadron sat in their cockpits, waiting for the flare that would announce it was their turn to launch. In front of them were the new Martinus *B-10 Castellums*, wearing the same blue-and-yellow paint jobs as their fighters. The aircraft were big, ungainly-looking things, with a bulbous nose turret holding a single .30-caliber gun. The pilot and topside gunner sat under ridge-like canopies. A further two machine guns stuck out from the gun position behind the pilot. Each of the bombers could carry more than two thousand pounds in bombs.

The twin engines were spooled up on the ten bombers to Marcus's front, and they took turns rolling down the runway and soaring into the air. As the last one rolled out, a Signifer stepped out of the control tower and fired a red flare, indicating it was time for Marcus and the rest of his *Eagles* to take off.

Marcus pulled his goggles down and advanced his throttles. He built up airspeed rapidly and was soon airborne. Behind him, the rest of the 212th Pursuit Squadron raced into the air to catch up with their charges.

It was going to be a very busy day.

AIRFIELD 237, DACIA
ABBASID LINES
OCTOBER 18TH, 2676 AUC

Faisal was jarred out of bed just after sunrise by his orderly.

"Sir, the front is reporting enemy air activity—a *lot* of air activity," the obsequious man said.

Faisal groaned awake. They had expected an attack for over a week now, which meant he and his men had been on continuous air patrols. He was weary to his core, for he had only fallen into bed just three hours before.

"I am awake, Masood. Is there any coffee or tea?"

The maddeningly dapper orderly produced a large steaming cup of black tea that just promised to be brimming with caffeine. Faisal took it gratefully and took a large sip, oblivious to the heat of the liquid. He put the cup down and lit a cigarette, then put his boots on. He hadn't taken his flight uniform off from the previous day, only bothering to remove his leather flight jacket.

"Sir, there has been a great deal of air activity over enemy lines," repeated Masood.

"I see. I assume everyone else is being woken up?"

"Yes, sir. The hangar crews are prepping the aircraft now."

Faisal shrugged back into his coat, took another drag on his cigarette, then hurriedly gulped down the rest of his chai.

"Very good, Masood. I can handle it from here."

He walked out of his small room and headed toward the flight line, already thinking ahead about the battle to come. Reaching his plane, he took a moment to confer with the crew chief. The Raqib had finished his instructions to the maintainers and turned to Faisal.

"Sir, your plane is fueled, and you have a full loadout for your guns. We have looked at your number two gun, and we think we have figured out why it was jamming on you previously, or at least we are ninety percent sure."

"What was the problem?"

"There was an indentation in the receiver. We banged it out and hope that takes care of the problem."

Faisal walked over to the port side gun well and looked in.

"Could we not swap it out for a new gun?"

"Unfortunately, we are out of new guns. With all the major preparations, we have used up our on-hand supplies."

"Understood, Raqib. Thank you for doing what you could."

Faisal mounted the small ladder and boosted himself up into the cockpit of his fighter. All around him, other aircraft were starting their engines or running down the taxiway towards the runway. Faisal's ground crew got his engine running, and he also taxied to the runway. The signal was given for him and his squadron to launch.

The air tasted sweet to Faisal as his plane raced down the runway, then lifted into the air. The sun was up, and he turned the nose of his aircraft toward the west, where they expected to meet the Roman forces that were even now winging toward them. Around him, the rest of his squadron had formed up into a V formation, with his aircraft taking point. He was glad for the darkened goggles over his eyes, which helped to cut down some of the glare from the rising sun.

"Naqeeb, look over there," came a tinny voice on the wireless. "I can see an airship at our ten o'clock."

Faisal glanced in the direction indicated, and sure enough, an enormous airship was emerging from a cloudbank. *It must still be more than four or five miles away;* damn, *I wish we had the incendiary rounds for this.*

"Okay, flight, follow me in: we will make a pass on it from topside, working it over from nose to stern. Stay away from the ship's guns and keep a sharp eye out for enemy fighters—they must be nearby."

A chorus of replies told Faisal that everyone had received and understood their orders. He pulled back on his stick, bringing his *Sahir's* nose up until he judged that they were three thousand feet higher than the airship. The air was sharp with cold and stank of gasoline exhaust off his engine. Scanning around, Faisal didn't see any enemy fighters, but there were also sporadic dense clouds that they could be hiding in.

Marcus and the rest of his squadron observed the enemy fighters below them. The aircraft maintained their formation, even as they turned toward the airship *Mercury*. The 212th wasn't alone, either, for *Mercury's* four parasite fighters also formed up with intent to strike the 'Sid fliers below. He waited until the Caliphate fighters were passing close to the cloudbank he was in when he waggled his wings and then dove.

Marcus lined up his sights on the aircraft that formed the rightmost edge of the enemy V. The Caliphate pilots seemed oblivious to their approach, and so Marcus waited until the enemy fighter grew large in his sights. He squeezed his trigger, and a burst of machine gun fire shot into the enemy plane, killing its pilot instantly. Marcus saw at least two more enemy machines fall from the sky, in addition to his kill. The surviving Caliphate fighters broke formation, trying to escape the Romans.

The *Mercury* was not idle, either. Its own machine guns streaked the sky with tracers as more than one Caliphate squadron swooped in to attack it. Marcus watched as the biggest aerial dogfight he had ever seen broke out. His friend Caeso managed to wing a Caliphate fighter; though it didn't fall from the sky, it was still forced to dive for the safety of the ground. Caeso didn't give chase, instead mixing it up with another fighter that had risen to challenge him.

Damn, there are so many of them!

"Naqeeb, there are too many of them," came the panicked voice of Molazim Ayoub.

Before Faisal could respond, the man's plane exploded, though from what, Faisal wasn't sure.

They have killed half of my squadron. We can't keep this up.

Faisal lined up on a Roman *Eagle,* and leading it ever so slightly, he depressed his trigger, a fierce grin lighting up his face as the enemy machine began to spew smoke and flames from its huge engine. Faisal saw the enemy pilot push himself up and out of his cockpit to tumble into the air. Faisal lost sight of the other pilot for a minute until he saw a parachute open, indicating that the man still lived.

We really need to adopt those. Also, I had better stop philosophizing before I get my ass shot off.

Faisal found himself alone for the moment, with no enemy fighters engaging him. He observed one of the small parasite biplanes pass below him, evidently intent on a *Sahir* trying to line up on the airship.

Those were not supposed to be here. These must be newer airships, and not the obsolete ones we were promised.

Faisal dropped his nose, lined up on the enemy plane, and again sent a stream of bullets into an enemy aircraft. This Roman pilot was less fortunate than his fellow, for his biplane exploded.

"Naqeeb, enemy bombers sighted," radioed Sharaf. "There is a large formation of them at our two o'clock high."

"I see them. All right, new plan: ignore the airships, since our rounds aren't having much in the way of an effect on them. Flak will have to deal with them. Concentrate on the bombers."

"Understood, sir," radioed the remainder of his flight.

Faisal's remaining five fighters slew around and up towards the flight of *B-10s* steadily approaching Popesti. Angry black bursts of flak dotted the sky all around both his fighters and the Roman aircraft.

"Those damn gunners are shooting at everything," radioed Sharaf.

Looking down, Faisal could see why; they were now over the main marshalling yard for the 3rd Armor Division. The four hundred tanks were still neatly parked in rows, though Faisal could see personnel on the ground scampering around the tanks. He didn't have a lot of time to spare thinking about the tankers below, though, for he could see a detachment of Roman fighters descending toward his group.

We really need to put radios in these aircraft, Marcus thought.

He and the remnants of the 212th formed up to give chase to a group of *Sahirs* arrowing toward the *B-10s* that he was charged with protecting. The bombers closed up tight to provide protective fields of fire for each other. Beside his aircraft, Caeso was flying close formation on his right wing while Decius and one of the replacements formed up on his left. Behind his flight, the airship *Diana* exploded, causing Marcus to blanch.

"The flak is getting better," he gritted out loud.

Marcus pointed at the lead pair of *Sahirs* after getting Caeso's attention; he indicated to the other pilot that he would take the left fighter while Caeso was to take the right. Caeso nodded his understanding, and both pilots dived into the attack.

The fighter that Marcus tried to line up on was maneuvering violently so that he couldn't get a good fix on it.

"Come on, get in there," muttered Marcus.

Just as he thought he had it, the other pilot jerked back on his stick and applied his flaps, effectively jinking the fighter up and braking it so that he could get behind Marcus. For his part, Marcus rolled his fighter left and down, then jerked his stick over to put his plane up on its right wing. Doing this brought both Marcus and the Caliphate pilot down to under five thousand feet. The men on the ground fired their rifles up at the aircraft, not bothering to distinguish friend from foe. A machine gun on top of one of the tanks spat fire into the air toward Marcus.

Marcus's fighter staggered as rounds impacted it, though he couldn't tell where he had been hit. To his surprise, the controls still seemed to be just as responsive, and he jerked his fighter out of the line of fire. He took that moment to drop both of his 150lb bombs on the enemy troops below, more out of annoyance than because he thought he was going to have any great effect. Even over his engine noise, Marcus could hear the *whump, whump* of the bombs bursting behind him.

He looked at the mirrors he had previously installed around the rim of his windscreen. He saw the enemy fighter peel away from him. Marcus brought his fighter around and saw that the enemy pilot was driving for all his worth toward the *B-10s* that were closing in on their target.

"In your desperation, you have made a mistake, my friend," Marcus said quietly.

———

"Damn, damn, damn, damn," muttered Faisal.

The enemy bombers were almost over their targets, and worse, he had had to break off his attack on the Roman fighter to try and break up the bombing formation. Tracers began to streak toward him from the noses of the enemy bombers.

If they can range on me, I can range on them.

Faisal depressed his trigger. There was a bang from his right gun, but it wasn't the right tone. Worse, no tracers spat from it.

"Allah be merciful," Faisal cried out.

He depressed his trigger again, and again, fire only came from his left gun. The tracers impacted the lead *B-10,* but seemingly to no effect. Faisal had little time to reflect on that, however, as his plane was seemingly kicked from behind. He could feel several impacts on his plane, and his stick suddenly became very sluggish. Faisal fought his controls, trying to keep the aircraft in the air. More streaks of fire flashed passed Faisal's face, some impacting on the wing to his right.

To his horror, he saw a crack forming between the impact holes in his right wing, starting at his cockpit and stretching up and over the top. He briefly saw the Roman fighter flying off his right side, its pilot looking over at him.

"I am undone, my friend, and you were the luckier pilot this time," Faisal said aloud to the enemy fighter.

Then the right wing separated.

———

Marcus watched the enemy plane fold up like a broken kite and spiral into the ground. It exploded as it impacted beside an enemy tank. The tank crew that had been by the vehicle were caught in the explosion.

"There but for the grace of Mithras, I commend your soul to whatever gods you believe in, my friend."

Looking around, Marcus saw that there were no more enemy fighters left nearby, but he also couldn't find Caeso's plane in the sky. Over the vehicle park, the *B-10s* dropped their deadly mixture of high explosive and incendiary bombs. Great gouts of earth, men, and machines were tossed up as the bombs exploded on the ground.

Worse for the Abbasids, the remaining airships also contributed their loads of bombs and light cannon fire to the spreading conflagration that had been a vehicle park. Marcus's exaltation at seeing the destruction was tempered by the uncertainty of the fate of his friend Caeso. He formed up with the remaining two fighters in his squadron and turned for his airfield.

Mithras protect my friends and fellow pilots. See them safely home.

AUTHOR'S NOTE

Part of the fun of writing alternate history is deciding how to make changes to the world to get to where you are by the time of your story. As you can see there were a lot of changes to get to where we are by the time the story takes place, but chief among them is the survival of the Western Roman Empire, and the Abbasid Caliphate. I chose the Abbasid Caliphate due to its importance in history. The loss of the universities and libraries in the Mongol sack of Baghdad in 1258 is perhaps one of the largest losses of human knowledge, eclipsing that of the loss of the Library of Alexandria. I would suggest further reading on the Abbasid Caliphate to my readers, for their history is fascinating.

For the purposes of this story, I chose to number the years by Roman reckoning of Ab Urbe Condita, or AUC, which is the number of years since the founding of Rome in 753 BC. The year 1 AD would be 754 AUC. This brings us to the dates of the story, which correspond to a version of WWI lasting more than 16 years.

The planes that I modelled my aircraft on are the *P-26 Peashooter* for the Roman *Eagles*, and the *Westland Wizard* for the Abbasid *Sahir*. Additionally, I did choose to use the fighter or bomber number designation from our timeline so that if one were so inclined, they could do a quick internet search to see what the aircraft looked like, though I have changed their names. Additionally, I have used Roman ranks, as well as the Arabic translation for ranks in the story so for example a Decurion is roughly equivalent to a modern captain, while Naqeeb is the Jordanian Army rank for captain.

I hope you enjoyed this story!

ABOUT PHILIP WOHLRAB

Philip Wohlrab has spent time in the United State Coast Guard and has served for more than 18 years in the Virginia Army National Guard. Serving as a medic attached to an infantry company, he earned the title "Doc" the hard way while serving across two tours in Iraq. He came home and continued his education, earning a Master of Public Health degree in 2016. He has written short stories in Mil-SF, Hard SF, fantasy, and alternate history. He currently works as a wargame designer for the United States Marine Corps and has also designed and executed wargames for the USAF, USN, USSF, and the Intelligence Community. He also does game design work for the civilian market. When not crafting new stories or new games he can be found hiking in Appalachia or attending Sci-Fi Cons.

https://www.amazon.com/stores/author/B01HTBZ57A

AIRACUDA!

Lee Allred

AIRACUDA!

May, 1938
Buffalo, NY

There were only three truly beautiful things in this ugly world, beautiful because they symbolized Man's triumph against Nature's tyrannies. Because they embodied the perfect curves Nature abhorred and the straight lines it forbade. Because even at rest, they suggested the blur of streamlined speed, as if poised to leap past the constraints of gravity and inertia.

Those three things were the streamlined Vanderbilt Commodore locomotive, the low-slung Cord coffin-nosed roadster, and the gleaming *Bell YFM-1 Airacuda* multi-place fighter aircraft.

Of the three, Captain Rory Sampson reckoned the *Airacuda* he piloted the most beautiful.

Pity it was such a flying deathtrap.

Flying a *Model 7 Airacuda* over the middle of Lake Ontario was about as suicidal as it gets, given its proclivity to fall from the sky if you breathed hard on it.

Maybe Sampson was so appreciative of beauty that gave Nature the raspberry because of the job Nature had done on him. Sampson had a phiz that looked like it'd gone ten rounds with Joe Lewis. He could use a little of those perfect lines.

"Coming up on dogleg checkpoint," co-pilot and navigator Brigham "Brig" Card announced. Brig's family came from Alberta somewhere, which made things a little rough, but he was a good egg. Sampson had taken on the rail-thin lieutenant as his number two when nobody else dared. Brig sat in the number-two cockpit position just behind Sampson.

Simpson acknowledged and gingerly eased the great silver beast into a slight turn to port towards the Canadian shoreline to the North. The city of Kingston, Ontario, and her ports could be seen as a dark smudge on the horizon.

Aviation industrialist Larry Bell had wanted to start making a big splash with his new aircraft company, so he'd had his engineers whip up a real futuristic Buck Rogers job for the company's first aircraft. Too bad his engineers hadn't designed one that could fly.

Bell had taken the challenge of a new Air Corps design specification nobody else in the aviation world had wanted to touch with a ten-foot slide rule: a multi-place fighter, a flying anti-aircraft gun platform that could fill the fighter role, as well.

Instead of simply designing a plane and sticking guns on it, Old Man Bell had built a plane around its weapons: two long-range 37mm cannons that could swat down bombers from beyond the range of their machine gun defenses.

To do this, Bell had turned the *Airacuda's* twin engines around backwards in a pusher configuration. Now the front of the wing nacelles could house a manned gunnery compartment out of which the long, long barrels of the .37 cannons protruded.

The result was the sleekest-looking plane in the air. The round noses of the glass-canopied nacelles mirrored that of the fuselage, giving the aircraft a triple-fuselage trimaran look to it, resulting in the sleekest-looking plane in the air. An Art Deco masterpiece and an engineering marvel, as well.

Rather than leaving the fire of cannons to the by-guess-and-by-golly of the "gunners" manning the nacelles, Bell's designers had added a fire-controller position just aft of the pilot. The co-pilot/navigator would be the ones firing the cannons by means of Sperry Instrument's new Flash Gordon toy: its Thermionic fire-control system. The nacelle "gunners" were there simply to reload and clear jams.

Sampson turned his head for a quick check on his two gunners. Their compartments were eye-level with him and just a few feet behind.

There they both sat perched in their wing-mounted coffins, bored out of their skulls. Young Williams in the port nacelle was still green enough to be making a half-hearted attempt at craning his neck to check for Canadian fighters. "Hog" Dempsey, the starboard side gunner, had long ago given up on that. Seeing Sampson, Dempsey grinned a face-splitting grin and mimed knocking back a beer. Knowing Dempsey, there could very well be an empty bottle rattling around his feet in the compartment.

If there were, Sampson would rip a strip off his hide when they landed, even though he couldn't really blame the man if he had snuck booze aboard; Sampson would have to get himself well and truly squiffed before *he'd* ever climb into that flying foxhole. The plane's pusher-prop configuration meant Dempsey had no way to bail out of the nacelle without getting sucked into the spinning props behind.

The cannons Dempsey and Williams risked certain death to babysit weren't the *'Cuda's* only armament. A pair of .30-caliber popguns were mounted on the nose of the plane under Sampson's control, if the need arose to fight like a conventional fighter aircraft.

Back behind Brig's number-two chair laid the waist gunner's compartment. Two waist blisters like those on a Navy Catalina flying boat framed either side. Solly Garfinkel could shift his pintle-mounted M2 Browning .50 cal from one to the other if he needed to knock a bandit off their tail.

If he were awake, that is. More than likely, Solly was racked out on the floor sawing logs. Sure, there was a war on, if you could call it that, but neither side was fighting.

Depression-wracked America and Canada were like two old drunks who'd talked themselves into going out back of the bar to settle things. Neither one wanted a fight, but neither could back down. So far, all the war had amounted to was a lot of angry speeches and military planes buzzing around each other's border.

Not that an early-model *Airacuda* could ever be accused of buzzing.

Its twin Allison engines—despite its revolutionary superchargers—were anemic to the point of catatonic. Instead of speeds of 300+ mph its designers had envisioned, the plane could barely manage 240 with a strong tail wind. To stick everything Bell had wanted on the plane, the fighter had ended up the size of a medium bomber. A sleek bomber-sized fighter, to be sure—silver and streamlined like something out of that H. G. Wells movie, *Things to Come*—but a wallowing pig of a plane, all the same. All the maneuverability and climb of a brick.

Worse, the early model *YFM-1* was catastrophically unstable in flight.

She'd pitch violently whenever power was applied to the engines. Just flying straight and level was a white-knuckled affair requiring constant finicking with both throttle and yoke wheel. (That she had a bomber's steering wheel on her control yoke instead of a joystick showed what the designers actually thought of her "fighter" designation.)

The plane droned on. The only positive thing Sampson could say about the pusher configuration was it put the engine noise aft so it bothered the waist gunner instead of the pilot.

"Captain!" Brig shouted over the intercom. "I'm getting a drop in—"

The ship suddenly went dead, the intercom along with it.

Sampson lost all electrical power.

That innovative Auxiliary Power Unit the designers had saddled the *'Cuda* with powered all the on-board electrics, so if the APU ever flickered or faltered—and it did on a regular basis, just like now—the plane lost *all* electrics. Instrumentation, hydraulics, flaps, fuel pumps, little sundries like that.

Oh, and spark plugs.

The Allison engines clattered to a stop.

Sampson heaved back on the suddenly-dead control yoke with all his strength, trying to keep the nose up. Back behind him, Brig had swung his stowed secondary control yoke out from the bulkhead, and heaved along with Sampson. The yoke still refused to budge.

The APU flickered back to life.

Willing himself calm, Sampson thumbed both starters, and for a miracle, both Allisons caught and resumed running. One engine was worse than none at all.

Another little flaw: it couldn't fly on one engine alone. Should one engine fail, the plane would auger into the ground despite anything a pilot could do. The term deathtrap was actually an understatement.

Sampson wiped sweat out of his eyes. "Lock your yolk back, Brig," he told his co-pilot. "I've got her."

He chanced a glance at his gunners. Dempsey looked over and attempted a grin. His face was a sickly greenish-white.

Williams, too green to know how close he'd been to death, was still craning his neck around looking for Canuck planes as if nothing had happened.

The *'Cuda* continued droning north-northeast.

"Coming up on target, Skipper," Brig said a few minutes later.

Kingston looked like more than just a smudge on the horizon now.

Sampson touched his throat mic. "Captain to waist gunner. Wake up, Solly. Time to earn your pay. Break out your brownie."

A sleepy mumble came back over the intercom.

The aircraft suddenly lurched up and to the left.

Solly had opened one of the waist blister canopies. The sudden change in airflow had caused the unstable plane to jerk left, and Sampson's hand on the wheel jerked with it, causing the plane's nose to pitch upwards violently.

Sampson stomped on the rudder and applied more power, finally getting the plane it back into control.

"You jackwall!" he shouted at Solly when he finally had a hand free to trigger his throat mic. "I told you to warn me before you opened up!"

"Sorry, Skip." A pause. "You want I should take pictures now?"

They were about as close to Kingston harbor as they were likely to get.

The small port of Kingston laid on the east end of Lake Ontario and served as the gateway to the St. Lawrence River and the Atlantic beyond, making the port a reconnaissance target.

That was about all a *Model 7 Airacuda* was good for.

Taking photos.

Simpson banked the plane to give Solly a better camera angle, the *'Cuda* fighting him until it settled into its new groove. He risked taking one hand off the yoke wheel and fumbled for his own binoculars. He scanned the docks.

Brig must've been doing the same. "Skipper, you see what I see?" he yelled.

The port was crammed with ore barges and the like, the kind that plied the five Great Lakes, some of them 500 feet in length. More surprising were the cargo nets draped over the sides of the barges. Crowds of men were climbing down the cargo nets into small boats below. The men wore the brownish-green battle dress of the Canadian army.

They were practicing for amphibious operations. Somewhere along the American shore of Lake Ontario was about to receive visitors. The war was about to turn hot and very, very nasty.

Sampson fingered his throat mic. "Tell me you're getting all this, Solly?"

"Am I ever!" the excited reply came back. Hopefully, Solly had remembered film this time.

William's voice cut in. "Skipper, we got company." Good boy! At least somebody was keeping watch in all this excitement.

Two Canadian Royal Air Force *Hawker Demon* biplanes were coming up to play. The two-seaters were straining to gain height. Seemed they really didn't like Yanks looking their docks over.

"Solly, close 'er up."

The *'Cuda* jerked again as the blister canopy slammed home, but this time Sampson was ready and the jerk merely added to the banking curve Simpson was already making.

Sampson considered his choices.

He could fight. True, the *Airacuda's* cannons outranged any popguns the Demons carried, but that that presupposed the *Airacuda* would hang together and the APU wouldn't conk out again. The *Model 7 'Cuda* may be a beautiful ship, but nothing you wanted to dogfight in.

Or he could run. The top speed of a *Demon* was maybe 180 mph. The *'Cuda* could push 270 in a pinch, nearly a hundred miles an hour faster.

Getting those photos back was more important than knocking down a couple aging biplanes.

Decision made.

He firewalled the throttle. The supercharged Allisons screamed in protest as the *'Cuda* blazed through the sky.

"We're pulling away, Skipper," Sully hollered. "They're dropping back and turning for home."

Sampson throttled back to a saner speed, nosing his plane west for Buffalo.

At least one crew member disagreed with his decision to turn tail, however.

"Should let me work 'em over," Dempsey complained. The compartment gunners could, in an emergency, take manual control of the cannons, but it'd have to be a pretty dire emergency. Whether on manual or remote, firing the .37mm cannon filled the compartment with smoke, blinding the gunner, and more likely than not asphyxiating him, as well.

Not for the first time did Sampson wish he could haul the engineers who designed the *Model 7* aboard and see how they like riding in the nacelle-coffins of a plane that couldn't fight, fly, or even stay in the air.

"Keep your meathooks off the gun, Dempsey. Any shooting to be done, fire control will do it," he told the crazy Irishman, but Dempsey wasn't any crazier than the engineers who'd dreamed up this aircraft.

In a sane world, they'd have grounded the early *'Cudas* by now. But then again, in a sane world, the Danzig Treaty would never have come into force.

Like the 1927 Washington Naval Treaty that limited the size and number of battleships and cruisers in the hopes of preventing a naval arms race, the 1936 Danzig Treaty limited the types of aircraft the Great Powers could fly.

The aviation world stood on the cusp of a generational leap in aviation technology. Metal monoplanes capable of 300 miles-an-hour, perhaps even 400-plus. Bombers that could carry a whole air fleet's worth of bombs across oceans.

The Treaty put a stop to all that. It banned all future designs and then went through existing designs on a case-by-case basis, essentially banning everything but existing biplanes and a few first-generation monoplanes. Fighters, bombers, auxiliary types—the proscribed list was long and exacting.

Except for one clerical error.

They'd accidentally left the *YFM-1 Airacuda's* unique category—fighter, multiplaced—off the proscribed list.

A diplomatic donnybrook and lengthy Treaty adjudication followed. The US was allowed to keep her flaw-ridden *YFM-1 Airacudas*, which had by this time gone through development and emerged as the *FM-1D* production model, a generation ahead of any Treaty plane. The fly in the ointment was that the US had to keep its YFM prototypes in operational service if it wanted to keep the production models.

Sampson got saddled flying one of the old prototype jobs. He was due for one of the *Jendrassik D* models soon, with all the *'Cuda* flaws fixed and then some.

When he did, he'd be back for a rematch.

———

The western end of Lake Ontario hove into view. The city of Buffalo, thirty miles to the south of it, was a smudge-line on the shore of Lake Eire.

The industrial powerhouse—home to not only steel and iron works, but to Curtiss Aircraft, which built Navy fighters, and the Bell Aviation plants which built the *Airacuda*—was about as poorly sited as could be for a war with Canada. The Niagara River, with its famous ,falls ran northward from Lakes Eire to Ontario and Buffalo, and its outlying communities crowded the length of that river's east bank. Canada laid on the west bank.

With Buffalo wide open to Canadian attack from three directions, the river bank and both lakeshores were lined with shore batteries and anti-aircraft emplacements manned by green crews with itchy trigger fingers.

No place Sampson wanted to fly over without radioing ahead first.

He called Wheatfield tower.

"Acknowleged, Able Charlie Four," a bored voice answered. Presumably, the very bored voice would telephone ahead and let the gun pits know he was coming.

He swung wide of the lake and to line himself up for landing approach. Several miles south of the shoreline laid Wheatfield. Bell Aircraft had set up its new plant with its cruciform of runways. The military had all but taken it over and turned it into an airbase. Row upon row of olive drab tents filled the open space surrounding the plant.

A glint of silver in the air ahead of him proved to be Sandy Ferguson in one of the newer *YFM-1A* jobs, a prototype that had swapped out simpler waist hatches for blisters and taildragger configuration for tricycle landing gear while keeping unfixed most of the rest of the *'Cuda's* flaws.

Sampson slotted his plane in behind Ferguson' s left wing, getting a little formation landing practice in as the two planes began their descent, coming in low and slow over the lakeshore.

Suddenly, the entire shoreline opened fire on them.

Greasy-grey puffs of anti-aircraft fire burst all around the two airplanes. A crashing noise, a slamming jerk, and Sampson's starboard wing was trailing fuel. Oil streamed from the sputtering engine. The nacelle canopy had shattered panes, and Dempsey was clutching one arm.

Another jolt and a rattle-like hail striking a tin roof sounded from the rear of the plane. Solly squawked in panic.

Then both *'Cudas* were past the gun pits and coming up fast on Wheatfield airstrip. Sandy's tricycle job looked untouched, and he flared his plane for a textbook landing.

Sampson's plane seemed to skid all over the sky and he couldn't correct. He had no engine power starboard side. His rudder was sluggish and he had no elevators at all. With Brig's help on the auxiliary yoke, he managed to manhandle it into the groove. His taildragger *'Cuda* bounced once, twice, three times like a pregnant kangaroo before he finally set down for good.

He chopped his crippled starboard engine and coaxed his plane onto the taxiway with just his portside prop before his portside temperature gauge redlined and he had to shut completely down.

A final flaw in the *Airacuda's* long list of defects was that without the propwash from a pusher-prop configuration, the otherwise reliable pusher-configured Allison air-cooled engines overheated on the ground. A *'Cuda* couldn't taxi on or off the field—it had to be towed.

In the sudden quiet, Sampson could hear the tinny bell of a crash truck approaching.

Dempsey was cursing and fumbling at his compartment hatch, but couldn't work it one-handed.

"Brig," Sampson called over his shoulder. "Looks like Dempsey got hit. See to him."

Brig acknowledged and opened the waist door. He and Solly jumped out and helped the swearing Irishman down to the ground. Williams had popped his hatch open and, puppy-eager, lent his unwanted aid.

Sampson wearily unbuckled himself and slid the pilot hatch cover out and down. Spring-recessed toeholds in the hatch cover functioned as a ladder down to the tarmac.

"Dempsey's okay," Brig said. "Superficial bleeding. Just got pinked in the bicep from flying glass. Solly says our entire tail surface got shot away, though."

Not quite that bad. Most of the tail assembly was still there, only it looked like it'd been run through a colander. One elevator hung crazily, tenuously attached to the rest of the tail. That it hadn't fallen off during landing was a miracle

The crash truck screeched up, clanging bell and all. Other vehicles followed in the truck's wake. A crew truck to haul them back and—sure as death and taxes—a buff-colored Cord convertible roadster belonging to the airfield's odious Head Proctor. Proctor Crane had come to access Sampson's crew's patriotic fervor or lack thereof and otherwise stick his needle-nosed beak into places it didn't belong.

Not for the first time did Sampson wondered how the United States had slid so low it now had Soviet-style political commissars.

President Henry Wallace had used the war as a pretext to jam his Progressive Party bully-boys not just into the noses of the harried civilian sector, but now the military branches, as well.

We used to be a nation of free men. Now, not so much.

Not so much for the rest of the world, either.

The world was nothing but one big prison camp these days. Fascist or

Bolshevik, what did it matter? It varied only in what dictator stared down at you from their giant banners. Trotsky, Earnest Rhoem, Mussolini, Darlan, Mosley, Quisling, Franco.

President Wallace was only a half-step behind and lickspittles like Head Proctor Crane were doing their utmost to catch him up.

Crane came tearing over to their plane, barking about how a sloppy landing like that demonstrated complete lack of patriotic fervor, not that how Sampson landed a plane was any of his business.

He was well into his second chorus when the wounded Dempsey splayed a bloody hand in the proctor face. "Patriotic fervor just got us all shot to pieces," he roared. "How about less fervor and more target recognition so we don't get shot up by our own side?"

Crane's head swiveled from Dempsey's bloody arm to the flak-riddled tail. "Shot? Your plane was shot? By our own men?"

"Well, it weren't no termites!"

Crane's mouth worked soundlessly like a landed mackerel. "Treachery!" he managed to bleat. "Sabotage! *Treason!*" He jumped in his car and tore off down the tarmac, tires squealing.

Solly spat on the ground. "Five to one says some poor gunner's mate is a guest of a People's workcamp by noon tomorrow."

Sampson could only nod. Crane was the sort who looked for treason when there was none. No, Crane was the sort who *found* treason when there was none.

A gum-chewing private leaned out of the driver's seat of the crew truck. "Hey, youse guys getting in or what? Ain't got all day."

Simpson chivvied his crew into the truck. Debriefing next. Higher echelon needed to know about those barges.

Higher echelon didn't want to hear of barges or Canadian troops climbing down cargo nets. Higher echelon had proctors assigned them, too, proctors that toed the current line from the Wallace administration that the Canucks were too afraid to come out and fight. Nobody with brass on their hat wanted evidence or testimony to the contrary.

"They're like the three wise monkeys," Sampson complained over a highball. "See no evil, hear no evil, file no evil reports."

He sat with his old boss, Larry Bell, in what had been the Bell Aircraft canteen and was now an Officer's Club. Not caring a fig if it interfered with aircraft output, the Army and Navy had jointly commandeered the Wheatfield Bell Aircraft plant complex for use as Buffalo Military District Headquarters.

They'd commandeered one Rory Sampson, too.

Sampson had been Bell's top test pilot on the *Airacudas*. The Army had stuck him in uniform, put captain bars on his collars, and set him to flying the same *Airacudas* from the same Bell airstrip on one-tenth his civilian pay.

"What do you want me to do about it, Rory?" the heavyset Bell asked. The executive was on his third whiskey sour.

"Stop them from sending us out in the old YF deathtraps, for one thing."

Bell snorted. "Think I haven't tried? My own factory, and the only thing I'm the boss of around here is when I visit the men's room."

He tinkled the ice in his glass. The threat of possible invasion had really shaken him. The Bell plant and building his planes was everything to him.

"I've been trying like the dickens to get them to let me relocate *Airacuda* assembly down to the Marietta, Georgia plant where it's safe, but will they listen? Defeatist talk, they say. At least I managed to slip the duplicate jigs and work drawings away before they stopped me."

The factory owner stiff-wristed the last of his drink and got to his feet. "I'll see what I can do about getting you assigned a production model. Least I owe you."

That was something, at least. Beat a hole in the head.

Sampson sat there nursing what was left of his highball, listening to the tinny sounds of Harry James on the jukebox and watching headquarter staff digging into steak dinners or whooping it up with their female civilian typists.

He hadn't quite decided to get another drink when a grey-haired navy commander sat down at his table. Husband Kimmel.

If you looked closely, you could just see fade patterns on his jacket cuffs where admiral stripes had once been sewn. Kimmel had run afoul of the proctors at the start of this phony war for actually trying to do his job. At least they hadn't cashiered him.

"Hello, Sampson-with-a-P."

"Hello, Kim. Sink any ships lately?"

"Ours or theirs?" Kimmel's voice still held traces of his Kentucky origins. "Heard you picked up a little friendly flak today. General Short is currently running amok up and down the halls of CINCBUFF over it, thinking up bright ideas to show the proctors he cares."

Short commanded the Buffalo Military District Headquarters and an apter surname nobody ever had. Not short in height, but short in brains. Brains, temper, and sightedness. Short didn't need Proctor Crane to suggest sabotage and enemy infiltrators. Finding Canucks under the bed was Short's pet hobby.

"Yeah, I heard his newest bright idea. Line up our planes wingtip to wingtip, the better to watch for sabotage." The better to be bombed and strafed by enemy planes, but Short understood airplanes like Ugg the Caveman understood integral calculus. "Bell managed to scotch that." The operational *'Cudas* were still in their sandbag revetments. The old silver YF junk heaps were now wing to wing, though.

"He has a newer one. He's handed out rifles to half the ground crews. Half your mechanics are now out playing infantry guarding the airstrip."

"Wonderful." Half the mechanics meant half the maintenance, and early *'Cudas* needed all the maintenance they could get.

"That's not what I wanted to talk to you about, though." Kimmel's eyes did a quick check of the room and his voice lowered to a Proctor-proof whisper. "You on the level about those barges?"

"Should all be there in the photos. Check 'em yourself."

"Can't. They mysteriously met the business end of a match shortly after the powers-that-be got a look at them."

Sampson put his face in his hands and shook his head. They'd risked death-by-APU for those photos, and for what?

He told Kimmel what they'd seen.

Kimmel nodded. "That checks with other reports I'm getting. They've gathered up ore barges from the other Great Lakes, as well. They could land a division anywhere they want, anytime they want."

Here or Detroit. Or Cleveland. Toledo. Milwaukee. Chicago, even.

Wallace had raided the Treasury for his social schemes. He'd cut the standing Army from two hundred thousand men to a bare ninety thousand —and less than half of those were actual combat troops. The Army had maybe three divisions, tops, to cover the entire Great Lakes shore line, neverminded the 49th parallel or the New England borders.

"Do they want?" he asked Kimmel.

"Boys in crypto think so."

"Wonderful. Preceded by bombing raids, I take it."

"There's a reason our gun pits were so trigger-happy today. Navy

Department sent a preliminary warning to all shore batteries before the proctors put the kibosh on."

"And word spread to the Army flak pits." Sampson waggled his empty glass. He definitely needed another. "Well, the word didn't reach Air Corps." Always the last to know. *We're just the boys who'll have to fly out to meet the Canucks.*

Kimmel spread his hands. "I advised General Short to pass it on to you. I was told in a string of four-letter words to stick to my knitting."

"Well, don't get yourself busted down again for our sakes, Kim," Sampson said. Joes like Kimmel who cared about their jobs were the ones who ended up holding the bag after things went wrong. It was the Cranes of the world who always managed to skate away clean.

Any reply Kimmel might have made was cut off by a sudden commotion in the back of the club.

Kimmel squinted in the direction of the noise. "Isn't that your pet Hungarian?"

Cheese and crackers and other comestibles.

It was indeed Jozsef Jendrassik, Bell Aircraft's chief design engineer. The Hungarian was sounding off very drunkenly and very loudly about things that shouldn't be sounded off about, not in range of a proctor rate. Luckily, most of his shouting was in Hungarian.

Kimmel raised one eyebrow. "You better drag him out of here before some Proctor finds a Hungarian dictionary."

Drag was the operative word. Sampson had to all but bodily carry Jendrassik out to his car.

"Let's get you home."

Jendrassik lived, if you could call it that, in an outbuilding next to the main plant that Larry Bell had fixed up into apartments for his engineers. The engineer was lucky to have that. Sampson's assigned quarters was an eight-man canvas tent near the plane revetments. The eight-man tent currently held sixteen *'Cuda* pilots.

The disheveled Jendrassik started pounding a fist on the car's glove box. "I escape from Nazis!" he declaimed.

"You certainly did." Hungary had been swallowed up by the Nazis bloodlessly, the way they'd swallowed up Austria, Czechoslovakia, and Denmark.

Jendrassik, brother of the famed Hungarian physicist/aviation inventor George Jendrassik and a genius aircraft designer in his own right, had managed to slip away to the putative freedom of Wallace's America.

"I escape Nazis, I land right back with Nazis!"

"You'll land right in front of my fist if you don't shut up."

"I would not like fist. I be quiet."

The drunken engineer managed to stay quiet all the way from the car to his apartment. Then the Hungarian started up again. "I take engine, I save engine from Nazis, but then like *idióta* I give to Nazis."

Sampson laid Jendrassik out on the Murphy bed. "You didn't give to Nazis, you gave to Mister Bell, a very fine gentleman." He got one of the Hungarian's shoes off.

"I give turboprop!"

"Yes, you did." The Hungarian escaped with not only the clothes on his back, but the plans and a working model of his brother's revolutionary new turboprop engine. Bell had teamed with Lycoming to whip up new engines for the *'Cudas*.

"Turboprop-p-p-prop!" the drunken Hungarian motorboated. "Stick on broken plane."

Other shoe off. "Yes, you did."

The *Lycoming-Jendrassik LJ-1* provided seventeen-hundred horses each for half the weight and none of the overheating. More than enough power to turn a sluggish *'Cuda* into a 400-mph beast.

"They show me broken plane. Backwards plane. I laugh. I fix tail!"

Jendrassik had taken one look at the *Airacuda* and said the plane's pitch problem when applying power stemmed from pusher prop airflow buffeting against tail elevators.

"I make V!" He made a V with his fingers.

Switching the tail surfaces from the standard cruciform to a "butterfly" V-tail placed the ruddervators, the v-angled surfaces doing the work of both rudder and elevator, out of the buffeting path.

"You make sleep now, is what you make." Sampson helped him the rest of the way out his clothes and covered him with a blanket.

Jendrassik passed out.

Sampson felt like doing the same. He went over to the kitchenette and a half-full bottle of what looked like vodka. He sniffed it. *Palinka*. Fruit brandy. Too sweet for his taste. He poured himself some, anyway.

Jendrassik had indeed fixed most of the problems of the *'Cudas*. The other fixes had just been common sense, like ditching the APU.

And like replacing the slow-firing, low-velocity .37mm cannon with a smaller, faster .20mm Hispano-Suiza rig, one that used a 100-round continuous belt feed rather than requiring a gunner to reload 5-round clips. This eliminated the need for the nacelle compartments gunners. The nacelle front was now a sleeker, slimmer affair, mostly an air scoop now for the turboprop and what housing the cannon needed.

The wing had been changed, too, given a Davis "teardrop" cross-section for more lift. They reversed the tapered leading edge/straight trailing edge wing shape and subbed it. With added power, lift, and response, these new *FM-1D* were nimble enough to dogfight and so didn't need a waist gunner, either.

Sampson looked over at the sleeping engineer. If the Canadians really were going to make a fight of things, this factory would be the first place they bombed. It wasn't just factory jigs and dies and plans that needed relocated. The people who designed and built the planes needed moved, as well.

He'd call Larry Bell in the morning. Get him to move Jendrassik and other key engineers and floor workers down to Marietta while there was still time.

Of course, if the powers-that-be really wanted to pull their ostrich heads out, they'd relocate Sampson's *'Cudas* south, too.

They didn't, of course.

A week later, the Canadians struck at dawn on a Sunday morning, on what came to be known as Detroit Day.

Detroit laid, like Buffalo, wedged between two Great Lakes just across the river from a slice of Canada. Canadian forces launched a full-scale air attack followed up by amphibious landings and a race to encircle the industrial metropolis.

Sampson didn't learn any of that until later. The first he knew of Detroit Day was the whistling whine and bone-shattering *crump* of falling bombs. He rushed out of his tent in his skivvies to gawk at the Canadian heavy bombers overhead.

Handley Page Heyford heavy bombers, they were, the most ungainly giraffe of a biplane bomber imaginable. *Heyfords* looked like a grab bag of airplane parts glued together by a dyspeptic schoolboy.

A biplane, yes, but instead of lower wing on lower fuselage and upper wing strutted high above, the plane's broad, boxy, bomb-laden bottom wing was attached to the spatted undercarriage at wheel-axle level. A long, long, long scaffolding of struts and braces separated that undercarriage from the body of the plane—the cockpit stood twenty-feet above the ground when parked. The upper wing sat level with the top of the long, pencil-shaped fuselage the way shoulder-winged monoplanes mounted their wing.

Most peculiar of all was its defensive guns. In addition to open-air nose and waist gun tubs, they had a long metal cylinder hanging from the middle of the plane, looking for all the world like a man-sized dustbin. This "dustbin" gun turret extended down nearly ten feet for combat and then retracted back into the fuselage when not in use.

As ungainly as the *Heyfords* looked—or flew, for that matter—they carried a ton of bombs each, and the squadron of six overhead were dropping those bombs with abandon.

With abandon, but not much effect.

The bombs completely missed the main factory, hitting instead a couple hangars and demolishing the outbuilding where Jendrassik had lived up until the day before. Either the Canadians were just as green as American pilots, or they were sparing the *Airacuda* plant for when they took over.

No sooner had the *Heyfords* gone by than a wave of light bombers followed. *Fairey Battles*, a three-man monoplane design that had just barely squeezed under the Danzig moratorium. They were about as modern a plane as Britain and her daughter Canada had under the Danzig Treaty. The plane had a speed roughly that of a *'Cuda* and nearly as many flaws.

The *Battles* came in fast and low, dropping their paltry bombload on the surfaced runway, hoping to crater it so as to prevent any *'Cudas* from taking off in pursuit.

As for the parked *'Cudas* themselves, the *Battles* strafed those, as well. A *Battle* had only a single forward-fixed .303 Browning in its right wing and most of the new models *'Cudas* were safe behind sandbag revetments, but a few of the early *'Cudas* were lined up wing-to-wing per Short's order.

The *Battles* turned their anemic fury on those, puncturing their metal skins but otherwise failing to seriously damage them. They did manage to hit the landing gear of the already-damaged Model 7 Sampson had flown to Kingston. The *'Cuda* slumped crazily on freshly bent wing.

The last *Battle* in line perforated the wing tank of one the tricycle-gear YFMs and it went up like a two-for-a-penny firecracker.

"Hey, that's my plane!" Ferguson shouted. He and Brig and the other pilots from the tent had tumbled out, as well. The red-haired lieutenant muttered a string of curses. Sampson didn't see it as much of a loss. Not as if they'd hit one of the V-tails.

"Here they come again!" shouted a half-dressed pilot. The *Battles* had doubled back.

Bullets stitched a line down the tent city and Sampson hit the dirt, covering his head with his arms. The planes screamed past and climbed for home.

Sampson got to his feet.

Brig was kneeling beside a blood-spattered body. "Ferguson. He's dead."

But Sampson was already ducking in the tent for his clothes.

"Get to your planes," he shouted as emerged, shoving sockless feet into untied boots. Fastening his pants as he ran, he sprinted for his new V-tailed *'Cuda*, Brig right behind him.

Sampson and Brig completed the world's hastiest pre-flight check, unchocking the wheels and waggling control surfaces and ignoring the rest of the list. He fired up the engines. The Lycomings spun up to a roar overlain with that high-pitched vacuum-cleaner whine peculiar to turboprops.

First out of the gate, Sampson taxied his V-tailed *'Cuda* down the runaway.

The Canucks had only managed to crater the far end that Sampson didn't need, anyway. The *Airacuda* clawed its way into the sky.

The Canuck planes were hightailing it north over the lake in the direction of their Toronto airbase. Instead of following north, Sampson banked due west instead, away from any gun pits. The American gun crews had finally woken up and were blasting away with abandon. Sampson didn't intend to give them a friendly target again.

The radio crackled unintelligibly, voices babbling over the top of each other, one of which was General Short, no doubt, demanding their flight plans in triplicate. A heterodyne whine and the radio conked out. The fool thing had been acting up. Maintenance had been too busy to fix it.

Sampson shrugged. He didn't need radio to tell him to chase after the Canucks at all possible speed.

He flew west, then cut north over the lake, confident in his *'Cuda's* ability to catch up. The clumsy *Heyford* heavies could barely crack 140 miles per; their cruise speed hardly topped 100. The faster *Battles*, he reckoned, were keeping close to the *Heyfords* as makeshift escort, providing what cover they could with their one fixed popgun forward and one .303 rear gunner.

"Anybody else manage to get their plane up?" he asked Brig when he had a moment.

"Not that I saw," Brig said over the earphones, but he didn't have any better a view reward than Sampson had. They shared the same cockpit canopy. *This is one time I actually missed the old* Model 7 *and having a gunner's set of eyeballs in the waist*, Sampson thought.

Off in the distance, two o' clock low at only a couple thousand feet, Sampson spotted six *Fairey Battles* plodding along. The *Heyfords* must be further ahead.

Sampson lowered his goggles over his eyes. "Here we go, Brig. Let's see if that Sperry gizmo of yours actually works."

He nosed the *'Cuda* into a screaming dive, the airspeed indicator needle quivering near three-eighty.

The Canucks spotted him before he got within cannon range. The six light bombers scattered in six different directions. Sampson chased after the Tail End Charlie.

He lined the *'Cuda* up on the *Battle's* tail.

Time to let Brig to work his magic with the Sperry. Brig was peeping through a belly-mounted periscope, aligning the *Battle* dead center in the periscope viewfinder's reticle. The Sperry's mechanical brain would then calculate a ballistic solution for drift, windage, parallax, shell drop and such, and slave the guns, which could pivot a 25-degree cone of fire to the stabilizing gyros.

All Sampson had to do was hold the *'Cuda* relatively steady and wait for Brig to pull the trigger.

Rather like an aerial tank: Brig worked the gun. Sampson was merely the bus driver.

Twin Hispano-Suizas barked. The short burst chewed up the *Battle's* duralumin skin-like tissue as it walked its way up the fuselage, smashing machine and frail human bodies alike. The *Battle* nosed over into a lakebound dive. *One down*.

Sampson danced his plane around in a g-pulling maneuver to line up on another fleeing *Battle*.

"Easy, easy," Brig crooned, and the cannons spat another burst. "Got him!" The *Battle's* engine erupted in a gout of flame. *Scratch number two*.

A panicked *Battle* angled across the nose of the *'Cuda*. Sampson mashed down his yoke trigger and the nose guns spat a .50 caliber hailstorm. White haze trailed from the bomber's left wing as the *'Cuda* flashed by. The haze turned to blue smoke.

The *'Cuda* found itself in the center of a knot of swerving *Battles*. Lines of red tracers tracked the *'Cuda's* progress as Sampson jinked to get clear.

A rattle like dry beans in a tin can danced down the *'Cuda's* fuselage. One of the Battle rear gunners had peppered them with his .303 Browning but had missed their vitals.

Sampson yanked up and away. He'd been a fool not to simply keep out of range and let the cannons do the work. Buck fever, he supposed.

"You okay, Brig?"

"Just shaken up, Skipper."

Sampson swung round behind the same plane he'd just plinked. Before Brig could fire again, the blue smoke trailing from the Battle's wing turned to greasy flame. The stricken plane rolled over on its back as the crew bailed out. The empty bomber plowed straight down into the lake below. *Three*.

The three remaining light bombers looked mighty tempting as they peeled away in panic, but Sampson saw even more tempting targets ahead: a formation of *Heyford* heavies creeping north at a turtle's pace.

"Portside cannon jammed in that last attack," Brig warned.

"We still have right side, don't we?" Those lumbering beasts ahead had to be as flimsy as they looked. Twenty-millimeter shells from even a single cannon should tear them to pieces.

The *Airacuda* loped ahead.

The heavy bombers kept to their formation rather than scatter, trusting the box pattern of their defensive guns to keep his *'Cuda* at bay.

If he'd been in a normal fighter operating normal machine guns, Sampson would have come up from below to face only one gun from the ventral dustbin instead of the two up top.

Sampson, however, had no intention of getting into the dustbin's range at all. This time, he'd just hang back and let Brig and the Sperry do all the work. After all, that was how the *Airacuda* was designed to fight: as a stand-off anti-aircraft platform.

It proved harder in practice than theory, however. The *Heyford's* cruise speed was barely faster than the V-tail *'Cuda's* stall speed.

He angled into position.

"Lining up on the one to the far left," he told Brig, beginning to wish he could fire the cannons himself like a regular fighter and be done with it. That Sperry was a mighty fine gizmo, but the two-man firing process was also proving exasperatingly clumsy.

The gears and cams of the Sperry seemed to take their own sweet time before Brig fired a burst from the only working cannon,

The *Heyford* was metal, not wood—Handley Page's first all-metal bomber—but that didn't save her.

A wooden plane would shatter into flinders. What Brig's shells did to the metal was nearly as catastrophic.

The twenty-millimeter shells sawed right through undercarriage support struts. The whole lower wing assembly flung itself away from the top half of the plane, spinning as it fell.

Stripped of half its lift, what remained of the *Heyford* plummeted like a stone. *Four.*

Sampson pulled up sharply. Streams of enemy red tracer fire curved after him, futile as he was out of range, but what else could the Canadians do?

A wide circle brought the *'Cuda* back into position for the next attack. Sampson lined up again, this time on the rearmost plane to the right.

"That big boy on the right," he told Brig.

Out of the corner of his eye, he saw the cannon muzzle quest side to side almost aimlessly, then stop askew, clearly not lined up on the target.

Brig yelled in frustration. "The gyros! I can't get them to clutch."

Sampson poured on the coals and pulled away, aborting the shot.

He could hear Brig fussing about behind him. "Going to try resetting the breaker." He clacked it open and shut a couple times.

Instruments quivered and the fuel pump sputtered under the sudden current drain. The *'Cuda* hiccupped in flight, but regained power.

Nearly bad as the old APU.

The huge electrical demands of the Sperry and the gyro-slaving mechanisms were what had prompted them to install a separate APU engine in the *Airacuda* in the first place. The turboprop Lycomings had power to spare to drive the plane's electrics, but the sudden applied load taxed them.

"Let's not do that again," he called to Brig.

He lined up the *'Cuda* again. "Same plane."

Again, the gyros tumbled.

Sampson pulled off to a safe distance.

This time, Brig flipped breakers one by one rather than all of once.

The *Airacuda* swung around once more. *Third time's the charm.*

"Come in slower, if you can," Brig ordered.

"Any slower and we'll stall," Sampson shot back, but he edged his speed down a further ten knots. The controls felt mushy as oatmeal.

The Hispano-Suiza barked at last, a long, lingering burst that caught the *Heyford's* portside Rolls-Royce Kestrel square. Chunks of shredded engine flew like shrapnel, and fire blossomed from the cowling.

The cannon clattered empty. Out of ammunition.

Still, the wounded *Heyford* refused to die. It continued on a single engine.

Did he dare risk getting in close to finish her off with nose guns? Silly-looking or not, Sampson had a healthy respect for that box formation. The *'Cuda* might be the one ending up in the drink.

"Skipper, we got company."

Seems Sampson had heard that those words before.

This time it wasn't just a couple of *Hawker Demons*, though.

A whole cloud of Canuck fighters arrowed south toward him and the bombers. The short-range fighters had come to escort the bombers home and swat any Yank plane pestering them in the bargain.

That settled it. He hated giving up on the crippled *Heyford* and reaching ace, but he banked the *Airacuda* hard left and away. He'd have to make ace some other day.

Just as he did so, the wounded bomber slid out of formation. The blazing engine vanished in a gout of explosion. The huge plane augured into the water.

Five and ace, after all.

Both cannons useless and a swarm of enemy fighters. Time to head for home. Not even the proctors could find fault with that.

Fires still sputtered fitfully at Wheatfield when Sampson landed. The acrid smell of smoke and ash penetrated the cockpit. South on the horizon where the city of Buffalo proper lay was nothing but a solid smear of black smoke and fire. The Canadians must really have plastered it in a second attack.

The *'Cuda* coasted to a stop. Sampson popped the hatch and deplaned, not to a hero's welcome but to General Short himself and a swarm of armed MPs.

A red-faced Short sputtered incoherently about Sampson and Brig and desertion in the face of the enemy. He ordered the pair of them dragged to the stockage and shot, not necessarily in that order. The MPs seemed only too happy to oblige.

They hauled Brig away separately, where, Sampson didn't know. As for Sampson himself, the MPs dumped him at the airfield's Proctor station. "We'll be back after they get through with you," the MP sergeant smirked as they threw Sampson into a windowless box of sheet-iron the proctors called the "cooler."

The iron door closed behind him with a band, and the outside bolt shot home.

Sampson sweated the next several miserable, stinking days in that steel box. Broiling hot during the day, freezing at night. Close and stuffy, it smelt of urine, some of it his. In the dim light, he saw scratched on the wall various scatological remarks about Wallace, proctors, and the US Army. Sampson added his own little ditty, feeling that General Short had been neglected.

Sampson repeatedly asked his proctor jailors what why he was being held, but for once, the proctors were silent as the grave.

All Sampson knew was that once a day, they shoved a plate of dry bread and a pannikin of water through a slot near the floor.

After a few days, even that stopped.

When he realized they weren't feeding him anymore, Sampson pounded on the door, shouted, screamed but no answer. Pressing ear to the wall, he heard no one, no one moving about in the corridor outside. No one in the station building at all.

He still heard the war going on. The drone of planes taking off and landing. The occasional bark of anti-aircraft guns. The occasional whistle-crash of falling bombs.

But nothing of the guards. One day, two. Two stretched into the beginning of three.

Had they abandoned their posts? Had they forgotten him? Or had the proctors just decided to just let him starve and save the expense of a bullet?

He gave up on banging on the walls to attract attention. He needed to save whatever strength he had. Hungry and thirsty, he rolled over and went to sleep.

———

The door bolt snicking back awakened him.

A pair of MPs grabbed him by each arm and hauled him out of the box.

No, not MPs. These weren't army—they were naval Shore Patrol.

Sampson blinked against the blinding light of a twenty-watt bulb dangling from the corridor ceiling above.

Standing before him were two men he certainly didn't expect to see. One was Brig, managing to look obscenely clean, well-fed, and smug. The other was Husband Kimmel, no longer wearing the stripes of a commander. His cuff held the broad band of a rear admiral again.

Kimmel looked him over. "So much for the military courtesy of a salute. For two cents, I'd throw you back to the proctors. Lucky for you, we're somewhat out of proctors." A grim smile crept over his face. "You were right. Short *did* chuck him in here and didn't tell anybody."

"C'mon, Rory," Brig said gruffly, taking his elbow. "How about we get you cleaned up?"

Sampson opened parched lips. "I'd settle for an explanation," he croaked.

———

An explanation he got, but not until after a shower, shave, and sandwich and about a gallon of water.

They sat in the Buffalo District Headquarters office of General Short himself, only Admiral Kimmel's nameplate was on Short's desk.

The room looked different from when it'd been Larry Bell's executive office. Faded wallpaper showed where Chamber of Commerce awards had hung. One of the window panes had been blown out by bomb concussion —a square of cardboard was taped in its place—but that wasn't the change that niggled him.

Then he realized there were no photos of Wallace on the wall or any sign of proctors.

Kimmel poured Sampson a generous splash of aged Kentucky bourbon

Kimmel must have been saving for a grand occasion. Considering Kimmel was pouring it out as new CINCBUFF, this must be that occasion.

"What happened to Short?" Sampson asked. Not the most pressing of Sampson's questions, but the first past his lips.

"Short got what he'd intended for you," Kimmel drawled, sipping his bourbon. "Proctors stood him up in front of a firing squad."

Sampson tossed off his drink and held out his empty glass. "He had me up for desertion."

"Would have stuck, too, you haring off to chase retreating bombers with Short radioing to go after the ones hitting Buffalo instead." Kimmel poured Sampson another shot. "If maintenance logs hadn't backed up Brig's story about your faulty radio, I'd have left you in that cooler. That whole Horatio Nelson ignoring orders bit is just the kind of stunt you'd pull."

"Wouldn't have made a lick of difference, one more plane," Brig said. Kind of feisty-like, Brig was, but he was wearing new squawking chickens on his collar. Colonel in charge of what was left of Buffalo District's air wing. Promotions all around, it seemed.

The new colonel frowned. "They really clobbered Buffalo hard. Wiped out the Curtiss plant completely."

"Which rather annoyed the Navy," Kimmel said, and so it would. The Navy's torpedo and dive bombers and half their fighters were all Curtiss jobs. "Which is why Navy's in charge here now."

"Not just here," Brig said, a touch of reproach in his voice.

Kimmel shot him a look. "Look, Nimitz is only running things temporarily. He's going down the Cabinet line of succession, trying to find a skunk that isn't too much of a skunk to risk swearing him in."

"Must be down to Postmaster General by now," Brig muttered.

"Something happened to Wallace?" Sampson asked.

"The US Navy happened to him, mister," Kimmel snapped. "'Least the part of the Navy that wasn't in his back pocket, and that means Nimitz."

Sampson eventually got the story out of them. The American populace didn't take the fall of Detroit well. Riots broke out, and when Wallace's proctors tried to clamp down, the American populous decided they'd had enough of proctors, as well. Started stringing them up from lampposts.

"If you want to know where our old friend Crane ended up, visit the corner of Clinton and Broadway," Brig said.

That must be how Sampson ended up abandoned in the cooler. The proctors were all dead and nobody else knew Sampson had been put there.

"Congress realized they were next in line for a necktie party," Kimmel continued. "They finally grew a pair and the Senate impeached Wallace. Only Wallce refused to budge, so Nimitz and the Navy gave him a 21-gun salute. Thus endeth the Sabbath lesson."

"So what now?"

"So now we win the war," Kimmel said. "Wallace was only play-acting at it. Too useful a cudgel against political opponents to let it end. But us, we've got no choice but to win."

Kimmel poured himself a healthy slug. "America, free American, has thrown off our shackles. The totalitarian powers of the world can't afford to let that stand. They can't afford let their captive populaces see it can be done. They'll eventually have to come at us hammer and tongs."

"And probably sickles," Brig added.

Sampson examined his empty glass. "You're saying we need to take on the entire world when we can't even handle Canada? How, with no army, navy or any airplanes worth mentioning? How?"

"By flipping the table over," Kimmel said. "We start building ourselves *real* airplanes. Non-treaty airplanes."

"That's crazy!" Sampson exploded. Sure, they could do it. They had the jigs and plans squirreled away of the planes the Danzig Treaty had axed. Every country had. But if you did that— "Every country in the world will follow suit."

"Exactly," Kimmel said, tossing back a shot. "The Great Powers of the world—Britain, Germany, France, Japan—are balanced on a knife edge. They hate each other. They'd be at each other's throats if they could project any military power beyond their borders. That's what the Washington and Danzig treaties were drawn up to prevent. We abrogate those treaties and the whole house of cards come crashing down. They'll be too busy fighting each other to come after us."

Sampson shook his head. Lovely theory, but theories have their own way of crashing down. Just ask Henry Wallace.

"So what now?" Sampson repeated. "I mean you, me. Us here. Buffalo."

"Now we hold on, same as we have been doing," Kimmel said. "Only not 'us.' You, Mister Sampson-with-a-P, are going to Marrietta to help Jendrassik and Kartveli and Kelly Johnson and Larry Bell build a whole new generation of planes. Not just the ones we mothballed, but the *next* generation of aviation. Turboprops and jets."

Brig nodded. "The slide rule boys *need* a combat pilot jogging their elbow so they don't build more planes that look great but can't fly."

"And you're going have to the rank to do just that," Kimmel said.

The admiral pulled a little felt box out from a drawer, the kind officer's insignia come in. Sampson snapped open the lid and snapped it back just as quickly. *You've got to be kidding.*

Brig touched two fingers to his brow in mock-salute.

"There's a medal coming with that," Kimmel added. "For both of you for your ace-in-a-day singlehanded daredevil stunt. Blue ribbon job. Dangly star. At least whenever we get a new president to sign it. Public could use something to cheer about right now."

The admiral handed Sampson typed orders. "You'll ship off in the morning. In the meantime, get some sack time. You'll be getting a lot of it in Georgia."

They saw him off at the railway station the next morning. The trains still ran to Buffalo, for now.

Sampson stood on the New York Central platform, the mighty *Empire State Express* chuffing waste steam as last-minute passengers boarded.

He'd gotten to see his third beautiful thing, after all. The "Commodore Vanderbilt" Hudson 4-6-4 locomotive still wore its Art Deco shroud, the metal cladding worn for function now rather than form. The railroad hoped the streamlined metal served might protect the engine against Canuck strafing.

Sampson wore his own concealing shroud of sorts. Civilian clothes. Army's orders: they didn't want it to appear an officer of Sampson's new rank was fleeing a sinking ship. Sampson felt just like a rat, slinking off instead flying combat with Brig.

Kimmel saw his frown and took it to mean something else. "You pilots. Never happy traveling unless you can fly and never happy flying unless you're piloting."

"Well, I *do* wish I could have flown a *'Cuda* down."

The Air Corps had already ferried the remaining *Airacudas* down to Marietta. They'd taken heavy losses defending the skies of Buffalo, and the Air Corps had withdrawn them from frontline service. They just weren't suitable for combat, Jendrassik's fixes notwithstanding.

Bell wanted to salvage the V-wing turboprop engines for something new he had in mind. They'd also sent the three surviving early model *YFMs* along, as well. For museums, if peace ever came again.

The admiral chuckled. "Funny thing about men and machines. You get attached to them, miss them when they're gone, and it's not their virtues that endear them in your memories but their flaws." A faraway look came over him. "The old *New York's* wardroom ceiling used to drip water, a plumbing leak we could never fix. Nuisance then—I look back on it rather fondly now." He wished Sampson luck, shook hands, and departed.

Sampson watched him go. "Sounded as if he was making final goodbyes. Think he can hold here?" Those ore barges and troops were still in Kingston harbor waiting to sail.

Brig chuckled. "That tough old bird? He'll hold. They can't surprise us with a sneak attack like they did Detroit. Given proper warning, Kimmel is the kind to come through with flags flying."

The locomotive's whistle shrilled.

Sampson shook Brig's hand. "Brig, you keep your head down, too, you hear?"

Brig smiled and shot him another mock-salute. "Go and build me some planes that actually fly."

"I will."

"No *Airacudas*?"

"No *Airacudas*."

He'd do his best, however, to see the new designs were as beautiful as the old girls. He owed them that, at least.

ABOUT LEE ALLRED

With nearly a hundred professional publication credits, Lee Allred's award-winning short fiction has appeared in *Asimov's Science Fiction Magazine*, anthologies, online magazines, and other venues. His debut novella "For the Strength of the Hills" was named a Sidewise Award for Alternate History finalist.

He's also scripted fan-favorite comic books for DC *(Batman '66, Batman Black and White, BUG! The Adventures of Forager*), Marvel (*Fantastic Four*), IDW (*Dick Tracy*), and Image Comics (*Madman Atomic Comics*).

Lee served three rotations in Iraq as part of Operation Iraqi Freedom for the United States Air Force and retired as a Master Sergeant. He now writes full time.

You can find out more information about Lee and his fiction by visiting his website at leeallred.com.

LONDONFALL

James Young

1

OF YANKS AND CIRCUSES

RAF Warmwell
1835 Local
18 August 1942

"Maybe next time we try to tell you about a new aircraft, you stupid bastards will listen to us. Curtiss *Hawks*, my ass."

Flight Lieutenant Adam Haynes briefly considered getting up to intervene at the ruckus he heard inside the small alert hut. It was clear that one of his countrymen was, as the British put it, "in a state of high dudgeon." Which was not surprising, given the day's events, stacked on top of many such days in the past two weeks. Still, in most situations, it would be considered improper to deliver a tongue-lashing to some poor bastard who clearly didn't deserve it.

No, I think I'll just let that continue to play out, Adam thought, keeping his eyes closed as he laid in the setting English sun. Odds were the angry speaker, intense Texas drawl and all, was probably going to stop just short of physical altercation.

Intelligence officers deserve a good flogging for thinking a bunch of men flying Spitfires *and* Hurricanes *would be flummoxed by a bunch of obsolescent, likely flown-out American birds*, Adam thought, reflecting on Fighter Command HQ's initial retort to pilots reporting a new *Luftwaffe* aircraft several months before.

"You seem far too pleased, sir," a heavily accented voice said from behind and above him. Indeed, so thick was the Polish tone to the words that Adam doubted most English speakers would have understood the sentence on the first try. On the other hand, spending a year with the bunch of displaced, near homicidal warriors without a country had adapted Adam's hearing.

"We're three months into a fight for England's life and the intelligence boffins are just now believing that the Focke-Wulf exists," Adam replied, sitting up as the American pilot continued to make disparaging remarks. He did not recognize the Polish officer standing before him as he kept speaking.

"Meanwhile, us pilots are busy dealing with at least *two* variants of that thing, the damn twin-engine fighters mauling us at random, and 109s with drop tanks," Adam snarled, standing up. "Which, I remind you, Intelligence swore was something that flat out could not happen."

He stopped and pointed upwards as a flight of *Hurricanes* flew at a couple thousand feet just over the grass runway.

"So we have to keep a flight of fighters above any active runway, lest eight or so of those twin-engine fighters show up to start shooting up the place with cannon and rockets," Adam finished, dropping his hand back to his side. "So, no, I don't really care if some other American has to sleep in the brig tonight before possibly going off to die tomorrow."

To Adam's surprise, the Polish officer looked nonplussed at his tirade.

"It is good that you remain so angry," the man replied with a smile, saluting now that Adam was standing. "Flight Officer Paley, 305 Squadron."

Adam returned the gesture, confusion on his face.

"The dispersal officer told me to report to the 'stout American dozing outside the alert hut,'" Paley said. "He said that you landed with five aircraft, and that I would make six."

Adam fought the urge to let out a primal scream at the absurdity of Fighter Command's current situation.

So many losses and mauled squadrons that we're reduced to pick up teams like we're playing playground baseball, Adam thought angrily as he looked Paley over. *Thanks to Leigh-Mallory and Douglas's idiocy, we can't even attempt to rotate pilots to the north anymore*.

"Where is the rest of your squadron?" Adam asked cautiously, looking around the airfield in the gathering dusk. He saw a lorry bouncing over the grass field towards the alert hut, a WAAF visible in the driver's seat.

At least we're going to get a last meal as the condemned, Adam thought wryly as Paley started to answer.

"At last report, three of us are at Debden," Paley said. "Two of us are making the way back by train from down at the coast. We took off today with ten."

"Well holy cow, look what the dog dropped off on the porch."

I guess the interview with the intelligence officer is over, Adam thought, turning to look at the irreverent speaker. Trevor Fesselier hailed from just outside Houston, Texas and was everything one would expect from his native state. Strikingly handsome with pale blue eyes and a full head of hair, Fesselier was a walking recruiting poster. Unfortunately, the striking good lucks were coupled with an outsized personality, something that made Adam glad the man was not in his squadron.

"Trevor," Adam said, nodding as he headed to walk into the hut. Fesselier moved to get in his way.

Now we may have a problem, Adam said, raising an eyebrow. Fesselier had always struck Adam as a hothead. A few weeks of watching his friends butchered by superior aircraft had apparently not helped his disposition.

"Come now, Adam, don't have a couple seconds to spare for one of your fellow Yanks?" Fesselier spat, fists clenching. Adam was about to speak when a stern voice cracked from behind the Texan in impeccable diction.

"Flight Officer Fesselier, it is common in our service to salute your superiors, not call them by their first name," a tall, thin older man in a RAF flight suit stated. Adam saw a red-faced, sweating NCO walking behind the superior officer.

"Group attention," Adam said, coming to the correct position. He saluted the unknown officer, the gesture returned as the individual continued to close.

"As for you, *Squadron Leader* Haynes, according to the orders telegraphed to this station about twenty minutes ago, you are out of uniform," the man stated, gesturing at Adam's rank.

"Wing Commander Holt, so good to see you, sir," a voice said from the hut's doorway. A slightly heavyset officer stood in the doorway, rubbing his glasses as he looked from the wing commander to Fesselier.

"Yes, well, I was informed my presence would be helpful," Holt said, staring intently at Fesselier. "There seemed to be some disagreement about intelligence operations in the Royal Air Force, *Leftenant* Duncan. I'm glad to see that discussion is complete."

Adam saw Fesselier's nostrils flare, but the Texan wisely decided to just give a nod.

"Then I am sure you can see your way to the officer's mess and then to our guest quarters, Flight Officer Fesselier," Holt continued. "I'm told we have a couple of other Eagle Squadron officers there already, a Blakeslee and a Fussner. They seem to have found another *Hurricane* pilot to form a flight with. Sergeant Blake will show you on your way."

Fesselier came to attention, recognizing when he'd been dismissed. With a salute that Holt returned, Fesselier followed the sergeant towards the flight mess. Wing Commander Holt watched the man go, his expression flat.

"Are you familiar with Bloody April, Squadron Leader Haynes?" Holt asked, turning towards Adam once he was certain Fesselier was out of earshot. The man began reaching in his pocket as Adam answered.

"Only from what I read in the books, sir," Adam replied sheepishly. "I was around for the First World War, but didn't talk really well and had a habit of crapping my pants."

Holt gave a thin smile at the slight joke.

"That makes two of us," Holt replied. "I think I had much different reasons, however, unless your upbringing was far more adventurous than most people's, involved machine guns, and seeing your playmates going down in flames."

The door slamming on the lorry caused Adam and Holt to both jump, interrupting the wing commander's recollection.

"Sorry, sir," the young woman who had been driving said. She wore overalls and riding boots, the mud spatters on her uniform providing some idea of why she'd chosen the clothing. "We had a slight problem getting back from the emergency dispersal field."

"I'd heard there was some German fighter bomber activity north of here," Holt replied grimly, returning the young lady's salute. "I trust that everyone was okay."

"They were after a train, sir," the woman replied, her voice sounding haunted for a moment. "In any case, we have sandwiches if anyone wants them."

That woman does not look like she's older than fifteen, Adam thought, his stomach dropping. *My God, this is really having "Rome as the Vandals are about to kick in the gates..." feelings to it.*

There were several other individuals hopping out of the back of the truck, a couple of them gingerly behind helped down by the handful of

WAAFs that had apparently gone on the sandwich run. Holt turned back to Adam, extending his closed fist in the universal gesture indicating he had something to give his subordinate. Adam cupped his hands underneath the fist, at which point Holt dropped insignia into his palm.

"You're the senior *Spitfire* present now," Holt said. "Once you're done talking to Duncan, I'm going to need you to meet me at the improvised command post."

Adam looked confused until Holt pointed towards a nearby copse of trees. Adam was startled to realize most of what he was looking at was camouflage netting and displaced tree limbs.

"Hopefully none of their folks get to comparing aerial photos with things a couple weeks ago," Holt muttered, glancing up at the sky. "Or else you might be talking to *my* replacement for the same reasons my predecessor is unavailable."

That's a very grim way of looking at things, Adam thought, glancing back towards where Warmwell's previous command post had been. It was not 303 Squadron's home airfield, but Adam had flown into the airbase while delivering a *Spitfire* shortly before the Second Battle of Britain had begun.

"The problem with forcing a bunch of chaps back to their home countries after you make peace with the Germans is they owe you no kindness if conflict resumes," Holt continued mournfully, realizing where Adam was gazing. "I do wonder just how many Dutch, French, and Norwegians have helped the *Luftwaffe* with targeting."

"Speaking for myself," Adam said, turning to his superior, "I'm pretty sure it wouldn't take much arm twisting, the way your government screwed them over."

Holt's expression darkened, and Adam wondered if he'd gone a little too far under the cover of "Yank bluntness."

"Yes, well, if bloody Churchill had just left well enough alone, it wouldn't matter," Holt replied angrily. "Funny how helping a bunch of Czechs kill a ranking Nazi caused the truce to fail."

Leftenant Duncan coughed from where he was standing behind Holt. The wing commander turned and gave the intelligence officer a polite smile.

Yes, while he's now the former *Prime Minister, it's still bad form to talk about him in front of us proles*, Adam thought, noticing that many of the other personnel in earshot were studiously looking elsewhere.

"Thank you, *Leftenant*," Holt said, gesturing for the two men to follow him away from where the others were eating. Adam glanced up as the first two *Hurricanes* that had been on air patrol came in for a landing. His stomach clenched as he glanced about nervously.

"Squadron Leader Haynes, are you all right?" Holt said, noting Adam's tenseness.

"My flight leader got killed when we were landing at Debden just like those guys are," Adam replied. "190 hit him and kept running out at low altitude."

"Yes, it's part of the reason you'll note the *Hurricanes* are landing in pairs rather than our standard line abreast," Holt replied, gesturing towards where the last two *Hurricanes* were lurking.

Hurricanes *have as much chance catching a Focke Wulf at low altitude as I do tackling Santa Claus on the roof of Buckingham Palace this Christmas*, Adam thought, still looking around as the section of fighters landed. *Not that I can do anything but point and yell if I do see something.*

"Parliament is meeting tonight for purposes of offering possible terms after what happened to Portsmouth this morning as well as Fighter Command casualties this past week," Holt stated grimly. His words drew a shocked gasp from Duncan. The wing commander ignored the man and looked at Adam.

"Let me guess: one of the possible terms involves foreign officers currently in the King's employ?" Adam asked, turning and looking towards the gathering of men and women eating sandwiches. Two of the former passengers wore Eagle Squadron unit flashes, while another had a Czech squadron's insignia.

"Yes," Holt replied simply. "I am told arrangements have been made to get as many of you out of the country as possible, should that come to pass."

I have no idea what arrangements those would be, Adam thought. *Unlike when France fell, there's nowhere close by for people to flee to. Which leaves going by ship and taking our chances with the U-boats.*

Holt looked over at Duncan.

"Good God, man, you look like you've seen Satan himself," Holt noted, shaking his head. "As Churchill said in his farewell speech two days ago, 'Even if fair Albion falls, my fervent hope is that the torch of freedom remains alight in the Commonwealth.'"

Duncan swallowed, then tried to return to a neutral expression. Adam could tell the young officer was still quite distraught.

First time being on the wrong side of a war? Adam thought, then felt guilty for his misplaced anger. The young man's service was getting manhandled and, if the German bombing raid on Portsmouth that morning was any indicator, its cities were soon to follow.

Just an inherent escalation of their fighter bombers roaming around and bombing things at will, Adam thought, his shoulders slumping. *Fucked up to just be strafing and rocketing anything on the rails or road, but it served its purpose.*

"In any case, you should probably finish your interview with intel, for what it's worth," Holt said. "I'll see all senior officers in thirty minutes."

You know, if anything, this is worse *than the end in Spain*, Adam thought a little over an hour later as he walked towards the revetment where his *Spitfire* was parked. The dense ground fog that had rolled over Warmwell shortly after sundown was a mixed blessing. On one hand, it all but guaranteed they wouldn't have to deal with German fighters flying intruder missions. Unfortunately, it also made walking around the airfield downright treacherous due to trigger-happy patrolling soldiers and the armament and fuel lorries that trundled from fighter to fighter.

Would be ironic to survive the madness upstairs only to be run down by a fuel truck, Adam thought, seeing the fighter's familiar shark-like form. *Guess the U-boats haven't quite gotten all the tankers.*

"Who goes there?" a voice called out from next to the *Spitfire*. Adam was glad that the person couldn't see him rolling his eyes.

"Not a Kraut," Adam replied wearily, moving cautiously closer.

"No, no, I guess not," the other voice replied, and then after a pause, "sir." A moment later, a short, stocky man wearing RAF coveralls materialized out of the thick haze. Between the haze and the darkness, Adam doubted he would've been able to pick the man out of a line-up the following morning.

If the Germans ever did try to infiltrate, coming in as ground crew would be the perfect cover for them, he thought.

"Wasn't expecting a Yank with this bird," the man continued, gesturing behind him. "You sure you have the right plane? *Hurricanes* are on the other side of the airfield."

"I'm not one of the Eagle Squadrons," Adam replied, waving away the directions. "I'm just your run-of-the-mill mercenary, nothing exemplary."

The man cocked his head at that statement, then shrugged.

"Right, then," he stated, turning back to the bird. "I'll cover the good news first: the engine's in tiptop shape for as many hours as it's got on it, we patched up the bullet holes in the tail, and it looks like the radio issue you reported was due to a nearly severed wire from where a 20mm shell went in and out."

Oh, boy, Adam thought, his stomach doing flip-flops. *I wasn't even aware of that hit*.

"Thankfully, we've got some great fitters here on the base, as the usual procedure manual says we should be taking the kite out of the line to make sure that dud shell didn't do any structural damage," the man continued.

"What's your name, if you don't mind me asking?" Adam asked, interrupting the stream of consciousness.

"If you don't mind, sir, I'd rather not," the other party replied. "Seems every time I've been introducing myself to one of you lot lately, you lads don't come back."

Adam was taken aback at that one.

"If you have to call me something, Sergeant Rook works," the man replied. "Not my actual name, but the mechanics will know who you're talking about."

Odd as hell, but he has a point about it not mattering now, Adam thought.

"In any case, the bad news," Rook continued without pausing. "We only had enough petrol on station to give you ninety percent of your capacity."

"Wait, what?" Adam said, looking at the *Spitfire*.

"Your choices were ninety percent of the 'fighter juice,' as the petrol boys call it, or full tanks of the bomber fuel," Rook replied. "I made a decision for you, but if you'd rather that extra ten percent, then we can pump it out before dawn."

That's the last time I'll assume enough tankers are making it through, Adam thought grimly. He suspected that "fighter juice" was the slang term the logistics folks were using for the 100-octane fuel that Shell Oil had been providing from the United States. Although the *Spitfire* would run just fine on the lower octane fuel, Adam was well aware of the numerous advantages that special aviation fuel was giving Fighter Command.

Hard enough dealing with the Focke Wulfs *with the better fuel*, he thought, wincing. *Not doing myself any favors worrying about a few dozen miles of range over friendly territory*.

"No, it's fine," Adam said. "I wasn't planning on going to Berlin tomorrow morning or anything."

"Probably a good thing," Rook replied. "Part of how we got in this mess, anyway, I hear."

"Yeah," Adam allowed. "Although I doubt I could get Himmler in my gunsights long enough to do any good."

"That brings me to my next bit of bad news," Rook continued. "You only have half your machine-gun ammunition."

"*What?*"

"If you had one of the *Spits* with .303, we have it in abundance," Rook replied. "Alas, you have a pair of .50-caliber machine guns, and we don't have nearly enough of that to go around."

Adam was about to say something, then resignedly closed his mouth. He had been so happy to get his new *Spitfire* with the enhanced armament of twin 20-mm cannons with a pair of .50-caliber machine guns just two weeks before. Now he was realizing the price of increased firepower and was not a fan.

Just another symptom of the U-boats, he thought. *I'm sure if the British weren't losing so many ships from each convoy, all those bullets would have arrived.* Rumor had it that the Germans' newest U-boats were just flat out faster than the escorts that guarded the convoys. Adam was no naval expert, but he could tell from the increased food rationing that things had taken another bad turn.

No wonder there was a no-confidence vote against Churchill...

"Sir?"

Adam jumped. "Sorry, I got distracted," he finally replied, shaking his head.

Before he could say anything else, there was the distant sound of massed propellers. Both men took a moment to listen to see if the sound grew closer, but it remained at a mid-level hum.

"Looks like night shift is early tonight," Rook noted grimly. "That can't bode well."

"No, it doesn't," Adam agreed. "Also means there's no fog across the Channel, whereas our night fighters can't get off the ground."

"In any case, sir, I need to get my lads together and plan out how we're going to keep fighters rotated tomorrow," Rook said. "It's been a horrible week."

Adam bit back the urge to snap at the other man. After a moment, he felt a bit of shame at nearly losing his temper.

It's gotta be even worse for them, he thought, gazing northward as anti-aircraft fire burst in the distant night sky. *They count us out, then have counted so many fewer of us in.*

"In any case, your normal crew chief has taken good care of your bird, sir," Rook noted. "We've had all sorts of birds come in here with obviously bad maintenance or faults that competent crew should be catching. Definitely buy that man a pint if you get an opportunity."

Adam nodded.

"Thank you, I am sure Sergeant Mickelson will appreciate the professional compliment," Adam replied. "I wasn't planning on ending up this far west today, but I appreciate you all taking good care of me."

"Sir, I do not pretend to have a better idea of how the war is going outside my little part of it," Rook said. "I just know I've had so many men that I respected and were good lads leave from this grass field never to be seen again in these last few months. I'm doing my best to make sure when I don't see *you* again, it's for good reasons."

Adam nodded at the crew chief's words.

"Let's hope so, Chief Rook," he said, thinking back to Holt's warning about peace terms. "For all our sakes, Fighter Command needs to stop the bleeding soon."

Caen, France
1935 Local
19 August 1942

Hauptmann Gregor Schwarz raised his arms and stretched, straining towards the ceiling in yet another vain attempt to pop his tightened back. The young officer had first noted the problem as the adrenaline was wearing off from his latest jaunt across southern England.

It's almost as if my body realizes I'm no longer over that godforsaken island, he thought, struggling to his feet against the dull throbbing along his spine.

"You really should go see a medic about that, Gregor," his companion, *Hauptmann* Silvan Schmitz, stated as he continued poring over the photographs in front of him. "It would not do for you to have it seize up tomorrow, of all days."

Gregor grunted at Silvan's comment, standing up and wincing at the pain.

"I wasn't aware that intelligence officers moonlighted as medical practitioners in their spare time," Gregor said, twisting side to side. The sharp pain that shot up his back nearly made him cry out.

Okay, this is...bad, he thought, gripping the table. *I didn't think I'd hurt myself, but apparently throwing a* Hornisse *around is a bit more strenuous than I realized.*

"So are you going to the flight surgeon or am I going to report you for hiding injuries...*again*?" Silvan asked, adjusting his glasses as he gave his companion a hard look. The intelligence officer looked like a stereotypical functionary of his profession, with his pale complexion, thinning hair, and round face. His allergies gave his eyes a perpetual wetness, while the handkerchiefs he was constantly going through testified to a constant struggle with mucus production.

"Shouldn't you be off writing reports and downgrading kills to probables?" Gregor snarled, dragging himself up to his full height and glowering at the smaller man.

"Yes," Silvan replied simply, looking utterly nonplussed at his friend's anger. "A task which can wait until tomorrow. That is, unless I'm helping box up your belongings to send to poor Maida."

Gregor gave Silvan hard look.

"Leave my sister out of this, you miscreant," he said, shaking his head. "You're just hoping that she would be vulnerable in her grief and finally acknowledge her love for you."

Silvan shrugged, coloring slightly.

"I am not above taking advantage of a fortuitous situation," he stated, his tone indicating an utter lack of future remorse if that happened. "Alas, let us not test her chastity nor my scruples: Go to the damn flight surgeon."

"After we go over this one more time," Gregor bit out. "We're the lead *Staffel* for the Circus tomorrow, and I'd hate to get us lost like last time."

Silvan smiled at Gregor's use of *Zerstörergeschwader* 22's unofficial nickname as he looked over the assembled photographs. They had been dubbed "Kesselring's Circus" due to the *Luftwaffe* High Command's propensity to shift them from airfield to airfield, depending on what missions they were supporting. Caen was their fifth home since the Second Battle of Britain.

"I am sure Major Heydrich learned a vital lesson about listening to his flight leaders that day," Silvan noted, his tone hushed as if he expected the senior official to just appear out of thin air behind him. "Now here you are, leading a *Staffel* of your own."

Yes, well, publicly disagreeing with Reinhard Heydrich was either the bravest or stupidest thing I've ever done, Gregor thought. *But I got us to Warmwell, and we caught the damn Tommies with their pants down.*

"Don't you gentlemen have something better you could be doing?" an unfamiliar voice called from the entryway. "Like perhaps taking advantage of the numerous young ladies hoping to bolster your morale from the surrounding countryside?"

"As I said to the last idiot who interrupted us, if I wanted to risk getting a case of the clap, I'm sure your sis..." Gregor started to say, grimacing as he turned to the door. Who he saw there killed the insult in his throat.

I may have truly just said the dumbest thing ever, he thought. He started to snap to attention, then gasped as his back simply denied the request.

"Mein Gott!" Silvan said, snapping to attention out of his chair as he, too, realized who was standing in the doorway. Gregor, annoyed at his body, gathered himself and also came to attention.

"Well, *Hauptmann*, if I had a sister, I might be deeply insulted," *Generalmajor* Adolf Galland replied easily, stepping forward as he glanced over at the second man who accompanied him into the room. "I'm certain *Generalmajor* Mölders will assume you weren't talking about the lovely Annemarie."

"No, sir," Gregor said. He could feel the sweat breaking out on his forehead as he fought against the agony of bracing his back.

Silvan is right, I should absolutely go see the flight surgeon.

"*Hauptmann*, are you well?" Mölders asked, stepping closer to look at Gregor. "At ease, at ease."

Gregor relaxed, still gripping the table.

What lie can I get away with? he wondered, shortly before he realized Silvan was having none of his deception.

"*Hauptmann* Schwarz injured his back this morning over the Channel, sir," Silvan replied. "He was talking about going to the flight surgeon after we finished looking over the aerial photos."

Mölders nodded at the report, then turned to Gregor.

"You're the one they call 'Mothkiller,' no?" Molder said, starting to grin.

Oh, God, Gregor thought, color rushing to his face.

"*Ja*, sir," Gregor said, his tone resigned. His peers had bestowed the name upon him after he'd shot down four *Tiger Moth* trainers during ZG 22's rampage across the Northlands.

I cannot believe that has been three months ago, Gregor thought, thinking back to when the Me-410s were first committed to operations during the Second Battle of Britain.

"It is always glad to meet a man who takes advantage of a good aircraft," Molder said with a smirk. "Even if it is a flying bus."

"A very deadly bus, sir," Gregor replied, recognizing Molder's teasing for what it was

I can't turn with your 109, Gregor thought, *but I can outrun you at sea level and don't have to spend the whole flight looking at my fuel gauge.*

A descendant of the Bf-110s that had come to grief during the First Battle of Britain, the *Hornisse* was emblematic of the radical production changes forced upon the Reich's defense industry by the Minister Albert Scheer. The original heavy fighter successor, the Me-210, had already been considered a failure when Fuhrer Himmler had ascended to his post. Allegedly, the head designer for that debacle and two of his engineers had been shot. The subsequent Me-310 had been a marginal improvement, for which the chief engineer had merely been sent to a penal colony somewhere in Norway. The *Hornisse*, unlike its predecessors, was faster, carried a heavier armament and, most importantly, could carry external drop tanks on the wings. Gaining almost two hundred miles in additional range from the already long-legged Bf-110 had greatly expanded the places where a *Schwarm* of *Hornisse* could just appear and shoot something.

"Well, I certainly hope so, given the plans for the next three days," Galland remarked, his face grim. "Unlike last time, *Luftwaffe* intelligence seems to have an accurate understanding of the losses we've inflicted."

Silvan stiffened at that remark, but wisely held his tongue. Like Gregor, the intelligence officer had just completed training at the tail end of the First Battle of Britain. Hermann Goering had heaped much of the responsibility for the defeat on the *Jagdflieger*, but the intelligence corps had come in for more than its fair share of abuse from the *Luftwaffe*'s late commander.

To hear some of the old hands talk, the best thing that man did was decide to kill himself in shame after what happened to the Führer, Gregor thought, glancing briefly at his friend. *Perhaps eventually they'll eventually let go of Goering's attitudes, as well.*

"Adolf, no need to be antagonistic," Mölders gently chided, drawing a hard look from his counterpart. "We'll know if the intelligence is right in three days or not."

"I think the gun cameras have gone a long way to confirming enemy losses, sir," Silvan said, his tone neutral. "Despite claims in some circles, we have only been disallowing kills if there is no clear evidence a *Spitfire* or *Hurricane* is damaged."

Mölders nodded, even as Galland made a scoffing noise.

"Ignore him, gentlemen," Mölders said, waving off Galland's disdain. "Someone is still upset he lost a coin toss this morning."

"It is not my fault that apparently God really does answer your prayers," Galland muttered.

Gregor looked at Silvan and saw that his friend was just as confused as he was. Galland sighed and began to explain.

"Field Marshal Kesselring is of the opinion that he does not want to risk both of us over England during what we hope is the final phase," Galland said. "Operation Londonfall is expected to take three days, so ol' Smiling Albert came up with a simple solution: we would flip to see who flew the first and third days, and the loser would get the second."

"You're only so smug about it because you won the toss, *Vati*," Galland replied. Gregor saw a brief flicker of anger across Molder's face before the other general responded.

"Almost certainly not," Mölders replied. "But alas, you'll have to hope this gentleman and his friends leave some *Spitfires* for you."

"I am sure that there will be enough Tommies to go around," Galland said grimly, then brightened his tone. "Besides, with your aim, I'm sure most of the ones you see will get away."

Mölders shook his head, smirking at Galland's jibing.

I wonder if the rumors are true that Kesselring only made Galland a general because Mölders would have kept flying combat every day just so Galland wouldn't catch him, Silvan thought, looking between the two men.

"Since you are burning the midnight oil, *Hauptmann* Schwarz," Mölders said, looking at the map. "Why don't you brief us on what your plan is?"

Well, that was unexpected, Gregor thought, looking briefly across at Silvan, then back to the map.

"Yes, sir, of course," he replied, starting to look around the table for his pointing stick. There were several seconds of awkward silence as he searched before Silvan gave an exclamation of surprise, bent over under the table, then arose with the stick. Gregor sheepishly took it from his friend.

"What you have before you is RAF Warmwell," Gregor began, then quickly did a rundown of the surrounding area and markers.

"Our task tomorrow is to interrupt refueling and rearming operations in support of the bombers' operations against targets in London," Gregor continued. "It is my intent to ingress at low altitude, making landfall towards the west of Warmwell."

"Why the west?" Galland asked. "That will add easily fifty miles to your trip."

"Because the photos indicate that the British have arranged their Bofors guns to the north and east facing in the Channel direction," Silvan answered, gesturing at two of the photos. "It would appear that they were rather annoyed about our last visit."

Galland nodded, gesturing for Gregor to continue.

"My second and third *Schwarm* will climb to 2500 meters as we are approaching so they can bounce any approaching fighters or the British standing patrol," Gregor resumed, drawing out the eight fighters' proposed paths. "Their orders will be to bounce anything once, then immediately flee southeast towards the sea."

Mölders chuckled.

"I am sure your men will be quite unhappy about that," Mölders noted.

"Our job is to disrupt their operations, not sit on top of them, sir," Gregor said. "One of the mistakes of the first Battle was Zerstörers thinking we are single-engine pilots."

Gregor colored slightly as he realized he might have spoken out of turn. To his great relief, Galland and Mölders nodded.

"It seems someone here has actually paid attention to the reports," Galland noted. "In any case, continue."

"My lead *Schwarm* will engage the anti-aircraft positions with rockets," Gregor stated.

"Which kind, out of curiosity?" Galland asked. "There has been a great deal of discussion about what weapons we need to prioritize for ground attack."

"White phosphorus and the new incendiary warhead," Gregor replied. "We have greatly appreciated the new, jettisonable rocket tubes."

Galland nodded at the last comment. The initial rocket mounts, being heavy and fixed at an upwards angle, had greatly slowed the *Hornisse* even after firing. Although the jettisonable tubes were in limited supply, they had more than proven their worth in the couple of operations ZG 22 had employed them.

One more month and we'd start running out of drop tanks and rockets, Gregor thought, recalling the *Gruppen* supply officer's briefing two days before. *However, if we're still fighting in a month, then we will have failed the Reich once more.*

"Why are you using the rockets on the anti-aircraft guns and not simply strafing them?" Mölders asked, then quickly held up his hand to stop Gregor's reply. "This is not saying you need to change your plans, just a question."

"We have found that strafing the guns doesn't ensure their suppression," Gregor replied. "I've lost two *Hornisse* crews from Bofors that we thought were strafed that either the crews recovered or we didn't hit them in the first place."

"So you're going to set them on fire," Galland said with a slight chuckle. "Effective, if you're accurate."

"I'd gas them if I could," Gregor replied simply.

Mölders and Galland shared a brief look, then turned back to Gregor.

I must have missed something, he thought, the butterflies that had been present the whole briefing supplanted with curiosity.

"Alas, the Reich has insufficient production capacity for gas at the *Staffel* level," Mölders muttered, then quickly gestured for Gregor to continue.

"My fourth flight will attack these revetments here," Gregor said, pointing, "with incendiary rockets from the first *Rotte*, then *Sprengbombe* from the second."

Hopefully the ***Sprengbombe*** *don't detonate early this time*, Gregor thought, recalling the last time the Circus had used the cluster munitions. Two *Hornisse*, officially deemed lost to anti-aircraft fire, had actually been destroyed by their weapons springing open shortly after release. *Luftwaffe* ordnance had assured ZG 22's commanding officer that this was most likely a production flaw, the lot had been inspected, and potentially dangerous weapons removed. Gregor had his doubts, but they were by far the most effective method for suppressing an enemy airfield.

"Are you going to engage any additional targets during your egress?" Galland asked, looking at some of the marks on the larger map.

"No, sir," Gregor said. "The longer we're in English airspace, the more likely we are to end up fighting *Hurricanes* or *Spitfires*. We can escape the latter, but only if we see them first. The latter can and will pursue us."

Galland pressed his lips into a thin line, even as Mölders nodded at the answer.

Herein we have the difference between wanton aggressiveness and judicious caution, Gregor thought, keeping his face expressionless. *Or more correctly, a man who has never been shot down and another who was a guest of the French for a few months*.

"I think you have prepared enough, *Hauptmann* Schwarz," Galland stated. "Come and spend some time with us and your comrades. I brought some surprise entertainment with us just for this occasion."

Ah yes, the singer you're rumored to be cavorting with, Gregor thought, nodding his understanding that Galland was giving a command, not an invitation.

"You can come along, as well, *Hauptmann*," Galland continued, gesturing at Silvan. "I'm sure there will be plenty of *fräulein* looking for a more...*intellectual* interaction tonight."

Gregor looked over at Silvas with a smile as the intelligence officer seemed slightly flustered.

"Of course, sir," his friend said aloud, taking his glasses off to clean them. "It has been a long time since I have seen a live performance."

You better not get anything my sister might catch later, Gregor thought, following the two senior officers out the door. *That is, once you two idiots finally acknowledge what's obvious to the rest of us*.

2

PASSES AND CHUTES

Kent, England
1035 Local
19 August

There was absolute chaos in the skies over Kent.

I don't mean to be uncharitable, Adam thought, wrenching his yoke into his abdomen, *but there really needs to be a course during training entitled, "Die Quieter, You're Clogging Up the Radio."*

The *Focke-Wulf 190* he was drawing a bead on apparently saw him at the last second, its port wing starting to snap up in the type's characteristic escape roll, even as the exhausts puffed additional smoke. Adam pressed the firing button, the *Spitfire*'s two 20mm cannon and matched pair of .50-caliber machine guns shaking the fighter's frame. The four streams of fire were harmonized to converge at two hundred yards, or twenty yards beyond where the 190 was. Rather than a fusillade that completely severed the fighter's wing, a half-dozen heavy-caliber bullets also smashed through the side of the fuselage and into the cockpit. Adam saw the glass shatter even as hurtled past, continuing his turn while frantically searching the skies around him.

The panorama he saw was a scene from Icarus's worst nightmares, with at least a couple dozen smoking and flaming comets falling towards the fields of Kent below. Unlike what the old hands had told him about the first battle, the *Luftwaffe* had not welded its fighters to the incoming bomber stream. This meant the massive train of twin-engine medium and heavy bombers pointing unerringly towards London served as an attractant for every British fighter for hundreds of miles.

Unfortunately, that particular honeypot was surrounded by literally hundreds of free-roaming Bf-109s and Fw-190s. If his particular piece of sky was any indication, the *Luftwaffe* was going all in while hoping that Fighter Command would do the same. It was a wager that was working so far.

Are those idiots actually still in Vics? Adam thought, seeing a squadron of *Hurricanes* hurtling south towards the oncoming German bombers. His headset was a cacophony of German marching music being jammed across Fighter Command's radio frequencies, controllers desperately trying to mass what fighters were available towards the German hammer blow, and the aforementioned young men dying noisily. Checking to make sure Paley was still with him, Adam began to climb as he briefly headed away from the mass of contrails heading southwest.

Smart to feint north then dogleg in towards the city, Adam thought, switching to the alternate Fighter Command frequency. *I'm betting half the controllers thought they were going for the Midlands aircraft factories again.*

"Dogbody Base to all available fighters! Dogbody Base to all available fighters!" a woman's voice carried over the radio. "Divert immediately to Point Truffles! Divert immediately..."

The woman's transmission was cut off by the sound of brief screams and an explosion. Adam swallowed as he heard several other controllers attempting to raise any available fighters to divert to other points. Looking at his map case, he felt a sense of dread wash over him.

Those bastards are targeting the sector stations, he thought. *Oh, fuck.*

"Bogeys, eight o'clock!" Pavey warned. Adam snapped his head to port just in time to see a gaggle of what appeared to be Bf-109s heading in the opposite direction, drop tanks falling off their airframes as they dived to attack another squadron of *Hurricanes* hurtling south.

"*Hurricanes* north of Point Onion, break left! Break left!" Adam shouted desperately, reefing his *Spitfire* around. A flight of 109s, seeing his motion, broke off as the lead two flights continued on their attack into the *Hurricanes*. Adam had brief moment to note an alternating red-yellow-red band pattern on the 109 leader before he was busy jinking to avoid enemy fire.

You bastards, we can dance with all day, Adam thought, reefing his *Spitfire* around as he and Pavey passed through the enemy flight. To his joy, he watched the lead 109 explode as two more flights of *Hurricanes* arrived from their port left. The second 109 in the *Schwarm* fell away into a spin, its tail shot off as the remainder of the *Hurricanes* followed their leader into the German flight. Adam continued his turn, putting the nose down to gain some more speed as he reversed back towards the initial 109s Pavey had sighted.

Oh shit, he thought, seeing a swarm of familiar, round black dots coming in from the east. *Looks like their cavalry has arrived.* Doing the geometry quickly and spotting the lead 109 as it dispatched a *Hurricane*, Adam realized he ***might*** be able to make one pass before it was time to run. Engine roaring, he focused on lining up on the 109 as it zoom-climbed upwards. The German fighter's nose puffed smoke as Adam watched its pilot turning to focus on finding another *Hurricane*.

"Tartan Leader, Tartan Leader, break!" Pavey called frantically.

Not yet, Adam thought. *Just a second more*.

The German pilot turned back towards Adam just in time to realize his danger, then the *Spitfire*'s guns were sending their greetings at point-blank range...and so was the 190 that Pavey had tried to warn him about. Adam felt his own fighter stagger from several hits, other tracers all around his cockpit as he snap-rolled inverted. His engine briefly cut out, the carburetor floating into negative-g as he brought the nose down. Just as it caught, there was the sound of hail hitting a tin roof, several more cannon impacts, then the sickening sound of tearing metal as the *Spitfire*'s tail ripped off.

Time to leave, Adam thought, his hands working like lightning to slam the canopy back. The *Spitfire* was starting to tumble as he released his straps, the force first pushing him into his chair, then flinging him out into the slipstream. The fighter's rear fuselage just missed hitting him, and then he was hurtling just over a passing *Fw-190*.

One thousand...two thousand...three thousand, Adam began counting. There had been numerous reports of Germans shooting RAF pilots in their parachutes, and Adam had no desire to find out their veracity. At twelve thousand, he pulled his ripcord...and had white-hot pain shoot through his body as the straps crushed into his groin.

Fuck me, he thought, groaning in agony from the impact. Fighting back the urge to vomit, he gingerly checked to make sure no lasting damage had occurred. Satisfied on that front, he glanced up at his chute to make sure it had fully opened, then down towards the green farms below.

About three thousand feet, he thought, glancing around the sky in front of him. In the distance, he could see a pair of twin-engined aircraft, likely German bombers, heading east as fast as they could. Desultory bursts of anti-aircraft fire appeared in the sky behind them, successive groups of anti-aircraft gunners misjudging their speed. Adam's eyes narrowed as he also saw the glint of sunlight off clouds of drifting metal strips below him.

What in the hell is that? he wondered. Looking down below him, he saw that the wind was carrying him towards a cluster of houses located near a crossroads. A lorry was tearing down the north south road towards him, men in back pointing excitedly towards his chute.

I'm gonna hope the Hatfields or McCoys down there aren't too trigger-happy, Adam thought as he tried to gauge whether he was going to end up in someone's living room. To his earnest relief, he just managed to clear the last of the houses before hitting like a sack of potatoes in meadow. Taking a moment to gather himself, Adam realized there was a slight stinging sensation at the back of his right arm. Feeling towards the source, his fingers came away with blood.

Wonderful, he thought. *Looks like I've gone and gotten myself winged again.* He had just enough time to make sure the limb functioned before there was the sound of running feet.

"Don't move or we'll shoot!" someone shouted.

"I imagine the King will be quite upset if you do!" Adam retorted, standing stock-still.

"Bloody Hell, it's a Yank!" someone shouted.

"At least you didn't call me a Colonial," Adam said. "Can I turn around now?"

"Certainly!"

There was a long pause.

"Do you realize you're bleeding?"

Thirty minutes and a drive later, Adam stood outside a cattle barn along with six other RAF pilots...and twelve *Luftwaffe* aircrew. The latter had already been removed of all their flight gear, standing sullenly looking at the RAF men enjoying some sandwiches and cigarettes. The half-dozen Home Guard that had directed them from the lorry to the barn had been replaced by a company of British regulars. The sound of distant engines and anti-aircraft fire had finally faded, with several aircraft having passed within view heading in various directions.

"All right, you lot, who is the senior man here?" a British Army captain asked as he came around the side of the barn. The gathered RAF pilots looked around at one another, and Adam realized they hadn't really figured that out yet.

"Squadron Leader Haynes," Adam stated. "303 Squadron."

"I think that trumps all of us, mate," one of the other men stated after a long silence.

"Right, then," the British captain continued, taking a deep breath. "I'm to take you lot immediately to Debden. Someone will collect you from th..."

The man was cut off by the approaching roar of several aircraft engines. Adam was the first to see the approaching aircraft, at least a dozen of them, low to the ground as they came in. Even as several of the British infantrymen started shouting for machine gunners, the group roared overhead, climbing as they went.

"Looks like eight *Ju-88s* and four of those twin-engine fighters," one of the RAF pilots muttered, watching the aircraft push off towards the south. Adam looked at his watch, then back at the aircraft.

They're going to catch some folks flat-footed as hell, he thought, looking around for someone in authority.

"If you know someone at Debden, best ring them and tell them trouble is coming," Adam barked at the British captain. The man looked at him as if he'd grown a third eye.

"Now, damn you!" Adam shouted. The British officer ran off towards the farmhouse as fast as his legs would carry him. Adam turned around to see one of the *Luftwaffe* men smiling as he watched the departing aircraft.

I ought to wipe that smile off your face, fucker, Adam thought, his hand moving towards his sidearm before he caught himself. Taking a deep breath, he, too, looked after the departing aircraft.

Don't think I'll be going to Debden today.

English Channel
1135 Local

We're late, we're late, Gregor thought angrily. He fought the urge to shove his throttle forward to war emergency power, knowing that it would only result in leaving his heavily laden fourth flight behind.

Goddamn bomber pilots! he fumed for at least the fourth time. His *Staffel* had been taxiing for takeoff when a damaged He-177 had come in, engine ablaze and the pilot ignoring the tower's orders to find another airfield.

I can't even have the satisfaction of the man being shot for insubordination, Gregor thought, glancing at his watch, then putting the *Hornisse* into a gentle starboard turn. *Although I'm sure burning to death after flipping his damn aircraft in a ground loop was sufficient punishment enough*.

"Aircraft to starboard!" his gunner, Obergefreiter Schafer, called out on the intercom. Gregor whipped his head around to look, then relaxed as he saw the twin engine aircraft moving at a high speed back out to sea.

"Don't know what they are, but they're heading away from us," Gregor noted, taking the opportunity to look over the other twelve aircraft. It was a minor miracle that all twelve of the original aircraft slotted to perform the mission had been able to take off, and for a brief moment, Gregor had considered taking the *Staffel*'s two spares. Being already twenty-five minutes behind schedule, Gregor had opted against it.

There's the final turn point, Gregor thought, sighting the railway bridge that served as the signal for the high cover to separate and begin climbing. His own wingmen extended their line abreast formation, the English countryside hurtling by beneath them.

"Anti-aircraft fire, ten o'clock!"

Guess they've sighted us, no point in maintaining radio silence, Gregor thought. His hands were sweaty within the flying gloves, the clear August sun turning his cockpit into a greenhouse. The uncharacteristically clear skies were a mixed blessing, making the advancing *Hornisse* easy to spot but also making it highly unlikely any RAF fighters would catch them unawares.

"*Achtung Spitfire!*"

The radio call caused Gregor's stomach to drop even further.

"Which way, you idiot?" someone called in return. Gregor didn't need the clarifying report, sighting the trio of British fighters crossing from ahead right to left. To his pleasant shock, he realized the British fighters either did not see his *Staffel* or, almost as likely, were too short on fuel and ammunition to tangle with them.

Two minutes...

"We are engaging enemy fighters!"

Hammel is a good flight leader, he will keep the patrol off us, Gregor thought as his fighter reached three hundred meters. There was a flash of orange above and to his front.

"*Horrido! Horrido!*"

That's at least one...no, two *Britishers down*, Gregor thought, seeing a single-engine aircraft cartwheeling down to smash into the ground about three miles off his port side. Turning back, he was startled to see RAF Warmwell before him, two aircraft heading down the runway as his *schwarm* went for their targets.

"Engaging enemy fighter!" Schafer called, followed immediately by the Me-410's machine guns firing from their barbettes aft of the cockpit. Gregor glanced in his rearview mirror before he realized Schafer meant the two fighters they'd just passed over. Then he swung his vision forward just in time to see the northernmost Bofors rotating around before him.

Oh no, you don't, he thought, kicking rudder to bring his nose in line with the gun. Squeezing the trigger on his yoke, he felt the *Hornisse* lurch and slow as all four rockets left their tube in a bright, smoky launch. The four 208mm rockets made a corkscrewing path in front of his fighter as Gregor put the large *Hornisse* into a sharp turn. The maneuver saved his and Schafer's life as a string of white puffs appeared where they would have been, had he continued on straight.

"Got them, sir!" Schafer cried in exultation. "Direct hit, look at the bastards burn!"

"Keep your eyes up!" Gregor responded, following his own advice in time to see three unfamiliar but clearly single-engine shapes curving in towards his fighter. He immediately jettisoned the rocket tubes, feeling the *Hornisse* lift without the extra drag.

Those aren't Spitfires...

Then the trio of fighters were in front of him, closing head-on with large air scoops visible under the nose and cannons sparkling in their wings. Their leader missed with his first burst, the tracers going just over the *Hornisse*. Gregor mashed his own trigger, the four 20mm cannons and pair of machine guns sending a concentrated cone of fire right into the rapidly swelling enemy aircraft. The British machine came apart, its wreckage hurtling towards Gregor. He ducked involuntarily as what appeared to be the engine hurtled just over his wing, other parts of the nose and prop slamming into the fuselage.

"Two is hit!" Schafer shouted, the report causing Gregor to turn around just in time to see his brand-new wingman's *Hornisse* smash into the English countryside below.

Goddammit, not another letter, he thought, nausea roiling his stomach. The young *Leutnant* whose name escaped Gregor in the moment had mentioned a new daughter. Now that child would never know her father, as Gregor had seen no chutes.

"What the...one of the Britishers is turning around!" Schafer shouted. The *Hornisse*'s engines thundering, Gregor was certain that they had enough of a lead that the...*whatever* that was would not catch them. The Daimler Benzs in each wing were the newest model, meaning that the *Hornisse* was well capable of over three hundred miles per hour on the deck. Yet, to his abject horror, the pursuing pair of fighters appeared to be growing larger.

"Bogeys, two o'clock high!"

We may have bit off more than we can chew, Gregor thought, his heart rising in his throat. The fear turned to exultation a moment later as the pair of Bf-109s, one sporting an alternating band of yellow-red-yellow on its spottled gray fuselage, executed a high-frontal pass on the pursuing pair of enemy fighters. Both hostile aircraft turned into the threat, breaking off their pursuit of Gregor's reduced *schwarm*.

Thank you, Herr Galland, Gregor thought, his hand shaking as he reduced the throttle and set course for the rendezvous point south of the Isle of Wight. Glancing in the rearview once more, he saw a distant pall of smoke rising from the direction of Warmwell.

Maybe we hit something important, he thought, taking a deep, shuddering breath as he started to count the circling Me-410s. It appeared that the *staffel* had lost two aircraft, with another one streaming smoke from its feathered engine. The pair of Bf-109s soon returned, waggling their wings in recognition as they took up cover above the group of *Zerstörer*s.

"Start a timer, Schafer," Gregor said. "Three minutes, we go home."

It was only as he taxied the *Hornisse* back towards its revetment that Gregor's back began to bother him once again. In the time it took to pull the fighter into its spot between the sandbags, the slight tingle that foretold of an expiring pain injection began to transition to full-scale fire. As the pair of engines shut down, the fire became a roaring inferno of spasms, nerves firing, and uncontrollable agony.

"Medic!" he dimly heard Schafer yell, clenching his mouth shut to avoid screaming uncontrollably. "Get the flight surgeon!"

It figures, Gregor thought, pounding the side of the cockpit in frustration. *At the moment we come back relatively unscathed, I end up almost certainly grounded.*

"Easy, *Hauptmann*," a familiar voice said from besides his cockpit. Gregor's embarrassment compounded further as he looked up to see General Galland looking in the *Hornisse*'s cockpit.

"Sorry if I don't stand up, sir," Gregor hissed, the pain so great he almost wanted to vomit. "But it appears my back has betrayed me."

"They have a way of doing that, yes," Galland said gently, then stepped aside as ZG 22's flight surgeon quickly leaned in.

"Help me get his uniform off," the surgeon barked, gesturing at Schafer and Galland. Gregor tried to help as much as he could as the three men stripped him down to his undershirt.

"You're going to feel a sting, then a burn," the surgeon said. "You're probably going to lose consciousness, but we need to get you immobilized as soon as possible."

"I thought you said it was just muscle damage yesterday," Schafer snapped, then realized the gathering group of *staffel* crew could hear. "Sir."

"It is muscle damage now," the surgeon replied evenly, completing the injection. "But if he keeps spasming like this, there is a chance..."

Gregor did not hear the man finish the sentence, as unconsciousness bounced him faster than the swiftest *Spitfire*.

3

BODY BLOWS

RAF Warmwell
1900 Local
20 August 1942

This can't go on, Adam thought, barely able to keep his eyes open as he once again waited his turn to talk with the intelligence officer. He was just getting ready to finally just let the exhaustion win when his left hamstring cramped terribly.

God fucking dammit, he thought, grunting at the pain. Fighting through the stiffening limb, he managed to stretch the offending muscle without letting out the scream the pain warranted.

"Sir, do you need water?" a female voice asked from behind him. Adam turned to see a blonde WAAF heading towards him, a large canteen in her hand. Adam nodded, not trusting himself to speak as he took the container from the medical corporal. Looking at him worriedly, the woman reached into a pouch at her waist. As he took a long pull of water, Adam glanced once more back at the Warmwell's battered flight line, then looked over towards the burnt-out grove of trees where the station's second command post had been.

"It was our command post," the woman said mournfully as she handed him two salt tablets. "The Germans bombed it yesterday."

Adam nodded, forcing the pills down with another swig of water.

"I flew out of here yesterday morning," Adam replied, drawing a look of recognition from his companion.

"Oh, wait, you're one of the Yanks," she replied, smiling. "One of those Eagle blokes!"

Adam shook his head mournfully.

"Afraid I'm not, actually," he replied, pointing towards the squadron flash on his uniform. "I'm with the Poles."

"Oh," the woman said, then blushed as she realized how disappointed she sounded. "Then I suppose you didn't know the Texan, um...Trevor, I think he said his name was?"

If he hadn't been so tired, Adam would have tried to keep a better poker face.

Yes, I know Trevor, he thought, thinking back to how his day had started over RAF Eastchurch. Quickly swigging his canteen in hopes that the woman had not seen his face, Adam realized the futility of his actions when she raised her hand to cover her mouth.

Goddammit.

"Oh," she said. "He had such a lovely singing voice."

"I'm sorry if you knew him well, Corporal..."

"Dunham, sir," the woman said, her face looking absolutely stricken. "Sorry to have bothered you about him."

I can't even lie and say it was quick, Adam thought, recalling the sight the flaming *Hurricane* had made as it was arcing out of the dogfight.

"If you'll excuse me," Dunham said quickly. "I...I have to go."

The corporal quickly turned as to leave.

"Don't forget the canteen," Adam said, extending the container. The young woman took it, her grasp almost violent, then turned to walk away. Adam could see Dunham's shoulders trembling as she went.

"I do hope you don't have a habit of making all women cry, Squadron Leader," Wing Commander Holt said from behind Adam. Feeling every bit of the three sorties he'd flown as he turned around, Adam was surprised to see Holt was also in flight garb. Like Adam's, his indicated a "rough day in the office."

"Sir, did you...?" Adam started to ask, then stopped before completing the obvious question.

"Kites are a bit faster than they were in 1917, but the general principles seem to hold," the man replied. "Not that I think I did any good, and my kite's a write-off."

Adam looked back towards where his damaged *Spitfire* sat in an improvised revetment.

"That seems to be going around," he said grimly, panning to look at the burned-out anti-aircraft gun position north of the runway.

"Bloody bastards came over with a bunch of those 410s," Holt explained. "Buggers are getting particularly adept at catching us in between operations if we're not careful."

"I was at Eastchurch this morning," Adam replied, pulling out a handkerchief to wipe his face. "For once, we caught them, but it was still bad." He continued on to explain what had upset Corporal Dunham, drawing a somber nod from Holt.

"I won't bore you with the details," Holt said, wringing his hands. "But it's starting to get grim. Are you familiar with boxing, Squadron Leader Haynes?"

"Yes, actually," Adam replied. "My father made sure I knew how to take care of myself in a fistfight."

Holt nodded at that as he continued.

"The damn Jerries and we are like a pair of boxers slugging it out in the middle of the ring. Problem is, we're just rearranging his face while he's pounding our ribs into kindling."

"Body blows, sir," Adam said, shaking his head. "Going for the head looks flashier, but it's the body blows that do you in."

"Precisely," Holt replied. "We can't get him in the body, damn Bomber Command got slaughtered the few times they tried, and now there's not enough petrol to go around."

Adam jerked his head up at that.

"That doesn't go any further," Holt said, looking slightly annoyed at himself. "But you're a Squadron Leader now; you're probably figuring out how bad it is."

"Yes, sir, I am," Adam replied.

"But I have some good news for you that you may *not* know," Holt said. "They're putting you in for a gong."

"What?" Adam asked, shaking his head.

"You shot down a very important man yesterday, at least according to your wingman's report," Holt replied. "Werner Mölders, one of their two Generals of Fighters."

"Wait, *what?*" Adam asked. Then he remembered the strangely colored Bf-109.

Guess that was worth hanging in there and nearly dying, after all, he thought, smiling.

"I see your memory is obviously catching up with you," Holt stated. "He's currently cooling his heels in the Tower of London between interrogations."

"I'm guessing that we're just politely asking him questions, alas," Adam replied, his grin growing broader.

"The King is a good sport and frowns upon him getting a true Tower of London experience."

Adam fought the urge to laugh.

"Yes, I suppose that would be bad form, especially if this continues to progress as it has been over the last 48 hours," Adam stated. "I heard they managed to knock out the sorting room at Fighter Command during that big raid on London, then nailed a couple of the sector control stations."

"Yes," Holt replied. "It's why we had to go to standing patrols over the airfields, at least."

That's also not good, given a shortage of gasoline, Adam thought. *Good as shooting down a couple dozen fighters if squadrons are stuck just making sure people can land and refuel.*

"There's rumors the Germans used gas bombs on some airfields today," Holt said. "We're still getting that confirmed, but wanted you to be aware so you can make sure your pilots keep their gas masks with them."

So the bastards have taken the gloves completely off, Adam seethed. *Maybe I should have let that soldier shoot that Kraut, after all.*

"In any case, try and get some sleep," Holt said, looking at his watch. "I am told you managed to bring part of your squadron with you this time, at least."

"Yes, sir," Adam said. "I have four of my own pilots."

"Very good," Holt stated. "We'll brief at predawn, but I think we're going to try something different to deal with these raiders."

Caen
2000 Local

Gregor startled awake, trying to sit up and finding himself restrained.

"It's about time you woke up," Silvan said, closing the book he'd had in his hands. Gregor looked down to see that he wasn't fully restrained, just with a belt across his chest. Looking around, he realized that he was in a solitary room, not the common hospital near the airfield.

I must have been truly out of it.

"Doctors immobilized your torso," Silvan continued. "You've been asleep for a little over twenty-four hours, and they brought you into the main hospital rather than the clinic out by our field."

"What?" Gregor croaked. "Why did they have me asleep for so long?"

"Turns out you might have cracked a vertebrae last week when you had that crash landing," Silvan said. "Something you'll note that I told you might need to be looked at."

Gregor rolled his eyes.

"It didn't hurt much at the time," Gregor replied. "Besides, in case you noticed, there's been a war on."

"A war, you'll note, that has gone on without you," Silvan replied, shrugging. "Quite well, in fact."

"I need some water if you're going to keep being your usual self," Gregor said, laying his head back onto the pillow. "Did they take X-rays while I was out?"

"No, they did not," Silvan replied, holding a glass over to Gregor, then waiting until his friend started to drink. "General Galland persuaded the surgeon that perhaps the first thing you needed was actual rest."

"Yes, well, so does everyone else," Gregor snapped, starting to reach for the restraining order.

"I would not do that," Silvan said simply, leaning back in the chair. "General Galland directed that if you got yourself out of that bed, you were to be transferred to an Army liaison unit within the week."

"What?" Gregor asked, nearly spilling his water.

"Yes, something about you'd probably find a *Storch* a bit hard to handle after throwing a *Hornisse* all over the sky," Silvan said, smirking. "I pointed out that clearly you weren't all that good at flying a *Hornisse*, so maybe the change would do you good."

You're lucky I'm restrained in this bed, Gregor thought, fixing his friend with a glare. Before he could respond to the intelligence officer, the door opened.

"Ahhh, *Frau* Steinhoff," Silvan said, nodding to the slim, raven-haired woman who walked into the room.

"*Hauptmann*," the woman replied coolly. "I see our patient is awake."

"Yes, and able to move around somewhat," Silvan said. "Looks like you'll get to take that catheter out today, after all."

Gregor winced at Silvan's comment, glancing down the bed at his gown.

"Just what drugs do you have me on?" Gregor asked, concerned. "Shouldn't I feel that?"

Steinhoff favored Silvan with a glare.

"We have you sedated with some nerve blockers so you didn't injure yourself worse in your sleep," Steinhoff said. "The doctors considered evacuating you to Berlin, but decided against it. If you pass some tests, they will return you to flight status in a couple of weeks."

"*A couple of weeks?*" Gregor asked, his tone causing Steinhoff to recoil in shock. Color rushed to his face.

"I am sorry, *Frau* Steinhoff," Gregor said sheepishly. "I didn't mean to yell at you."

"It is fine, *Hauptmann*," she replied, moving to the basin to wash her hands. "My husband is...*was* a fighter pilot."

"I am sorry," Gregor said, thinking of his wingman.

I wonder if they've notified his wife yet, he thought. *Wait, it's only been a day. Of course not.*

"You didn't shoot him down," Steinhoff replied airily, waving away the condolences. "In any case, are you feeling any pain?"

Gregor concentrated, realizing the narcotics he was on must be far stronger than he realized.

"No, no I am not," he replied.

"The doctor's orders were to remove your restraints, then have you walk to the latrine," Steinhoff said, then turned to Silvan. "I assume you can help him, *Hauptmann?*"

"I suppose I can for the Reich," Silvan joked, drawing a slight smile from the nurse. "Would not be the first time I've helped him stumble to a latrine."

"Well, first we have to remove some things," Steinhoff continued. "I apologize in advance for the pain."

Wait, wait, what are you...oh, no. The catheter.

"Would it help if I distract him, *Frau* Steinhoff?" Silvan asked, causing Gregor to turn to look at him.

"Distract me *how*?" he asked, concerned.

"Just look at me, Gregor," Silvan said. "We can talk about how Operation Londonfall is going."

Gregor raised an eyebrow, then turned to look as Steinhoff rolled back his hospital gown.

"I strongly doubt *Frau* Steinhoff is an English spy," Silvan said easily. "Allegedly, the Gestapo has caught a few of those as of late. Dour, humorless ladies, every one, not like the good nurse here."

Steinhoff outright giggled at that, a sound that caused Gregor a small amount of distress, given her current task.

"Sorry!" she stated, starting to blush.

"In any case, we have reportedly shot down two hundred British fighters over the last 48 hours," Silvan said, causing Gregor to whip his head back around. He was about to open his mouth when Steinhoff completed the painful portion of her task, eliciting a hissed curse from him.

"Sorry again," she said, this time somber as she began removing his restraints.

"Oddly enough, with the gun camera films that you pilots hate so much, it seems as if that claim is not far off," Silvan continued. "Of course, we won't talk about how many aircraft our side lost to pull that off."

Gregor noticed *Frau* Steinhoff paused briefly in her task, her shoulders stiffening before she continued.

"In any case, the next two days will be the hammer that we hope breaks the English psyche," Silvan said. "There are certain weather conditions that headquarters hopes to take advantage of over London."

Gas, Gregor thought, feeling slightly nauseous. *We're going to use gas on civilians. Maybe it's a good thing that I am unable to fly.* Using the horrible weapon on fighting men was one thing in his mind. Becoming a "*Terror Flieger*" was another.

"It would appear that the British are about to regret breaking the truce," *Frau* Steinhoff said. If a tone could be described as vengeful, hers was certainly that as she removed the last straps.

"There you go, free to walk down the hall," she said, then turned to Silvan. "I'll go fetch an orderly to make sure he doesn't fall."

"I am certain I would hear no end of it from his sister," Silvan noted, favoring Steinhoff with a smile. "Not to mention his mother would probably beat me."

"My mother has never raised a hand to you in over twenty years," Gregor said, smiling. "Even when you deserved it."

"I note that you did not say anything about your sister," Steinhoff responded, smiling herself.

She has a pretty smile, Gregor thought, meeting her eyes. The expression faded as she glanced downwards and away from his gaze.

"I'll go get Fritz," she said, turning quickly to walk out the door. Gregor watched her go, feeling somehow wrong.

"You know, you should definitely court her if she's interested," Silvan said, his tone conversational. "The fact she didn't laugh at the family jewels like all the others is a good sign."

Gregor whipped his head around to see his friend's conspiratorial expression briefly before Silvan resumed his poker face.

"I see you would take advantage of a wounded man," Gregor said, starting to lever himself out of the bed.

"This is probably the first time in all our days that I'd be able to beat you," Silvan replied. "Why would I not take advantage of it?"

"Because it would be to the detriment of the Reich to lose a fighter pilot right now?" Gregor retorted, incredulous.

"I honestly do not believe that you'll be anywhere close to flying before this is all over with, anyway, my friend," Silvan said. "Even if you account for General Mölders missing, it has been a great two days for you pilots."

"Wait, what happened to General Mölders?" Gregor asked.

Silvan was about to answer when a man Gregor assumed was "Fritz" appeared in the doorway.

Dr. Frankenstein is getting much better at making monsters, apparently, Gregor thought, looking at the massive orderly. *I will have to ask the hospital for help the next time I need to take off. Surely this man could throw a* Hornisse *if he had to.*

"In any case, Operation Londonfall is going apace," Silvan said, helping Gregor shuffle towards the door. "I believe the British will be suing for peace within a week."

I hope so, Gregor thought as he shuffled towards the latrine. *Then we can turn to the Reich's true enemy in the east.*

Author's Note: If you want to find out what happens next, check out the excerpt for Acts of War at the back of the anthology!

ABOUT JAMES YOUNG

James Young is an American author of science fiction, alternative history, and post-apocalyptic fiction. His primary series is the *Usurper's War*, which is set in an alternate history where Adolf Hitler is killed by an RAF bomb in November 1940. He is also the author of *The Vergassy Chronicles*, a military sci-fi universe set in the 3050s.

In addition to his own work, James has edited anthologies including bestselling authors Sarah Hoyt, S.M. Stirling, and David Weber. His non-fiction writing credits include *Eagles, Ravens, and Other Birds of Prey*, winning the United States Naval Institute's (USNI's) 2016 Cyberwarfare Essay Contest, and various articles in *Armor*, *The Journal of Military History*, and *Proceedings*.

LinkTree (i.e., one stop for everything - scan or click):
https://linktr.ee/jamesyoungauthor

Blog (i.e., the thing I wish I updated more often - scan or click the link):
Jamesyoungauthor.com

There's more on the next page...

SWORD OF THE SUN

A World Afire Story

William Alan Webb

1

0543 HOURS, 15 APRIL, 1943
VUNAKANAU AIRFIELD, 10 MILES WEST OF RABAUL, NEW BRITAIN

Crisp and white, the immaculate uniform of Admiral Yamamoto Isoroku appeared as a wraith in the predawn darkness of the repair shops along Rapopo Airfield. Accompanied by several staff officers, including Vice Admiral Kusaka Jinichi, his co-commander in the recent I-Go offensive, Yamamoto walked from revetment to revetment to thank the ground crews for their hard work and attention to detail in maintaining their aircraft. At least, that was his stated intention.

In fact, the Commander-in-Chief of the Combined Fleet wanted to determine for himself whether Operation I-Go had, in fact, been the major victory claimed by the air crews. Losses had been heavy, and if not catastrophic, it still cost Yamamoto some of his best remaining men. Such high cost could be justified if the Japanese had dealt the Americans a blow as severe as claimed, with the important word being *if*.

Sandbags stacked to a height beyond six feet outlined the next revetment in the line, with a large canvas canopy keeping the light of work lanterns and flashlights from acting like a beacon for night-prowling Allied raiders. Darkness lingered under the dense forest of palm trees on either side of the airfield, and inside the revetment, as well, as Yamamoto and his entourage paused to inspect the Mitsubishi G4M1 bomber inside.

Fuselage markings labeled it from the 705th Kōkūtai; the tail number read "323."

The uneven light made it difficult to pick out many details, but even in such conditions, Yamamoto saw the numerous bullet holes in the airplane's nose. Mechanics hovered over the starboard engine, and when the Admiral moved around to one side, he spotted the black streaks of oil smoke that stained the wing. G4Ms were notorious for catching fire, which usually proved fatal. That the pilots brought this one home at all indicated the high level of their skills.

Yamamoto half-turned to Vice Admiral Kusaka. "If it is operational, I would like this aircraft and crew to transport me to Ballale. That they could bring such a damaged aircraft home over such a distance testifies to their courage. I wish to express my admiration for their diligence and commitment to the Emperor."

Kusaka, the Commander of the Eleventh Air Fleet, leaned close to the shorter Yamamoto and dropped his voice. "Forgive me, but there are other aircraft available that have not been damaged and repaired, Admiral."

"That is good to know," Yamamoto said. He half-turned again, he smiled before continuing. "This tour is about instilling confidence, Admiral Kusaka. To do so, I must *be* confident. If this aircraft is not ready, then I shall require another. But if it is operational, then I wish to be transported by this particular aircraft. If it is safe enough for its crew, it is safe enough for me."

"Again, forgive me, sir, but you are more valuable to Japan than a mere bomber crew, or even one hundred bomber crews."

"We are all servants of the Emperor, are we not? A commander who does not share the risks of his men cannot gain their loyalty. I will share their risks."

Kusaka grunted. "As you wish, Admiral."

Kneeling on the wing with his attention fixed on the damaged engine, the crew chief looked up at the voices. Startled, he jumped to his feet and nearly fell off, snapping a salute to his brow.

"Chūi!"

Startled by the sudden command to "attention," men all around the revetment turned, spotted the group of officers, and came rigid with salutes. Gravely, Yamamoto raised his own return salute and held it, walking at a measured pace throughout the entire revetment to face each man individually. Once finished, he returned to his colleagues and dropped his hand.

"Please return to doing your excellent work," he said. "I merely watch in admiration of your skills."

Scuffing shoes signaled a figure rounding the aircraft's tail, wearing the insignia of a Flight Warrant Officer. Black smudges covered his uniform, face and hands. Trotting to the group of officers, he saluted.

"My crew and I are honored by your visit, Admiral."

"What is your name, Flight Warrant Officer?"

"Kotani Takeo."

"Where and when did your aircraft sustain so much damage, Flight Warrant Officer Kotani?"

"Three days ago over Port Moresby, Admiral. We bombed one of the airfields there with great effect and flew back almost to the northern shore near Lae before American fighters found us. They were P-40s. My top gunner shot down two, but they managed to strike the starboard engine multiple times. It caught fire, although the wind soon extinguished the flames."

"You brought such a crippled aircraft all the way home to Rabaul?"

"*Hai!*"

In a blatant breach of Japanese naval protocol, Yamamoto looked the man directly in the eyes, smiled, and placed his right hand on the flier's left shoulder.

"The Emperor is very proud of you, Flight Warrant Officer Kotani, and so am I. Only with men like you can we win this war."

1045 hours, 15 April 1945
Admiral Kusaka's underground Naval Headquarters, Rabaul, New Britain

Fresh flowers filled a vase on the far side of a rectangular room. Yamamoto's excellent sense of smell appreciated Admiral Kusaka's efforts to make his stay more pleasant, but doubted it would dampen tempers in the contentious meeting ahead. The subject he planned to broach was not one any Japanese officer would easily agree with—at least, not in public.

Approximately thirty feet long and ten wide, the walls slanted inward from waist height into an arched roof. Steel beams reinforced the shelter. If the Americans possessed a bomb or naval shell capable of penetrating deep enough to destroy Kusaka's headquarters, then they did so without the Japanese knowing.

The four men who comprised the Japanese brain trust in the southwest Pacific sat at a plain table, two on each side, with Yamamoto and his Chief of Staff, Rear Admiral Matome Ugaki, on one side, while Kusaka and Lieutenant General Imamura Hitoshi, Commander of the Eighth Army, faced them. Various aides and staff members stood nearby on all sides.

Yamamoto stood to open the conference, which for all its air of comradeship and friendliness, he still expected to be contentious. Eyeing his fellow commanders, as he so often did when opening a meeting, the Commander-in-Chief knew the conviviality would not last long once they understood his point of view.

Yamamoto adjusted his uniform, his expression calm but the set of his jaw betraying the gravity of what was to come. He glanced briefly at the notes on the table, then straightened, shoulders squared, every movement purposeful and composed, projecting an air of unshakeable confidence before addressing his officers.

"Today will be an open discussion of where I perceive our military situation in the Southeast Pacific to be at this point in time. What is said here today is to remain known only to those in this room. Is this understood?"

Glances among the participants matched nods all around.

"First, allow me to congratulate everyone involved in Operation I-Go for their hard work and diligence in the face of a determined enemy," he said. "I am satisfied with the results achieved. We have dealt the enemy a heavy blow." According to pilot reports and intelligence analysis, it was not a lie. Yamamoto felt no inclination to divulge that he strongly doubted the accuracy of such reports. "I have therefore concluded there is no reason to keep the carrier air groups at Rabaul any longer, and am ordering them to return to their carriers."

Pausing, he saw the twitch of relief on Ugaki's face. The Chief of Staff had opposed their commitment from the start, seeing no reason to risk such highly trained and carrier-landing qualified air crews in such an attack as I-Go. Kusaka and Imamura, however, reddened. The loss of the carrier aircraft effectively ended the operation. Without giving time for anyone to speak, Yamamoto nodded at one of his aides, a sub-Lieutenant who appeared barely out of his teens.

"The official results for Operation I-Go are as follows," the nervous young officer said in a voice slightly too loud for the small room. "The enemy lost one heavy cruiser of the *Northampton*-class, one *St. Louis*-class light cruiser, three destroyers, and 25 transports and other vessels sunk, with a further three cruisers, three destroyers and 18 smaller ships damaged. Our forces shot down 175 enemy aircraft. Our own losses were 39 aircraft lost without returning, and eight more aircraft declared unrepairable after returning to their bases."

"Thank you," Yamamoto said. "I find these results quite satisfactory...if they are accurate."

"Forgive me, sir, but do you question the truthfulness of my fliers?" Kusaka said.

"No, Admiral, your men are honest, brave and loyal warriors for the Emperor. I believe they are being completely truthful about what the results they observed. Yet we both know that claims are often inflated because of things such as double observations, obscured vision, and the general excitement of battle. Yet!" Yamamoto held up a finger to emphasize his next words. "Even if we discount the results by half, a great victory was still the result."

Given the chance to interject with their opinions, none of the others spoke right away. Only after a long ten seconds did Imamura clear his throat.

"In your estimation, Admiral, does this now mean that my troops at Lae can be regularly supplied by sea?"

Yamamoto turned to Kusaka, an indication for him to answer the question.

"The...*conditions*...that led to last month's unfortunate operation have not been fully rectified. Results from I-Go are promising, but must be studied."

"Is *now* not the perfect time to organize another convoy? If the American aircraft have been temporarily neutralized, does this not give us a temporary period of respite?"

When Kusake didn't answer, Imamura first turned to Ugaki, then to Yamamoto.

"Unfortunately, Admiral Kusaka is correct. Without definite knowledge of the enemies' strength, we cannot risk another disaster such as happened last month."

"Then what was the purpose of Operation I-Go?"

The directness of Imamura's question added to the implied insult. Yamamoto's left eye twitched as he bit back a sharp response. No Navy officer would have dared speak to him in such a manner, but relations with the Army were difficult in the best of times. Imamura's relationship with Admiral Kusaka had so far been cordial and cooperative, and Yamamoto had no desire to sever that tie.

"Perhaps there was a misunderstanding about the objectives of the operation, General Imamura? Allow me to once again explain my rationale. I desired to slow down the American advance, both in the Solomons and on New Guinea. As we know all too well, control of the air is critical for both sides. By destroying so many of their aircraft and sinking so many ships, we set back their timetable of attack for months."

Imamura nodded, as if to accept Yamamoto's explanation. His expression, however, betrayed skepticism.

"The time so dearly bought will bring great benefit to the convoy survivors at Lae," Imamura said, not bothering to hide his true feelings.

Once again, the room fell silent. As Yamamoto's nostrils flared, the surrounding junior officers cut their eyes to each other. The insult had cut deep, both because it had been unexpected and because it had been true. Before the Admiral could respond, however, Ugaki spoke first. Never known to be diplomatic, the fiery Ugaki did not temper his tone.

"No one has dealt the enemy crueler blows than the Commander-in-Chief!"

Imamura nodded. "I meant no disrespect, Admiral Ugaki. The Navy also suffered heavily in the Bismarck Sea action."

Once again, the General's words filled the room with tension, reminding everyone of yet another disaster that had befallen the Navy under Yamamoto's command. Wanting to rebuke Imamura personally, Yamamoto instead drew a deep breath. Despite his desire to refute the general's sarcastic implications, he couldn't. In truth, he believed I-Go to have failed. There would be no such admission, though, since morale would suffer. Yet, it was as good a time as any to broach his main topic.

"Yes, General, your words are true. Our losses in this war have been heavy and will continue to be so. One must recognize when a strategy no longer serves its purpose and have the courage to abandon it, no matter how hard-fought the effort. Acknowledging that you have not fully achieved your goals is bitter, but true growth comes from understanding and accepting such moments."

That brought around a round of knotted eyebrows and scowls, as Yamamoto had known it would. What he had in mind was nothing less than the complete dissolution of Japan's agreed-upon naval strategy for the future conduct of the war. It would generate strong resistance, and possibly even threats to his person, but he believed this change was Japan's only hope to avoid total defeat. Introducing his idea would have to be done in stages.

"What exactly do you mean, if I may ask?" Imamura said.

Taking a deep breath, Yamamoto straightened before sitting with hands placed palm down on the table. Realization came that the timing had not yet come for proposing radical changes in how the war was prosecuted.

"Only that a wise man considers all options. Now, let's us concern ourselves with how best to coordinate our efforts at defeating the enemy in the middle Solomons and eastern New Guinea."

2

1713 hours, 16 April 1943
Three miles west of Rabaul, New Britian

So far, his stay on New Britian left Yamamoto tired and depressed. The war against America was developing exactly as he'd feared it would, yet he remained vigilant not to show a public face of more than quiet confidence. Well aware of the esteem which the younger officers and men felt toward him, the Commander-in-Chief could only act as though everything was going according to plan when the truth was the opposite. If he allowed himself to dwell on the war situation, then deep within his soul, Yamamoto felt it as a betrayal of trust toward his men; no matter what they did, no matter how many of them sacrificed their lives for the Emperor, Japan could not win the war that he, Yamamoto, had been ordered to prosecute.

Now, after he'd finished addressing pilots from the porch of their command post, rousing them to greater efforts against the hated Yankees, Yamamoto and his entourage climbed back into the cars provided by General Imumura for the short ride back into Rabaul proper. Wearing the green Naval uniform instead of his white one, Yamamoto felt more at home among his men, more like a part of their everyday lives. Most of the time, he reveled in being the top officer in the Imperial Japanese Navy, and very much enjoyed wearing his famous snowy uniform, but lately, it had brought him less and less joy.

At his superior's request, Yamamoto's Aide-de-Camp, Commander Noboru Takata, drove the staff car instead of the Army Sergeant assigned the duty by Lt. General Imamura. Even in only for a few brief moments, Yamamoto wanted relief from the relentless necessity to guard his words. He trusted Noboru implicitly, and Vice Admiral Ugaki Matome in most matters.

"We have now finished our inspection tour, Admiral Ugaki," Yamamoto said. "What are your impressions?"

"My *honest* impressions?"

"You know that I would not have it otherwise."

"The men give their best—they do not slack from their work. The aircraft are all surprisingly well-maintained given the supply situation. Every man understands his place in the war effort, and is prepared to do his duty unto death. Overall, I was quite pleased with what I saw."

"But I do not believe that is the sum total of your impressions, is it?"

Ugaki shook his head. "No, sir. I wish that was. The men are not lacking in Samurai spirit, but some of them *are lacking* in—"

Yamamoto finished the sentence for him. "Training."

"Yes. The pilots are as brave as we could ask, but they do not have the skills of 1941. Too many of those men are gone now. It is not only pilots, though. The radioman who broadcast your travel itinerary should have known better. Now, it is far too dangerous to adhere to that schedule without change."

Ugaki was nothing if not aggressive, sometimes to the point of recklessness, so when he proposed that Yamamoto change his itinerary, the Commander-in-Chief considered the idea. He was not the sort to overly worry about enemy interference.

"I trust the men, Admiral. Leave things as they are."

But Ugaki was not finished. "Please allow me to openly disagree. *You* are the only officer capable of representing naval interests in a government dominated by the Army, sir. You, and only you. Perhaps you do not realize that you are a national hero?"

Yamamoto waved his hand, although he did, in fact, know that Ugaki spoke the truth.

"I am not going to survive this war."

"Perhaps you speak the truth, Admiral. Yet...may I speak plainly, sir?"

From the driver's seat, Yamamoto saw Noboru glance into the rearview mirror.

"Please do."

"Sir, the Americans certainly intercepted that radio signal. It was encoded, yes, that is true, but they would only need to break a few words of the code to discern your objective."

"The flight will have adequate fighter escort."

"Again, sir, forgive me, but six *Rei Shiki Sento Ki* seems quite a minimal escort for the Commander-in-Chief of the Combined Fleet. The Emperor is the Son of Heaven, but you are his sword. You are *our* sword, too—all the children of the Rising Sun."

"Perhaps so, but that is the very reason *not* to have more fighter escorts. Do you not see? By entrusting my life to so few, I show utmost confidence in their ability to protect me. And they are all veteran pilots, the best we have."

"And if the Americans do intercept your flight with overwhelming force?"

Yamamoto smiled and shrugged. "Then my prophecy of not surviving the war will be proven true." When his glib answer only deepened Ugaki's scowl, Yamamoto continued. "All will be well, Matome, you will see. And if it makes you more comfortable, you may tell the pilot not to risk flying if the damaged engine does not seem fully repaired."

Known as an inveterate gambler who often used hidden meanings in his words, Yamamoto's last sentence made Ugaki stop for a moment.

"And if it causes a slight delay that impedes your timetable?" the Vice Admiral finally said.

"Such things cannot be helped."

2133 hours, 16 April 1943
Flight officer barracks near Vunakanau Airfield

The room Flight Warrant Officer Kotani Takeo shared with his fellow pilot, Flight Petty Officer 2nd Class Hayashi Hiroshi, barely held their two simple cots. Yet, compared to the accommodations of their co-pilots, Chief Flight Seaman Ozaki Akiharu and Chief Flight Seaman Fujimoto Fumikatsu, the quarters were the equivalent of a posh hotel. Each man had enough room to angle his head to stare out the window into the night sky beyond. Tree limbs partially obscured the view, but that didn't matter, while breezes off nearby Keravia Bay made the sultry nights more tolerable. The briny odor carried on those light winds soon faded away from the men's sense of smell so they no longer noticed it.

Hands behind his head, Kotani laid still and stared at the bamboo beams across the low ceiling. A full stomach made him sleepy, while the flavor of the fresh-caught grouper remained a pleasant taste in his mouth. With Admirals Kusaka, Ugaki and Yamamoto joining the flight crews during their evening meal, the cooks had prepared the best food on hand, including a variety of fresh seafoods. Rice, kelp, pickled vegetables and other staples complemented what amounted to a feast.

"Did that feel like a final meal to you?" Hiroshi said.

"If it was, then I will die happy."

"Please don't misunderstand, Takeo. If they wish to feed us that way every night, I will be very happy. But I still cannot shake the feeling that we are not expected to come back from this mission."

Kotani leaned on one elbow to see his fellow pilot lying on his own bunk across a three-foot-wide space. Moonlight under a clear sky lit Hiroshi's legs, while his upper torso stayed hidden in shadow.

"If we return from *any* mission, Hayashi, it is only by the grace and protection of the Emperor's invention with the *kami*. Our lives became forfeit the day we joined the Navy."

"That does not mean that I cannot enjoy living!"

"No...that is true."

"And you should, too. I do not fear death, Takeo...I look forward to joining my brothers at Yasukuni Shrine. There is no higher honor than giving my life for the Emperor. What I fear is failure. You are flying the Commander-in-Chief of the Combined Fleet, a man who stood beside Admiral Togo when Japan defeated the Russians in 1905—"

"And lost two fingers."

"Yes! There is no one else in the Navy like Yamamoto. The Emperor will have his eyes on you, as will the entire nation."

"Thank you for making me even more nervous than I already was."

Both men laughed. Hiroshi lowered his voice and leaned toward Kotani.

"The Admiral's itinerary was broadcast over by radio to Ballale and Buin."

That penetrated Kotani's good humor. "Who told you that?"

"Fujimoto heard it from a friend at the radio center. Do you know what that means? If the Americans intercepted it, they may know the very minute we will appear over Bougainville."

"Was it not encrypted?"

"Well...yes, it was. But they might have broken our code."

Relief flooded Kotani in a rush of warmth. He exhaled a deep breath.

"And more likely they have not."

"No, but...I still think we should do something. Sergeant Asaki knows an armorer in the *204th Kōkūtai* who claims that we will have only six *Rei Shiki Sento Ki*. Six, Takeo. There should be at least a *Sentai*."

There could be no denying the alarming nature of Hiroshi's news, *if* it was true. Escorting such an important man as Yamamoto with only six fighters was nothing less than madness. Especially if Hiroshi's information about the itinerary turned out to be true.

Six.

Madness.

"Does the Commander-in-Chief know?"

"It is said that he trusts us to transport him safely regardless of what happens."

"But..."

Hiroshi held up a finger. "Let me take the lead, Takeo. Let me fly first. That is the spot usually reserved for the highest-ranking officer. If we are attacked by the Americans, they will think that my *Hamaki* is more important and shoot at me first."

Kotani found it hard to refute his friend's logic. If the Americans did ambush them, there might only be seconds to decide on maneuvers that would determine Admiral Yamamoto's fate, and there could be no question that the lead aircraft would be their first target. Yet, while the arrangement made perfect sense, it filled Kotani with a sense of shame, a sense of cowardice. Would the Admiral approve of staying alive at the cost of sacrificing someone else? Ambient moonlight lent Hiroshi's face a ghostly pallor as he awaited Kotani's reply.

"No," the senior pilot finally said. "I cannot do it, Hayashi. I will not do it. No self-respecting Japanese officer would. I appreciate your offer of self-sacrifice, but it would be dishonorable."

"You cannot think of yourself in this matter."

"Enough. I will fly in the lead aircraft. If we are attacked, I will dive to starboard while you dive to port."

"I beg you to reconsider, Takeo."

"No. The matter is settled."

Kotina's expression softened, then; he and Hiroshi had only known each other a few months, but in combat, that was a lifetime. As others in the *705th Kōkūtai* died and were replaced, Kotina and Hiroshi quickly rose to be the top veterans in the air group. A close friendship flourished, as both men realized it would probably be the last one they formed before they, too, fell under the guns of the Americans.

"Go to sleep, my friend," Kotina said. "Dream dreams of the feast that awaits when we return from Ballale."

"A feast, perhaps, but for who? Us, or the sharks?"

———

0102 hours, 17 April 1943
Rabaul, New Britain

Never one to outwardly betray doubt or disappointment, Admiral Yamamoto found himself glossing over more and more concerns about the future of the Japanese Empire. The nation that had once adhered strictly to the Meiji Constitution, with the Navy he'd joined and was prepared to give his life for, no longer existed. The formation of the February 26, 1936, cabinet had changed all that. It granted to the armed services an irrevocable veto power over the government's actions.

In return for the military's support, every prime minister agreed in advance either to serve as war minister and navy minister or to choose these two officials from within their respective organizations. This applied even when a general officer was serving as both prime minister and army minister; he could not also serve as navy minister unless he held a commission in the Navy General Staff. If either service chose to abstain from forming a cabinet or withdrew from one once formed, the ministry fell.

The Navy did not exploit this veto power. Since 1868, it had observed Emperor Meiji's rescript enjoining loyalty to the civil power. When necessary, naval ministers resigned rather than provoke a crisis by withdrawing support from the cabinet.

The Army showed no such self-restraint. By 1941, after five years of escalating political crises, only the generals were left standing. They manipulated the system so adroitly that they managed to seize complete control of the country without ever officially declaring martial law.

And by 1941, whether willing accomplices or unwilling dupes, the admirals had been maneuvered into a corner where they could do nothing but go along with the generals' decisions. Feeble gestures of resistance notwithstanding, the Imperial Japanese Navy understood there was no other choice but to lock arms with the Army and march ahead together.

Yamamoto had seen it all firsthand. He had fought and objected against what he knew to be a disastrous policy of making war against an unbeatable foe, but in the end he went along. The Emperor had acquiesced, which was the final word on the subject.

Now disaster loomed, and Yamamoto knew it. However long and hard they fought, however brave they might be or how many sacrifices might be made, defeat was now inevitable. Unless...

Unless Japan's shrinking offensive might could be hoarded to gain a naval force large enough to beat the Americans in a decisive battle. Instead of being frittered away trying to protect the outer defense perimeter in places like Lae, the Solomons, the Gilberts and the Marianas, the Navy would have to safeguard its capital ships and rebuild its carrier force until a crippling blow could be delivered. Only if that happened *might* the Americans negotiate a peace treaty that allowed Japan to keep some of her territorial gains. The chances were small, Yamamoto knew the American psyche too well to hold out much hope for such an outcome, but the only alternative was smashing defeat. *Bushido* did not make a man impervious to bullets.

Unable to sleep, he took up a stylus and wrote a poem to his mistress, Chiyoko Kawai. After changing several words, he sat back and reread the final draft out loud.

"The body is frail, yet with a mind firm with unshakable resolve. I will drive deep into the enemy's positions and let him see the blood of a Japanese man. Wait but a while, young men! One last battle, fought gallantly to the death, and I will be joining you!"

With a grunt of satisfaction, he locked it away in his personal safe and laid down to sleep. Fiery dreams brought no rest.

3

1452 HOURS, 17 APRIL 1943
RABAUL, NEW BRITAIN

A magnifying glass helped Admiral Yamamoto pick out details from aerial reconnaissance photos taken after the Port Moresby attack earlier in the month. Admiral Kusaka's intelligence analysts circled areas of supposed damage in numerous places, and Yamamoto did not question them, but he'd studied enough such photographs to know the level of exaggeration behind the damage claims. By any measure, Operation I-Go had fallen short of expectations.

Seated nearby while reading the latest reports, Commander Noboru glanced up when the office door opened. Senior Petty Officer Sato, the sort of leather-faced veteran who had run command headquarters in every army since the dawn of organized combat, stepped inside.

"An aircraft carrying Rear Admiral Joshima just touched down at Vunakanau. The Admiral has requested a private audience with you, Admiral Yamamoto."

Yamamoto grunted and turned to meet the eyes of his aide; clear understanding passed between them about the nature of Joshima's sudden visit. Once Sato left, Commander Noboru said, "He wants to prevent your flight tomorrow."

Again, Yamamoto grunted, which was his usual noncommittal answer.

Moments later, a sweating Joshima entered the room. Barely bothering with the customary bow, he only paused to remove a handkerchief and wipe his brow.

"Would you like some water, Admiral Joshima?" Yamamoto said. A broad smile reflected his genuine affection for the man.

"Thank you, Admiral Yamamoto. Perhaps in a moment."

Joshima then met Noboru's eyes in an unspoken request to leave the two senior officers alone. Catching it, Yamamoto prevented the move.

"I would like the commander to stay, Admiral Joshima. Please, sit down and tell me the purpose of your unexpected but wholly welcome visit. Did you come from Truk?"

"Yes, I did, sir."

"All is well there?"

"As well as anywhere. May I freely express my thoughts, Admiral Yamamoto?"

"Of course. I would have it no other way."

"I, Rear Admiral Joshima Takoji Joshima, am a very worried man. Sir, the news of your upcoming visit to Bougainville has driven me to the desperate action of flying here today. When I learned that your schedule was broadcast by radio, in code, from Rabaul to the various units you would be visiting, I could not believe my ears. It filled my heart with terror. This seems like an open invitation to the Americans."

He went on to say that while Rabaul was far from Truk, Joshima felt it was a journey he had to make. He made the arduous trip with a heavy heart but a determined purpose. Once at Rabaul, he'd lost no time in seeking an audience with Yamamoto.

"Sir," Joshima said earnestly, "you must understand that your proposed itinerary is not merely risky, but suicidal. I am here to plead with you to cancel your planned visits to the units at Ballale, Buin, and the Shortland Islands. You are practically assuring that the enemy will intercept you. They are too close, too numerous, and too dangerous. If you do this thing, you will die."

Yamamoto heard the words and nodded. Folding hands on the table, he leaned forward on his forearms and made certain that his face remained confident.

"Your concern for my well-being is touching, Admiral Joshima. I treasure your loyalty, and your friendship. But I have faith that my men will keep me safe.

"Please hear me, sir, I—"

"I *do* hear you," Yamamoto said, this time with an edge to his voice. He'd done little else except dwell on the upcoming tour for nearly three days, and rapidly grew tired of debating the matter. Did his subordinates think him oblivious to the danger? Inhaling deeply to calm himself, he continued. "If I cancelled this trip, Takoji, it would be an admission that I believe the Americans too strong to venture near, and how would morale suffer because of such a thing? That the Commander-in-Chief send the men forth to face the enemy, but dares not do so himself. Would that not harm their fighting spirit? Their faith in me?"

"I...but sir..."

"Yes?"

Joshima stammered, and grew quiet. "Could you not at least change your timetable?"

"No, I will *not* do such a thing, and for the same reasons." Then, seemingly without meaning to, Yamamoto let slip the notion that played with his dreams. "Only the pilot can change the timing now, based on the performance of his aircraft."

In his peripheral vision, Yamamoto saw Noboru cock his head, and then look away.

0457 HOURS, 18 APRIL, 1943
VUNAKANAU AIRFIELD, RABAUL, NEW BRITAIN

Flight Warrant Officer Kotani used a flashlight to finish his pre-flight inspection of G4M Number 323, the *hamaki* assigned to him as pilot. Hulking silent on the concrete runway, the cigar shape that spawned the bomber's *hamaki* nickname stood silhouetted by the pink eastern horizon. No clouds marred the sky, promising a fine day for flying in the New Britain area, although closer to Bougainville the forecast called for scattered rain squalls. The weather wasn't Kotani's chief concern, though —the Americans were.

Are we flying into a trap as Hiroshi and the other pilots claim? he thought. *If so, have I done everything possible to protect the Commander-in-Chief?*

Kotani had spent every daylight hour helping repair his aircraft, along with the rest of the flight crew. The ground mechanics had done an excellent job of patching and repainting the bullet holes from the previous week's near-fatal encounter over Port Moresby. No trace remained of the black smoke stains on both the upper and lower wing surfaces left by the flaming Mitsubishi Kasei 21 engine. Largest of Mitsubishi's 14-cylinder radials, it was geared, supercharged, and had optional water methanol injection, a true marvel of Japanese engineering. But without self-sealing fuel tanks, once set on fire, few bombers had survived the ensuing conflagration.

Night shadows had begun to vanish by the time Kotani finished his visual inspection. Inside the *hamaki*, co-pilot Chief Flight Seaman Ozaki had the task of testing the control and electrical systems. Satisfied with the plane's condition, Kotani once again thanked the ground crew for their hard work and climbed aboard. Before joining Ozaki and the navigator forward in the cockpit, he checked first on the rear gunner. Manning a 20mm cannon, the man in that position could mean the difference between survival and death, as the other defensive machine guns only fired 7.7mm rounds. All stations reported ready for the mission, as did the radioman and navigator. Since they carried no bombs, the bombardier stood by to help where needed.

"Everything is in order," Ozaki said. "Fuel, oil and hydraulic levels all register as full. Electrical systems test as working."

"What about that tightness in the rudder control?"

"I'm afraid that is still there. The mechanics thought they had found the problem, but it appears they did not."

Kotani settled into the pilot's seat and pulled on his flight cap. Goggles came next, pushed high on his forehead. Chief Radioman Ito Hiroshi leaned in and handed Kotani a steaming cup of tea made from roots and leaves, according to a native recipe. Most of the Japanese found it tolerable when compared to the common green tea known as *Sencha*, but Kotani actually preferred the local brew. He nodded once in thanks, sipped from a chipped ceramic mug that still bore the emblem of Rabaul's previous owners, the Royal Australian Navy, and set the mug on a small shelf to his left.

"Prime the engine."

"Primed," Ozaki said. "Fuel flow looks good."

"Ignition on."

"On. Magnetos engaged."

Kotani inhaled a deep, noisy breath. "Start port engine."

Like most radial engines, the Kasei 21 took several revolutions before catching. When it did, gouts of black smoke spiraled backward as the propeller created a wind tunnel. The airframe vibrated. A deep roar filled the fuselage.

"Everything is normal," Ozaki cried over the engine noise.

The two men's eyes met; now came the moment of truth. They had tested the damaged engine several times after affecting the repairs, but that was no guarantee it would work properly now.

"Start the starboard engine," Kotani said, loud enough to be heard.

Ozaki pushed the electric starter once, twice, thrice, four times, five... on the sixth try, it caught for three revolutions, but then stopped. Ozaki glanced at his commander.

"Again, Flight Warrant Officer?"

"Yes, damn it. Again!"

The propeller spun several times...and caught. Within seconds, spouts of flame and smoke poured from the exhaust. The aircraft vibrated, as if settling into a well-choreographed *odori* dance routine.

"Engine temperature is normal."

Kotani nodded, although he could read the gauge for himself. Glare from the lightening morning outside made it difficult for Kotani to see the oil pressure dial, so he asked Ozaki what it showed.

"The pressure is a little low," came the answer, edged with a hint of concern.

While it bore watching, that didn't surprise Kotani. His co-pilot had far fewer hours in a G4M, and so did not understand the quirks of a Kasei 21, especially one that had recently been repaired. Replacement hoses and other parts often took several hours under load to reach optimum performance.

"Keep me informed if it does not come to normal within 10 minutes of takeoff."

"But Flight Warrant Officer, should we not be certain *before* takeoff?"

"We *should*, yes, but Admiral Yamamoto keeps to a very strict itinerary."

Clearly unhappy, Ozaki nodded acquiescence. "*Hai!* Yes, sir."

4

0542 hours, 18 April 1943
Vunakanau Airfield, Rabaul

There was an iridescence to the light of predawn that invigorated Yamamoto Isoroku with a childlike wonder of the natural world. Stepping out of the staff car into the grass that lined the concrete runway, the Admiral paused for five seconds to inhale the salt air swirling inland off Blanche Bay. Maybe the Americans would be waiting for Yamamoto somewhere along his route of travel, and maybe he would indeed be shot down and killed, but if so, he could not think of a nicer day on which to die.

The idling growl of the G4M engines brought him back to the present. A glance at his watch showed them right on schedule. Led by Commander Noboru, Yamamoto followed Rear Admiral Takata Rokurō and Commander Toibana Kurio toward the aircraft. Each officer saluted the ground crew and other personnel on their way to the three-step ladder into the fuselage. Flight Warrant Officer Kotani met each of them inside the fuselage with a deep bow.

"You honor me with your presence, sirs."

Yamamoto grunted. "You honor the Emperor with your distinguished service, Flight Warrant Officer. There can be no higher praise."

G4M number 323 already had seats installed for the use of Admiral

Kusaka and his staff. This accommodation reduced the plane's bombload capacity, but allowed Noboru and Yamamoto ample room to sit during the flight. Close behind were the dorsal 7.7mm gun blisters, while at the rear, Yamamoto could see the 20mm gunner already at his position.

"Is the damaged engine performing well?" Noboru asked, which earned a disapproving glance from Yamamoto. It implied a recklessness on the part of the air crew; such a question showed doubt in the pilot, which damaged morale. He would have to speak to Noboru in private about the matter. Yet, a slight hesitation from Flight Warrant Officer Kotani caught his attention.

"The oil pressure is not ideal," the nervous young flier said. "But it is slowly coming up to normal, Commander. In my experience, this is normal after an engine overhaul. I believe we are safe to take off."

Noboru pressed the point. "How long do you anticipate it will take to become normal?"

"Ten minutes, no more than fifteen. I...I did not want to delay the Admiral's schedule."

Noboru gave a nod of understanding, and then turned to Yamamoto. Much as he hated being late, Yamamoto understood that sometimes things happened to prevent plans from unfolding as designed, but that day of all days? Could the gods have stepped into the matter?

"Delay is preferable to disaster," he said.

Kotani bowed. "*Hai!*"

0951 hours, 18 April, 1943
Coast of Bougainville near Kunau

The mission's code name was *Kogeki 1* (Attack 1). The effort at deception was typical for the Japanese Navy: direct and simple while simultaneously deceptive. Flight Warrant Officer Kotani hoped that it worked.

Having delayed takeoff from Rabaul until 0627 hours, Kotani and Uzaki had pushed the G4M as far as they dared to make up time. Unfortunately for Admiral Yamamoto's penchant for punctuality, a moderate headwind kept them nearly 15 minutes behind schedule. The second G4M flew above Number 323 to the upper right rear, with two V-formations of three Type 1 fighters stacked above the two bombers.

So far, everything had been quiet. Buin and Ballale both reported clear skies with no sign of the enemy. Ballale put up a combat air patrol just in case, but they had not seen anything, either. It looked like the Admiral's intuition proved better than the worries of his doubters.

Until the formation entered the northern limits of Empress Augusta Bay. Both Kotani and Uzaki went rigid when the radioman called out a transmission from RXZ, the callsign for Ballale Airfield.

"RXZ calling *Kogeki 1* with an urgent message. Patrol craft report American aircraft circling low over the water west of Cape Torokina. Estimated number is fifteen or twenty airplanes of the twin-engine type. We are sending help."

Uzaki's eyebrows raised along with his goggles. "Could they be part of an attack? B-25s, like at Lae?"

The possibility *did* exist. The Americans possessed numerous twin-engine bomber types, and had even more if you counted the Australians. And most American fighters did not have the long range of Japanese fighters, meaning they could not reach Bougainville, even with drop tanks...*most could not.*

One might, though—the fast and deadly model called *Ni-Sentoki* or Two-Body Type. The Americans called it the P-38. Using extra fuel pods, the *Ni-Sentoki* might have enough range. Kotani had no intention of finding out. He called out to the bombardier to inform Yamamoto and his entourage they had flown into a trap and were turning back for Buin. Then, without waiting for permission, he banked hard to port and came to course due north. Dropping to 200 feet, Kotani pushed the throttle as far forward as it would move.

"Radioman, inform the rest of the flight we are making for Buin. Request air cover. Tell them about the message from RXZ."

"*Hai!*" came the answer, quickly followed by, "Fighter leader reports American aircraft in sight and moving toward our position. They are breaking to intercept."

"*Chikushou!*" Kotani swore.

It was going to be close.

As the G4M banked to the left, Admiral Yamamoto leaned forward on his ceremonial sword, as was his wont when the situation called for a serene example. The green and turquoise waters below rushed up to meet the aircraft, until he could count individual fronds on the palm trees lining the white beach. Sandbars trapped water in tidal pools, in which Yamamoto envisioned trapped crustaceans waiting to be harvested for *Tokiyaki* or some similarly delicious snack. Instead, it was the marine birds who would feast on the bounty.

"I am sorry," Yamamoto said to his companions, nearly shouting to be heard over the guttural roar of the engines. "I have put you all in grave danger."

When Rear Admiral Takata and Commander Toibana did not respond, Commander Noboru did.

"Sharing danger with you is a great honor, sir."

Characteristically, Yamamoto grunted.

The *hamaki* suddenly slewed from side to side, forcing Yamamoto to grab his chair. Images of trees and water flashed past the large waist blisters in smears of blue and green. Behind the passengers came staccato metallic hammering from the Type 99 20mm cannon at the rear, followed seconds later by the various Type 92 7.7mm machine guns located around the plane.

Thuds hammered along the fuselage as .50-caliber bullets ripped through the G4M's thin metal skin. Something warm and wet splashed the back of Yamamoto's head, and he turned to see Commander Noboru slump over against the bulkhead. To his left, Rear Admiral Takata laid half-in, half-out of his chair, with most of his head blown away above the right ear. Commander Toibana appeared unhurt, but in shock; he sat frozen, staring at the grotesque ruin that had been his superior officer.

Wind whipped through holes in the glass of the blister, while blood spattered the interior. Coughing, Yamamoto brought up his sleeve to breathe as smoke drifted through the enclosed space. Glimpsed as it leveled out for another firing pass, an American fighter bore down on the wounded bomber and opened fire. Yamamoto saw flashes along its nose, and heard bullets striking the starboard wing. Flames trailed backward from the previously damaged engine. The *hamaki* lost altitude as violent twists shook the airframe.

Then the world went dark.

The crew members of G4M Number 323 fell silent one by one. Soon, only the rear gunner operating the 20mm cannon remained alive to call out new attacks, although by now, there was nothing Flight Warrant Officer

Kotani could do to avoid them. Skimming barely 50 feet over the surf, it took all of his concentration to keep the *hamaki* airborne. Flying to Buin now seemed impossible.

"We're going to crash!" Chief Flight Seaman Uzaki yelled.

Both he and Kotani gripped the shuddering flight controls in a vain attempt to keep the mortally wounded bomber aloft. Kotani recognized splashes in the water dead ahead as overshoots from another American fighter attack; seconds later, the aircraft staggered as more .50-caliber rounds tore through its vital spaces. Kotani turned to Uzaki just as bullets tore through the cockpit. Glass shattered and the co-pilot's torso jerked under the impact of numerous heavy caliber bullets that left ragged holes and shredded Uzaki's body into bloody fragments. Blood and bone fragments spattered the entire cockpit area, including Kotani.

Looking beyond what remained of his co-pilot, Kotani saw fire streaming from the starboard engine, just like over Port Moresby...except this time, the fire spread to the wing. Once it reached the fuel tanks, the resulting explosion would rip off the wing to send the G4M into a cartwheeling crash from which there could be no survival.

Kotani's flying goggles kept most of the sweat from his eyes. Smells of feces, ocean brine, smoke, blood and urine made him gag, and Uzaki's brain matter made the control surfaces slick. Acting by instinct, he pushed forward on the controls and prayed.

5

Despite Kotani's best efforts to keep the nose up, the G4M struck the shallow surf mere yards from the beach in a nose-down position. The force of striking the water sent everything inside the aircraft crashing forward, while simultaneously shattering the windscreens. The big bomber wound up on its back.

Water filled the cockpit halfway to the floor, which was now the ceiling. Kotani woke up hanging upside down from his seat straps, with his head and shoulders underwater. In a panic, he managed to unbuckle and float to the surface, spitting out water contaminated with fuel, oil and bits of human body parts. Kotani's brain screamed for escape from the deathtrap, and he was about to swim through the gaping holes in the canopy when he remembered his mission: to get Admiral Yamamoto safely to Ballale. Saving his own life counted as nothing toward saving Yamamoto's, although the chances that any of the passengers had survived seemed poor.

Pushing through the flotsam, Kotani half-swam, half-walked toward the passenger seats. The gore of mangled humanity he ignored, although the glint of a gold ring on a severed finger did momentarily cause Kotani's stomach to heave.

He found Yamamoto floating face-up near the blown-out starboard blister. In the semi-darkness of the fuselage, Kotani could not see if the Admiral yet lived. He needed to leverage the Admiral outside into sunlight, and with fuel burning across the water's surface, there was an acute need for urgency. Grabbing Yamamoto under the armpits, he tried to back out through the shattered blister. In the lapping waves that lifted and lowered the bomber, however, it was nearly impossible.

As if by a miracle, Kotani saw the face of Petty Officer First Class Higuchi Tsuyoshi appear in the darkness. Higuchi was the 20mm cannon operator.

"I shot down two of them, Flight Warrant Officer!" Higuchi said. On seeing who Kotani was trying to pull out of the wreckage, though, the Petty Officer's smile vanished.

"Oh!"

Kotani went to speak, but a wave washed foul-tasting water into his mouth and drowned out the words. Spitting several times, he said, "Help me get him onto the beach."

Once outside the aircraft, Kotani stood in waist-deep water. Distant engines buzzed overhead. Shading his eyes, Kotani saw aircraft dancing and spiraling high overhead, both American and Japanese...too many Japanese to be merely the six escort fighters of *Kogeki 1*. Reinforcements from Buin or Ballale had arrived.

A deep gash lined Yamamoto's forehead, oozing blood that washed away in the seawater. A hand laid on Yamamoto's chest revealed rapid shallow breaths; the Admiral lived. Coordinating with Higuchi, the two men pushed and pulled Yamamoto shoreward. Once onto the hard-packed sand, they both looped one of his arms around their necks and dragged him toward the treeline.

At that moment, Kotani heard powerful engines drawing closer. Diving toward them, half-hidden in sunlight's glare, came the unmistakable shape of an American P-38. Drawn no doubt by the pall of smoke boiling skyward from the burning G4M, the American pilot must have had orders to kill any crash survivors.

Still more than 50 feet from safety, they could never make it in time. Kotani could either drop the Admiral and run for his life, or...

"Put him down!" he commanded, laying Yamamoto facedown in the sand. Higuchi hesitated, forcing Kotani to repeat the order. Kotani then ordered Higuchi to run for the trees while covering the Admiral's body with his own.

Multiple heavy machine guns opened up with their distinctive explosive sound. Sand kicked up in founts, running toward the helpless men. At the last instant, Higuchi jumped on top of Kotani as the bullets reached them.

Kotani felt a searing pain in his right side and left calf, like someone had driven a red-hot spike into his body. Warm fluid soaked his back and ran down his side. From underneath Higuchi's shoulder, he spotted the P-38 that had just strafed them pulling up for another run, an attack they could not possibly survive.

Out of Kotani's line of sight, however, something fired tracers at the big twin-engine fighter. The American aircraft flew right into their arc and staggered in midair as 20mm cannon shells ripped along its wings from right to left. Both engines began to smoke. The aircraft lifted straight up, stalled, and spun into the water offshore. Secondary explosions followed. A second pall of smoke marked its grave.

Higuchi's weight pressed on Kotani, making it hard to breathe. Trapped under both men, there was a very real worry that Yamamoto could be suffocated.

"He is gone," Kotani said. "Get up, Higuchi, I cannot breathe."

But Higuchi did not move. Nor would he do so ever again.

Pain wracked Kotani's body as he strained to push away the dead man's weight. The bullets that had struck the Flight Warrant Officer had first ripped through Higuchi, killing him instantly. Only by straining and wiggling could Kotani slide out from under Higuchi. Kneeling beside the two men still stacked on the beach, he pushed Higuchi off and dragged Yamamoto as far up the beach as strength allowed.

Blinking, still short of the trees, Kotani found his vision blurring into a spray of red stars. The world began to spin. Consciousness faded.

0922 HOURS, 21 APRIL 1943
RABAUL NAVAL HOSPITAL, RABAUL, NEW BRITAIN

Dim light sifted through closed eyes as Flight Warrant Officer Kotani gradually became aware of his surroundings. Snores and low voices coalesced into recognizable sounds, and the air had a pungent chemical smell.

This cannot be Yasukuni Shrine.

The slightest moves caused pain to shoot through his side and groin, while his left leg felt as it had once before, when he'd fractured it as a boy.

No, definitely not Yasukuni. There is no pain in the afterlife.

Blinking, it took several moments to recognize the sounds of a hospital wardroom. Where was he? How was he still alive?

Rain pattered on the hospital roof as Kotani struggled up on one elbow. In the far corner of the room, a man with a notepad moved from bed to bed.

"Where am I?" Kotani called out. The man looked up, and it took him a few seconds to find Kotani among the dozens of patients. Spotting the Flight Warrant Officer, the orderly hurried to Kotani's side.

"You are awake, this is good. The Admiral has ordered to see you as soon as you are able."

"Admiral?"

"Yes, the Commander-in-Chief."

"Admiral Yamamoto is alive?"

"Yes, thanks to you. Do you wish something, sir?"

"Water?"

"Of course."

The man hurried away, and Kotani laid down.

Yamamoto lives!

Kotani had done his duty; whatever happened now was by the grace of the gods. A few minutes later, something clattered across the wood floor, accompanied by the cry of *chūi!* Once again propping himself on a forearm, Kotani could not believe what he saw: Admiral Yamamoto, seated in a wheelchair with a bandage wrapped around his head, was being pushed toward Kotani's bed. Embarrassed at still being prone, Kotani swung his legs over the side and tried not to grimace. Only then did he notice the heavy bandages wrapped around his right calf.

"No, stay in your bed," Yamamoto said, holding out a hand. "You have earned your rest, Ensign Kotani. I need you alive and well."

"Sir, I am not an Ensign, I am a Flight Warrant Officer."

"Since when is it permissible for a junior officer to correct his Commander-in-Chief?" Yamamoto said. His voice carried an angry edge, accompanied by a fierce scowl. That only lasted for a few seconds before fading into a broad grin. "Please forgive my having a little fun at your expense, Ensign Kotani. You have earned far more than a promotion—you have earned my gratitude. You and your brave crew kept me alive when I should have died. I need men like you, and wish for you to join my staff. The war is about to enter its most critical phase. It will require all of our efforts to defeat such a powerful enemy as America. Will you help me to do this?"

"I am honored, sir."

"To begin with, I want you to be my personal pilot."

"Hai!"

"Good. Now recover quickly, Ensign Kotani. We have much work to do, and little time to do it."

ABOUT WILLIAM ALLEN WEBB

William Alan Webb grew up devouring history books, often wondering what might have happened had things gotten just a little bit different... this led him to major in History and Creative Writing at the University of Memphis. World War Two has always been Webb's primary area of study. In addition to being published in *World War Two* magazine, Webb is the author of the three books in the *Killing Hitler's Reich* non-fiction series. His Alternate History series *The Last Brigade* has sold more than 100,000 copies, while future series include the World War Two epic *A World Afire*, and the Roman series *The Unbroken Lion.* Webb lives in West Tennessee with his wife and five dogs.

At his website: www.thelastbrigade.com
On Patreon: https://www.patreon.com/c/WilliamAlanWebb
On facebook: https://www.facebook.com/keepyouupallnightbooks

MORNING SUNS

William Stroock

MORNING SUNS

William Stroock

USS Sunny broke the calm water and roiled to the surface. Through three years of war and two captains, *Sunny* had been dinged and battered, her hull repaired numerous times. During the last war patrol in the summer of 1945, she'd been bombed by a *Zeke* off the coast of Formosa. The deck around the forward hatch still showed scorch marks. The yard crew at Mare Island had replaced the hatch, but they hadn't had time to replace the planking, which still showed the scorch marks. *Sunny* was needed for lifeguard patrol for the New Year's aerial campaign against Japan.

Chief Lemon had stenciled nineteen tiny Japanese flags on the conning tower, two of them earned in the waters northeast of Formosa.

Within *Sunny's* conning tower, he looked at the depth gage and nodded. "Surfaced, Commander."

"SD radar?" Commander Martinelli asked.

"Clear, Commander."

"No *Zekes?*"

"None."

"SJ Radar?"

"No surface contacts."

"Okay, Lem, open the hatch," Commander Martinelli ordered.

Chief Lemon climbed up the ladder and turned the crank and opened the conning tower hatch. Cold sea water poured down into the conning tower. He hopped back down to the deck with his usual energy.

"Lookouts," Martinelli ordered.

Two lookouts climbed up the later and took their stations atop the conning tower. They scanned the nightscape for blips of light or dots on the sea.

"All clear!"

"All clear!"

"Your peacoat, Commander," said Lemon.

Martinelli wearily took his well-worn peacoat from the chief and put it on his lanky frame.

"Thanks, Lem."

"After you, Commander," Lemon said, and motioned toward the hatch.

"This is one hell of a way to ring in the new year," Martinelli said dourly. "Happy 1946."

Martinelli climbed up the ladder and into the cold night. Chief Lemon, clad in a brown wool sweater, went up after Martinelli, and then Lieutenant Commander Byrne, wearing only his Navy-issue lightweight jacket.

He hadn't packed for the winter before being posted to *Sunny*. Chief Lemon had been laughing at the lieutenant commander ever since. "Think you were cruising the tropics, did you...sir?" he'd teased. Of course, Lemon had laughed at Commander Martinelli when he first arrived as the boat's new XO two years before. Lemon tolerated him now, he kidded, despite Martinelli being a Massachusetts man and Lemon being a Washingtonian.

Martinelli took his station on the bridge, exhaled and saw his breath in the dark. He breathed deeper, enjoying the feel of the cool air in his lungs. *Sunny's* nightly surfacing was the best part of the day, when he could escape the cramped confines of the boat and get fresh air. The sky was mostly clear and moonless. Martinelli saw the stars and took comfort in the constellations above. He'd sailed a schooner under them in his youth and had taught the constellations to his sons. He liked to think the boys were looking up at Orion's Belt at the same time as he, even though it was daytime back in Massachusetts.

Martinelli could barely make out the Japanese coastline. *Sunny* laid a thousand yards off Kyushu. Martinelli knew from the maps and recon photos provided after their Midway stopover, as well as their own periscope survey earlier in the day, that the coast, hilly and craggy, rose slightly before leveling off inland. A river estuary and a few shallow inlets laid a few hundred meters to the east.

A quay for fishing boats jutted out into the sea. Those had been machine-gunned to pieces by Army Air Corps B-25 *Mitchells* armed with a half-dozen .50 caliber machine guns. Now the Japanese only fished at night. Even then, flights of B-25s cruised the water, attacking Japanese fishing trawlers revealed by flares. *Sunny* had reported a few scows to the Army Air Corps.

Martinelli sighed in resignation. He'd half-hoped sonar would detect a Japanese sub hunter. Even a scow would have required him to call off the mission. No such luck.

Martinelli called down to the radio room. "Radio, report our position."

"Aye, aye," Lieutenant Brady replied.

"I don't want to get strafed by our own guys again."

Three nights before, a B-25 had dropped a flare and dove on *Sunny*. The boat's experienced lookouts had heard the twin engine *Mitchell*. Martinelli had ordered, "Clear the bridge!" before it even dropped the flare. The last they'd heard of the bomber was a volley of .50 caliber ammo ricocheting off the conning tower.

'Damn flyboys," Lemon had cursed. "Don't they know a *Gato* when they see one?"

"They're trigger-happy," Martinelli said. "When the war's over I'll sue the pilots for malpractice."

He looked about. "No flares, Lem."

"Nope," Lemon replied.

"Probably no more boats to machine-gun I expect," Byrne said.

"Do you?" Chief Lemon replied. "Sir.'

"Lem..." Martinelli cautioned.

Byrne breathed in "I..." he began, but the chief shushed him.

"Listen," the Chief said.

They heard a vague but steady hum in the distance and knew from experience what it was: hundreds of 20th Air Force B-29s were making their way southeast back to their bases in the Marianas. *Sunny* had been on lifeguard station in the spring of 1945 along their return path.

Chief Lemon whistled.

"Those B-29 raids ain't never gonna stop impressing me," he said. "I was at Midway when we thought a couple of dozen B-17s was gonna stop the Japanese." Chief Lemon strained to listen. 'They're northeast of us."

"That's right, Chief," Byrne said.

Lemon made a face, as if he needed confirmation from that young Annapolis grad XO who'd spent most of the war at Annapolis and Pearl and only transferred to *Sunny* so he could get a combat ribbon when it was all over, or so he thought. Lemon began the war in an S-Boat patrolling Philippine waters. He loathed Byrne and wasn't afraid to show it. "That fresh-faced kid can barely grow a beard," Chief Lemon had told Martinelli when Byrne joined the crew while brushing his own gray whiskers.

The officers aboard *Sunny* mostly kept their distance from the Annapolis grad. "He can't start a sentence without saying 'when I was at Annapolis,'" Brady said, only half-kidding.

The B-29s gradually faded southeast.

"There goes the night shift," Lemon said.

Throughout the autumn of 1945, the 20th and 8th Air Forces had been alternating raids against Japan. Even with their new B-29 bombers, the 8th Air Force under Jimmy Doolittle preferred bombing during the day, as they had in Europe. Lemay's 20th Air Force continued bombing at night, creating great conflagrations that could be seen on *Sunny's* bridge over the horizon. Down the coast, the city of Nobeoka laid in fire-charred ruins, bombed multiple times by the 8th Air Force during the war, most recently three days ago. Martinelli sniffed, and swore he could still get a whiff of the destruction in the air.

"Why they sending all them planes to do a job one plane can do now?" Lemon asked.

Byrne said, "Well, back at Mare Island, I read in *The Atlantic*..." When he saw no one was listening, Byrne stopped talking. He put his hands in his pockets against the cold and said, 'There's a glow now coming over the mountains." He nodded west toward the Kyushu coast.

The three men looked, and indeed, the night was now slightly lit by a faint glow coming over the Japanese coast.

Martinelli pondered the horizon. He knew the layout of Kyushu, after a war patrol on the west coast in 1944, back when he was merely *Sunny's* XO . "They hit the north coast. Fukokoka, most likely," he said.

"Could be Kurume," Lemon offered.

"Na, Doolittle's boys firebombed Kurume last week," Martinelli replied. 'No need to hit it again so soon."

"Maybe Oita?" Byrne offered.

"Oita is more the east coast."

Ain't you learned nothing yet? Lemon thought.

"Sir," Chief Lemon said. "The night shift has been bombing over that way," Lemon pointed in the general direction of northern Kyushu.

They listened as the B-29s bombers gradually trailed off to the southeast.

Lemon grimaced. "Hope nobody has to make an emergency landing in our lifeguard old sector."

Sunny had been on lifeguard duty for four days. They had even pulled a flyer from the drink two days before and drafted him into the mess room where he'd been pressed into peeling potatoes. The next day *Sunny* received orders for this new mission. Martinelli had taken the teletype message from ComSubPac and read grimly:

SUNNY WILL PROCEDE TO A POSTION EAST OF KYUSHU
APROX 20 NAUTICAL MILES NORTH OF NOBEOKA
LISTEN TO MESSAGE PURPORTED TO BE FROM DOWNED AMERICA AIRMAN
ATTEMPT RESCUE IF PRACTICAL
NOTIFY COMSUBPAC SOONEST

At that moment, Martinelli wished a B-29 would have dropped an atomic bomb on ComSubPac...

"What time you got, Chief?" Martinelli asked.

Martinelli took a red flashlight out of his pocket and shined it on his watch.

"Twenty-three-forty-nine."

"Eleven minutes," Martinelli said. He sighed

"What's wrong, Skipper?" Lemon asked

"Just thinking about what Captain White had promised back at Mare Island."

No convoy attacks, he thought. *No hunting convoy escorts, just sitting and waiting to rescue downed pilots...*

"He told me, 'I know it's been a long war for you and the boat,so I'm giving *Sunny* a lifeguard station off Kyushu.'"

Lemon snorted.

"I asked him 'Why they hell don't they keep dropping A-Bombs on Japan?'" Martinelli recalled, shaking his head. "He reminded me that President Truman hadn't taken him into his confidence."

Martinelli looked out into the darkness.

"Worst part about hit was having to go home and tell Maggy," the skipper said, sighing. "We'd been anticipating me getting back to being a lawyer, working on getting all my clients back. All those deals I made prewar, all that work gone, and I couldn't even blame them for it

"Midnight, Skipper," said Lemon, interrupting his captain.

I was starting to ramble a bit there, wasn't I? Martinelli thought. *Definitely time to get some rest*.

"All right, I'm going down," Martinelli said. "You have the conn, Byrne. Keep an eye on him, Lem."

"Aye, aye, Skipper."

Chief Lemon grinned.

Martinelli climbed down the ladder and went to the radio room. Brady stood at the radio with Signalmen Spier. Next to him was Ensign LaFrance, the *Hellcat* flyer they'd rescued two nights before. He was in his old uniform now, after borrowing one of Byrne's. The laundry detail had stitched up LaFrance's uniform as best he could with pieces of cloth from about the boat. The man looked like a Raggedy Andy doll standing next to Brady.

"Anything yet?" Martinelli asked.

Brady replied. "Not yet. I wonder..."

The radio crackled, "Hello, hello,' a distant voice said.

"There it is," said Brady.

"Shhh!" Lemon said.

"This this is Lieutenant Saul Rosen, United Stated Army Air Corps, broadcasting in the clear. I'm being held at the village of Ito in Oita prefecture on the Island of Kyushu. My captors are willing to let me go, provided their demands are met. They want to speak with an America officer. You can respond on this frequency..."

"That was different than last night's message," Brady said. ComSubPac had radioed a transcript to *Sunny*.

"So it's not a recording," said Martinelli.

"No."

"But is he one of ours?" Brady asked. "Or a Japanese impersonator?"

"What do you make of it, LaFrance?"

LaFrance shrugged. "What do you want me to say, Commander? He sounded like a flyer, I suppose. But I don't know anything about the 8th Air Force."

"Well, that's useful," Martinelli said.

"Hey, a year ago I was graduating flight school," LaFrance said.

"Orders were to make contact," Martinelli sighed. He took the mic.

"Lt. Rosen, this is Commander Michael M. Martinelli, USN, responding to your call."

They waited several seconds for a response.

"Hello!" the voice came back. "This is Lt. Saul Rosen, United States Army Air Corps. Hello!"

Maritnelli looked at Brady and Lemon, made a confused face, and shrugged. "Go ahead."

"As I said, I am being held at the village of Ito in the Oita prefecture. The village head says he'll let us go in an exchange. A trade."

Martinelli looked at Lemon and shrugged again. "What do you think, Lem?" he asked.

"Never heard anything like it, Skipper."

Martinelli keyed the mic. "How do I know you're who you say you are?"

"Rosen, Saul." He gave his serial number. "333rd Bombardment Group out of Kadena, Okinawa."

"Hold on..."

Hmmmm... Martinelli thought.

Lemon said quietly, "They could have got that off of some dead man's dog tags."

"I know." Martinelli keyed the mic. "You like baseball?"

"Sure," the voice said. "What do you want to know? I like the Yankees. What should I tell you? Babe Ruth's homerun record? What did Lou Gehrig die of?"

"I would have preferred Joe DiMaggio," Martinelli said to Lemon.

"You would. Sticking with your own kind." Lemon grinned.

"Of course—I'm a Boston man." Martinelli said to Lemon. Martinelli keyed the mic, , "That's a start, Rosen."

"Babe Ruth hit sixty homeruns," Rosen replied. "And Lou Gehrig died of Lou Gehrig's Disease. I don't know what the real name of the disease is."

A skeptical Lemon said, "The Yankees would be the team the Japanese would know about. Who hasn't heard of the Yankees? Goddamn New York Yankees," the native Washingtonian muttered.

"Are you from New York?" Martinelli asked.

"Yeah," the voice said. "Tremont Avenue, just off the Grand Concourse, about twenty blocks from Yankee Stadium. I used to be out in the right field bleachers watching the Babe. I went to Horace Mann Prep in Bronx."

"I don't know much about New York City," said Martinelli. He looked to Lemon. "You?"

"Not outside Brooklyn Navy yard."

Rosen added, "Want to know my shoe size?"

Martinelli looked at Lemon, who said, "Maybe he's a Japanese who lived in New York City."

"Now you're being paranoid, Lem," Martinelli replied.

Lemon snapped his fingers. 'Rosen. Ain't that a Jew name?"

Maritn pointed to Lemon. "You're right." He keyed the mic. "Are you Jewish?"

"I am," the voice replied. "Want to check if I'm circumcised?"

"Hold on," Martinelli said.

"You ain't a Jew, is you, Skipper?"

"How long have you known me, Lem?" the skipper replied. "And does Martinelli sound Jewish? I'm Catholic." Martinelli laughed, "Heck, Maggy and I were married in a nice respectable Episcopalian church. Her Boston Brahmin father insisted."

Brady asked, "Lem, anyone onboard Jewish?"

Lemon replied, "Ain't Siggy a Jew?"

Martinelli said. "I don't know. Siegfried? Maybe? Could be Jewish. Sounds German to me. You know, the Siegfried Line?"

"Weren't some Krauts Jewish?" Lemon asked. "Ain't that where Hitler got started?"

Martinelli nodded. "If Siggy is Jewish, maybe he can figure out if this guy's telling the truth. Get him up here. Let's do our due diligence."

Lemon picked up the 1MC mic. "Siggy to the radio room right now."

Martinelli called to Rosen, "Wait one."

"I've been waiting for three days now."

"Sarcastic fella, ain't he?" said Lemon.

Martinelli said, "This mission keeps getting weirder."

Lemon laughed.

"What's that, sir?' Brady asked.

"We're sitting here on the coast of Kyushu waiting to find out if some guy I'm talking to on the radio is a Jew."

"Yeah," Brady said. "But it beats the Formosa patrol."

"Does it?" Martinelli asked. "It's been a long goddamn war."

He momentarily recalled the sense of hope *Sunny's* crew had felt at Midway when word of the three atomic bombings came over the radio. Everyone thought they were going home. Then the Japanese army overthrew the emperor and declared Japan would fight till they end, even after they dropped the third bomb. Japan fought 'til New Years with no end in sight. At least they'd returned to Mare Island before the new war patrol.

Siegfried reported to the radio room. He was a one of the kids, as Martinelli and Lemon called the new personnel assigned to the boat after their last refit at Mare Island. Siegfried was eighteen, or so he claimed, but Lemon doubted he was even that old. Martinelli wondered how he got past the draft board, Lemon replied that with the war sure to last until the late forties now, the draft board probably didn't care.

"Siggy, are you Jewish?" Martinelli asked.

Lemon looked over Siegfreid like he was appraising an antique. Siegfreid was thin and pale like everyone else on the boat after a couple of weeks at sea. He had black hair and close-set black eyes, a prominent brow and nose.

"He's a Jew," Lemon nodded.

'Uh, sure," Seaman Siegfried said. *"Baruch Hashem."*

"Baruch Hashem?" Martinelli asked.

"Blessed God,' Siegfried said. "Or thank God, depending on the translation."

"Is that Hebrew?'

"Yeah."

Martinelli said, "Okay, so we have an American on the other end here." He held up the mic. "He says he's a Jew. Name's Rosen."

"That's a Jewish name," Siegfried said. "We had a Rosen family down the street from us in Milwaukee."

"Okay, so talk to him."

Martinelli gave Siegfried the mic. He took it and said, "Hello?"

"Hello," the voice on the other end said.

"This is Yeoman Sam Siegfried..."

There was a pause, then, "Great, a fellow Hebrew."

"Baruch Hashem."

"Baruch Hashem," Rosen said back.

Siegfried went on, "The skipper here wants us to talk Hebrew to each other to prove you're not a Japanese spy."

"Okay," the voice said. *"Baruch Ata Adonai...eleheinu melech H'alom."*

"Was that Hebrew?" Martinelli asked.

Siegfried nodded.

"What'd he say?" asked Lemon.

Siegfried translated, "Blessed are you, Lord our God. King of the universe."

"Have him say more of the Jew stuff," Lemon said.

Siegfried said, "My chief wants you to pray more."

Lemon added, 'You start one of them funny prayers.'

"Okay. *Henei ma tov umanaim...*"

Rosen finished the prayer. *"Shevet achim gam Yachad."*

Siegfried looked at Lemon and asked, "You want us to go on?'

"Never mind that," Lemon said. He pointed to the mic. "So this guy's a Jew?"

Siegfried said. "He's doing a heck of an impersonation if he isn't."

"Don't you people know where the rest of you people are?" asked the chief.

"Sure, Chief. We get a new map every year, like the phonebook."

Lemon smacked Siegfried about the head.

"I never heard of Jews in Japan," Siegfried said.

"Ain't you people everywhere?" Lemon asked.

"We *were*," Siegfried deadpanned.

"Oh, right," Lemon replied. "The Krauts."

'My people were from Poland," Siegfried said.

Brady offered, "There was a big Christian population in Nagasaki."

"There *was*," Lemon snickered. "Till we dropped the bomb. Any of you Jews there, Siggy?"

"Not as far as I know, Chief."

Maritn shot Lemon the disapproving look he gave him whenever he thought he was speaking out of line or stupidly. He took the mic from Siegfried and spoke. "Okay, Rosen. You're an American."

"I'm glad I could prove myself."

Time for due diligence. "You're not the only American?"

"No."

"How many are you?"

"They won't let me say."

"Why not?"

"I guess they're keeping secrets."

That's smart negotiating, Martinelli thought. *I'd be crazy to sign off on this if it were a legal agreement.*

"So what the hell do they want?" Martinelli asked.

"Easy, like I said in the broadcast these last few nights. We're in the village of Ito. The people here are holding us. They'll release us, but they want to do an exchange."

Martinelli asked. "Japanese prisoners? We don't have any."

"No, Commander, they want food."

"They want food?"

"Yep?" Rosen replied. "There's not a lot to eat here. I can confirm that."

"Really?"

"It's bad here, Commander."

"Holy hell," Martinelli said. "All right, give me a minute."

What the hell? Martinelli thought. Then to Rosen, "Well, how much food do they want?"

"I don't know. Hold on a second..."

There was talking on the other end.

"They want to talk to you directly. They want you to come to the village."

Chief Lemon shook his head. 'No way."

Martinelli shot Lemon a glance. "Chief, I will negotiate this."

Lemon held up his hands in surrender.

Martinelli thought for a moment.

I've gone to the other council's legal offices to make a deal. I suppose I can do that now.

"Okay. But how the hell am I supposed to get it there? And how do I get you guys out here?"

"Uh, well, the village head said they'll send a skiff out to you."

"How will they know my pos?"

"They say they can see you in the water right now. These people are fisherman and say they know the waters."

Martinelli looked at the chief, who nodded and said, "That's right. I knew every rock and shoal in the Chesapeake, that's for sure. If something was floating past Kent Island that shouldn't be there, I sure as hell would've known."

"All right, give us a minute," Martinelli said.

"Okay."

"What do you think, Lem?"

"Could be a trap. I suppose." He rubbed the whiskers on his chin. "But if they know we're here, they could already have blown us right out of the water."

"We know they have some of our guys," Martinelli said.

"The flight captain is probably dead," said LaFrance. "That's why the copilot is speaking. And all they want is food...they're starving." said LaFrance.

Brady offered, "That's the plan, wasn't it, Skipper? After the atomic bombs. Blockade Japan to starve them into surrender. I guess it's working."

Sigfried held up a finger. "Ah, but if we're trying to starve Japan into surrender, wouldn't we be helping them by giving them food?"

Lemon glared at Siegfried. "Ain't nobody ask you," he said. *"Yeoman."*

"Sorry, Chief," Siegfried replied. "It's an ethical issue and I spent all that time studying the Talmud. The rebbes asked us ethical questions like this all the time in Yeshiva."

Martinelli said, "Knock it off, Lem. Siggy has a point."

"Giving a little food to get one of our guys back seems like a pretty good deal," Brady said.

Martinelli looked off into the distance for a moment. Then he nodded and keyed the mic, "Okay, Rosen. Tell them to send a boat out, but nothing big. You Army Air Corps boys might spot it and blow it out of the water. Lord knows they're trigger-happy."

"I don't think they have anything larger than a skiff, but I'll tell them," Rosen replied.

"We'll move in closer to shore."

Rosen said, "What? Hold on... They say you can come to about a hundred yards. There's a shore quay you'll be able to see. The boat will come from there."

"Right, we've seen the quay already," Martinelli replied. "You'll be in the boat?"

"Uh, no. They said food, then you can see me."

"Tell them no deal," Martinelli replied. "I need proof of life."

I wouldn't be a very good lawyer if I didn't demand that.

"They're not going to like that," replied Rosen.

"They don't get anything without proving you're alive. I must see you in the flesh."

"Hold on."

"They gotta be talking it over," Lemon said. "Think they're deal makers? Car salesmen?"

"I hope so," Martinelli said. "In '39, I talked a salesman off his rack rate and then kept bidding him down. Always be prepared to walk away. Works the same in law. Always be prepared to go to trial."

"Will you walk away, Skipper?" Lemon asked.

"If I think the risk to the boat is too great? Absolutely," Martinelli said. "Why, I once...

Rosen came back on. "They say all right. I'll go out. But I have to bring back the food."

"Negative," Martinelli said. "You'll come out and bring me back to see how many of our guys are there. Then we'll talk about how much food they get."

"Hold on."

Lemon asked, "Just what the hell are you thinking, Skipper? Still negotiating?"

"I'm not risking the boat without knowing just what I'm getting back in return," Martinelli said. "So I'm going to see things for myself."

"You sure as hell aren't going ashore alone," Lemon said.

"Are you coming, Lem?"

"Try and stop me," the chief replied. "Sir."

"You're willing to leave Byrne in charge of the boat, Lem?" Martinelli joked.

"Aw hell, Skipper. The kid's gonna have to grow up sometime. Might as well be now."

They waited till Rosen called back. "Okay. Bring the boat close to shore, Commander. We'll come out to you."

"See you soon." Martinelli secured the mic.

He shouted up to the bridge. 'Byrne, get ready to take her close to shore!"

"Aye, aye, Skipper," Lt. Bryne shouted back.

Byrne shouted orders, and the boat got underway.

"Skipper," Lemon said, "Don't you think we better be ready for a fight?"

Martinelli asked, 'You want me to order battle stations? Man the deck guns. Get everybody topside and armed?"

"No. But I would like to be up there with my Thompson."

Marin nodded. "If it makes you feel better, Lem."

Lemon excused himself and went down to the arms locker. Martinelli and Siegfried went up to the bridge.

"Take her to a hundred yards off the quay, Lt. Commander."

Byrne held his hands in his jacket and stomped his feet against the cold. He slowed the boat and brought her about at a hundred yards from the shore. They were close enough that they could see the white caps in the river inlet and even the dark silhouette of the quay.

Lemon came up to the bridge with what he always called his "Tommy gun." He'd brought it aboard himself when he was posted to *Sunny.* The Thompson was an older model with a barrel clip. Martinelli wondered if Lemon had been a mobster before the war. He never did say where he got "his Thompson."

Martinelli said, "Chief, me and you and Siggy here will go aboard the Japanese skiff."

"Me?" Siegfried said.

"Why not? You can confirm Rosen's identity," Martinelli said. "And someone's got to lug the food around."

Lemon said, "Good thinking, Skipper." He turned to Siegfried. "You Jews can sniff each other out, right, Siggy?"

"Sure, Chief," Siegfried laughed. "I can always spot a Jew."

The stern lookout called, "Commander, firing to the north."

Martinelli looked north up the Kyushu coast and saw the far horizon flashing.

"Lem, you hear anything?"

Chief Lemon shook his head. "Listen," Lemon said.

The bridge stayed quiet for several seconds till they heard a faint booming sound, like someone banging a gigantic kettle drum.

"I think it's *New Jersey* again, Skipper," Byrne said.

"That's good," Chief Lemon replied. "Sir."

For a couple of weeks, the Navy had been running a pair of battleship patrols. They cruised up and down the coast looking for targets of opportunity. The bridge watched the yellow light coming over the northern horizon and listened to the boom for a few more seconds.

"You know," Martinelli said. "I think you're right, Byrne."

"She's been hammering the Japanese coast for a couple of days now, hasn't she, Skipper?" said Byrne.

"Scuttlebutt was they're clearing the way for the Marines."

Byrne whistled.

"I knew guys at Tarawa and Iwo...sir," Lemon said. 'Them guns ain't gonna do much for the Marines. Rock is awful tough even against sixteen-inch shells."

The port lookout said, "Contact dead ahead, Skipper."

They saw the outline of a boat coming out from the quay and heard paddling.

"Can't you call him, Siggy?" Chief Lemon asked.

"Like what would I call, Chief?"

"Don't you people have some sort of...signal?"

"What are we?" Siegfried asked. "Indians?"

Lemon laughed.

"Maybe I should blow a shofar."

"Shofar?" Byrne asked.

"A horn. A ram's horn used to ring in the new year."

"Well, it's New Year's," offered Byrne.

"Not the gentile New Year. *Our* New Year. Rosh Hashanah. That was..." Siegfried thought for a moment. "September last year."

"Oh."

"The chief's right," Martinelli said as the boat drew closer. "Try something, Siggy."

Siegfried closed his eyes and said slowly, soulfully, *"Shema Israel, Adonai Eleheinu, Adonoi Ehad..."* The prayer echoed in the night, drowning up the drumbeat of *New Jersey's* guns.

"Wow, a regular Tommy Dorsey," said Lemon.

Rosen called back with the Shema.

"Does it check out, Siggy?" Lemon asked.

"It was the exact same prayer that I said."

Martinelli shouted, "Okay, approach!"

Lemon chambered a round and level the Thompson at the oncoming skiff. 'You never know, Skipper. That skiff could be loaded with soldiers."

"I haven't said the Shema since I enlisted," Siegfried said.

"Shhh," Lemon said.

The skiff drew closer.

Lemon climbed down to the deck, Thompson in hand. Siegfried went with him and cast out a line to the skiff. Rosen caught the line and pulled the skiff toward the boat till they pulled alongside. Lemon took a red flashlight out of his shirt pocket and shined it on the skiff. The light revealed an American in an olive drab flight suit sitting on the prow.

"You Rosen?"

"Yeah."

Lemon shined the light on the Japanese man at the oars. "Who's he?"

"That's Hideki."

"I speak English," Hideki said.

"I didn't ask you nuthin'," Lemon said.

"Which one of you is Siegfried?" Rosen asked.

Siegfried raised his hand. *"Shalom."*

"Shalom," Rosen said.

"You two gonna have a Jew reunion right here?" Lemon asked. "Sir!" He called up to the bridge, "It's okay to come down, Skipper."

Martinelli came down to the deck and walked up to the skiff. Rosen saw him and saluted. Martinelli saluted back.

"This is a hell of situation," Martinelli said.

"Sorry, sir," Rosen replied. "It wasn't our idea to get shot down."

Martinelli put his hands on his hips and worried his lip. "No, I suppose not. When did you guys go down?"

"Three days ago in the Nobeoka raid."

"Where'd you get a radio to call us?"

"They had one in Ito."

"So you're here, Rosen," Martinelli said. "What's the situation?"

"There are seven of us. The captain and two gunners were killed when we ditched in the water, right over there." He pointed to the east. "G2 back at Kadema said we should locate Japanese authorities right away. Well, the rest of us swam to shore, these villagers met us on the rocks. There must have been a couple dozen of them, all armed with pitchforks and rapiers. I mean, we had out .45's but even if we shot our way out, the army would hear, and..."

Martinelli held up a hand. "I got it."

"So they took us back to their village." He pointed to the river. "It's a few hundred yards up the river there."

"How they treating you?" Lemon asked.

"Not bad, under the circumstances."

"What circumstances?" Martinelli probed.

"There's hardly any food. That's why they want to trade us for food. I don't even know how to describe what we've seen, Commander," Rosen said. "You'll just have to see for yourself."

"I intend to."

"I'm going with you," Lemon insisted.

Martinelli looked at Hideki. 'Is that okay with you?"

"Bring food," Hideki said.

"Not without a deal."

"No food, no deal," Hideki said.

Martinelli wondered if he was dealing with a fellow lawyer.

"Maybe a sign of goodwill, Skipper?" Lemon said. "Get things moving?"

"There's a lot of kids in the village, Commander," Rosen said. "Trust me, if you've ever seen starving kids..."

"Get a sack of potatoes from the mess, Lem."

"Right, Skipper."

"And Lem, leave the Thompson here."

Lemon glared at the skipper, who held his gaze and glared back. "You heard what I said, Lem."

"Fine." Lemon walked up to the bridge. "Lieutenant Commander Byrne, take my Thompson." Byrne took the gun and looked down at it. "You sure you can handle one of those things?" Lemon asked. "Sir?"

"I can shoot."

"I'd just sling that thing over my shoulder if I were you...sir."

From the bridge, Byrne shouted, "Skipper, you sure this is a good idea?"

"No, but it's been a long a war."

"Okay, Skipper."

Martinelli walked over to the bridge.

"You have the conn, Byne. If we're not back in..." He looked back to Rosen. "How long would you say it take us to get there, see things for ourselves, and get back?"

Rosen shrugged and made a face. "It took us ten minutes to row out here."

"One hour then," Martinelli said.

"If you're not back you want me to sail out?"

"No," Martinelli replied. "I want you to order battle stations and blast the village to smithereens."

"Okay, Skipper," Byrne said enthusiastically.

Lemon came back with a sack of potatoes slung over his shoulder.

"Give them to Siegfried," Martinelli said.

Lemon threw the sack of potatoes into Siegried's gut. "Oof," he said and slung the sack over his shoulders.

"All right, let's get in," Martinelli said.

"All aboard," Siegfried joked.

Martinell, Lemon, and Siegfried got in the skiff with Rosen and Hideki. Lemon took his red light out and shined it into Hideki's face. He held up a hand and blinked against the red light.

'Show me your face," Lemon said. "I want a good look at the man who's rowing me to Japan."

Hideki lowered his arm. His face was gaunt. His jowls sagging a bit. Big bags sagged under his eyes, as well.

"You look sick," Lemon said.

Hideki glowered at Lemon.

"Put the light away, Lem," Martinelli said.

Lemon pocketed the flashlight and pushed off the hull of the boat. Hideki used an oar to turn the skiff about and began rowing back to the quay. To the north, the horizon flashed with the fire of *New Jersey*'s sixteen-inch guns.

When the prow touched the quay, Lemon grabbed it, found a cleat and tied a line to it. He held the skiff steady while everyone else climbed onto the quay.

"Lead the way," Martinelli said to Hideki.

"Come with me," Hideki said.

Lemon was the first to follow Hideki, but after a few steps he put out hand and said, "Hold on, Skipper."

"What is it?" Martinelli asked.

"You smell that?" Lemon asked. "Something ain't right."

Martinelli inhaled deeply. "Now that you mentioned it…" He smelled rot and something else, like being in a hospital with a sick person.

"Yuck," Siegfried said.

"Oh!" Rosen snapped his fingers. "I'd already gotten used to that stench," he said glumly.

"It's not bodies," Lemon said. "I smelled plenty of them before. It's…"

"Famine," Rosen said. "Famine and disease."

"But not corpses?" Martinelli said.

Hideki turned around angrily. "You may not allow us to feed our children, but we can still bury our dead."

"Okay," Martinelli said. "Take us to Ito then."

The party of four walked along the quay in silence. They came to a gravel path which ran along the river and set foot on the ground. Lemon stopped.

"Well, son of a bitch," he said.

"What's the matter, Lem?" Martinelli asked.

"We just invaded Japan."

Martinelli looked down at the ground beneath his feet.

"Before we go…" Lemon turned around and looked back upon the water.

"What are you doing, Lem?" Martinelli asked.

"I just want to make sure Byrne hasn't sunk the boat."

Siegfried laughed and pulled the sack of potatoes over his shoulder.

"Jesus, Lem," Martinelli said. "Anything else?"

"Nothing I can think of, Skipper."

They walked on, coming to a vast rice paddy divided by dirt berms, with a high, wide berm running up the center of the paddy. At the far end, they saw several darkened buildings. The rice paddy smelled of rancid, dirty water.

Rosen said, "Hideki told me there was no harvest this autumn. He said the Army Air Corps firebombed the rice paddy. Wasn't my group. Must have been the new guys in the 20th Air Force."

Hideki took the party along the central berm. At the end, he stopped and shouted something in Japanese.

In the distance, a voice shouted back in Japanese.

"Come on," Hideki said to the three Americans.

They veered off the riverbank past several trees and walked till they saw someone standing along the path with an oil lamp.

"He's the head of the village," Hideki said. "Igawa-*san*."

Igawa said something in Japanese and then walked past Hideki. He stopped at Lemon and held up the lamp to him.

"Carful there," Lemon said.

Igawa said something in rapid-fire Japanese. Hideki said something back and then, 'Where is the food you promised?"

Martinelli said, "Siggy?"

"Okay, Skipper."

Siegfried came forward and dropped the potato sack at Igawa's feet. Igawa considered the sack of potatoes at his feet and picked it up. Igawa said something in Japanese.

"He says to follow him."

With the sack of potatoes in hand, Igawa led them through the village past one-story wood homes with peaked roofs and wires leading to telephone poles. Despite the electrical wiring, the village was dark. People looked out of windows and stood in doorways, watching as the small group walked past. Igawa dropped the potato sack in front of the last house and spoke. Two women came out and took the sack. They opened it and looked inside. One of the women cried out, *"Jaigamo!"* She turned to face the door and said it again. *"Jaigamo."*

"I guess we know the Japanese word for potato," said Lemon.

Onlookers gawked as the Americans walked past.

"Don't you wish you had brought guns now, Skipper?" Lemon asked.

"No." Martinelli shook his head.

They came to a small one-story brick building. A group of men met them there, all carrying pitch forks and farming implements.

"What about now, sir?"

"Lem, shut up."

The Japanese men parted for the Americans. Igawa and Hideki led them inside the school. A few lit candles were on the windowsill and Igawa's lamp lit up the inside. It looked like an American schoolroom, with a chalkboard at the head and a Japanese flag in the corner. The desks were all pushed to the back, though.

Six American flyers were sitting cross legged on the floor or leaning against the walls.

"I'll be damned," one of them said. "Lieutenant Rosen made it back."

Martinelli said, "I'm Commander Michael M. Martinelli, *USS Sunny*.

The flyers rose to their feet. A couple of the flyers cheered. One whistled. Another clapped.

"We're rescued!" one shouted.

"Oh, thank the Lord," another said.

Martinelli held up his hand and said, "Hold on, it's not that easy. We still have to negotiate. So just hold on."

"Hey, Skipper?" Lemon said.

"Yeah, Chief."

"Maybe Siggy here ought to negotiate?"

"What the hell for?" Martinelli asked.

"Yeah, why me?"

"Ain't you a banker or one of them financiers?"

Siegfried doubled over laughing.

For once, Chief Lemon felt embarrassed and didn't know what to say.

"Yeah, okay, Chief," Siegfred said.

"What's funny?"

"My father is a Rebbe at a schul in Milwaukee," he said. "My eight siblings and I share a room in our apartment. I had a nice mattress on the floor with my next oldest brother."

"Knock it off," Martinelli said. He looked at Hideki. "How about another sack of potatoes for the rest of the guys?"

Start with a lowball offer. Martinelli had learned that while practicing law.

Hideki translated. Without needing translation, Martinelli knew Igawa rejected the offer. His expression said "no." He spoke in Japanese.

"Uh, Commander," Lemon said. "Hate to interrupt—I can tell you're enjoying this back and forth and all, but we told Byrne to sail the boat in here and start blasting if we ain't back in an hour."

"Quite right," Martinelli said.

Igawa spoke again.

Hideki said, "Igawa says one sack of potatoes per man."

Martinelli said, "You've got seven of our guys. I'll give you six potato sacks, including the one I just brought. And as my chief just reminded me, if I'm not back in an hour, my boat's going to show up here with a deck full of angry and well-armed sailors."

Hideki translated.

Igawa nodded and said, *"Hai."*

"Okay, that means yes," Martinelli said. 'Tell Igawa he's got a deal." He looked to the flyers. "Come on, guys, let's go."

They walked out of the school.

The village head spoke, and Hideki said, "He says I'll row you back."

"Tell him he's coming with us to the quay."

Hideki translated. Igawa spoke.

"Why? He asked."

"Tell Igawa he's our insurance policy in case someone decides to get cute. No Igawa, no potatoes. Tell him."

Hideki told him, Igawa spoke back.

"He wants to know why he should trust you to send the potatoes."

Martinelli walked up to Igawa and said, "I give you my word as an officer in the United States Navy."

Hideki translated.

"And as a lawyer," Martinelli added. "Tell him I'm a member of the Massachusetts State Bar Association."

Hideki translated.

Igawa nodded. *"Hai."*

Martinelli nodded back.

Igawa led the Americans out of the village and to the quay. Lemon peered into the dark. "I see *Sunny*'s outline," he said.

"You say that as if you think she might not be there."

Lemon shrugged. "With Byrne, you never know."

Martinelli walked to the far edge of the quay and called out to the boat. "Byrne, this is Martinelli!"

"I hear you, Skipper!" Byrne called back.

"We're coming!"

"Okay!"

In all, eleven men got in the small skiff. Two men sat on each bennch and the rest on the deck.

"Crowded like a lifeboat," Lemon said. He put both hands on the quay and shoved off with a grunt. Hideki rowed hard.

Rosen and Siegfried sat across from one another. "Hey, Siegfried! Funny running into a fellow Jew all the way out here."

Siegfreid laughed. 'We're the set-up to a joke."

"Oh, yeah, what's that?" Rosen asked.

"Two Jews walk onto a *Gato* sub..."

Behind them, Chief Lemon doubled over laughing.

"Lem?" Martinelli asked.

The chief got control of himself and sat upright. "Sorry, Skipper. Siggy, I always heard you Jews were funny."

"Thanks, Chief," Siegfried said.

"You two go to the same temple or something?"

"I doubt it," Siegfried said. "I'm Lubavitch. You're not Lubavitch, are you, Rosen?"

Rosen sniffed. "Reform."

"A what?" Lemon asked.

"Really religious," Siegfried said. "Like those Bible thumpers down south. My father wouldn't even consider Rosen here a Jew. Hell, I'm supposed to be at a synagogue in Brooklyn studying Torah all day."

"Then what the hell is you doin' here?" Lemon asked.

"Wanted to get away from Dad. I lied and said I was eighteen and enlisted."

"Ha!" Lemon said. "I knew you wasn't eighteen."

"They'll take anyone these days." Rosen shook his head. "That's okay. My dad hates you Lubavitch. Says you should join us in the twentieth century."

As the skiff approached *Sunny*, Martinelli saw the 40mm gun was manned and a dozen sailors were on deck wearing helmets and carrying firearms. When the skiff drew close to the boat, a man threw a line out and pulled it parallel to the sub.

"Welcome back, Skipper!" Bryne shouted from the bridge.

Martinelli stepped onto the deck. "I see you turned out the crew."

"You were running out of time," Byrne said. He looked down at his watch. "Eleven minutes before I was to take *Sunny* into the estuary and start blasting."

"Good thinking, Commander," Lemon said.

He turned around and held a hand on the prow of the skiff to steady it. One by one, Rosen's rescued crewmen stepped onto *Sunny*.

"Byrne, have the mess ring up five more bags of potatoes."

"Okay, Skipper," Byrne said. "Stow all the gear and prepare to get underway."

"You heard the skipper!" Lemon shouted.

The mess crew came down to the deck with sacks of potatoes slung over their shoulders. On Lemon's word, they tossed them into skiff at Hideki's feet.

"Hey, Skipper," Siegfried said. "Don't you think we should give them the seventh sack?"

Martinelli looked at the yeoman and asked, "What the hell for, Siggy?"

"Seven flyers. Seven sacks. And besides, that village is starving. You saw the way those women acted when they saw *one* sack of potatoes."

Martinelli folded his arms. "Yeah, I guess you're right. Lem!"

"I heard," Lemon said.

"Hey, Lem!" Siegfried shouted. "Maybe a little salt, vinegar and sugar, too."

"You heard him, Lem!" Martinelli shouted.

Siegfried continued, "And how bought some..."

"Don't push your luck, Siggy," Martinelli said.

"Sorry, Skipper. The rebbes told us to always try to do good."

"You already did."

A steward brought another sack of potatoes up from the galley. Martinelli took it and walked it over to the skiff. He tossed it in and said to Hideki. 'I guess that's it."

Martinelli unceremoniously put a foot on the prow of the skiff and pushed it off. Without a word, Hideki turned the skiff around and rowed back to Ito.

Lemon stood next to Martinelli. The two men watched the skiff disappear into the night.

Martinelli put his hands on his hips and said, "This has to be the strangest goddamn mission of the war."

"Yep."

Lemon looked back to the seven flyers climbing aboard the bridge.

"It's going to be crowded."

The two men walked down the deck and climbed aboard the bridge.

"Let's get underway, Mr. Byrne."

"Aye, eye, sir."

Byrne gave orders to helm to come about ninety degrees.

"Lt. Commander Byrne. Have radio raise ComSubPac. Tell 'em mission accomplished. We'll drop these guys off at Okinawa."

"Right, sir," Byrne said.

He started down the hatch.

"And nice work, Lieutenant Commander."

"Thank you, sir!"

"You could head below, Skipper," Byrne said. "Get some rest?"

"Nah, I'll stay up here, enjoy the night, wait for the morning," Martinelli replied. "You go."

"Okay, Skipper. Thanks."

Byrne went below, but Lemon stayed up on the bridge.

"Why don't you sack out, Lem?"

"Where you go, I go, Skipper."

Sunny sailed east for a few minutes at ten knots, putting distance between itself and the coast, then south at ten knots. After 0500 hours, the eastern sky turned gray.

"Anything, lookouts?" Martinelli asked.

"Nope."

"Some specks in the distance," the port lookout said. "Off the stern, due north about...five thousand."

Martinelli trained his binoculars north. "Spotter aircraft?"

"I expect," said Lemon. "But those are coming from the southeast. That's 20th Air Force. They're usually the night shift."

"Well, *New Jersey* was bombarding targets overnight. Maybe they're changing tactics?"

After 0600 hours, the sun peeked over the horizon, casting beams that shimmered off the water.

"I always like this time of the day," Lemon said. "New day. New things."

Sunny sailed past the city of Nobeoka, recently bombed by the 8th Air Force. Soot and smoke still rose from the burnt-out buildings.

"So that's what we smelled," Lemon joked.

"Knock off the macabre crap, would you, Lem?"

"It's a little late in the war to worry about that, don't you think?"

Soon after came the city of Hyuga, set alight by the 20th Air Force the previous October. Martinelli put his binoculars to his eyes and trained them on the city. The buildings were gone, reduced to piles of ashen wreckage. Martinelli saw hundreds of specks on the beach and dozens of wisps of smoke.

"Tents and campfires," he said. "Those poor bastards are living on the beach."

There followed Miyazaki, a blackened husk after a sustained December campaign by the 8th Air Force. The entrance to the Oyodo river was blocked by blackened and overturned ships. Martinelli counted a pair of freighters and a capsized oil tanker.

"The *Mitchells* must have had fun with them," Lemon whistled.

"Contact!" the port lookout said. "Multple contacts. Way up...30,000, I'd say. B-29s."

Lemon trained his binoculars on the contacts. "Yep, six of em. 30,000 feet...huh. They're breaking off now. Into three groups."

They followed the contacts for several minutes.

"Looks like they're headed in different directions," Lemon said. "West, northwest, one's coming southwest toward us..."

Martinelli shrugged. "Some kind of reconnaissance?"

The two B-29s shimmered in the clear morning sky as they passed over the shattered city of Miyazaki, and flew inland, following the Oyodo River.

"Miyazakie isn't their target?" Martinelli said.

"Nope."

"What's further inland, Lem? Miyakanojo, right?"

"Right," Lemon replied. "Wonder what's so important in Miyakanojo that they need fresh pics of it?"

"You know, Lem," Martinelli said. "We're sailing passed our third bombed-out city of the morning. Lemay's guys bombed it. Doolittle's guys bombed it..."

"Yeah, and then they bombed it again just to be a son of a bitch," said Lemon.

"Do we even need the atomic bomb?"

Lemon shrugged.

Martinelli looked out upon the water and said, "I could make the case either way."

Behind the mountains west of Miyazakie, the sky flashed white, so bright that everyone topside winced and turned away for the moment.

"What the hell was..."

Before Lemon could finish, they saw a great blast of orange mushrooming up from behind the mountains.

"Holy hell," Martinelli said.

"Is that an atomic bomb?"

"I..." The blast wave hit the boat, a slight concussion of air at that distance. Then they heard a large *bang* and finally, a low persistent rumble.

"I don't know what the hell else that could be," Lemon said as the cloud mushroomed higher and higher into the sky.

The starboard lookout said, "There's another one of those clouds to the northeast. And another one due north."

"Three atomic bombs, Skipper," Lemon whistled. "I guess that answers your question."

ABOUT WILLIAM STROOCK

William Stroock is the author of more than 20 novels and two history books. He is a former teacher and adjunct professor of history. Will has published dozens of military history articles with magazines in North America and Europe including *Strategy & Tactics, History Magazine*, *Military Heritage*, *Civil War Quarterly, Medieval Warfare, Ancient Warfare*, *Military History Matters* and many others. Will lives in northern New Jersey with his wife and three daughters.

Will blogs at Stroock's Books (they rhyme) and Substack. His novels are available at Amazon.

RED TAILED TIGERS

Justin Watson

RED TAILED TIGERS

Justin Watson

Benny rocked as the C-47's wheels hit the tarmac. Standing five-foot-eight and a heavily muscled one hundred sixty pounds, Benny had caramel skin and refined, patrician features, thanks to his Creole mother. Until three days ago, he'd also been an Air Force officer with a promising career ahead of him.

The cargo plane rolled for about five more minutes, Benny swaying miserably in his seat the whole way before the roar of the engines turned into a whine and then came to a full stop. Benny ran a hand across his brow and wiped the accumulated perspiration on the gooney bird's canvas seat before lurching to his feet. Benjamin Jakes and Robin Olds were the only other passengers; the rest of the hold was filled with crates of .50 caliber ammunition. Benny gave Olds a baleful look.

"What? It's no worse than the Philippines," Olds said, retrieving his duffel bag. "Aren't you from Louisiana?"

"I feel like I'm drinking the air," Benny said.

"Bitch, bitch, bitch," Olds said.

"Gentlemen," the C-47 pilot said as he stepped out of the cockpit. "Welcome to Gia Lam Airport, jewel of Hanoi. The temperature is five degrees hotter than hell and it's humid enough to drown a fucking fish. If you head down the gangway and take a left, the 4th AVG building is right there. No offense, fellas, but shake a leg. I can't get out of this hellhole until they come unload all this ammo."

The pilot was a middle-aged man with thinning gray hair.

"All right, buddy, we're moving," Olds said. "High risk of air raid here, I take it?"

"Nah," the cargo pilot said, tapping out a cigarette and lighting it. "The war is all out on the frontier with Laos and Cambodia. Both sides are leaving the rear areas alone for the moment."

"So why are you in such a hurry?" Benny said.

The pilot took a drag off his cigarette and chuckled.

"Because I fucking hate it here," he said.

The sun was blinding after the dim cargo hold, and it cooked Benny's head and shoulders unmercifully as they trekked across the tarmac. On their way to an oversized Quonset hut, with a simple wooden sign that read, "4th AVG," Benny counted sixteen straight-winged, smooth nosed P-80 jets waiting on the flight line, and twice that number, each, of single-propeller driven P-51 *Mustangs*, P-47 *Thunderbolts* and fork-tailed P-38 *Lightnings*.

"You had to deck that colonel," Olds said.

Benny glared at Olds. His friend was a solid five inches taller than him and seemed as wide as a barn door with a broad, square face that bore no hint of chagrin.

"He tried to deck me," Benny said. "*After* you provoked him."

Olds shrugged.

"He shouldn't have called you a nigger," Olds said.

"That's my fight, Robin," Benny said. "Do you want fly jets or go around punching every bigot in the Air Force? The latter is going to take you a lot of time."

"They both sound fun, to be honest," Olds said. "Look, are you going to keep bitching at me, or can we check in and start flying jets?"

"You brought it up."

Benny and Olds continued their trek across the tarmac.

"They've got a nice little Air Force going here," Olds said.

"Yeah," Benny said, pulling the door to the hut open. "Wonder what all the French have got on the other side. Besides the 262s, of course."

The clattering of typewriters and static-ridden radio chatter greeted them as they stepped inside. The layout was familiar, with maps and charts dominating large tables in the center of the space, illuminated by intermittent bulbs hung from the peak of the arced ceiling.

"Okay, tell the bombers we'll have escort up in five minutes." A deep

Texas drawl drew Benny's eyes to a radio set on the other side of a massive map of Vietnam. "They can sortie now, and we'll get ahead of them."

The speaker was a tall, lean man with a broad face and over-prominent ears. He looked up from the radio just in time to see Benny and Olds step through the door.

"Olds, Jakes," he said. "They told me ya'll were coming. Good: now we've got a four-ship."

"Sir?" Benny said.

"This ain't the Air Force, Jakes, I'm the boss, David Miller," he said. "Call me Tex. And I'm glad you're in flight suits, because we've got a mission."

"Sir, what?" Olds said. "We just got here—"

"And now that I have you, that makes four P-80 qualified pilots between you me and Jesus over there." Miller pronounced the name *Hey-soos*, and pointed to a swarthy man bent over the map. Jesus looked up and gave them both a toothy grin.

Benny exchanged a look with Olds, who shrugged.

"What's the mission, sir?" Olds said.

"I told ya'll call me Tex," Miller said. "The Viet Minh have a company of Frenchies pinned on our side of the border. We're sending a passel of Jugs to hammer 'em real good. The P-51s will sweep ahead and level, we four are going to fly outlaw high, and surprise them sonsabitches if they show up in their German jets.

"Here, I'll show you the route on the map..."

Benny applied a bit of pressure to his stick and compensated with the opposite rudder pedal to drop his P-80's left wing while maintaining course. Several thousand feet below, he saw flights of P-47 *Thunderbolts* diving on the jungle like piston-driven angels of vengeance. Explosions reverberated through the thick jungle air as the verdant treetop canopy was alternately consumed by clouds of fire from bombs, then perforated by hailstorms of .50-caliber rounds. At this altitude, he couldn't make out anything of the enemy ground force, but if the Jugs were even remotely accurate, the French were not having a good day.

"Eight Bandits, ten o'clock low," Hill announced. "Olds, Jakes, you got high flight, we'll take low. Dive in on them, then lay on the throttle and get some distance before you reengage. If you get into real trouble, climb as soon as you can extend; we got 'em beat for speed and ceiling."

Benny saw two flights of four Me 262s staggered in altitude by about two thousand feet, laterally by about five thousand. Rather than the Buck Rogers shape of the P-80s, the Me 262s followed much the same pattern as the propeller-driven planes of the '40s. Their graceful lines were marred only by the massive jet engines slung under each wing. The French pilots were boring in on the P-47s, probably intent on relieving their comrades on the ground.

"Roger, acknowledge all. Tally Bandits," Olds answered. "Engaging."

Benny felt his stomach lurch in negative G as he put his P-80's nose below the horizon and followed Olds's dive. They didn't need to talk, automatically sub-dividing their targets as they had a hundred times before in training.

As they came close enough to see roundels on the Messerschmidt's wings, Benny adjusted his approach to a more lateral vector. It added deflection to the shot, which made it trickier, but would allow him to engage the second target more easily.

Applying fractional adjustments on the stick and rudder pedals, Benny put the gunsight piper right over the 262's wing joint and squeezed the trigger on his control stick. Metallic clatter filled his ears, the sky before him burned with muzzle flashes, and the cockpit rocked with the recoil of six .50-caliber machine guns each firing twenty rounds per second. Red tracers lanced through the sky and tore into the first French jet's fuselage. Benny was rewarded with an orange and black explosion, followed by the sight of the 262's right wing falling away. The remainder of the jet spun off toward the distant ground.

That's five. Benny grinned behind his oxygen mask. *I'm a bona fide fucking ace!*

In his peripheral vision, Benny saw Olds's target burst into flames and plummet. The surviving French jets banked hard left, then split, one climbing, the other diving. Benny yanked his stick until his wings were perpendicular to the horizon to stay on the low man. Acceleration pressed him into his seat, and his G-suit constricted around him, slowing the flow of blood toward his feet. He grunted as he fought the pipper out in front of the enemy. Once he judged the lead sufficient, he squeezed the trigger again, sending another burst from his six machine guns arcing toward his enemy. His P-80 was only one hundred meters away from the Frenchman when the 262's canopy shattered from the impact of several dozen .50 caliber rounds, sending glittering fragments all about. The plane inverted less than a second later and began to spin to the ground.

Six, Benny thought, as he pulled his P-80 about and climbed to regain his position on Olds's tail. *This is shaping up to be a good war.*

"Benny, get up here," Olds said, his voice calm but strained. "I got a bandit at six."

Scanning the skies, it took Benny precious seconds to spot the 262 on Olds's tail. Olds was maneuvering violently, but the French pilot was staying with him, using his lower speed and tighter turn radius to keep Olds in front of him as they scissored back and forth across the sky. Benny opened his throttle to close the gap, his P-80 shooting up into the sky at thirty-five meters per second.

"Break right and climb, Rob," Benny said. "I've got him."

Olds's P-80 banked hard, and its nose shot skyward as instructed. This Me 262 pilot had better situational awareness than his friends, though. After a missed snapshot at Olds, the jet dropped into a split S, falling out of Benny's sight picture just as he pulled the trigger.

Damn. Gravity pulled Benny against his restraints as he inverted his jet to get a better look down. Enemy in sight, he pulled his stick back and sacrificed altitude for energy, closing on the 262 in a dive. The 262 was still on his guard, though, and the Frenchman's hard bank took him out of Benny's gun sight again, forcing Benny to level off to maintain pursuit.

This guy is a good stick, Benny thought. As he brought his nose up from the dive, the enemy pilot attempted another high-G bank, trying to get Benny to overshoot. Benny countered by pulling his nose up and then into a roll, completing a high yo-yo. It prevented an overshoot, but only barely, as the 262 now filled Benny's forward canopy and his plane shook with the enemy's jetwash. At this range, there was no need to worry about the gun sight. Benny mashed the trigger, cutting his enemy to ribbons with a point-blank stream of .50-caliber rounds.

There was no time to avoid the resultant fireball and cloud of debris; dozens of chunks of molten hot steel clattered against his fuselage. Something big enough to jerk the P-80's nose hard right impacted with a loud *BANG* as he cleared the cloud. A bare three seconds later, his engine began to sputter, his plane shook, and then the cockpit was filled with deadly silence as the roar of his jet engine died.

Benny gently pulled his stick and pressed the rudder pedals until his nose was pointed east, deeper into Vietnam.

"My engine is dead," Benny reported, sounding calmer than he felt. "I'm on glide path east. Going to bail out before I go into a spin."

"Roger, Benny," Tex answered him. "We've got friendlies all over the area. Stay calm, we'll have search and rescue to you in no time."

"Acknowledged," Benny said. "See you later, guys!"

Grunting with effort, Benny worked the canopy release lever. The mechanism gave way with a pop, and the glass and steel canopy flew away into the sky. He was buffeted with hot wind as he undid his restraints, and clumsily hauled himself out of his seat. A carpet of green tree tops rushed upward to meet him. Heart pounding, hands shaking, Benny made his way out of the cockpit and onto the wing and unceremoniously fell off, plummeting toward the ground like a rock.

Oh, Jesus Christ!

Fighting the panic, Benny struggled against swirling atmosphere and his own momentum to get into a flat arched position, arms and legs splayed to each side. It took precious seconds of effort and hundreds of feet of altitude before he stabilized. He tasted bile in the back of his mouth, and he was pretty certain his pants were now soaked in his own piss, but at least he was alive. In the distance, he saw his P-80's angle of descent steepen, then go nearly perpendicular to the ground as it crashed into the jungle, the secondary explosion lighting up the treetops.

Benny yanked the ripcord, and his parachute harness dug violently into his groin and shoulders, drawing another grunt from him. Dangling from the silk, risers in hand, he finally was able to draw several deep breaths and take stock of the situation around him.

The bombing and strafing had ceased. He could see the P-47s vanishing east, back toward the airfields. The dogfight seemed to be over, too. The three P-80s were flying a wide racetrack orbit around him, close enough to see, far enough not to catch his chute in jetwash. Glad to have friends close by, he turned his attention to his next task: figuring out where the hell he was going to land.

Gaps in the jungle canopy were few and narrow. Picking the best of bad options, Benny pulled down on his left riser, trying to steer towards something other than solid treetop. Despite his efforts, tree branches pummeled his legs and torso as he fell into the jungle. Benny struggled to keep his feet and knees together. The branches batted and scraped at him, taking scraps of flightsuit and swaths of skin from him on his way down.

Finally, he broke through the lowest branches and crumpled to the jungle floor like a sack of shit. Miraculously, his chute hadn't caught in the trees. Battered from both high-G maneuvering and his descent through the treetops, Benny hit the releases on his parachute and laid back in the thick grass. The humidity and heat were oppressive, but he took a few breaths to enjoy the quiet, anyway.

Running feet and voices shouting in a singsong language shattered his calm. Springing to his feet, he looked around and saw that green palm fronds and bush cut visibility to mere feet in every direction. He was debating whether or not to hide when three short men in too-baggy green fatigues burst through the bushes to his left, rifles leveled at him. They were shouting in the same singsong language he couldn't understand. He noted that the rifles were M1 Carbines, the fatigues clearly American cast offs.

Benny put his hands in the air. *Now if only I can convince them not to shoot me.*

"Hey, guys," he said. "Same side. I'm here to shoot down French jets."

The tallest of the three men advanced on Benny, almond-shaped eyes wide with anger and adrenaline.

"Hold on, now," Benny said, hands still up. "Just wait—"

The man slammed the butt of his carbine into the side of Benny's face. Benny's vision went white, then black, then puckered with sparkling gold stars as the interwoven branches and leaves of the jungle canopy started to come back into focus. As if through a funnel, he heard another voice. This one was definitely American, with a corn belt rasp.

"Goddamn it, Dat, he's an American." The voice was shouting in English before switching to the native patois. *"Người Pháp không để người da đen bay máy bay, Thang cho de!"*

Benny was only vaguely aware of hands lifting him off the soft jungle floor and carrying him...somewhere. Somewhere in the jungle with a large cloud of yellow smoke, and a...a massive ceiling fan? What the hell...

The long swim up from the depths started with a dull pain in his lower back, then another sharper one in his head. Light crept in at the seams of his eyelids, then muffled voices that sounded as if they originated on the other side of a thin door. The air around him smelled of ethanol and iron. Cracking a single eye, bright morning sun penetrated his pupil like a lance into his brain, eliciting an involuntary croak from him.

He heard footsteps on tile and one of the voices growing closer, more distinct. The voice was pleasant, feminine and...French?

Forcing his eyelids open and accepting the resultant stabbing pain, Benny appraised his surroundings. He was lying on a hard mattress with rough linens at the end of a long line of beds, about half of them occupied. An intravenous needle was lodged in his left arm, its tube leading up to a glass bottle full of clear solution, and he wasn't wearing anything besides a pair of skivvy shorts.

The first person he saw was a woman who strode rapidly toward his bedside. She was clothed in green fatigues, with the sleeves rolled to her elbows. Her chestnut hair was bound up neatly in a tight bun, and she smiled at him warmly. Benny found himself staring into her large, dark eyes. She was such an incongruously lovely vision for a war zone.

"Good Morning, Mr. Jakes," she said, her English clear but heavily French-accented. "I'm so happy you've elected to rejoin us."

Benny tried to straighten up in bed, his expression hardening.

"*Bonjour*, Mademoiselle," Benny said, his parched throat grating the French words before they could escape his lips. *"Suis-je un prisonnier, alors?"*

She chuckled as she reached for a pitcher of water and glass from a shelf behind his bed.

"No, you are certainly not," she said as she poured the glass and held it out to him. "Though I understand your confusion, I am one of many free Frenchmen and women here in Indochina aiding our Vietnamese and American friends."

Benny didn't take the glass. Incredulity marred his features.

"You're aiding us against your own people?" he said.

"They are no longer my people," she said, thrusting the glass at him. "They are Nazis. Take this—you must rehydrate. You have been asleep for more than a day, and saline solution isn't as good as drinking your fill."

He accepted the glass with a chagrined expression and drained it in one draught.

"Forgive me if I've offended you," he said, handing the glass back to her. "The narcotics must have made me stupid. Is the doctor available? I feel much better, and I want to get back to my unit."

She arched a dark brown eyebrow at him and accepted the empty glass.

"*I* am the doctor, Mr. Jakes," she said. "Dr. Margot Durand, at your service. And no, you are not leaving. You suffered a significant head trauma. Your waking wasn't a forgone conclusion, not to mention the lacerations you suffered. If you don't let those heal up properly, you are asking for some nasty infections."

"Oh, sure, give the lazy bastard an excuse to lay about some more," a familiar booming voice interrupted from the door.

Benny turned his head just enough to see Robin Olds's bulk filling the doorframe at the near end of the ward. He was dressed in a green flight suit, a grin on his big blunt face.

"Mr. Olds," Durand said. "I will thank you to lower your voice. I have patients resting in this ward."

"Oh, I'm very sorry, Doctor," Olds said, with no discernible change in volume. "I'm just glad to see my friend here awake."

Durand's expression was suddenly much more stern, and she didn't bother to hide her asperity when she spoke again.

"Very well," she said. "I will give you ten minutes to chat, but no more. Mr. Jakes also needs rest."

She turned to leave, but before she could go, Benny spoke up.

"Dr. Durand, would it be possible to speak to the chopper pilot who flew me out?" he said.

Durand turned back to him, a slight smile on her full lips.

"This is possible," she said. "What would you say?"

"Well, anyone with the...gumption...to fly that tinker toy into combat deserves at least a drink for it," Benny said. "He's a braver man than me."

"I'll pass that along," she said. Her smile hardened into something more severe when she turned her eyes on Olds. "Ten minutes."

Olds was chuckling even as he spared an appreciative glance at Durand's retreating form. Even the baggy fatigue pants didn't hide her curves and the sway of her hips as she walked. Benny found himself annoyed with Olds and then annoyed that he was annoyed.

"What are you laughing about?" Benny asked.

"She flew the helicopter, buddy boy," Olds said.

"What?" Benny said, sitting up straighter. "Stop screwing with me."

"Cross my heart and hope to die, Benny," Olds said, grinning. "A body like that and she can fly, too. A helicopter, no less. Frankly, I'm not sure how it generates enough lift to keep her big brass ovaries in the air."

"No shit," Benny said. "They sent a Frenchwoman to flight school?"

"Not so much," Olds said. "The Agency let her finish medical school and come here as a surgeon. She convinced the head of the whirlybird detachment to teach her to fly. Then she started flying search and rescue with no one's permission. Feldman tried to stop her, but she's rescued sixty-three men, and operated on twenty-six of them, so he gave up on that. The guys around here worship her."

"Sweet Jesus," Benny said.

"Yeah, the lady gets what she wants," Olds said. "I mean, do you think you'd have any luck saying no to her?"

Benny didn't answer that. He knew better than to get infatuated with a white woman.

"How did we make out, anyway?" Benny said. "You're here, I assume Tex and Jesus made it back, too?"

"They did," Olds said. "We didn't even lose any Jugs. You're the only one who took a walk. I asked Hill if you counted as your own kill since you basically shot yourself down."

"Ass," Benny said with no real heat.

"Guilty," Olds said. "Regardless, you, me and Tex are the first Americans with jet kills. You've got three confirmed from yesterday, I downed two and a half, Jesus got one and Tex got three and a half. Congratulations, Ace."

"Wow, we really mauled them," Benny said.

"Sure did, half a squadron gone for one of our planes," Olds said. "We can trade eight for one all day, especially if we get our pilot back, anyway."

A Texas drawl interjected.

"Woulda' been eight for ought if y'all had listened to what the hell I told you." Tex Hill stepped through the door. He was dressed in a sweat-stained flight suit and looked tired and exasperated rather than exultant.

"Come on, Tex," Olds said. "We nailed them, didn't we?"

"You nailed 'em because you're both shit hot on the stick," Hill said, his drawl becoming more pronounced as he grew angrier. "But if you'd made one pass, dived and used your speed to create a gap before you reengaged, like I damned well told you to, I'd have sixteen P-80s instead of fifteen."

Benny frowned. It felt wrong getting a lecture after he'd just become an ace, but he saw Hill's point. If they'd listened, they wouldn't have had to dogfight the French at all for their kills.

"You're right, sir," Benny said before Robin could speak. "No excuse."

Tex's expression relaxed.

"Oh, can the kay-det crap, Benny," Tex said. "Truth is, you flew great, and I appreciate aggression. Just keep in mind, you're about to be taking new guys into combat. They see you taking unnecessary risks, they might put themselves in a situation where you can pull it out of the fire, but they can't."

Olds exhaled, visibly letting go of a counterargument.

"Hell, you're right, Tex," Olds said. "I'm sorry, too."

"Sorry don't kill Messerschmitts, boys. Just learn," Tex said. "And do better."

Movement in his peripheral vision drew Benny's eye away from Tex to Durand, who stepped next to his bed, clearing her throat.

"Pardon me, gentlemen," Durand said. "But I need to examine him and then he will need to rest."

"Of course, ma'am," Tex said. "How long do you think he'll be out?"

"At least a week," Durand said. "I need to evaluate the effects of his head trauma and his wounds need to close up properly before he returns to the cockpit."

Tex frowned, but he didn't argue.

"All right, then," he said. "I suppose a week of vacation for making ace isn't too much to ask. I'll check in on you later, Jakes. Come on, Olds, you heard the doctor."

"See you later, Benny," Olds said.

Durand pulled a small flashlight from a fatigue pocket and sat down on Benny's bed next to him. Taking his wrist in her hands, she found his vein with her fingers, and he saw her nodding as she counted his pulse. Benny realized, of course, that she was just being a medical professional, but his body took her touch in all the wrong ways. He took a deep breath, trying to slow his heartrate, and thought of penguins. Apparently satisfied, Durand dropped his wrist without comment and put her left hand on his cheek, tilting his eyes toward her and leaned in close, shining the flashlight in his eyes.

"Your eyes are dilating properly," she said, putting away the flashlight and pulling a fountain pen from her breast pocket. "This is very good. Please now follow my pen without moving your head."

Benny tracked the tip of the pen without issue as she moved it right and left, up and down in front of his face. The pen stopped in front of her nose, and when she dropped it, he was staring into her eyes again. She met his gaze for a long moment, her chin tilted just slightly to the side, a hint of mischief tugging her lips into a smile.

"Also very good," she said, unscrewing the cap of the fountain pen and reaching for a clipboard hanging from a nail beside his bed.

"Thank you," Benny said. "For saving my life, I mean."

"For flying my 'tinker toy' into combat to get you, you mean?" Durand said, an impish smile blossoming on her face. "It wasn't as dramatic as all that. The boys had the enemy on the run. I didn't even take small arms fire."

Benny snorted and shook his head. *Brass ovaries indeed.*

"What?" Durand said. "Several men tried to kill you yesterday, and you don't seem perturbed by the fact. Why should I feel differently?"

"You've got me there," Benny admitted. "Thank you, nonetheless."

Durand finished what she was writing with a bold stroke and recapped her pen before answering him.

"You are most welcome," she said. "Now tell me, where did you learn to speak French so well?"

"My family is from New Orleans," Benny said. "My mother made sure I could speak French. My grandmother didn't even speak English."

"It's an interesting accent," Durand said. "It reminds me of my grandfather. He was a country farmer and always spoke a bit rougher than his cousins from Paris. *Tres masculin.*"

As she reached out to put the clipboard back on its nail, Benny noticed a tattoo on her forearm. It was nothing artistic, just a long series of small black numbers. Durand saw him staring at it, and her smile vanished. Realizing he'd upset her, though not why, Benny dropped his gaze.

"I'm sorry," he muttered. "I didn't mean to make you uncomfortable."

"It's all right," Durand said. "I'll check in on you later. If there's anything you need while I'm out of the ward, just let one of the nurses know and they'll take care of you."

"Thank you again," Benny said.

"It is my pleasure again," Durand said, making her tone light with visible effort. "Perhaps when you are not my patient anymore, I'll let you buy that drink you owe me."

"Oh, you don't have to—" Benny said, "I mean, I didn't know you were a... That is, I wouldn't want to embarrass you or..."

Benny Jakes, flying ace and stammering idiot.

"Embarrass me how? Are you reneging on your debt, Mr. Jakes?" Durand said.

"Of course not," Benny said. "I just wouldn't want anyone to gossip, if you were seen socializing with, well, with me outside of a professional setting."

"Oh, Mr. Jakes," Durand said, disarming smile back in place. "I'm a big girl and I socialize with whomever I please. You rest now. We'll chat more later."

Six weeks later, Benny and his three charges were cruising eastward, closing on a final approach back to Gia Lam in a standard finger-four formation.

He smiled behind his oxygen mask. Four French Stukas were smoking wrecks just on the Laotian side of the border; they'd been dead before they'd known they were in danger.

The hunting was a lot thinner these days. The French became careful about how and when they employed their airpower, taking pains to avoid the threat from the P-80 squadron. They sent their Sturmvogel ground-attack Me 262s only for quick bombing raids wherever the P-80s weren't.

On the bright side, American planes and volunteer pilots continued to flow into Vietnam. Between Free Vietnamese Air Force and AVG pilots, they now had sixteen qualified P-80 pilots and eighteen operational airframes. Initially, Tex had divided out the American and Vietnamese pilots evenly amongst the four flights. Each flight got three Americans and one Vietnamese pilot.

As it turned out, though, Benny was the only leader who spoke decent French. The other three flight leads became quickly frustrated by the language barrier, and Tex reassigned all three Vietnamese pilots to Benny's flight.

At first, he'd found his new subordinates to be competent pilots, but on the timid side and entirely too deferential for fighter jocks. However, three weeks getting to know them revealed they suffered no deficit of killer instinct and, while still scrupulously polite, they each displayed keen and quirky humor the longer they were in the flight.

Earlier that morning when he'd walked out to the flight line, he'd noted that his four ships had a new coat of paint on the tail. Tex Miller had insisted on shark's teeth on all the P-80s, but only Benny's birds had a bright red coat of paint on the tail.

When he'd asked his maintenance chief, Sergeant Hernandez, about the surprise aesthetic modification, the man had looked at Benny like the answer was obvious.

"Well, sir, you were in the 332nd in the War, and you guys kicked ass," Hernandez had stated. "I figured it would be good luck."

"Excellent travail aujourd'hui, les hommes," Benny told his men. "Now let's give them a show. Keep it tight."

"D'accord," each of his men acknowledged the order.

Switching back to English to talk to the Tower, he announced his intentions.

"Tower, this is Tiger Four on final approach," Benny said. "Stand by for victory loop."

"Tiger Four," the Tower operator responded in a clipped Boston accent. "You are cleared for loop."

Benny kicked his plane into a wide cork-screwing series of turns over the runway, his men following him perfectly. His grin grew wider as the Gs pulled him this way and that against the restraints. As the end of the runway passed beneath him, he leveled out for three seconds before pulling his nose hard up, shooting into the air, all the way over into a loop that put them back on approach to Gia Lam.

"Good show, boys," Benny said. "Now let's get into our normal landing pattern. I'll see you all at the O Club tonight. Drinks on me."

The O Club's turntable was connected to some surprisingly good speakers, so they had jazz records piped in with their meal. The décor was all rich browns and golds, definitely an artifact of the Club's previous owners. Robin and two of his guys were mangling a waltz with three of the nurses on the dance floor while Benny and his pilots celebrated the day's victories on the second-floor balcony.

"We're tied at four kills, Tran," Ngo Than Duc, the oldest and shortest of the three Vietnamese said. "But you're still a *trinh nữ* in jets."

"Eat shit," Tran Hien Vo, the youngest, replied. "I'll put five thousand piastres against your sister's virtue that I'll be the first Vietnamese ace."

"That's a losing bet," Lee Phi Hung, Benny's wingman and the middle "child" of his pilots, said. "No way something as battered as his sister's virtue is worth five thousand piastres."

All four pilots roared at that.

"Ngo, what's a 'trin new?'" Benny said when they'd stopped laughing. His Vietnamese was improving, but his guys still talked mostly French around him out of courtesy.

"It's, ah..." Ngo stopped. "I don't know the French word."

"Sir, it means he's never, ah..." Lee made a circle with left thumb and forefinger and poked his index finger through it in universal sign language.

"I see," Benny said, laughing again.

A figure in a dark red dress caught Benny's eye, approaching the bar below. Conversation forgotten, he stared like a moonstruck schoolboy. He'd thought Margot beautiful from the first time he'd laid eyes on her, but in a red, form-fitting silk dress, she appeared as something from a dream.

Benny frowned. He'd taken lunch several times with Margot Durand, always accompanied by Robin and one of Margot's nurses or another woman for proper chaperonage. Margot seemed amused by Benny's insistence on the propriety, but she was no less charming and interesting for it. They shared an affinity for Victor Hugo, and Jazz, and enjoyed their disagreements regarding the merits of Camus and Sartre's works—those published before World War II, or smuggled out following both men's executions in 1945.

Damn Vichy, Benny thought. As Margot moved around the room, his thoughts turned back to the French doctor. He was drawn to her, but wary. Miscegenation was still illegal in most of the United States. Openly romancing a white woman could get him arrested; hell, even sharing a table with Margot, as he'd already done, could get him murdered back home in Louisiana. This wasn't Louisiana by several decimal places, but survival habits died hard.

But women like Margot don't grow on trees.

When he pulled his eyes off Margot, he saw that all three of his men were grinning knowingly at him.

"*Dai uy*, why don't you go wish Dr. Margot a pleasant evening?" Ngo said. "We'll be all right up here."

"No, no," Benny said. "I shouldn't—"

"No, sir, really, go ahead," Tran chimed in. "Unless you're afraid..."

"Go to hell, Tran," Benny said. "I hope Ngo does get his fifth kill before you do."

The table erupted in laughter again as Benny stood up, drawing Margot's eye to their table.

Well, I'm pot-committed now.

Margot followed him down the stairs with her eyes, all the way to the bar, an inviting smile on her face the whole time.

"Benny," she said, her accent inflecting the y at the end of his name in a manner he'd come to appreciate. "I saw the victory loop; you broke the dry streak today. Congratulations."

"Merci beaucoup," Benny said, returning her smile. "You look especially lovely tonight, Margot."

"You are too kind," Margot said, her wide, dark eyes reflecting the warm incandescent light of the club.

"I am too honest," Benny said, shaking his head. "And I must be crazy."

"Why? Because you find yourself interested in a woman? This is a strange definition of insanity, Benjamin," Margot said.

"Do I really have to spell it out for you?" Benny said. "Is France really that progressive, that it just doesn't matter? Or did you miss the fact that I'm black as the as the ace of spades?"

"You are most certainly not," Margot said, lifting her chin. "You are a lovely chocolate and caramel shade; I find it most appealing."

"Oh, for Christ's sake, Margot," Benny said, putting a hand to his face and rubbing his forehead.

A dark line appeared between Margot's eyebrows and something not entirely pleasant flickered in her lovely eyes. She was quiet for a moment, staring at Benny. Suddenly she thrust out her right forearm, palm up to show the ivory skin covering her veins and the series of numbers he'd seen that first day in the hospital.

"You saw this in the hospital," Margot said. "You didn't ask what it was."

"You seemed upset when I noticed," Benny said. "I didn't want to distress you."

"That's very polite," She said. "It is from Ravensbruck. Is this a place you have heard of?"

It sounds familiar...oh... Oh.

"My God," Benny said. "The camps—"

"Yes, the camps," Margot said, dropping her arm. "I was at Ravensbruck from 1943 until 1945, when your government negotiated our release."

"I didn't even know you were Jewish," Benny said. "I'm so sorry, I can't even imagine--"

"I am not Jewish," She cut him off. "I left medical school to fight with the resistance. I had already killed four policemen and a collaborating mayor. When I tried for an SS Obergruppenfuhrer, it did not go as well."

Benny felt respect conflating with terror as he looked at her.

"I'll spare you the details of everything they did to me," Margot continued. "Afterward, I thought that I was broken by it, that they had turned me into something worth less than a whore. After we were deported, I spent months feeling sorry for myself. One day, though, I realized that I am a survivor. The French fighting for the Reich? *They* are the whores."

She paused, visibly taking an effort to calm herself.

"Your people would not put me in a position to fight them," she said. "So I rescue warriors, heal you so you can kill them for me. Through all that pain, I learned to reach for what I want, Benjamin."

Benny heard the determination in her voice and could almost guess what was coming next.

"When I say I do not care what others think when we are together, allow me to be absolutely clear: I do not give a single *fuck* what anyone else thinks of us," Margot said. "I have faced much worse than them. I like you, and I think you like me, too. If that isn't true, then by all means, I shall not trouble you further."

Margot took a step back and started to turn on her heel. Benny reached out and put a hand on her arm.

"Margot, wait," he said.

"Wait for what, Benny? You to get a chaperone so we can continue this conversation without offending bigots?"

Benny thought furiously. He didn't know what to say. Five minutes ago, he'd thought their relationship impossible; now it seemed nothing in the world mattered more than convincing her to stay. In the background, the record changed and Fred Astaire's voice filled the room to a smooth bass and piano accompaniment.

"They all laughed at Christopher Columbus,
When he said the world was round..."

"Dr. Durand, would you dance with me?" Benny said.

Removing his right hand from her arm, he extended his left hand palm up in a time-honored courtly gesture. Margot's eyes widened for a long moment. Then, slowly, she smiled again and the light returning to her eyes seared his anxiety away. She placed her right hand in his left.

"Yes, Mr. Jakes," she said. "I would love to dance."

Benny led her to the dance floor, aware of every eye following them. Only Margot, her hand still warm and gripping his firmly, allowed him to ignore them all. She flowed into his arms, assuming an elegant, strong frame against his. They moved into an easy foxtrot together, gliding across the floor with a stride that was simultaneously jaunty and graceful. She picked up on the rhythm naturally and followed his lead without a missed step.

"You know how to dance," Benny said.

"So do you," Margot said.

Benny twirled Margot into an underarm turn and back into his arms, then a reverse turn to shadow position for a few counts, her back to him with his hand on her stomach. He picked up the floral scent of shampoo on her chestnut hair before she returned to his arms to glide across the floor once again.

Everyone else in the world fell away. There was only Margot and the music.

They opened up into a promenade. Margot's shapely legs flashed as they strode across the floor, and as they came back together for the final beat of the song, she pressed her body fully against his, drawing a sharp breath of surprise from him.

"That's not part of the foxtrot," Benny said.

Margot batted her eyes and leaned up to whisper in his ear.

"It is in France."

Applause and a wolf whistle pierced the spell of the dance. He spared a glance for the room. Robin Olds was standing near the turn table, grinning broadly and clapping; upstairs, Tran, Ngo and Lee were likewise applauding. The rest of the officers in the club and their dates were torn: some smiling and clapping, some looked uncomfortable, and a handful glared.

To hell with you, gentlemen, Benny thought as he bowed to the crowd and Margot curtsied like a born queen. *For once, you just wish you were me.*

The next morning as he stepped into 4th AVG headquarters, Benny could hear explosions and gunfire over the radio speakers, along with the voices of men doing their best to maintain laconic professionalism under fire.

"Tiger Main, this is Ajax Main," a static ridden midwestern voice announced. "We have one company engaged with a battalion in the hamlets three kilometers to our direct east. Another company has been cut off on the northeast bank of the lake, five klicks out. We estimate at least two enemy battalions. Ajax Main and Ajax North are both under intermittent indirect fire, over."

"Understood, Ajax," Tex said. "We're loading bombs now. ETA one hour, over."

"We need you ASAP, Tiger," a note of fear crept into the voice from the other end. "That company on the lake can't last long."

"Roger, Ajax," Tex said. "My staff will be monitoring this net. Send updates. We'll be there as soon as we can. Tiger Main, out."

Robin stepped into the building behind Benny, followed by Jesus.

"What's going on, Tex?" Robin said, his usually cheerful face grim.

"The base at Pleiku and the outpost at Kon Tum are under attack," Tex said. "The French crossed the border in division strength an hour ago. We're loading bombs now and sortieing the whole squadron because we can get there faster than anyone else. Ground intercept radar doesn't report any enemy air, but we'll be cautious. When we get there, Benny and Jesus will take the first bomb runs, while Olds and me fly high cover, then we'll switch. Eventually, the prop birds will catch up and we can rotate out to refuel and rearm. Get to your birds."

Benny pulled his stick back and leveled out twenty feet above the treetops. Ahead of him, breaking up the green jungle-infested hills of the highlands was a massive blue lake. On the northeast bank of the lake he caught muzzle flashes in between the tiny gaps in the vegetation, but couldn't make out any of the human shapes beneath the canopy.

"Ajax Main, this is Tiger Four checking in," Benny announced over the advisor's frequency. He was answered immediately.

"Glad to hear it, Tiger Four," the same midwestern voice he'd heard back at the AVG answered. "Stand by for the advisor on the scene. Ajax One-Six, we have air, over."

"Roger, Ajax Main," said another voice, this one with a French accent. "Tiger Four, this is Ajax One-Six. Recommend you make your run northeast to southwest, parallel to our position, initial point on or north of Zebra-Baker Zero-One-Zero, One-Five-Two. That pattern should keep you clear of the gun-target line from the artillery at Ajax Main."

Cool customer. Benny could hear intense machine gun fire, thuds, explosions, and the screams of the wounded, but Ajax One-Six's voice was steady as a rock and he had the presence of mind to try and deconflict friendly artillery with air. Benny relayed the new plan to Tran, Ngo and Lee in French, then switched back to English to talk to Ajax One-Six.

"Ajax One-Six, roger," Benny said. "You have sixteen P-80s with two thousand-pound bombs each. We can't see shit through the canopy. Can you mark your forward position and the enemy's approximate center of mass?"

"Roger, Tiger," the voice answered. "Marking our forward position first."

A few seconds later, a plume of green smoke drifted through the treetops, about two hundred meters from the riverbed.

"One-Six, I see green smoke," Benny said. "Confirm green smoke, over."

"Roger, Tiger," One-Six said. "Green smoke, stand by for enemy center of mass."

Even in the cockpit, he heard the report of the howitzer from over in Pleiku. Thirty seconds later, a much larger cloud of white smoke billowed into existence *over* the treetops, about four hundred meters north and east of the green smoke.

"Ajax One-Six, I tally white smoke," Benny said. "I say again, white smoke. Be advised target mark is well within danger close of your position."

"Roger, Tiger Four," the same calm tone replied. "I confirm white smoke on the target, acknowledge danger close."

"I have visual on friendly markings, I tally target marking," Benny said. "I am at the IP now. Four-ship in the initial pass."

"Roger, Tiger Four, you are cleared hot," One-Six confirmed.

"Get small, Ajax," Benny said. "This is going to be close."

Benny dropped down to five feet off the tree tops and throttled back to just shy of stall speed. Dropping bombs without a bombsight was very much an art form. As the lead, his steadiness and judgment would dictate the effectiveness of the planes following him. He kept his eyes on the center of the smoke as he made tiny rudder and stick adjustments to maintain level flight against the turbulence bouncing him around the cockpit.

Almost there...right...about...DROP.

Benny hit the bomb release and pulled up and right, opening his throttle to regain airspeed. Even roaring away at hundreds of miles per hour, the detonation of nearly eight thousand pounds of high explosive rattled him in his cockpit.

"Good drop," Ajax One-Six reported. "Keep laying it on."

"All right, Benny, you head to thirty thousand feet and keep an eye out," Tex said. "Robin, head for the IP."

"Much obliged, Tigers," One-Six said after the last flight, Tex's own, had dropped. "We're still taking fire, but we've got some breathing room."

"Can you make it back to friendly lines, One-Six?" Tex asked.

"We're certainly going to try, Tiger," One-Six said. "We've got a lot of wounded, though."

"Stand by," a feminine voice interjected. "This is Angel Three-Five. We are a flight of three Ravens. Meet me at the clearing on the riverbank one hundred meters south by southeast of your green smoke. My rotor cone will fit there. I can take your wounded first, then drop my litters and ferry the rest of your men on the skids."

Margot!

Sure enough, low and to the east, he saw three tiny shapes darting over the canopy toward the river. It took every ounce of professionalism in Benny's body not to tell Margot to get the hell out of here.

Let the woman do her job. You do yours.

"Roger, Angel Three-Five," the advisor on the ground said. "Thanks a lot, both of you. I take back every unkind word I've ever said about flyboys."

"All elements, this is Ajax Main," the plain midwestern voice from earlier blared onto the net. "Ground control radar reports sixteen bogeys coming in from the west. Too fast for propeller-driven birds, bearing two-eight-three."

"Roger, Ajax, coming to two-eight three," Tex acknowledged, his Texas drawl betraying a hint of eagerness. "Tigers, spread out and climb to thirty thousand feet and we'll see if we can dive on these bastards."

Benny relayed the orders in French to his flight and pulled his stick back, following the rest of the squadron up to an altitude the Me 262s couldn't reach. He was surprised the French would sortie their limited number of jets when they had to know the P-80s were in play. They must have really wanted this attack to succeed.

Which means we may be facing a full-scale invasion, not a glorified raid.

With guidance from the radars, they vectored in on the approaching enemy. Three minutes into the approach, Benny spotted a series of black dots against the horizon.

"Tiger One, Tiger Four," Benny said. "I have visual on eight bandits, ten o'clock low."

"Tally, Tiger Four," Tex said. "Maintain altitude until we get a little closer—"

As Tex spoke, all eight dots shot up into the air, followed by eight more. They climbed fast, faster than any Me 262 he'd ever seen, and as the miles between them evaporated. Benny began to see the profile on the approaching enemy didn't fit the cross of a straight-winged jet, but was more of a V.

"Tiger One, those aren't 262s," Benny said. "Those are swept wing. I say again, swept wing airframes."

"Holy shit," Van Camp, one of the newer American pilots, said. "Those are fucking Me 503s."

"Can it, Tiger Three-Two," Tex snapped.

Benny understood the younger pilot's reaction. Intelligence swore on a stack of Bibles that the Germans were retaining the Me 503, the most advanced fighter in Europe, maybe in the world, strictly for Luftwaffe squadrons. Yet here they were. Worse, they were seconds away from effective range now, and the 503s had out-climbed them.

"Wait for them to dive," Tex said. "Then try a defensive roll, see if you can force an overshoot."

Benny translated the orders once again for his flight. It was a liability having to repeat everything in two languages, but it was better than flying three pilots short. In seconds, Benny had the unnerving honor of getting to look right up into a German jet intake, and though he couldn't make them out, he knew the ports for the 503's thirty-millimeter cannons were trained on him.

Don't panic...not yet...NOW.

"Roll," Benny said, matching deed to word. He was thrown against the side of his cockpit as he violently pitched his jet up and out of plane and back down again, Tran, Ngo and Lee following close behind, just as four streams of furious red tracers stitched the sky where they'd been.

The two lead 503s overshot, ending at Benny's one o'clock low. As he pulled his nose violently over, centripetal force and Mother Earth's gravity well cooperated to pull the blood from his brain, opposed instantly by the grip of his g-suit on his abdomen and thighs. Grunting against the pressure, ignoring the gray at the edges of his vision, Benny fought the gun-sight piper onto the lead 503's flight path and fired.

Six streams of tracers erupted from the nose of his craft, lancing through the sky towards the nimble, swept-wing fighter. Benny was rewarded with an orange flash and the sight of the lead Frenchman spinning off toward the jungle below. He gasped in relief as he came out of the high-G turn, only to see the trail 503 perform an impossibly fast and tight bank right out of his firing solution.

Holy shit, those things are nimble.

A part of his brain processed the radio chatter as he tried to keep up with the Messerschmidt.

"Tex, bandit at your six, break right and dive," Robin said.

"Affirm— Ah, shit." Tex's voice cut off abruptly, replaced by Robin swearing briefly and vehemently.

Benny pushed grief away without conscious effort. Nothing he could do for Tex now.

"Two Bandits on our six." Ngo's voice remained steady, if strained. "They're on us tight. Damn it, Tran is down."

Benny spotted the fireball of Tran's P-80 plummeting toward the Earth and Ngo's jet yanking and banking violently, trying to avoid the agile killers on his tail.

"Lee, stay on this one," Benny ordered as he banked hard right to try and save Ngo. The 503s on Ngo's six had *both* focused on the kill, the wingman having forgotten, if only momentarily, that his purpose in life was to watch the leader's six.

Benny made that mistake their last. Lining up the gun sight with relative ease, he sprayed the leader's cockpit with .50 caliber rounds, then gave the wingman the same treatment as he obligingly flew into Benny's sight picture.

"Thanks, Tiger Four." Ngo's relief was palpable, but there was no time to celebrate.

"Jesus, watch your six," Van Camp shouted, "Fuck, Jesus is down!"

"All Tigers, this is Tiger Three," Robin's voice said, still steady amidst the chaos. "Let's set up a weave; we've got to get some distance on these assholes—"

"Tiger Three, this is Hellcat One," a new voice cut in. "Stand by, we're almost there."

"Two 503s are breaking off," VanCamp announced. "They're headed toward the river."

Fuck!

"Angel Three-Five," Benny shouted as he came around, desperately trying to close the gap and get his gun sight on the two runners. "Get the hell out of here. Messerschmitts are closing on you."

"Roger, Tiger Four," Margot answered, but even as she did, the 503s were within range, and they started blazing away at the helicopter formation. He saw the far-right skeletal machine, two men hanging on each skid, shudder, then burst into flames and spin out of control into the river. The center bird sparked with impacts, as well. It skidded on the opposite bank of the river, coming to a stop without a secondary explosion by some miracle.

"Margot!" Benny shouted, just as he aligned his nose on the trail 503 and mashed the trigger for his .50 cals. Despite the impressiveness of their machines, lack of situational awareness killed their pilots all the same. The trail 503 joined its victim in the river. The lead 503 broke hard left and laid on the acceleration.

Benny tried to keep the 503 in his sight, but it was no use. The damn thing was just too fast and agile when aware of a threat. If he split his attention, the bastard would get away, if he didn't maintain situational awareness, he became a target.

As if from nowhere, dozens of tracer streams raced overhead. Benny looked back over his shoulder and saw the sky was filled with sleek P-51s, robust P-47s and fork-tailed P-38s. Superior design or not, the Me 503s now faced the remaining P-80s and several dozen older prop-driven fighters. The French pilots exercised the better part of valor and fled west, faster than any of their enemies could pursue.

Which didn't mean they didn't want to.

"This is Hellcat One," the P-51 squadron leader announced. "We are pursuing."

"Negative, Hellcat One," Robin remonstrated. "They'll lure you until you're low on fuel then sortie the rest of their fighters and cut you to pieces."

"Roger, Tiger Three." The P-51 driver sounded pissed, but he wasn't stupid.

"Angel Three-Five, Angel Three-Five, do you read?" *God, please let her be alive.* "Margot? Do you read?"

Several heartbreaking seconds passed in silence. Benny hit the transmit button again, but before he could talk his radio crackled to life.

"Benny, I'm all right," Margot said. "I'm walking out with the boys. I'll see you back home."

"Roger," Benny croaked, his throat unaccountably tight. "Be safe."

"All right Tigers," Robin's voice cut through. "We're pushing Bingo. Return to base."

Benny's heart expanded in his chest; he took a deep shuddering breath as he formed up on Olds. For the remainder of the flight, he prayed, silently but fervently.

Robin and Benny stood on the flight line as the sun set on Gia Lam airfield, tallying the butcher's bill and discussing how to proceed. Robin was the next most senior after Hill, now deceased, and Jesus, now deceased, so he would assume command of the entire group. Benny would take what was left of the P-80 squadron, which was really just two flights. The Me 503s had downed eight of the P-80s at the cost of only five of their own. If the prop-driven squadrons hadn't arrived when they did, it would have been worse.

Long after the decisions were made, Benny remained on the flight line, waiting. Knowing there was no point in trying to talk Benny into resting, Robin merely patted his friend on the shoulder and headed for the showers himself. Benny remained standing, stock-still next to the waiting ambulances until after sundown. Finally, the drone of a gooney-bird's twin engines filled the night sky.

Benny waited patiently as the cargo plane landed and taxied, as patients in various state of disrepair and dishevelment hobbled or were carried painfully down the C-47's ramp. He even restrained himself when a familiar mane of thick, dark brown hair poked out of the plane door, and Margot made her way down the ramp. She was talking to nurses and medics about care for wounded men; he would not interrupt that.

He waited until the C-47's engines died and Margot stood, alone at least for a moment, and then he could wait no more.

"Margot," he called, trying, and failing, not to break into a jog to reach her.

She turned to face him. Even in the moonlight, her relief at seeing him was evident in her eyes as she likewise jogged to him. They stopped mere inches from one another, unsure of what to do next.

"I'm so glad you're all right," he said.

Margot's hands twitched as if she wanted to reach for him, but she kept them at her sides.

"I know," she said. "I was afraid those new jets would cut you to shreds."

They stood for a long silent moment. Benny was lost in her eyes, a depth of feeling he'd never experienced before welling up inside him as the adrenaline dump of combat, his fear for Margot and his affection for her all washed over him like breaking tidal waves.

"My patients," Margot said, finally. "I should—"

Benny gathered her into his arms and pressed his lips to hers, kissing her intently. Margot did not stiffen, did not protest, but flowed into his arms just as she had on the dance floor and matched his intensity, returning the kiss with a will.

After several blissfully sweet seconds, Margot pulled away from him and took a deep breath, then gave a throaty little chuckle.

"Oh, *mon amour*," she said, caressing Benny's cheek with her fingers. "You have the worst timing."

She tilted her head back and drew his lips down to hers, kissing him once again just as fiercely, albeit more briefly, before pushing him away with both hands.

"Now, go away," she said. "You are very distracting, and I *must* work."

Benny watched her walk away for a few seconds, before turning his steps toward home.

Well, as far as wars go, it could be a lot worse.

ABOUT JUSTIN WATSON

Justin Watson was the last member admitted to West Point's Class of 2005, though, thankfully, he didn't graduate in the same slot. Justin commissioned into the Field Artillery and spent his career with line Field Artillery and Infantry units, deploying twice to Iraq and once to Afghanistan. Justin was medically retired from the Army in 2015.

Justin settled in Houston with his wife Michele and their four kids where he doubled down on his lifelong writing aspirations.

He is the author, with Kacey Ezell and Tom Kratman, of the Romanov Rescue and its upcoming sequel 1919: The Romanov Rising.

You can see his work at www.justinwatsonbooks.com.

FOOLISH GAMES

Eric G. Swedin

FOOLISH GAMES

Eric G. Swedin

"We are now at DefCon-2."

Those words brought Rigby to instant alertness. He pushed himself up and looked at his watch. The hands read ten o'clock, exactly when he was supposed to be awakened.

"Why?" he asked, his single word a bit more slurred than he expected. He was awake, but he had only slept about six hours, not the eight he sought. The other pilots had been too noisy in the officer's quarters, forcing him to seek an empty cot in the ready room.

"You didn't hear it from me," Truss said. "But I have it on excellent authority that we will start bombing Cuba in five or six hours."

Rigby nodded. Washington was in the same time zone as Cuba, both four hours ahead of Fairbanks. The attack would begin at dawn, approximately 3:30 in the morning in Alaska.

Truss was a man trusted to not spread rumors that weren't well-founded. He cultivated a network of reliable sources where the currency was accuracy, a trait he had displayed even back in the camps in North Korea. They had been guests of the communists just a decade earlier, and rarely saw each other then because of the long stretches each spent in solitary confinement. Still, they shared a unique bond.

"Is my flight still scheduled?" Rigby asked.

"Indeed, it is."

"Even with a shooting war about to start?"

"SAC says that it's even more important now than before."

"How so?"

"That's how SAC thinks. Always aggressive. They say that we need to know what the Russkies are up to in their nuclear program."

"Yeah, we need to know right now because whatever I find will make a difference in the next few weeks." Rigby didn't know why he was arguing. He loved to fly. The cockpit was his refuge from all that had gone wrong in his life.

The officer's mess hall at Eielson Air Force Base served a special meal for him: steak and scrambled eggs, plus mixed vegetables, all washed down with coffee. The meal was high-protein/low-residue, designed to take a long time to digest, since his flight was planned for nine hours. The *Fairbanks Daily News Miner* was a small newspaper in a small city, but he read it, anyway; he liked to read when eating. Its headlines about the Cuban Missile Crisis reflected the concerns of an entire planet on the brink.

Rigby liked history, and Alaska proved to be a good place to catch up on his stack of books. Yesterday, he had finished reading *The Guns of August*, a bestseller the president had been so impressed with that he instructed copies be sent to every military base. Rigby was not a fan of Kennedy, having not voted for him, but agreed with the president on the importance of the book.

World War One had killed at least ten million soldiers as it upended Europe and the war started mostly by accident. Three men could have stopped the war at any moment as Europe lurched towards mutual suicide, if only one had decided to stop. The 83-year-old Emperor of Austria-Hungary failed because he still lived in the nineteenth century and lacked any understanding of modern machines. He had not even liked his nephew. Even so, the emperor had allowed his government to humiliate Serbia as revenge for the assassination of the archduke.

The Kaiser of Germany had also failed. He was so certain that bullying Serbia would not lead to war that he didn't even delay his annual summer cruise in the Norwegian fjords on his yacht. The Tsar of Russia had chosen war even though his army was poorly equipped and unprepared to fight. That all three empires had disappeared into war's rubble was ironically satisfying, but in no way compensated for all the dead.

All three emperors had played a game of chicken. In that game, someone needed to blink or a crash was inevitable. Today, Khrushchev and Kennedy were playing chicken over Cuba. This was much more dangerous than the Berlin Airlift of 1948 or the Berlin Crisis of last year. It was more dangerous than the Korean War. The chance of accidental war was real, just like in 1914. Would Khrushchev and JFK prove to be greater leaders than the three emperors?

Neither side had blinked yet...or swerved, and war grew ever closer. If Truss was right, a man who was almost always right, then war was about to begin. Would the war remain confined to Cuba?

Attacking Cuba was not like the limited war in Korea. In Korea, the Soviets had sat on the sidelines, for the most part, though they lent fighter pilots to the North Korean side. The Soviets denied that those pilots existed, which meant that when they died in combat, they still didn't exist. In Cuba, the pilots and thousands of soldiers on the ground were known to be Soviets. How do you keep a war limited when your own men were dying?

Even worse, now there were nuclear weapons. Rigby had been about to start his senior year in high school when the radio broke the news of the atomic bombs dropped on two cities in Japan. He was glad the war was over, but the black and white photographs of Hiroshima and Nagasaki in *Life* magazine, showing cities that had been erased, had horrified him. That was only a small taste of the potential consequences if the two superpowers unleashed the nuclear genie.

As was normal, the local radio station was being piped into the mess. "Monster Mash" was playing. Rigby liked the singer's deep and ominous voice, with the backing girl chorus. He didn't care for monster movies anymore—he had seen enough real monsters—but he liked them when he was younger. A catchy tune, really just a silly pop song, but the most popular song in the nation, probably because Halloween was only five days away. This was the kind of song his sister back in Omaha would listen to.

Every week, his kid sister sent him a letter, often little more than a stream of consciousness about her thoughts and life; she was fourteen and obsessed with boys and music. She was born after he left for college, a late life surprise for his parents, and he knew her mostly through her letters.

Rigby went to the ready room assigned to his squadron. Truss and the intelligence and navigation officers waited for him. Rigby sat down next to a green tank and pulled an oxygen mask over his face. He was flying high enough that he required extra oxygen for an hour before the flight. He breathed calmly, aware that his breathing was now loud enough for the other men to hear, which always made him feel a little embarrassed, like he was farting repeatedly.

The J-2 went over the same material that he always went over. Protocol must be followed. The Soviets had resumed testing atomic and hydrogen devices just a bit over a year ago, breaking a three-year mutual moratorium. They had tested over a hundred devices, exceeding the total tested in the 1950s.

Those tests even included the Tsar Bomba, the biggest weapon ever detonated, yielding somewhere in the neighborhood of fifty megatons. Most of the testing was in Kazakhstan, deep inside the Soviet empire, but some of the tests were on islands in the Arctic Ocean, such as Severny Island, where the Tsar Bomba had been released.

The goal of the U-2 flights over the North Pole was to collect aerial samples of radioactive material so that the smart boys in labcoats could learn more about the Soviet weapons.

Rigby pulled aside the mask. "No more intel on Cuba?"

The officer adjusted his glasses. "Not anything more I'm aware of."

The President had shocked the nation just four days earlier with his televised announcement that the Soviets were putting nuclear-armed missiles on Cuba. The somber president had also announced a quarantine to prevent more weapons from arriving. It was not a good sign that Truss was better informed than the J-2, but also not a surprise.

Again, the mask. "Do you know if the 435th Tactical Fighter Squadron out of Georgia has deployed?"

The J-2 had a pained expression on his face. Rigby asked him this every day, and the J-2 brushed him off every time. He was not interested in finding out if Rigby's younger brother was part of the planned attack on Cuba.

Truss spoke up. "He's a 104 driver, right?"

Rigby nodded.

"They're at Key West now, at the naval air station there."

Another nod. He hadn't seen his younger brother for over a year, but he still felt protective about him. They were peas in a pod when it came to their mutual love of flying.

The J-2 stepped aside, and a navigation officer brought over a sheaf of maps to Rigby. The flight path was drawn across the largest map, north to Barter Island, then to the North Pole, turn to a reverse course back to Barter Island, then home. Nine hours in the cold night. The important maps showed him the location of stars that would be aligned with his sextant at specific times on the journey. Magnetic compasses were useless that far north.

With the briefing over, a cart carrying the pressure suit was wheeled in. Normally, two airmen helped Rigby get dressed, but one was sick, so Truss helped. First went on the padding to help keep him warm, then pulling and tugging at the pressure suit to get it on. A man alone could not dress himself. One of the airmen wheeled over a dolly with an oxygen tank and attached a hose to his helmet. As the airman placed the helmet on, Rigby felt that familiar sense of isolation that came from hearing only his own breathing, like what he imagined a polio patient felt when trapped in an iron lung. He could not hear anything outside of the helmet.

Truss plugged in the comm line. "Copy, copy, you hear me?"

"Confirm."

The process was similar to the routine the Mercury astronauts went through, because going into space was similar to flying at 70,000 feet. The early U-2 pilots had experienced examinations and qualifying tests quite similar to what the Mercury astronauts endured. The fifth Mercury flight, with Walter M. Schirra doing six orbits, had taken place earlier just that month.

Rigby had been invited to try out to be one of the Mercury Seven, since he had been a military test pilot with over 1,500 hours of flight time, which were the main requirements. He was cut early in the process, which irritated him. He wanted to fly the latest and fastest, and the Mercury program had promised that. He wasn't sure why he was dropped, but his enthusiasm to be an astronaut had waned as he watched reporters inundate the seven men and their families. They had no privacy left. He valued his own privacy and avoided public events.

This personal trait had been reconfirmed when he returned to his hometown after his time as a POW in North Korea. The town insisted on a quickly arranged parade, using floats from past July Fourth celebrations hauled out of garages. The whole town had a fine time while he stood and smiled awkwardly, wishing to be anywhere else. He passed on applying for the second group of astronauts that NASA had selected. He was okay with not riding a rocket into space, especially since he was flying on the edge of space every time he went up in a U-2.

With Truss and the airman assisting him, Rigby walked through the building to the door nearest the flight line. He looked out the window. His aircraft had been pulled out of the hangar and waited on the tarmac. Spotlights lit up the airplane as if she were a beauty on a stage, though the beauty was in the lines, not the grey paint. It was an airplane that wanted to fly, fifty feet from tip to tail, and wings that stretched eighty feet from tip to tip, the size of wings normally found on sailplanes.

Truss pulled open the door and tugged his coat closer together as he led the group out into the night of the Alaskan winter. Rigby followed the footprints Truss left in the frost. Normally, Rigby preferred to walk around his airplane, checking all the details, running a checklist in his mind, but that was too difficult in the suit. He relied on the ground crew to have done everything correctly.

Truss and the airman helped Rigby into the cockpit and switched over his oxygen line to the airplane. The radio line followed. The U-2 was a tight fit, even for his slight five-feet-seven-inch frame, especially in his pressure suit.

One of the last items on the preflight checklist was to remove a pin from the right side of his seat that blocked the ejection seat from firing. Like many of the other U-2 pilots, he chose to keep the pin in. Ejection seats had saved many lives, but they had also killed some, including a good friend four years ago.

One of the unique problems for the U-2 was that it flew so high that the plexiglass canopy grew rock hard from exposure to the freezing temperatures at high altitudes. Since the ejection seats could not always break through the canopy, three pointed metal spikes were located on the rail on the back of his seat to shatter the frozen canopy.

He took off at midnight exactly. Being off schedule by more than a few minutes would throw off his star charts. The U-2 had only wheels on the centerline, so temporary wheels called pogos were required to keep the tips of the wings from dragging on the ground. The pogos dropped off as the plane left the ground. Landing was always a challenge, forcing the pilot to keep the U-2 perfectly level until finally stopping and tipping over to rest one wing on the ground.

His airplane carried over six tons of fuel, almost as much as the U-2 weighed empty, a special blend created just for this airplane because of the high altitude and cold temperatures. The single jet engine pushed him ever higher into the dark sky, and he felt the familiar sense of solitude, where only he and the cockpit existed, with dim glowing lights on the control panels. He pushed the heating control to maximum. The heater kept him alive. If it failed, that would be an immediate mission abort and the faint hope that he would be able to get back to base before freezing to death.

Overhead stretched the heavens in all their magnificence, sharp points of light standing out in sharp relief; the new moon had just passed, and the moon was only a bare hint of a crescent, hardly any light at all. His wings were darker shadows under the starlight. The ground was a dark mass below him, with no lights in the wilderness of northern Alaska.

His course was 357, several degrees from true zero, heading for Barter Island, just off the northern coast of Alaska in the Arctic Ocean. He settled into a cruising speed of 410 knots. A familiar feeling of peace came over him, a sense of purpose that he usually felt when flying, where he and the airplane were one. He trusted himself and the airplane trusted him. The U-2 was very sensitive to stalling if he allowed his speed to drop by as little as five knots, a tight margin for mistakes.

A Duck Butt was orbiting about Barter Island. The search and rescue aircraft was an older four-engine aircraft, a SC-54D, which carried four droppable rescue kits and four parajumpers. It had enough fuel that the airplane would remain there during Rigby's whole flight. Everyone hoped it wasn't going to be needed.

He once asked a parajumper what he would do if he was forced to jump over the ice. The master sergeant was quite serious in his answer: he would not pull the ripcord. Rigby regretted asking the question, since ahead of him was only ice.

Rigby checked in with the Duck Butt crew, checked the radio beacon from the island, adjusted his gyro compass to match, then turned slightly to head directly for the North Pole. Three and a half hours before he reached the North Pole.

As he left land behind, he leaned forward and looked through the driftsight set on the top of his cockpit control panel. It was an odd contraption unique to the U-2, which allowed him to look through a reverse periscope and see out the bottom of his aircraft. There was nothing to see in the dark. The sextant built into the driftsight allowed him to find and fix a star in front of him. The maps were so important because they exactly matched his precisely timed sightings, and he then adjusted the gyro compass to compensate for drift.

It was time to do science. He pushed a lever to open a small aperture on the nose of his airplane, which allowed air from outside to flow into a small cavity containing six bottles. He had a button for each bottle, to open it and close it. Inside the bottle, cotton filters coated with a sticky goo trapped minute particles. Some of those particles would be radioactive fallout from Soviet nuclear tests. A scientist in the initial briefing months ago had explained that the different types of radioactive particles could tell the scientists what kind of bombs the Soviets had tested. Useful stuff to know.

This was hot-sampling, and every two weeks Rigby had to have his blood drawn to check if he was accumulating a radioactive dosage. While getting radiation sickness was frightening enough, with hair falling out and cells failing, he figured that the real risk was just flying the U-2.

The sky was brightening. So odd. Then he saw the Aurora Borealis for the first time. Bright green ribbons of light danced across the sky. He had wanted to see the northern lights and the past two months had not rewarded his desire; now the sky was full of splendor.

Time for another star fix. He checked the chart, saw the star that he was supposed to measure, and could not find it. The ribbons of light were like curtains blocking stars, or fading in and out as the light flickered. He knew where the star should be, so he shot the angle and adjusted his gyro, hoping to correct any errors on the next fix. It was time to close a sample bottle, change altitude, and open another bottle.

His mind wandered, part of it always on task with the mission and the art of flying, the other part lightly surfing over memories or musings about that which preoccupied or worried him.

Oddly enough, he thought about Eileen, his ex-wife. She had loyally waited for him while he was a prisoner of war, but after the war, they had seemed to be strangers. They had tried, but he could not find a way to connect with her, so he turned to flying, putting in even more time than necessary. Then came the Thunderbirds, where he was gone almost every week, and she hated living in Las Vegas, so they did what seemed inconceivable: they divorced. He still loved her, but not in a possessive way, and when she remarried, he was glad. He was even glad when she had the children that they had not ever gotten around to. Time to switch thoughts.

He looked at the clock on his dashboard. 3:30 AM. Sunrise in Key West, Florida. He offered a brief prayer for his brother.

Captain Rigby liked flying the Zipper. The F-104 Starfighter was lean, a silver tube with two stubby wings that looked like they could barely keep the aircraft in the air. It was built for speed and altitude and had set both world records, as well as a series of time-to-climb records. Just three years earlier, an F-104 had cracked the 100,000 foot ceiling.

Newer airplanes were now setting records, and the F-104 was already considered obsolete. In fact, all of the F-104s were transferred to Air National Guard units, but the Cuban Missile Crisis prompted the Air Force to reclaim some of those aircraft and assign them to pilots who were already rated on the planes.

A week ago, Rigby had been flying the F-102 Delta Dart in Georgia, part of an interceptor squadron defending the nation against the threat of Soviet bombers. Now he sat in a Zipper at Key West Naval Air Station, where the runways splayed out like a misshapen star. The other three Zippers in his flight lined up behind him.

The snug cockpit, with a tilted seat that made him feel like he was resting in an easy chair, did not feel claustrophobic. The engine growled, sending vibrations through the airframe, even when taxiing, reminding Rigby that the Zipper deserved its other nickname: Man in a Missile.

The F-104 was the opposite of the U-2 that his brother flew. Probably no airplane had less wingspan in proportion to the airplane than the F-104 and probably no airplane had more wingspan in proportion to the airplane than the U-2. The only exception to that second comparison would be the Flying Wing, which was not an active airplane.

Dawn was about to break on the eastern horizon.

He checked his watch. A dozen F-100 Super Sabre fighter-bombers had taken off from Homestead Air Force base, south of Miami, ten minutes ago. According to the plan he received the previous day, named Operation Hot Plate, his own flight was supposed to now take off. Rigby checked his compass: 318 magnetic. One of the details that tickled him about Key West was that the runway had an elevation of only three feet. His altimeter didn't even adjust that tightly.

Rigby pressed the key for his radio. "Key West, Yankee One requesting permission to take-off from runway thirty-two."

"Confirm, Yankee One, Key West permission granted for runway thirty-two. Other Yankee airplanes are clear to follow in turn."

Rigby's F-104 raced down the runway, the power of its engine focused with purpose. The other F-104s followed, eight fighters in all. Minutes later, Rigby's two flights were bound south for Cuba, flying cover at 20,000 feet over the Super Sabres who flew two thousand feet below them. Other than a needle on a dial, there was no indication of breaking the sound barrier as the airplanes accelerated.

The dawning day revealed the coast of Cuba on the far horizon. It was only 106 miles from Key West to Havana, though they were not bound for the capital. Their target was San Julián Air Base, on the far western end of the island, built by the Americans during World War II, oddly enough. Recon flights had found Soviet Ilyushin-28 Beagle medium bombers at the field, a first-generation jet with long turbojets under each wing, initially deployed in 1950, making it old technology in the rapidly changing world of jet aircraft. The Beagles could reach deep into the United States, so they were a priority for neutralization.

The operations order required the strike force to stay thirty-five miles away from the coast of Cuba until the attack. When the leader of the Super Sabres turned to the west, Rigby also turned, and each leader's pack of sleek aircraft followed obediently. Flying at eight hundred miles an hour ate up miles quickly, and ten minutes later, they followed the coast as it turned towards the south. Upon reaching the sea outside of Guadiana Bay, the strike force slowed down and began to rapidly lose altitude. As he dropped below the speed of sound, Rigby heard the familiar rush of air that came as the shockwave trailing the airplane rushed past the slowing craft.

There had been a lot of discussion in the ready room and at meals over the best ways to avoid the new threat of SAMs. The Soviet SA-2 anti-aircraft missiles were big beasts, 35 feet long and able to fly over twenty miles, designed to shoot down high-flying aircraft. One of those missiles had shot down Gary Powers.

Recon showed an SA-2 site near San Julián, so the operations plan required the attacking aircraft to come in at 500 feet. A good idea, but it made the aircraft vulnerable to anti-aircraft guns and Rigby had seen a classified report that described the four Soviet motorized rifle regiments on the island, but had no idea how many AA units there were.

The Super Sabres led the way across the bay and across the beach. The landscape was a smear of green, with occasional lines of sugar cane on plantations, and small hamlets. A dozen miles inland was the air base. Rigby guided his pilots into a pattern that would orbit the airfield, about two miles out, providing protection if the MiG-21 fighters that the Soviets had sneaked into the island interfered. Flying at 500 feet required focused attention; a slip of the arm on the joystick could send a jet into the ground so fast that the pilot would have only moments to react or feel a stab of fear at their end.

Bubbles of flame erupted from the airfield as the Super Sabres each took their turn at bombing runs. Rigby had missed the Korean War and had never seen bombs used outside of a bombing range, and those were usually dummy bombs, which thudded into the ground. He found it difficult to resist watching the show, even though he was flying his own plane, watching out for enemy fighters, and trying to keep track of the other fighters under his command.

"Yankee One, we have bandits coming in," came the excited voice of his wingman. "East. On your five."

Rigby twisted to look back. The sun blinded him, and he pulled up instinctively, aware of how close he was to the ground. "Yankee Three, Yankee Seven, go for them." That would send two fighters and their wingmen, Yankee Four and Yankee Eight, into the fight.

He concentrated on flying, maintaining his path in orbit about the airfield. The op plan authorized fighting the Soviet MiGs, but required his pilots to break off if the Russians ran. Apparently, the planners were still trying to limit the mission to an attack on an airfield, and that didn't make much sense to Rigby. Dropping bombs seemed to be a definitive act of war.

He listened to the chatter on the radio as Yankee Four and Yankee Eight both launched Sidewinders at the incoming Soviet fighters. So much was happening; he tried to keep track of it all and failed. It took too long to look in the right direction and seek out small specks that were fast-moving jets. He couldn't fly his own plane and perform his own tasks and keep track of the pilots for whom he was responsible.

"Jeff, on your four! Coming in high."

Rigby recognized the voice of his wingman and glanced back to his right and up and saw to his astonishment a MiG-21 coming towards him. A flash under its left wing indicated that it had just launched a missile towards him. The standard tactic would be to light his afterburner and dive, but he was too close to the ground for that. Within a fraction of a second, he took the opposite tack, pulling back on his stick to climb and dumped extra fuel into his jet pipe.

The F-104 flashed upwards as a stream of flame roared out of its rear. His vision turned red, and he struggled to stay conscious as five times his own weight pressed down on him. He wanted to ease over to reduce the pressure, but feared that the missile was too close. He must escape.

A moment later, he looked out through groggy eyes, struggling to make his brain work. He had passed out and now felt that his aircraft was falling. The roar of the afterburner was gone. He heard the shouted words of his wingman, could detect the fear in the voice, but couldn't process the sounds into words. No idea what his friend was saying.

Training took over. He didn't try to look around and orient himself, but concentrated on finding his artificial horizon and focusing on the floating bubble. He nudged the stick over, relying on muscle memory to tease the airplane back into level flight. Experience saved him as the airplane calmed down. He looked at his altimeter and was alarmed to see that he was under two thousand feet, so he tugged back to gain altitude. A glance at his compass showed him flying south. Not a good idea, nothing in that direction except empty ocean. He needed to head northeast.

As he turned on a better heading, he lifted his eyes to look around. The sky was a big place, with lots to take in. Off to his left, several dozen miles away, he saw smoke rising from the airfield bombing. He saw specks in the skies above, swarming about like insects. That was the fight, he had to rejoin it, so he nudged his stick over. His airspeed was somewhat above five hundred miles per hour.

Glancing behind and to the right, he was pleased to see his wingman coming up to take his place on his five. He had never felt more exhausted. The high-G turn had taken a lot out of him, and his legs still ached from the tight squeeze of the air bladders in his G-suit.

He nursed his F-104 back to Key West, worried about the fuel situation, and landed first. Their celebration over having shot down three MiGs was marred by having lost one of their mates. Flying was no longer fun.

Major Rigby tried to take another star fix. The shimmering light was too strong, and he guessed at the location of the star again. Time to change sample bottles again, so he ascended to 55,000 feet and pressed the next button.

He was now halfway through his mission. Somewhere down there was the North Pole, with nothing to distinguish it from anywhere on the ice except for maybe some flagpoles and flags from explorers lying encrusted in the ice. He recalled that the USS *Nautilus* had traveled to the North Pole just seven years ago, powered by a nuclear reactor, but the submarine had not tried to surface through the ice. Rigby turned left ninety degrees, then 270 degrees to the right; now he should be retracing his path back to Barter Island. He was too far away to pick up any radio traffic that could provide a destination to home in on.

He tried to take another star fix. The green light still blocked his effort. Nothing to do but follow the protocol and pray that he would find his way home.

Three hours later, he knew that he should be close to Barter Island. He made a call for the Duck Butt and couldn't get through. He was cruising at 70,000 feet. The minutes rolled past on the clock in the center of his control panel. He should be passing Barter Island right then, but there was no response on the radio. The mission was timed so tightly that the search and rescue aircraft was supposed to be shooting off flares to help him find them. As much as he squinted in the darkness, he could not see any flares.

He was lost.

He flicked through the different radio bands: VHF, UHF, and HF. There was something. Faint, hard to understand. He switched back and listened carefully. It was a radio station, playing music, now an announcer. The radio suddenly came in clear.

It was Russian.

It seemed to be a commercial radio station. Was it far away? Had an odd layer of the atmosphere bounced a signal a thousand miles or more? Or was it so strong because he was right on top of it? He switched to the Duck Butt frequency and requested a response. Nothing. He sent multiple messages to Eielson, but heard nothing in response.

Then to his surprise, a voice came, speaking in oddly accented English. "Charlie Niner, turn right thirty degrees. Repeat: Charlie Niner, welcome home, turn right thirty degrees."

That didn't feel right. That the voice was unfamiliar was not surprising, since there was regular turnover in the air control tower at Eielson. Fortunately, his orders had a protocol for this situation.

"Charlie Niner here, give me a Whiskey Tango," Rigby said.

"Charlie Niner, welcome home—turn right thirty degrees."

Wrong answer. Eielson was supposed to respond with November Romeo. He switched to the frequency used by Soviet air defense forces and found Russian voices talking in excited tones. He didn't know any of the words, but he recognized what excited pilots sounded like. Perhaps war had come, but the more probable answer was that the hounds were homing in on the hare.

He didn't like being the hare.

Major Truss looked at his watch again. Rigby was forty minutes overdue at Barter Island, and the Duck Butt had seen nothing. The U-2 was running out of fuel. Had he crashed? Was he lost? Minutes counted. There was only so much fuel.

Eielson had a much more powerful transmitter than the U-2 did, so while Rigby could not contact home, perhaps they could contact him. But contacting him was useless unless they had a helpful message for him.

Truss picked up the phone, opened a small black book that he carried, and dialed a number he had known about for the past month. His unit had only been at Eielson for the past two months, flying almost every night with one of their three U-2 aircraft, but in that time, Truss had worked his connections, always eager for information.

"Hello." The voice sounded wary, as if he was surprised that his telephone had rang.

"Hello. My name is Major Aaron Truss, Air Force, OL-5 detachment from the 4080th Squadron. This is an open line, but I don't have a choice —a pilot's life is at severe risk. We fly U-2 recon airplanes. One of our airplanes is overdue on a sampling trip to the North Pole. Do you know where it is?"

"Why are you telling me this?"

"I assume that he's lost. I hope he is lost, otherwise that would mean that he went down. I need to know where he is right now, so that we can send him instructions to get home."

"Why ask me?"

"Don't play games." Truss was about to grow angry, but he restrained himself, choosing to beg. "I know that you are NSA and that you have an advanced radar system that can see a lot farther than our radars. I know that you are copied on our flight plans. Do you know where he is?"

The voice on the other end of the line remained silent.

"He's an American. A war hero. He spent almost two years as a POW in North Korea. I was there with him; he has given enough already. Just tell me where he is."

"You asked for information that is codeword level only, way past Top Secret."

"I am asking you to save a man's life."

The voice sighed. "You never heard this from me. He's over Chukotka."

"Please, no!" Chukotka was the peninsula on the other side of the Bering Strait, in the Soviet Union. An isolated region, but useful as a transit point on the way by sea to the Kolyma River, where gulag prisoners had extracted a fortune in gold. There were a couple of air bases with fighters in the region, part of Soviet air defenses, with the mission to shoot down incoming American strategic bombers. A U-2 would look like a high-flying bomber.

"Sorry, buddy. A pair of interceptors have launched from Pevek Airport, two more from Wrangel Island, and another two from Anadyr. We think that they are MiG-21s."

Truss knew that the fighters could zoom-climb to 60,000 feet in less than two minutes. They wouldn't catch the U-2 if he was flying at maximum altitude, but he might be lower.

"What heading will take the U-2 back to Alaska?"

Another pause. "Turn left ninety-five degrees."

"Thank you. Please hold and tell me if he is turning."

Truss put the phone down on the table and stepped to the radio. "Give me maximum power," he instructed the radio technician.

He picked up the microphone and thumbed the key. "Charlie Niner, turn left niner-five. Charlie Niner, repeat, turn left niner-five. Jeff, buddy, you know who this is. We were mutual guests of Kim Il-sung. Turn left niner-five."

He picked up the telephone. "Is he turning?"

A shout went up from the other end. "Yes, he's turning."

"How far is he from Alaska?"

"About four hundred miles. He is six hundred and thirty miles from Galena."

"And the MiGs?"

Another pause. "Oh, damn, about forty minutes from intercepting him. Can he fly faster?"

"No." Truss swore. "Wait a moment."

He picked up another phone and grabbed a phone directory. Galena Air Force Station was 270 miles west of Eielson. Alaska Air Defense had fighters on hot stand-by there. He called the duty officer for the Alaska Air Defense and explained that he needed fighters to scramble to protect the U-2. He explained that Soviet MiGs were in hot pursuit.

Within two minutes, he received confirmation that a pair of F-102 Delta Daggers had launched and were bound for the Soviet Union at 800 miles per hour, followed by the crack of the sound barrier being broken across the Alaskan wilderness.

Truss picked up the microphone. "Charlie Niner, we have two Delta

Daggers inbound to protect you. Repeat, Charlie Niner, we have two Delta Daggers inbound to protect you."

He knew that Rigby was too far away to respond.

Rigby appreciated his friend contacting him. Hope had replaced despair, but the news that he needed protection meant that the Soviet fighters were getting close to him. He had no way to fight back or even maneuver to avoid the Soviets. He was like a big whale waiting to be speared, if they could get close enough.

He remembered the day that he had been shot down over North Korea, when a pair of Mig-15s darted across the Yalu River from their safe haven in China and angled to dive out of the sun, blowing holes in his beautiful new F-86 Sabre. The airplane was just weeks out of the factory, and the cannon round that went through his engine had proved to be a fatal wound.

He had bailed out to become a prisoner of the North Koreans for six hundred days. He had lived on bowls of rice, sprinkled with flakes of what might be fish, growing bone lean. There was no medical care, and he remembered the foul smell of gangrene from other prisoners who had infections that leaked fluids. A Chinese officer had tortured him for information about the F-86 Sabre, but the man seemed almost bored with his task as he went through the motions. Rigby kept his mouth shut, finding strength in his pride, and focusing on getting through each day.

He did not want to become a guest of the Soviets.

Rigby switched over his radio to the frequency for the Alaskan Air Defense Command. It was scratchy, but he heard the air traffic controller. "Bravo Two Three, you are authorized to use the Two-Six Falcon."

The pilot responded. "Confirmed. Ding-dong, it is."

The words crushed Rigby's spirit. He knew what the codewords meant. The F-102 Delta Dagger was armed with an AIM-26 Falcon, an air-to-air missile that carried a nuclear warhead. It was not big, as nukes went, only a sub-kiloton yield, equal to 250 tons of TNT. It was designed to knock multiple enemy airplanes out of the sky. DefCon-3 required that nuclear warheads be placed on the interceptors, and the nation was at DefCon-2.

The FUEL LOW LEVEL red warning light came on. He had less than fifty gallons left. About three minutes of engine power. The needle quivered on the bottom of his fuel gauge. The U-2 could glide for about two hundred and fifty miles, depending on his luck, gradually losing altitude as he soared towards Alaska. Rigby knew that he could fly higher than the Soviet airplanes, but only if he had a engine propelling him. He could easily lose enough altitude so that the Soviets could get him, whether that was before the Delta Daggers arrived, he could not know.

He realized that it didn't really matter. Bigger consequences than his own life were at play here. If the Americans used their Falcons to rescue him or to avenge him after he had been shot down, a threshold would have been crossed. The AIM-26 Falcon was a small warhead, but it was nuclear, a profound escalation over the use of a conventional weapon.

He shut down his engine, choosing to preserve enough fuel to have some options in the future, especially if he had to land. Those options looked limited. Was this going to be a repeat of *The Guns of August*, where the emperors who had a choice made the wrong choices? Rigby was no emperor, just a lowly major, but he had choices. Choices that could make a difference for the whole world.

He would not be the cause of a nuclear weapon used in anger. The decision came quickly. He flicked the radio key: "Bravo Two Three, Charlie Niner is going down. Repeat, I'm going down. Abort your mission." He repeated himself.

The F-102 pilot responded. "Charlie Niner, Bravo Two Three, roger that."

Rigby noticed that the southeastern horizon was getting brighter. Dawn was coming. With his engine off, the cockpit was silent; he felt alone in the world.

He refused to be party to escalating the crisis, but he did not need to be a martyr. Life had been hard, but life had also been sweet, and he had no desire to die. He turned the control column to the right, losing altitude as he turned away from the sun to head deeper into the Soviet Union. If he was going to bail out, then he preferred to be over land, and he was not sure how close he was to the Bering Strait.

Switching to the Soviet frequency, Rigby called out, "Mayday, mayday, I'm going down. Mayday, mayday."

He hoped that the Soviet pilots understood his words and held their fire. As he drifted lower in a sixty-degree banked spiral, a technique to lose altitude as quickly as possible, he removed the ejection safety pin from the right side of his seat. The needle on the altimeter circled rapidly, like water going down a drain. The sky continued to grow lighter as the sun rose, and it finally peeked over the horizon and he could see around him.

A MiG-21 picked that moment to fly close to him. Rigby looked at the pilot and was surprised to see a friendly salute from the man. He returned it, though he knew that it was not a harbinger of the future. If he survived ejection and was found by the Soviets before freezing or starving to death, he would be a prisoner again. He wanted this war to be short.

He prayed for hope.

The altimeter was drawing close to 10,000 feet. The surface below him was still in shadow, but it was clearly land, not sea. He straightened out the airplane and touched the instrument panel briefly, as if saying goodbye to a loyal steed. Major Jeff Rigby leaned back to brace his neck against the back of his seat and then reached down to pull the ejection handle between his knees.

AFTERWORD

This story is set within the events of my novel, *When Angels Wept: A What-If History of the Cuban Missile Crisis* (Potomac, 2010). Major Chuck Maultsby really did fly a U-2 over the pole during the crisis and get lost over Siberia on his return. Fortunately, he was able to return, and an incident was avoided. I changed the date of the flight and used the timeline from the novel. The attack on San Julián to destroy Il-28 Beagle bombers was actually part of the bombing campaigns Operation Hot Plate and Operation Scabbards, planned by the Air Force if the Cuban Missile Crisis heated up. The declassified plans are available online in the National Security Archive at George Mason University. Historical flight manuals for the U-2 aircraft are available on the web. Michael Dobbs's *One Minute to Midnight: Kennedy, Khrushchev, and Castro on the Brink of Nuclear War* (Knopf, 2008) is a useful account of the Cuban Missile Crisis.

ABOUT ERIC G. SWEDIN

Eric G. Swedin is a professor of history at Weber State University. His doctorate is in the history of science and technology. His publications include numerous articles, seven history books, four science fiction novels, and a historical mystery novel. His *When Angels Wept: A What-If History of the Cuban Missile Crisis* won the 2010 Sidewise Award for Best Long-Form Alternate History. The short story in this volume, "Foolish Games," is set in the same timeline.

Eric lives with his family in a house built in 1881.

His website is http://www.swedin.org/.

ZERO DARK 30

JL Curtis

ZERO DARK 30

JL Curtis

May 18, 1985
Moffett Field, California 0400Z

The tactical grey P-3 Orion bumped through the night skies, descending over San Jose, California, toward Moffett Field Naval Air Station after a nine-hour flight from Seattle, Washington.

"Charlie Fox 232, cleared to land 32 right," crackled through the radio.

Lieutenant Commander Randy Hathaway nudged the rudder as Senior Chief "Scoop" Vessels, the flight engineer, and Lieutenant Commander "Fast Eddie" Miller, the copilot, reviewed the lineup. Lieutenant "Tip" Adams leaned forward from his position behind Randy and double-checked the cockpit even though he didn't have the landing. Fast Eddie replied, "232, cleared on the right. Say winds."

"260 at 12."

"Speeds are 18 and 21, Randy. Landing checklist complete."

"Okay, pilot's power, Scoop."

"You got it."

Scoop looked over his shoulder at Chief "Hairy" Harris and motioned for him to reset the oil tank circuit breakers. Harry did so and shoved a thumbs up in front of Scoop.

At the TACCO's station, Lieutenant Commander Kevin James "KJ" Martin looked out the window making sure the gear was down; rechecked his harness, looked over at Lieutenant Commander Barney "Rubble" Roberts and received a thumbs-up. He keyed the ICS and said, "Five is set in the back; gear looks good."

"Roger that, KJ," Fast Eddie replied.

Randy called, "Short final, flaps to land."

"Flaps to land, speed is 118."

"Okay."

Randy finessed the P-3 the last thirty feet down to the runway, but it still flopped down the last fifteen feet.

"Six thousand remaining."

"Four good Beta lights."

"'Kay, full reverse."

"Charlie Fox 232, right off approved when able, contact ground 236.8."

"232 switching: night, Moffett."

Randy steered the P-3 off the runway and keyed the ICS. "Just another day at the office, guys. Crew's released, KJ: let em know we're home, and get us a spot."

KJ double-keyed the ICS in acknowledgment, noted the land time on his log and did the arithmetic for total flight time. He waited for Barney to complete the in report to the ASW Operations Center and switch to the squadron's base frequency. Barney gave him a thumbs up, and KJ keyed UHF2, called maintenance and gave the time, status and asked for a parking spot. The maintenance chief told him to park it in front of the hangar as the bird was due for a periodic maintenance inspection.

Meanwhile, Chief Iverson, the in-flight technician, strolled up with the first aid kit and his helmet on sideways. KJ smiled and pointed to the flight station, Iverson assumed the persona of an injured person and limped into the flight station. "Anybody up here need this? We only need a couple of ambulances for the guys in back."

Randy shrugged as Fast Eddie, Tip and Scoop laughed. "Sorry 'bout that. I didn't do it on purpose. Any major gripes?"

"Nope, we're up and up in the back, Sir, but this ain't a 747—we're a little closer to the ground. Just saying," Iverson replied.

KJ came over the ICS, saying, "Randy, put it right in front of the hangar; no gas, no covers. Scoop, they're gonna do an inspection."

He keyed the PA, telling everyone to pick up all loose gear, secure their stations, and clear all codes. Barney and Tip walked through the airplane clearing all the secure equipment codes, inventoried the Communications box, and signed it off.

Chief Clark, the senior Anti-submarine Warfare Operator, asked who had to go to debrief. KJ replied, "Well, since we debriefed at Whidbey, I don't see any reason for any of y'all to go, Randy and I can handle it."

"Sure about that, TACCO? After all, it took you seven minutes to get the torp off after we told you where the boat was," the chief replied with a smile.

Chuckling, KJ shot back, "All right, Charlie, you can come along and keep us straight."

"Naw, boss, we trust you to get it right. We'll be waitin' in the parking lot."

The bird was parked and turned over to maintenance, and Randy and KJ went to ASW Operations Center to turn in the operational message blank, debrief with the watch officer, and turn in all the classified material. Chief Clark, the Ordnance chief and the ordnance men cleaned up the bomb bay and did a walkthrough on the bird. Scoop and the second engineer did their post-flight, went into to maintenance to write up the gripes on the plane, and sign off the daily inspection.

An hour later, the crews gathered at KJ's rental car in front of Hangar Two for the parking lot debrief. KJ started things off by handing out beers and cokes, then did a round robin of each crewmember for comments, complaints, and plans.

As a Master Augmentation Unit crew, they didn't work or fly on the same schedule as a standard reserve crew. They flew their own aircraft or one loaned by an operational squadron. Since most of the crew lived and worked in the Bay Area, most of them were headed home until next month, as they had no squadron support flights or operational commitments scheduled.

KJ and Randy walked back into the MAU's space in the hangar and were approached by the Ops boss. "Nice flight, guys. The Skipper wants to see you both in his office."

"Okay, Willie. Hope to hell something hasn't come up, since I just let the crew go," KJ replied.

Commander Furness looked up as KJ and Randy knocked on the door. "Come on in, guys—nice flight. Seven minutes from COMEX to weapon is a new record for us, KJ. How the hell do you do it? Especially with a reserve crew? Most of the fleet squadrons can't even do that well."

Randy and KJ looked at each other, and Randy replied, "Shit, Skipper, look at the qualifications and experience we've got here. Fast Eddie and Tip both had crews in the fleet, KJ and Barney were both first-tour mission commanders, Chief Clark has seventeen years as an acoustic operator, Henerson and Macklin both have over fifteen, Iverson is a wizard with the gear, Vessels and Harris both are old B model flight engineers who know ASW as well as or better than we do, and 'Pops' Kanaka did his last fleet tour with PMTC as the Research and Development ordnance shop Leading Petty Officer before he flipped over to the civilian side. There isn't a fleet crew that could come close to that, much less stay together for five years like we have."

"Guess so, but you guys never cease to amaze me. Randy, what's your schedule?"

"Seven in the morning, here to LA, layover, then Sydney and back."

"When are you going to upgrade? Or is United holding you back?"

"Hell, I don't know, and no, they aren't. Flying right seat on a 747 ain't bad. Plus, if I upgrade to Captain on the 75, it would mean moving back to LA, and Julie would shoot me," Randy replied.

Commander Furness laughed and nodded at KJ. "What about you: still looking for a real job?"

KJ rolled his eyes, chuckled, and answered, "Why get a job, Skipper? It would just ruin my social life. Seriously, I finished up a security job yesterday, and I'm headed back to Bradenton tomorrow morning. We're doing pretty well with the FBO business, and Dad's having a ball, which lets me run around and do other things."

The skipper shook his head and said, "I'll never understand how the Navy didn't let you fly."

KJ grimaced and replied, "Shit, they claimed I wasn't 20-20. Said I was 20-25 in the right eye, and you know how that goes: one chance and that's it. I decided to try the NFO route since I was already there. Besides which, if I'd gone home, the old man would've killed me. You know how he feels about doing your time."

"You guys need your rest, so thanks for a great job, and see ya next month. Your crew should be doing an ASWEX with VP-19."

Reflections: CDR Bob Furness

Those two guys are damn good, maybe the best I've seen in twenty years. Too bad we couldn't keep them on active duty. Randy's a known entity: steady, happily married and loves flying for the airlines. KJ's a different story altogether: his record is outstanding from the start. A real golden boy in his first tour, special missions certified and every possible important job. A tactical wizard—that's what his skipper said. I wonder what would have happened if KJ's wife hadn't been killed during his first shore tour and he hadn't resigned to take care of his daughter. Wonder if KJ will ever get a real job. He's so damn talented it's not funny, but he plays with airplanes, has this KJM Consulting, which he won't talk about but seems to make money, has some connection with his dad's Fixed Base Operation at Bradenton, Florida; lives in Florida but drills in California. Aw, hell: I guess I shouldn't look two damn good gift horses in the mouth. I'll just take 'em and run.

Randy and KJ got up and headed out the door, logging out with the Duty Officer to ensure their drill time was counted. In the parking lot, they coordinated the call tree for next month, said their goodbyes, and KJ jumped in his rental and headed back for the Airport Crowne Plaza. He had paperwork to do and was looking forward to a good night's sleep and getting home to his now-teenaged daughter, Jonna, who was thirteen going on thirty-one, or so she thought. He just hoped she'd behaved, as Mom had promised to have a "girl" talk with her.

May 22, 1985
Washington, DC 1300Z

Third assistant agricultural attaché and KGB Lieutenant Cornel Sergei Rostov picked up the *Washington Post* and scanned the headlines, immediately focusing on the arrest of John Walker in Norfolk, VA, for spying. He slammed the chair down and hurried down to the secure room to find out what had happened.

CINCLANTFLT Compound,
Norfolk, Virginia 1500Z

Chief' Downs had his feet up on the watch desk, idly watching the staff in the watch center starting their turnovers, when the secure phone on his desk rang. He sighed as he reached for it and said, "Watch Officer."

A couple of seconds later, his feet hit the floor, and he was writing quickly on the pad by the phone as the voice on the other end identified himself as the deputy director of the FBI. He said, "Sir, I'm the watch officer. I need to get this information to the chain of command. Will someone be there in the next half-hour or so? Yes, sir. I'll have them call you back."

He jumped up and headed for the door, telling the commander on the submarine ops desk, "Shit's gonna hit the fan. FBI caught a spy with classified Navy carrier data. I'm going up to the flag office. You've got the desk."

The commander nodded and got up, moving to the watch desk as Downs banged through the door. A couple of minutes later, he stood in front of the Flag Aide's desk. "Commander, I need to see the boss right now. We got a problem."

"What kind of problem, Chief?"

Chief glanced around before answering softly, "A spy, caught with classified carrier plans."

"You're not kidding, are you?"

Chief shook his head. "Not in the slightest."

"C'mon." The aide got up, went to the admiral's door and knocked. "Admiral, Chief Downs from the watch floor with a hot one. Chief, go right in."

May 26, 1985
Chief of Naval Operations office,
the Pentagon 1400Z

The CNO turned toward the deputy director of the FBI. "So you're telling me he's *admitted* they've been passing all our crypto to the Soviets?"

"Yes, sir. He says they've never asked for hardware, only the codes."

The CNO leaned back against his desk, scrubbing his hands over his face. "So...as of now, we have to believe the Soviets are reading all our traffic, including the encrypted traffic. And we have no alternative but to destroy all the current crypto in the entire Navy and reissue all new." He glanced at the Vice CNO. "How long?"

"Thirty days, maybe forty-five. Depends on the courier delivery to overseas. What do we do in the meantime about the boomers?"

"Recall them. We need them out of harm's way. We need to do a secure... Shit, I'm not even sure we *can* do secure voice, either." He pushed off the desk, pointed at the deputy director and said, "You need to come with me; we need to go brief the Secretary and Chairman of the Joint Chiefs. I hope you didn't have anything planned this morning."

"No, sir. I didn't. We planned to give the other services courtesy briefs once we found out the level of compromise to our systems."

The CNO looked at the Vice CNO. "Mark, get with your counterparts, figure out what crypto we have in common, and let them know about the compromise. We're not going to downplay this. It is too important."

Admiral of the Soviet Fleet Gorchakov's office, the Kremlin 1100Z

"So we have lost our naval spy," asked Admiral Gorchakov.

"It appears so, sir. Comrade Rostov in Washington was able to confirm he has been picked up, along with his son and other members of his cell."

"So now we go to work. Are there any units we can pick off before the Americans know about it?"

His chief of staff unrolled a chart on his desk, pointing at an area in the north Atlantic off Norway. "There is one. The USS *Michigan* is on patrol here. *Kursk* and K-324 have been detached from the operations off Murmansk and are en route, pending your approval. They should be there in eighteen hours. K-123, an *Alfa,* is already in the area and believes she has had a couple of sniffs of contact. We have positioned her in a patrol box southwest of that position."

"Send an *Udaloy* ASW Destroyer, also. If we can get her up, the *Udaloy* can hold her hostage."

"It will be done, Admiral."

May 27, 1985
USS Michigan, North Atlantic 0300Z

Captain Thomas stuck his head in Sonar. "What you got, Chief?"

"*Alfa* is still south of us. I think we've got one or two *Victor* IIIs coming down from the north. They're a couple of convergence zones out yet." He pointed to a couple of dim lines on one of the screens.

"So they're trying to box us. Dammit, we can't go further west—no water. I think we'll move east and see if we can sneak down the coast."

"We gonna stay deep, Skipper?"

"Unless I hear different, Chief. No reason to go up on the roof since we got the recall and to terminate comms. Something bad is going down, and I've got a feeling our comms might be compromised."

"That Walker thing that was on the feed?"

"Yep. Keep us honest, Chief. I'll be in Conn."

"Will do, sir."

NAVY OPS CENTER, THE PENTAGON 1700Z

The various Navy department heads sat around the conference table, empty coffee cups and wax paper cups filling the trash cans as Captain Montfort, the lead planner, asked tiredly, "Any other options? There sure as hell isn't anything in the contingency plans covering this level of clusterfuck."

The LANTFLT rep on the VTC said, "We've got a carrier underway from the Med, but she's a couple of days away, at best. We really don't know where *Michigan* is or if she's still in her patrol box. Everybody else is accounted for and headed home but her, and we've grounded all Naval Air outside the US, for obvious reasons."

Montfort heard a grumble from down the table and said, "What?"

Captain Tobin looked up in irritation. "And that's BS. There is no reason to ground the P-3s. We could have been out there locating *Michigan* and giving her a hand. We routinely communicate with subs at sea."

"You don't work with boomers, and the Soviet's posture right now is to try to provoke a situation. You saw the report where the MiG hit the Norwegian P-3," the SUBLANT chief of staff countered.

"I don't remember anything in the SOPs that says we can't communicate with boomers, and you guys *supposedly* have the same pubs and the same buoys aboard."

"Well, they aren't allowed to use those."

Montfort made a chopping motion. "Knock it off, you two. Who *did* authorize the grounding of the P-3s and why?"

MAY 28, 1985
TEST CENTER, NAS PATUXENT RIVER,
MARYLAND 0000Z

The P-3 taxiing into the transient line with one engine feathered stopped suddenly, then turned and taxied to a hangar on the Test Center side of the field. It came to a stop in front of a hangar as the doors slid slowly open, and a tow crew and tractor hooked up to the airplane. Minutes later, the hangar doors rumbled closed behind the airplane. As the crew trooped off, they were loaded on a crew bus and taken to base housing, with the mission commander being told he would be notified when the P-3 was ready for a test flight.

Once the crew was gone, a group of civilians came out of various offices and started moving equipment into place on the unmarked P-3 in the other half of the hangar. Four torpedoes were pushed from behind a bank of storage containers as the bomb bay on that P-3 whined open.

Tactical Support Center,
NAS Patuxent River,
Maryland 0200Z

KJ led the rest of the officers and the three Anti-Submarine Warfare chiefs into the briefing room, and they quietly took chairs, staring at each other. Finally, Charlie Clark said, "Still no idea what is going on, TACCO?"

KJ shrugged. "Your guess is as good as mine. We weren't supposed to be on the hook for another three weeks, much less here. I guess we'll find out, since we're obviously going flying somewhere tonight."

The door opened, and a grizzled chief stuck his head in. "I see this is the mushroom locker. Kept in the dark and fed shit, as usual."

Randy started up, bristling, but KJ jumped up. "Dusty! What the hell are you doing here?"

They shook hands, and that devolved into beating each other on the back as Dusty said, "SSDD, I'm workin' out of here now. Looks like I'm going with you."

KJ cocked his head. "I've already got—"

"We're taking 323. It's here, and full up."

Charlie walked over. "Hey, you old reprobate. You ain't getting my seat."

They shook hands as Dusty replied, "Don't need to—I got my own. Your ordy will lose; he gets the galley seat."

Somebody said, "Attention on deck!" and everyone popped to attention as two older men in civvies walked into the briefing room.

One was RADM Gallo, the current Patrol Wings Commander, and he said, "At ease. Seats, guys." The second civilian walked forward, a briefcase in hand, as the admiral made sure the door was locked. "Gents, this is Vice Admiral Mark Kalenberg. He's the VCNO, and he's going to brief you."

The Vice Admiral nodded and popped the latches on his briefcase, pulling two sealed envelopes from it and setting them aside. He pulled a third sealed envelope out and slit the end open, extracting a number of pages. "Gentlemen, we are in serious trouble. Our entire encryption system, Navywide, is compromised. We have an SSBN currently trapped off the coast of Norway by three Soviet submarines and an *Udaloy* DDG. The sub popped a position today, and she is not in extremis, but she can't get home without help."

He slid the two sealed envelopes across the table. "You folks are the help. You're off the books, so to speak, not tied to any squadron, and apparently pretty damn good at putting torps on submarines."

P-3 #323,
NAS Patuxent River,
Maryland 0300Z

The crew bus deposited a very sober group at the hangar after the brief. KJ and the others were all positively identified before being allowed in the hangar, and the first thing he noted was there were two identically painted P-3s sitting side by side. *So this is how they're doing this... Shades of the old days.*

Pops Kanaka came out of the bomb bay and waved to him, motioning him over. KJ told Barney, "I'll be there in a minute. Looks like I've got a checklist to run." Barney nodded and headed up the ladder with the rest of the crew.

"Hey, Pops. Guess you got a surprise, didn't you?"

Pops handed him the checklist. "To put it mildly. These are war shots. And brand-new MK-50s. These aren't even approved yet, but we're carrying four of them?"

"I'll explain at planeside. Let's run this checklist. Gotta admit, it's the first time I've done one in a hangar."

"And I was told no final checker. We do everything in here, then close the bomb bay and go."

"Then let's get to it. Item one—"

. . .

May 29, 1985
Tactical Support Center,
NAS Keflavik, Iceland 0000Z

The debriefing officer looked across the table at KJ and Randy. "So you guys have a mission brief you're not allowed to share with me, and we're laying on three other flights fifteen minutes apart to cover whatever the hell it is you're doing? Is that what you're telling me?"

KJ looked levelly at him. "That's right, Lieutenant. This was tasked by higher than you or I are cleared for. If you've got a problem..."

The DBO threw up his arms. "Oh, screw it. At this point, none of us know what is going on. We're not getting shit over any secure circuit, and...oh, never mind. You're scheduled for a zero-dark-thirty go, take off at 0230 local. You are Mike Kilo 21. No tactical callsign, since we aren't doing shit. Go forth and do whatever it is you're supposed to do. That's all I've got."

"Thanks, Lieutenant. Don't feel bad. You're not the only one in the dark, trust me on this." As they walked out, KJ asked, "You got our track points and times to give to 22? And remind him to change voices when reporting for us, right?"

Randy rolled his eyes, "I may be a pilot, but I can accomplish something this simple, KJ. Don't sweat the petty stuff, and don't pet the sweaty stuff."

KJ laughed. "Okay, see you at planeside."

May 29, 1985
USS Michigan,
North Atlantic 0200Z

Captain Thomas sat in the wardroom nursing a cup of coffee and wracking his brain for a way out of the box they were in. He'd even thought about using a couple of decoys to see if he could confuse people enough to slip away, but that would have given away his hideyhole.

So far, even the intermittent pings from either the subs or the Soviet Destroyer had failed to spook him, but the crew was coming closer and closer to the breaking point. Four days of being constantly on pins and needles was impacting morale and the crew's ability to get rest. Plus, they had to look at possible rationing for food and consumables, like toilet paper. No showers and no laundry for four days was beginning to become apparent, and the boat was starting to stink.

Lieutenant Ryerson, the Communications Officer, came in with the tear sheet from the broadcast they had just copied. "Nothing new, Skipper, but somebody back in Norfolk fucked up the sports again."

"How, this time?"

"Chief caught it—it's item six, and he circled it," he said, laying the tear sheet in front of the captain.

He quickly scanned the tear sheet, then read item six: FOR THE TROOPS UP NORTH, THE SUSPENDED GAME BETWEEN THE YANKEES AND BEARS WILL RECOMMENCE AT 0800 WITH THE SCORE YANKEES 5-BEARS 2.

"Yeah, whoever did the sports obviously isn't a fan. Yankees would never play the Bears. Two different sports." He shook his head. "Put out the other stuff, but leave that one off." The Supply Officer stepped into the wardroom, and the captain said, "I need some time with SUPO."

The Communications Officer got up quickly. "Yes, sir." He threw a look of commiseration at the Supply Officer on his way out, thinking, *Better him than me. I just get fucked-up sports, not trying to figure out how to cut rations.*'

P-3 #323,
200NM SOUTHEAST OF ICELAND 0330Z

KJ keyed the ICS. "Okay, we're out of radar coverage. Time to go see if we get to start World War Three. Randy, make sure 22's got our comms. I'm dropping a fly-to point for you."

He heard the VHF radio key, "22, this is 21."

"21, go."

"We're chopping. You've got our comms."

"Good luck, whatever you're doing. We got it."

KJ came over the PA. "Crew, TACCO: set EMCON, darken ship. We're going down below 1000 feet, floatation gear required. We've got two hours to on-station. Pops says breakfast will be?"

He heard a pop and chuckle over the ICS from Pops. "Whatever the flight kitchen packed. No crew box on here, TACCO."

Various boos and hisses were heard, and Scoop keyed up. "I hope there are hard-boiled eggs!"

Randy keyed the PA. "Hairy, check the breakfasts. If there are any hard-boiled eggs, *dump them immediately!*" He pulled the power back, looked over at Scoop and Eddie and said, "Descent checklist, let's take it down to the deck. I don't want to depressurize unless we have to go to free-fall on buoys." He keyed the PA again. "We're emcon up here. IFF is off, DVARS is off, lights are off."

KJ noted the EMCON on his log, shook his head, unstrapped and stretched.

No gahdamn eggs for Scoop! I don't think I've ever smelled anything that vile in my life, and I sure as hell don't want to again. He looked over at Barney and mimed drinking a cup of coffee, and Barney nodded. Getting up, he headed for the galley and the coffeepot. *At least we got a coffeepot.*

As he walked aft, he checked with each of the operators and got a thumbs-up as they completed their systems checks. Dusty was cocked back in the aft observer's seat, sound asleep, as usual. KJ laughed to himself and checked the extra sensor station in front of Dusty. As always, there was a sticky with an up arrow on it. *Some things never change. I wonder if anything actually bothers Dusty?*

Pops Kanaka was sorting through the boxes of food from the flight line kitchen with Hairy and smiled, "No hard-boiled eggs, TACCO. Looks like omelets and meat du jure in the oven."

Hairy nodded. "At least I can get some sleep before I go back in the seat."

Randy came back, dropped the rack down and climbed in. "I'm down until we go on-station. Tim's in the left seat, and Eddie's in the right." He stuck earplugs in and rolled over, away from the galley light, wiggling to try to get comfortable on the thin mat as the airplane bumped down through the light cloud cover.

The Battle Cab,
the Pentagon 0600Z

The captain and colonel watch officers were on pins and needles as the Chairman, Joint Chiefs of Staff, and the service chiefs followed him into the cab and took seats in the back. One of the Army colonels whispered to the current Air Force watch officer, "Any idea what is going on?"

"Not a fucking clue," said the watch officer.

The chairman tapped the microphone at his seat. "This thing on? Focus on the GIUK gap, please. All air, surface, and subsurface assets, please."

As the picture zoomed in, the Chief of the Air Force asked, "Status on AWACS and tankers?"

The Air Force watch officer used a laser pointer. "AWACS is proceeding to a northern Norwegian Sea patrol, and there is one Tanker, Ploy 87, on a Faroes Island refueling track, sir. But I have no scheduled ops for that track."

The Chief nodded. "Status of 57th FIS?"

"Four F-4s on alert 30, four on alert 60. Weather is projected to be good."

The Chief looked down at his notepad. "493rd?"

The colonel flipped through his notebook. "Four F-111Fs on alert 30, four on alert 60. Weather is marginal."

The Chairman leaned over. "Russ, can they go if they need to?"

"Yeah, they are zero-zero capable. It'll suck if something breaks, but they can launch."

P-3 #323, 1000 FEET,
30NM OFF THE NORWEGIAN COAST 0630Z

Randy keyed up the PA. "Crew, we're inbound to the first fly-to point. TACCO, we're stable at 180 knots, 1000 feet; going to loiter number one. Aft observer, check in."

Chief Isaacson keyed his ICS. "Port aft, standing by." KJ looked out his window as he felt the shudder of the prop feathering, and heard the chief. "Good feather, good X."

KJ looked at the scope and keyed the ICS. "Okay, we're on-station now. One minute to the first buoy drop. Mac, you got anything on ESM?"

"Intermittent Top Plate. Some Soviet combatant. Might be an *Udaloy* or *Krivak*. Still points north, no cross bearing available."

"Charlie, Stretch, Dusty, standby for channels one and 12, and then we're going to run up the channels as we go. Wide spacing, as we discussed."

They all felt the thump of the buoy firing externally and the second internally. KJ heard the rattle of the high-speed printer as Barney dumped the position while Pops opened the chute and pulled the empty launch container out. "Two buoys away."

The tube of the P-3 filled with the odor of cordite, and Dusty crowed, "Ah, the smell, the smell! Let the hunt begin!"

KJ smiled, remembering when he and Dusty were on the special missions' crew and running all over the Atlantic and Mediterranean doing various operations. "Two minutes to next drop, channel two."

A half-hour later, the entire pattern was in the water, and Charlie and Stretch were sending data on two different subs. "Which is which, Charlie?"

"TACCO, the one to the south of nine is the *Alfa*." There was a minute of silence, and he continued, "The one to the west of 12, well, between five and 12, is the *Victor*."

"Nothing else?"

Dusty chimed in, "TACCO, low poss on an *Oscar* 030 off buoy two. Sniff on our guy east of 15."

The Hot Line,
Washington, DC 0700Z

"I have the Kremlin on the line, sir."

"Mr. President, I have a statement to read and will wait for it to be translated and your reply."

"Da."

"Mr. President, we know that you have compromised our secure communications cryptographic systems for now and that you have isolated and are attempting to either capture or board one of our ballistic missile submarines in international waters in the north Atlantic. You have one hour to contact your units and turn them north, removing the blockade on our unit. If you do not do so, I will authorize torpedoes to be used against your units in the area. This is not negotiable."

A simultaneous translation was heard, then a spate of Russian, and the translator said, "We categorically deny that we are attempting anything. We do not admit anything. We are operating in international waters and will continue to do so."

"Mr. President, you know that is a lie. You have one hour. This line will continue to be monitored until 0800 Zulu." He turned to the others in the room. "Come get me if they decide to talk. Otherwise, I'll be in my office," the President said.

P-3 #323, 1000 FEET,
30NM OFF THE NORWEGIAN COAST 0705Z

"TACCO, Jez. I wonder if the reason we're not seeing the *Oscar* is they are using depth separation."

"Hold that thought. Flight, new fly-to: gimme a right 270 after this line. Pops, I'll put this pattern out external. Going to put a containment around the *Victor*, then the *Alfa*, then we'll go look for that *Oscar*."

"Flight, aye."

As the third buoy spat, Mac said, "Got another hit on that Top Plate in sector scan. Sending a cross fix. Looks to be about 30 miles north of us, but I think it's coming south."

A fix popped in on KJ's scope, and he nodded. "Good call. 32 miles. Flight, let's take it down to 500. I want to stay below his radar horizon, just in case."

Randy keyed the PA. "Crew, going below 1000, floatation required." He dropped back to ICS and continued, "Looks like a sea state of one or two. Winds are probably 290 at around ten. Swells look like they are from about 270."

Barney keyed up. "Got it, thanks. Nav is looking pretty good. Minimal split between the inertial systems."

Chief Iverson came forward with two cups of coffee, handing one to Barney and the other to KJ. "Looking good in the back. I just hope Dusty's shit doesn't break. I don't know jack about it."

KJ nodded his thanks. "Don't worry about it. He's an expert on those and actually is building them in his dayjob." He took a sip of the coffee and grimaced. "Maxwell House, again?"

"Sorry, we already drank all the Folgers I brought. And I never got to the commissary." The airplane started bumping and bouncing as they leveled at 500 feet, and the chief sighed. "Once more into the bumps we go. Why can't we *ever* get a smooth flight?"

Barney laughed. "It's a P-3, whatta you expect, Chief?"

THE BATTLE CAB,
THE PENTAGON 0715Z

"Fighter launch, Murmansk. Estimate four MIG-25s. Possible launch IL-78 Midas," came over the speakers in the cab.

The Air Force chief spoke into the mic at his chair. "Bring 57th and 493rd to Alert Five and Alert 15, please. Notify AWACS and Ploy 87 of the MiG launch. Launch the Alert Tanker from Lakenheath."

The Air Force watch officer spun around and quickly made the calls. Once they were done, the Army watch officer leaned over again. "I wish I knew what the fuck is going on! We're *never* supposed to be out of the loop. *Never*!"

The Air Force watch officer shrugged. "Well, we obviously are, in this case. And if we are, I'm not real sure I really want to know."

The Chiefs watched, and as soon as the MIGs turned west, the Chairman asked, "Should we launch our guys?"

The Air Force Chief spoke into his mic and asked, "Do we have a speed on the MIGs yet?"

The colonel said, "Appears to be supersonic, sir."

"Shit. Scramble the 57th, point them at AWACS. Scramble the 493rd and point them north to intercept the MIGs. Launch the Alert 15s from both locations as soon as possible and point them at the Faroes Tanker." He leaned over to the Chairman. "We...it's going to be tight. Might have waited too long."

Alert Barns,
Keflavik and Lakenheath, 0728Z

Klaxons blared in both locations as pilots and WSOs scrambled to man their aircraft, and PAs clicked on. "Immediate launch, immediate launch. Alert Five, Alert 15, immediate launch. Standby for coordinates on common after launch." The message repeated twice more, and the klaxons sounded again but were quickly drowned out by the rising scream of jet carts, then the jets themselves.

Six minutes later, the first pair of F-4s lifted off from Keflavik, cleared unrestricted climb to flight level 280, and speed restrictions lifted. Two minutes later, the first F-111s lifted off from Lakenheath and climbed into the low clouds, clawing for altitude in the rough air. In Reaper 01, the RIO was cursing as he tried to get his systems online in the turbulence and suddenly sat back. "Damn, Roscoe, whatever is going on, it looks like it's for real."

Just as he said that, the British controller came on the radio. "Reaper flight, you are cleared unrestricted to FL280, cleared direct the ADIZ heading 000. Speed restrictions are lifted. We are clearing a corridor for you."

Captain "Roscoe" Booker keyed his radio. "Ah, Departure, Reaper flight copies all. Passing flight level 180 for flight level 280, coming to 000 at this time." They heard the other three aircraft roger the course change, and he said, "What are you talking about, Mongo?"

"I've got Link Four with an AWACS that's up. Four MIG-25s coming around the horn of North Cape with their hair on fire, and we've got 1300 miles to intercept point. I don't know if we're going to beat them there. And not a fucking clue why the intercept point is over the water."

Roscoe looked over at him in amazement. "You got to be shitting me!"

Mongo stared back at him and said carefully, "Roscoe, this *is not* a drill. I think the shit is about to hit the fan for real." He glanced quickly down. "And you're about to break our altitude."

They broke out of the clouds, and he dumped the nose over, skirting the tops of the cloud deck as the other three F-111s broke out. Keying his radio, he said, "London, Reaper flight level flight level 280." London acknowledged, and he keyed up on common. "Reapers, pin the wings back. We got a long way to go and not much time to get there. Confirm Link Four is up and operating."

The Hot Line,
Washington, DC 0750Z

"Have we heard anything back yet?"

"No, sir. Not a peep."

"Do we go back to them again?"

"I wouldn't, sir. You were pretty unequivocal in your statement. If you ask now, I believe you would be showing weakness."

"Probably. Dammit! Why do they have to be so damn stubborn when they are well and truly caught out?"

"Bluster and bullshit, sir. It's been that way since Khrushchev. If they back down, they potentially lose control."

"And they don't care if people die, correct?"

"As long as it's not them, no."

"Do we have comms with the Pentagon?"

"Yes, sir. They are standing by."

The Battle Cab,
the Pentagon 0801Z

The Chairman's face turned white as he listened to the phone, then said, "Yes, sir. I understand. We will give them the launch code, sir. I agree, sir. There will most probably be a loss of life, possibly on both sides. No, sir. Thank you, sir." He hung up and swiped a hand across his face, then turned to the CNO. "It's a go. Do you want to send the message?"

The CNO nodded. "They're my people. It's only fair that I send the message that may get them killed."

The Chairman opened a sealed binder and pulled out one code. "Launch code, correct?" he asked as he passed it down to each chief. They all agreed and passed it back.

He handed it to the CNO, who keyed his mic. "Can I have the secure HF on my phone, please?" A few seconds later, the light above the handset lit up, and he heard the hissing of HF as he put it to his ear and squeezed the handset switch. They all looked up at the big screen as four blue flights sped into the north Atlantic to meet the oncoming red flight, which tracked further and further south.

P-3 #323, 500 feet,
30nm off the Norwegian Coast 0804Z

KJ heard a sudden pop in his ear and faintly heard their callsign. He looked at Barney, who was looking back, both hands clamped over his ears, and keyed the ICS. "Getting a call on HF One. Everybody copy, please." He reached up and killed all of the radios except HF One and heard, "Mike Kilo Two One, Mike Kilo Two One, this is November Charlie Alpha. How copy?"

He glanced at Barney, who pointed at him and handed him the sealed packet from the comm box. He keyed his mic. "November Charlie Alpha, this is Mike Kilo Two One. Copy you, weak but readable. How me?"

"Mike Kilo Two One, November Charlie Alpha, copy you same. Stand by for code word."

"Mike Kilo Two One, standing by."

Mike Kilo Two One, November Charlie Alpha, code word is fastball. I say again: fastball. How copy."

"Mike Kilo Two One, November Charlie Alpha, copy code word fastball." KJ slit the package open as he keyed the ICS. "I copied fastball. Everybody else get that?"

Randy looked around the cockpit and got thumbs-up from everyone. "Flight station agrees."

"Jez, agrees."

"IFT, yep. Fastball."

KJ pulled out the envelope that said Fastball across the front, showed it to Barney, who nodded. He carefully slit it open and pulled out the authentication sequence. He showed that to Barney, who nodded again, and keyed the mic. "November Charlie Alpha, Mike Kilo Two One, request you authenticate Romeo Juliet."

"Mike Kilo Two One, November Charlie Alpha, authenticates Papa Kilo Xray."

KJ keyed his ICS. "Did y'all get Papa Kilo Xray?"

A flurry of double clicks answered him, and he keyed his mic. "November Charlie Alpha, Mike Kilo Two One, confirming authentication. Executing."

"Mike Kilo Two One, November Charlie Alpha, understands executing. Be advised four MIG-two fives en route your position. God go with you."

"Mike Kilo Two One copies all." KJ looked at the tasking order for a moment, then keyed the PA. "Crew, listen up. Our tasking is to launch our torpedoes against the Soviet subs. This is not a drill. I'm afraid we *are* about to start World War Three. And there are apparently MIG-25s inbound, probably to try to stop us. Pops, gimme a signal buoy in the chute. Code five. Flight, take us down to 200. I'd also suggest we think about getting in poopy suits in case this all goes to shit and we end up in the water."

"Buoy's loaded, TACCO." KJ gave the flight station a fly-to point east of where the Soviet subs were and activated it, feeling the airplane bank that way as it bounced lower.

Barney was struggling into his poopy suit, and KJ smiled as he reached behind the seat for his. *Now I will not only be hot; I'll be uncomfortable as hell as I try to get this shit right.* Royster came forward in his suit, carrying Scoop's in his hand, and he smiled wanly as he walked by KJ.

"Pops, weapons checklist. We'll go mid-depth first for the *Victor*, then

I want to go deep for the *Alfa*. We'll reevaluate on the *Oscar* at that point."

Randy said, "Got comms on 243.0, Reaper flight. They want to know where we are."

KJ shrugged. "Handle it. Fifteen seconds to drop."

"Signal buoy away." He activated the first weapons fly to and said, "Flight, come right. I want you to hit that weapons fly-to heading south."

"Got it."

"Mac, get the MAD warmed up. We get a MAD, I'll drop on it."

"Copy. Be advised I've got Saphir radar in search mode, TACCO. Bearing is north."

"Flight, set five. We're about to be in the shit. MiG-25 with look down, shoot down inbound. Only good thing is the *Foxbats* don't have a gun!"

Randy keyed the PA. "Crew, set five, strap in now! Man the aft windows, keep looking for anything coming down on us from above."

Iverson asked, "What is the bottom of the cloud deck?"

KJ looked at his notes and said, "4000. Don't plan on seeing the *Foxbats*. They can stay high and pop off missiles at us."

USS Michigan,
North Atlantic 0811Z

"Conn, Sonar. I've got a code buoy pinging!"

The captain asked, "One of ours?"

"Yes, sir. A code five. What the hell is—?"

The captain suddenly realized what it meant and yelled, "Take us up! Take us up! Keel depth 50 feet! Try not to broach." He ran to sonar. "Chief, let me know if you hear torpedoes."

The sonar chief turned white. "Torps?"

The captain nodded grimly. "And I don't think they are going to be EX-torps. I think they will be war shots."

P-3 #323, 200 feet,
30nm off the Norwegian Coast 0816Z

KJ keyed the ICS. "Two minutes to drop. Come left 160, flight. MAD standby."

"Bomb bay doors coming open," Randy said. "Checklist complete."

KJ saw movement in the passageway and saw Pops crouching over the bomb bay window. He yelled, "What the fuck are you doing, Pops? Get in a seat!"

Pops yelled back, "Gotta make sure it goes. I can roll into a ditching station right here."

Just as KJ started to say standby, Mac yelled, "MADMAN, MADMAN, MADMAN."

KJ punched the button, and the torpedo fell free. "Weapon away, 0818."

Mac yelled again, "Saphir in fire control mode. They've locked us up! Bearing north."

Randy already had the bomb bay doors closing, and he rolled the P-3 seventy degrees and pulled almost three Gs, turning to the left and back into the MiGs.

Iverson groaned. "Got a white streak coming down out of the clouds. It's...went over us."

Barney yelled, "*Aphid*? No radar?" He dumped the HSP again.

"Probably," KJ yelled back and heard a groan in the aisle.

Chief Clark and Dusty both said, "Torp lit off. High speed screws."

Mac came on again. "Saphir in search mode, bearing 180 from us."

KJ made a snap decision. Rolling his cursor over the suspected track of the *Alfa*, he dropped another weapons fly-to point and said, "Flight, hit that if we have time. Five, six minutes out if you reverse now."

Randy rolled the airplane hard again as Chief Clark said, "*Victor* is running. Got decoys in the water. Looks like he's turning northward."

KJ double-clicked the mic and started setting up the second torpedo's programming as Randy stabilized the airplane heading more or less south. He heard a groan again and looked back to see Pops sprawled in the aisle with his left leg going in an unnatural direction. He keyed the PA. "Dusty, Ivy, can y'all come get Pops and put him in the ditching station by the overwing hatch? I think his leg's broken."

He heard, "On it." Seconds later, the two of them were lifting Pops carefully and dragging him toward the back of the airplane.

Randy said, "Reapers are three minutes out; they're going to stay high. Knights are four minutes out, descending. They're going to come down to 3000."

KJ looked at the checklist, made the last selection and said, "Weapon is programmed. All we need is the bomb bay doors. Two minutes out."

He got a double click and Mac said, "Bearing reversal. Saphir in search mode still bearing now 000." A minute later he said, "Looks like the *Foxbats* split. One set of bearings now 330, the other...shit! Saphir lock again!"

Randy said, "KJ?"

"Gimme fifteen seconds." He rolled the scale down and said, "Fuck it, weapon away 0823. Your airplane, Flight."

Randy rolled the airplane violently again just as Mac said, "New radar, terminal home mode! 000 bearing!"

"*Acrid*, AA-6," Barney yelled as he dumped another round of HSP.

Suddenly, Dusty came over the ICS singing, "Fins to the left, fins to the right..."

KJ burst out laughing and glanced over at Barney, who was smiling and shaking his head. He keyed the PA. "Yeah, we get it, Dusty." He leaned across and yelled at Barney, "He ain't never been right in the head."

Iverson came on quietly. "Something hit the water a couple of hundred yards seven o'clock from us."

"Terminal homing radar lost," Mac added. Then he said, "Bearing reversal on Saphir lock up."

KJ looked at his scope, "Flight, keeping heading northwest. Buoy Four, I'm going to put a torp out up there. Maybe we can get the *Oscar's* attention."

Dusty said, "I've got the *Oscar* 330 out of Four. He's fairly close to the buoy."

Randy asked, "How long? They seem to be locking us up every couple of minutes."

"Three, maybe four. Programming now."

A minute or two later, Eddie yelled, "Visual! Looks like...two MiGs off the nose, high."

Mac chimed in, "Saphir lock up, 330, off the nose. Other set 240, search mode."

Randy replied, "We're going to keep running at them. I don't think they can lock us up and get a weapon off before we... Shit... Missile launch, right down our throat. Hang on, folks."

KJ calmly said, "Gimme bomb bay doors." He heard them cycle open and punched the third torp away. "Weapon away. 0828, line of bearing search."

Dusty came on the ICS. "Hey, flight, that ship we just went by is shooting at us. It's an *Udaloy*."

Mac said, "Bearing reversal."

Just as Randy and Eddie said, "Missile went high, MiGs just went over us."

"Aphid again," Barney added.

"Flight, gimme a left 270; I'm going to put the last torp on that damn *Udaloy*. Let's see how he likes it." KJ quickly worked through the programming, and as Randy straightened the P-3 on the new course, he hit the weapons release one more time. "Weapon away, torp four, 0829. And we're Winchester at this time."

"Saphir lock up, bearing 180, Flight!"

Randy rolled the P-3 sharply right, saying, "Right turns aren't natural. Eddie, don't let me hit the water, okay?"

Scoop pushed up power. "Ain't gonna happen, boss. I'll slap the shit outta you, you crash my airplane."

Randy couldn't help but laugh as he continued pulling almost three Gs to get the airplane on a southern heading. This time, he saw the two MiGs first. "Visual, off the nose. Two MiGs, one of them is in a dive, it looks like. Missile away, inbound!"

Mac yelled, "Terminal homing!"

Charlie said, "Explosion, buoy 11, no other sounds."

"Copy. Don't worry about them right now. Everybody cinch your belts down."

The P-3 was rocked hard left, and it was all Randy could do to keep it from rolling completely over as the missile hit the water and exploded underneath the right wing. "Lost aileron effectiveness. Eddie, we still got a wing out there?"

"Yeah, but number four is on fire."

USS Michigan,
North Atlantic 0830Z

"Conn, Sonar. Fourth torp in the water, bearing 030 relative."

Captain Thomas whistled softly as he looked at the plot. "Wonder what the fourth drop was on?" He looked at the plot again and smiled slowly. "High diddle, diddle."

The XO, Commander Green, looked over at him. "Sir?"

"Whoever that was opened the middle up for us." Pointing at the relative bearing lines to the torpedo noises, he continued, "Helm, make your course 245 True. Make turns for one half-knot below cavitation speed. Weaps open outer doors, prep Mk-48s for snapshot."

"Helm, aye," was the response, and he felt the deck tilt slightly and the thrum of the propulsor increase.

"Weaps, aye."

"We're going to run southwest, right through the middle. I think that was the intent." He stepped over to the scope. "Scope up." He caught it about waist high, spinning around as the tube rose higher, until he was standing straight up. "Close aboard is clear."

He turned toward the bow and increased the magnification to the maximum, moving back and forth. "Might be a P-3 out there. Distant. Some...jets, too. And...that one looked like an F-4. Smoke trails. Somebody is catching hell. Just saw an explosion. Bearing, mark! Second explosion, bearing, mark!"

"243 True, 238 True, Captain."

"Tell Sonar to listen down bearing 243." He slapped the handles up and retracted the scope. "XO, you have the conn."

Reaper and Black Knight
Flights 0830Z

"Reaper, Knight 01, we've got a tally on two Foxbats down here. Oh, wait, make that *one* Foxbat. The second just splashed itself. One P-3, on fire...it's turning west. We're intercepting remaining Foxbat."

"Knight, Reaper's got two Foxbats turning tail up here. We're at flight level 240 on top. Current heading, 000 true."

"And Reaper, Knight. This guy doesn't want to play. He's...in the cloud, coming around on 000. I still have a lock. Coming upstairs, I'll stop at 200. Go air-air 29."

"29."

"I've gotcha 190 at ten. I *think* this guy is going to pop out in front of you."

"Roger. We'll pull it back a bit to make sure."

P-3 #323, 200 feet,
40nm off the Norwegian Coast 0832Z

Scoop E-handled the number four engine, and Eddie said, "Good feather."

"Fire light, number four. Check me, fire bottle selected."

Randy said, "Number Four. Hit it." Scoop hit the fire extinguisher.

Dusty came in the ICS. "Flight, I see fuel streaming out from under the wing between three and four. And I still see fire in what's left of number four."

Eddie said, "Still seeing flames."

Scoop sighed. "Selecting alternate fire bottle. This is our last shot."

Eddie said, "Alternate selected."

Scoop fired it and watched as Eddie looked out the side window. "No joy."

Dusty yelled, "Flight, lots of flames out from under the wing, outboard of number three!"

Randy keyed the PA, "Crew, prepare for ditching. We don't have any choice." He turned the P-3 slowly south, paralleling the waves and said, "Fuck it. Send a distress message."

Barney keyed the HF as KJ keyed the UHF on guard. Barney put out the standard ditching message as KJ said quickly, "Knight, Mike Kilo 21, we're going in. How about relaying to somebody to come get us?"

He heard a quick, breathless response. "Knight 02, copy. We see you. SOBs?"

KJ answered, "Thirteen, one three. Souls on board. One injured, broken leg. Time 0834."

"Knight 02, copy."

Randy keyed the PA. "Standby for ditch." One long ring of the command bell followed, and he said, "Brace!"

KJ glanced over at Barney as he put his head down, saying a quick prayer as the P-3 hit the water, then bounced, bounced again, and slewed violently to the right. KJ vaguely remembered throwing up his arm, and then nothing.

He came to as Barney and Tim dragged him down the aisle, and he moaned in pain. Tim said, "Where are you hurt?"

"My arm. I can walk, I think." Water sloshed back and forth as it bubbled deeper and deeper, and he asked, "Everybody out?"

"Randy's checking. We're the last from up front."

The next thing he remembered was lying in the raft, and Dusty, his face covered in blood, bitching, "I brode by dam node agin. Dam parachood."

He looked around. "Where's Pop?"

Randy leaned over him. "He's in the other raft. We're all out. Iverson broke his foot falling in the hydraulic service center. Here, take this aspirin," Randy said, sticking it between his lips and holding a baby bottle full of water up to his lips.

KJ choked it down, and coughed. "Thanks. What happened?"

Eddie laughed ironically. "Right wing outboard of number three came off. Hooked a wave. Six of us in here, the other seven in the twelve-man. We're tied together. Knights said they'd notify sea air rescue. They had to leave; they were out of gas and needed to tank to get home."

KJ propped himself up a little. "So what have we got for radios and rats?"

Hairy replied, "Standard raft fare, and the rate we're drifting, we might make Norway before anyone finds us. So far, five, maybe six working radios, plus the two radios on the raft. One radio watch, one lookout. Two hours at a time."

USS Michigan,
North Atlantic 1230Z

Chief of the Boat Handfield swung the periscope and flipped to maximum magnification, then sang out, "I've got a life raft. Bearing, mark!"

The navigator said, "243 true."

"Somebody go wake up the captain." He ran the cross hairs down and said, "Range 1100 yards. Second raft sighted." He looked over at the helm, "Make turns for slow ahead. Steer 235."

"Helm, aye."

He had just taken a second mark when Captain Taylor stumbled onto into the conn, rubbing his face. "Whatcha got, COB?"

"Two rafts. They're drifting down on us. Range 800." He stepped away from the periscope and said, "Bearing about 239."

The captain hooked his forearms over the scope handles, made a quick full sweep, then a second, and finally turned to the heading. "Yep, looks like two rafts. Shall we offer them a ride?" he asked rhetorically.

The COB almost choked while trying to keep from laughing as the XO ran into the conn. "XO, you have the conn. Let's get up on the roof and see if these guys want a lift home. Muster the rescue party, and get them ready, if you will."

He felt the deck tilt as he hurried back to his stateroom, grabbing his float coat off the back of the door. He started back out, then reached back and crammed his ballcap on his head.

Five minutes later, he stood on the bridge, bullhorn in hand, as he conned the sub between the two rafts, catching the line on the conning tower. He turned to the talker. "All stop. Rescue party on deck, please." He clicked on the bullhorn and cleared his throat. "Ah, gentlemen in the rafts, may I have your attention?" A couple of heads popped out, and he smiled as he continued, "We were in the neighborhood and wondered if you might like a ride."

June 9, 1985
Kings Bay, Georgia 0300Z

The tugs nestled the USS *Michigan up* to her berth at the pier, and the brow was swung over and fastened into place. Rear Admiral Owens, the submarine squadron commander, closely followed by three other officers, came up the brow and stepped on board before the watch had a chance to challenge them.

Rear Admiral Owens told the topside watch, "Gents, this boat is on lockdown. Nobody on or off until you are released. Speak to no one, and don't announce us. Understood?"

The three watch standers came to attention and said in chorus, "Yes, sir."

As the officers passed, one of the watch standers whispered to another, "Did you see that middle guy? How many stars did he have, three, or four?"

The other watch stander shook his head. "Don't know, and ain't asking."

The four went down the ladder and into the passageway, marching forward, much to the surprise of the sailors on the ship. A ripple of "Attention on deck" was passed forward as they advanced on the conn.

Captain Thomas was surprised to see Rear Admiral Owens step into the conn, and even more surprised when Vice Admiral Mark Kalenberg stepped in. The VCNO nodded. "Admiral Owens has a brief for you and the crew. Where are the aviators?"

"They're all in the wardroom, Admiral. XO, would you escort the admiral, please?"

As they stepped into the wardroom, KJ looked up and called, "Attention on deck!"

The crew was rising when the VCNO said, "At ease, keep your seats. Gentlemen, I'll make this short and to the point. You were injured by a freak wave while you were onboard a fishing boat off Brunswick. You were brought here for medical treatment. Your luggage is here. Your TAD never happened, you left Patuxent River, flew to NAS Jacksonville and broke the airplane." He turned to his flag aide, who handed him thirteen pink sheets. "Take one, pass them around and sign them. You know what they are. Unofficially, you did a helluva job, even if all the Soviet subs made it back to port. Officially," he shrugged, "nothing ever happened."

Chief Clark muttered, "Didn't think so. The explosions were all timeouts, then. Dammit."

Dusty asked, "So even though we got a MiG, we don't get to paint a silhouette on a P-3, sir?"

The admiral laughed as the flag aide looked at Dusty in horror. "No, son. You don't. Not even on a model. Ever."

ABOUT JL CURTIS

JL Curtis is a retired Naval Flight Officer, serving over 20 years all over the world. He is also a retired engineer in the defense industry, specializing in Research and Development testing. A long time NRA instructor, he now lives in north Texas writing full time. JL Curtis has thirteen novels out in three different series, The Grey Man (urban fiction), Rimworld (military science fiction), and a new series, Showdown on the River (western). He also has written a number of novellas and short stories for over sixteen different anthologies.

He has also been a moderator and panelist at various conventions, including LibertyCon, LTUE, FantaSci, and others. He enjoys helping new authors to NOT make the same mistakes he has made.

He can be found at his blog- http://oldnfo.org or at his Amazon author page- https://amzn.to/4gAk8nU

PER ARDUA AD ASTRA

Jan Niemczyk

1

7th May 2005.
Thorpe on the Hill,
Lincolnshire, England.

> *"When Saturday 7th May dawned, it was Day 15 of World War Three; it was also Day 22 after mobilisation. Fatigue was beginning to set in on both sides. Today, it is not particularly remembered, it was neither a 'Hardest Day,' nor a 'Battle of Britain Day,' like the battle of the Last War. It was simply 'Another Day at the Office' for the men and women assigned to the defence of the UK, and while the day might not have been remembered or marked as being historic, it would be long remembered by most of those who were there."*

Extract from *The Aerial Conflict over the United Kingdom and Republic of Ireland, Volume IV of the Official History of the Third World War* (Government Official History Series, London 2020), by Marshal of the Royal Air Force Lord Foster of High Wycombe, RAF (Retired) and Dr. Lawrence Marksman.

David 'Gambo' Gambon, husband, father, Squadron Leader in No. 615 (County of Surrey 'Churchill's Own') Squadron, rolled over in the bed of the budget travel hotel. It took a moment for him to realise that he was not in his Haslemere home lying next to his wife Roberta.

If I was going to spend a night away from my wife in a hotel, I'd have hoped for better circumstances than this. The hotel had been requisitioned by the RAF a week ago after the Soviets had bombed the housing areas of a number of RAF Stations. Gambon was of the opinion that the action should have been a long time ago rather than requiring several dozen dead to be implemented.

Stupid bean counters will be the death of us all, he thought, stretching and heading into the latrine for his morning routine. Gambon was the Tactical Director of a Sentry AEW.1 crew, meaning he was the senior man aboard the aircraft. He also was the Officer Commanding A Flight, No. 615 Squadron, a Royal Auxiliary Air Force (RAuxAF) unit that provided additional air and ground crew for the RAF's Sentry force. As an auxiliary, No. 615 had no aircraft of its own, although No. 8 Squadron had been kind enough to paint one of their *Sentries*' port side with the markings of 615.

Regulars sure have been a lot kinder to us than I expected, Gambon thought as he began shaving. *Might be because the fighter boys have gotten them used to part-timers.*

While 615 Squadron did not have aircraft of its own, most of the other RAuxAF flying squadrons that had re-appeared during the late 1990s as part of the strengthening of Britain's defences did. That included seven of No. 11 (Fighter) Group's seventeen interceptor and fighter squadrons, their *Tornado F.3*s flown and maintained by volunteers. As the Americans had proven in the '70s and '80s, the old argument that part-timers could not operate sophisticated jet aircraft had just not held up to reality. The RAF had been glad to realise the cost savings involved.

Only reason we're still in the war, Gambon thought grimly. *Would not have been enough fighters to go around otherwise.* With that sobering thought, he headed down to get himself breakfast.

"Wakey, wakey, everybody!" a gruff RAF corporal stated from the front of the coach. It seemed like only a couple of seconds after Gambon had closed his eyes after boarding the vehicle in front of the hotel. "Have your passes ready for inspection!"

Bloody hell, these twenty minutes get shorter and shorter every day, Gambon thought, looking around the shuttle from the hotel. Getting his bearings, he began to rummage through the pockets of his flight suit. Outside his window, other RAFP 'Snowdrops' inspected the vehicle while being covered by the rifles of RAF Regiment Gunners.

I doubt we'd get hijacked in eight miles, but better to be safe than sorry, Gambon thought. He looked at the police escort that waited just outside of the base's gate to resume escorting the coach when it returned with the outgoing *Sentry* crews.

Then again, if they get past all of those police, then a few gate guards probably won't even slow them down. Gambon handed over his pass while hoping *that* disquieting thought didn't show on his face.

"I really wish they'd properly disposed of '108, Flight," Gambon observed, gesturing towards a burnt-out aircraft through the crew bus window. "Hardly conducive to our morale."

The Sentry that bore the serial number ZH108 had been destroyed in a Soviet air raid a week ago. Its burned-out carcass had been bulldozed onto a patch of grass between the main hardstand and a taxiway, where it was still visible to all. Thankfully, the RAF had had enough foresight to disperse its seven precious *Sentries* around the UK so that only a couple had been on the ground at Waddington when it had been attacked.

"At least nobody was killed aboard her, Sir," Flight Sergeant Max Phillips replied as the crew bus pulled up to *Sentry* ZH 107. "Shame to lose her, though; always thought she was amongst the best of the bunch."

Forty-five minutes later, ZH 107 was climbing to take her position over the North Sea. Gambon listened as the flight crew began coordinating with the *Tristar* tanker that would top off her tanks.

It's going to be a long day.

2

RAF LEUCHARS,
FIFE, SCOTLAND

Wing Commander John 'Jack' Foster, RAF, Commanding Officer of 43 (Fighter) Squadron, tried to focus on shaving rather than his imminent duties that day.

I'd rather face a flight of Flankers *than this lot*, he thought. The Ministry of Defence had authorised a group press visit in the hope of getting some good, morale-raising coverage that could also be used in the propaganda war.

Here's to hoping it will at least be partially *successful*, Foster thought uncharitably. He'd never been a big fan of the media. If the correspondent wasn't a blithering airhead who had never served, then they were generally officers who had retired so long ago that they considered the *Hawker Hunter* to have been the apex of modern fighter technology.

If I'd known making ace would lead to this, I might have let that last Fencer *get away*. Air Commodore Forbes-Hamilton, the Station Commander, had insisted that as the RAF's first modern ace, he should be the one to show around the print and television reporters. At least some of the print journalists were from aviation magazines, which meant they *should* know what they were talking about. Well, apart from a few individuals who still wrote of the *Tornado F3* as if it was the same aircraft that had first been delivered to the Air Force in 1985.

"Ow! Bugger!" he said, the thought of the latter idiots having apparently led to him pressing a little too hard on the razor. The *Tornado* pilots had been fed up with 'professional' aviation journalists calling their aircraft 'inadequate', or at best 'barely adequate for the task' prior to the conflict. In the twenty years since the *Tornado F3* had entered service, it had become virtually a different aircraft, capable of standing up to the best fighters in the world.

Some people don't keep up with the times, he thought, dabbing at the blood welling up from his chin.

---

43 Squadron's crew room was a different place than it had been a few hours ago. Located in the hardened squadron headquarters, it was usually full of pizza boxes and detritus from takeaways ordered from local restaurants.

Thank goodness they got the 'lad' and 'ladette' magazines out, he thought, looking at the magazine rack located between the crew couches. In their place were a number of aviation magazines, a few copies of *RAF News*, and the latest editions of the newspapers that the print journalists wrote for. Pictures on the walls of scantily clad persons of both genders had been replaced by aviation prints and aircraft recognition pictures.

"Because they could be scrambled at any time, I'm afraid I can't introduce you to the aircrew on alert, but I can let you speak to others who are off-duty at the moment," Foster told the journalists. "They should be happy enough to answer any questions you have for them."

"Before we start, Wing Commander, can I ask how it feels to be the RAF's first ace since the Last War?"

"It's an honour; however, it's one I share with my navigator, Squadron Leader Wilkinson," Foster replied. "It was also very much a team effort. Without the ground crew, my *Tornado* could never have gotten off the ground in the first place, and without those working in the radar stations and AWACS aircraft, we would never have been able to find our targets in the first place."

Foster paused to give some of the reporters time to scribble down what he was saying.

"I'm very much a cog in a much larger machine. I also hope you'll remember that there are a lot of aircrew out there doing the same job as me—I'm not anything special," Foster said.

"Can I ask how your aircrew feel flying an aircraft considered inferior to enemy aircraft?"

There was a rustle of paper and clicking of cameras as Foster turned to look at the questioner. Foster recognised the questioner as the defence correspondent of a national newspaper, a man called Mel Rippert. He was renowned for his opinionated and critical articles on UK defence procurement; the last one Foster could recall had suggested that the *Typhoon* was a waste of money, and that the RAF should have bought the *Super Hornet* instead. Buying American was something of a theme for him, and Foster often wondered if he was paid by the US defence industry to promote their products and rubbish their British and European rivals.

Foster thought uncharitably as he fixed the man with a hard gaze. After a few awkward moments of silence, the man broke eye contact.

"The *Tornado F.3* is in no way inferior to any enemy aircraft we can expect to encounter," Foster replied, his tone precise. "Indeed, last year at an exercise in Nevada, crews from this squadron and Treble One racked up a kill ratio of twelve to one against American Aggressor squadrons simulating Soviet fighters."

"Yes, but the *F.3* can't dogfight in the same way as American aircraft like the *Hornet*, or Russian ones like the MiG-29," Rippert persisted, as if he had not heard Foster's previous answer.

Foster gave the man a thin smile.

"Our main enemies are cruise missiles, *Backfire* and *Fencer* bombers, none of which are agile enemies. However, we have fought several successful engagements with Su-27 *'Flankers.'* I'm sure you saw in the briefing packet that I've killed two and my squadron has downed eighteen total."

Foster paused, his look making it clear he was expecting a response. When the correspondent murmured something, Foster moved on.

"Yes, the *F.3* is not a traditional agile fighter aircraft—it is an interceptor. Moreover, in my opinion, when you are armed with weapons like the *AMRAAM* and *ASRAAM*, you have done something wrong if you are forced into a dogfight."

He swept over the gathered audience, then went in for the finish.

"This is 2005, not 1940; we like to kill our enemies before he can see us or knows that we are there. Our tactics essentially make the agility of an enemy irrelevant."

The journalist did not look happy with the answer, principally because it did not fit his preconceptions. He was about to make another point when one of his colleagues jumped in first.

"If I may ask a question, how do the female aircrew cope with living in a male-dominated environment?" she asked.

Oh, Lord, not this again.

"Perhaps I'm not the best person to answer that. After all, I have the wrong equipment," Foster replied. A few of the journalists, but not the questioner, chuckled.

No sense of humour, some people.

"However, I have always been of the opinion that there are only two kinds of aircrew on this squadron: pilots and navigators, or Weapon Systems Operators, as we are now supposed to call them. Neither aircraft nor weapons care whether someone keeps their reproductive equipment on the inside or outside."

He looked up to see two of his squadron mates' faces fixed with thin smiles.

They hate these questions as much as I do, he thought. *Sorry, Bubbles and Mamba.*

"I'm sure that any of our female aircrew will be happy to share their experiences with you. Now are there any more questions before I pass you on?"

A journalist from a tabloid put up his hand.

"I wonder if I might ask a couple of personal questions, Wing Commander? It's just that our readers would like to know a bit more about the people behind the uniform."

"Ask away, but I don't guarantee to answer if it's a bit too personal," Foster said with a grin.

"Can I ask if you are married?"

"Not yet, but I am engaged."

"How does your fiancée feel about your job?"

"Well...at the moment, she's eating her heart out with jealousy," Foster said laughing. "She's also a pilot, though at the moment she's on a ground posting because of a back injury she got during an ejection."

There was a slight murmur of sympathy from the gathered journalists.

You'd be more sympathetic if you knew how much fun it is dealing with the cross between a cornered wild cat and disturbed wasp nest at home, Foster thought.

"She's a better pilot than me and I'm pretty sure she would have made ace well before I did if given the opportunity."

Once again, he paused as the reporters wrote this information down. He looked at his watch.

"Given the time, I'll let you loose on the aircrew because I'm pretty sure you've heard enough of my voice." Foster paused for a moment, just in case there were any questions. "Good: let me know when you are done, or if you have any trouble."

Foster sighed in relief once the journalists had dispersed to seek new victims. He knew fine well that his aircrew had been dreading this visit.

I'll just have to tell them the same thing they told me when I complained: "It will give you invaluable experience in speaking to the media and thus help with your professional development."

"Bet you're glad to get shot of that lot, boss," Squadron Leader George Wilkinson, the squadron's senior navigator, remarked.

"Where have you been hiding, George?" Foster asked, startled by the navigator's appearance. "I'm pretty sure that our esteemed visitors from the media would want to interview the other half of the first *Tornado* crew to become aces."

"I've got paperwork to catch up on, Boss, and then I need to inventory my personal kit and clean my SIG pistol. I'm afraid I don't really have the time, sorry."

Foster laughed.

"Nice try, George. I'm afraid you have to share the misery with the rest of us."

"Ah, well, worth a shot," the navigator conceded.

The door opened as an orderly from the Sector headquarters walked in with a message. Foster noted the red folder.

"Sir, could you please sign for this?" the young Corporal asked. Foster nodded, scribbling quickly on the requisite message form. Once that was done, he took the folder and checked to make sure no journalists could see what was inside. A quick scan caused him to purse his lips.

"Clear the journos," he stated. "It looks like we're about to be busy."

Thirty minutes later, Foster put the journalists out of his mind as his *Tornado* F.3 taxied out of the Hardened Aircraft Shelter (HAS). He needed to concentrate on the task ahead.

"Leuchars Tower, Delta One Three Alpha requesting permission to depart, over."

"Delta One Three Alpha, Leuchars Tower, you are clear to depart; contact Buchan once airborne. Good luck, sir."

"Thank you, and good day, tower."

3

Sentry AEW.1 ZH107,
over the North Sea

Squadron Leader Gambon was halfway through a cup of tea and a bacon-and-egg roll when his working day began.

"Tactical director, surveillance controller: we have what looks like a possible raid developing over the eastern Baltic," Sergeant Harris, one of the ZH107's NCOs, stated. "Have designated as RAID BRAVO ONE THREE, currently composed of sixteen aircraft."

"I can see it on my screen," Gabon replied. "What makes you think it is a threat to the UKADR? Could be heading for a target in the Central Region."

"The aircraft of RAID BRAVO ONE THREE have conducted what looks like air-to-air refuelling. A raid heading for the Central Region is not likely to need to do that," the controller replied.

"Your assessment would be a raid of *Fencers* or *Fullbacks*, then?"

"Affirmative," Harris said. "We also have what looks like a raid of *Backfires* coming out of the Leningrad Military District."

"Well, if it rains it pours," Gabon commented.

He consulted one of the other displays to check which RAF fighters were in the best position to intercept, then made sure that the data-link system was transmitting the most up-to-date information to them. While the Sentry could control the air battle, for the moment, it would be up to the controllers at the two Sector Operations Centres, RAF Buchan and RAF Neatishead, that would make the decisions regarding aircraft allocation.

Of course, if they get knocked out, it's on us, he thought, looking at the *Backfires*.

HQ RAF Strike Command,
RAF High Wycombe, Buckinghamshire.

Air Chief Marshal Sir Michael Johnson's day had also started early; he had risen from the narrow cot in the room provided for him in the station's bunker, shaved, eaten a rather Spartan breakfast, then taken his daily walk outside. The fact that he was accompanied by four armed members of the RAF Regiment and that even his ADC, Flight Lieutenant Victoria "Vicky" Jackson carried a sidearm, had not spoiled his enjoyment of the fresh air. Well, not too much.

As CINCUKAIR—the Commander in Chief UK Air Forces—Johnson controlled all NATO aircraft based in, or transiting through, the UK. His job had been onerous enough in peacetime. Now that certain people kept trying to bomb his command, the responsibilities had grown exponentially.

"Let's go to the Air Defence Operations Centre," Johnson said, feeling much more refreshed. "Always good to show one's face before things get too hectic."

Vicky and his security detachment laughed politely at his joke as they walked towards the bunker.

"Morning, Colin, how goes it?" Johnson asked the senior officer on duty as he stepped through the final blast door.

"Good morning, sir," Group Captain Colin Kenneth replied. "Their day shift has put in an appearance a little earlier. We've got several raids appearing already—Frontal Aviation stuff coming out of East Germany, plus Long-Range Aviation *Backfires* out of Leningrad and the Kola Peninsula. Danes and Dutch might get some of the Frontal Aviation stuff, but we can't bank on it, given operations over the Central Front."

CINCUKAIR looked at the large display on the far wall, which showed all of the radar tracking information available to the ADOC superimposed on an electronic map before he replied. He was also able to take in the virtual "tote board" alongside, which showed the readiness state of every squadron under his command. The racetrack traces of aircraft on Combat Air Patrol, tanker trails and AEW positions could also be clearly seen on the big display.

"The *Fencers* and *Fullbacks* will probably be escorted," Kenneth continued. "So we'll have the Tiffies go after them and send the Tonkas after the *Backfires*," he said, using the nicknames for the *Typhoon FGR.2* and *Tornado F.3*.

"Best use for them, Colin, although I do recall that Tonkas have still managed to give *Flanker* escorts quite a surprise, just as they did to *Eagles* at Red Flag last year," Johnson said.

If we ever wanted proof that the upgrades were worth it, beating up those American Eagles *provided it*, Johnson thought. *Still, not keen on having the* Tornadoes *fight* Flankers *too often.*

"Well, Colin, I'm due to call John Hazel, so I'll let you get on with it. I'll pop in this afternoon, though, and see how things are going. But if you need me give me a bell..."

"Will do, sir."

Technology is a grand thing, Johnson thought. Air Vice Marshal William "Bill" Hazel, Air Officer Commanding 11(Fighter) Group, stood looking into the video camera at RAF Bentley Priory. The station where Air Marshal Dowding had commanded the previous Battle of Britain, Bentley Priory had seen a great deal of updates since 1940. The Standby Air Defence Operations Centre (SADOC) that Hazel currently stood in was heavily computerized, giving him the ability to conduct a video conference with Air Chief Marshal Johnson as if the two had been in the same room.

This is a lot for former fighter jocks to take in, Johnson thought. Hazel had been a *Phantom* driver, while Johnson had flown the *Lightning*. There was more computing technology in the laptop running the conference than whole squadrons of either fighter could have boasted.

At least Hazel has remained somewhat current, Johnson thought, remembering that he'd had to forbid Hazel from flying either *Tornado F.3* and *Hawk T.2* sorties after the man had done both the first day of the war.

"Good morning, sir," AVM Hazel stated. "I hope you are well."

"Morning, Bill, I'm not bad, thanks," ACM Johnson replied. "I see it looks like our visitors are arriving a bit earlier today as intelligence suggested. Anything we should be worrying about?"

"They went after a few of my mobile ground radars during the night; Neatishead lost one and Boulmer had an emitter damaged," Hazel reported. "However, replacements are now operational, and I don't have any gaps in ground radar coverage."

Johnson saw the man's gaze shift as he looked at the map that was likely located just behind the SAOC's video feed.

"I'd expect the Soviets to try again during the day. I've ordered that as many of the emitters as possible be relocated to make locating them that bit harder."

"Could explain the extra *Backfires*," Johnson replied. "You need me to shift any fighters or ask the Americans for some of their *Eagles*?"

"No, sir," Hazel replied quickly, as if he'd anticipated the question. "The American deep strikes need escorts, and I don't have any concerns about the fighter force and our ground defences. I could do with more of both, but I'm sure every commander has said the same during wartime."

Johnson chuckled.

"Absolutely, Bill. We're lucky to have as much as we do, though."

Both men shared a grim smile at that one, well aware of the politics that had nearly gutted Britain's defence spending in the past. Thankfully, politicians in the 1980s and 1990s had stopped the rot.

"If today is going to be a maximum effort from the other side, I fully expect them to go after our main HQs," Johnson said. "So there is every chance that you may need to take over; after all, you are my current designated deputy if anything happens to High Wycombe."

"You don't have to worry on that account, sir," Hazel replied. "We're fully ready to take over here, if need be. And as the navy toast goes: 'Here's to bloody wars and sickly seasons.'"

CINCUKAIR chuckled at the reference.

"You'll not be getting a promotion today, I hope," he replied. "Either through disease or AS-6."

"Don't jinx yourself, sir," Hazel replied, drawing an involuntary snort from Victoria.

"That reminds me—no flying operationally," Johnson said. "I know you took a *Tornado* up the other day. I expect to be talking to you in a few hours, not hearing from Gwendolyn that the SAR are still trying to fish you out of the North Sea. Good luck to you and your people."

4

Over the North Sea

Flight Lieutenant Katherine Catz, known by her squadronmates as 'Katy Cat', or just 'KC', loved flying the *Typhoon FGR.2*.

Still the greatest aircraft ever built, she thought. *Period*. It was her second tour on the *Typhoon*, and her current tour with 74 (Tiger) Squadron was quite different than her previous stint with 92 Squadron at RAF Wildenrath in West Germany.

I don't think it's being a lead, either, she thought. Her experience at Wildenrath had qualified her to lead a flight. She'd led three other *Typhoons* off the runway at RAF Wattisham in Suffolk, and now the two pairs were split at their station over the North Sea. It'd been about an hour flying a lazy figure-eight pattern before her data link had beeped at her.

Looks like trade, Catz thought, her pulse picking up. She glanced over at her wingman, Flight Lieutenant Steve Carr, and saw he was waggling his wings to acknowledge he'd received the message, as well. It was time to go engage the formation of Soviet aircraft designated 'RAID BRAVO ONE THREE,' a group of sixteen contacts that could be a mixture of various threats.

Don't know how they did it with Skyflash, *never mind* Red Top *on the* Lightning, Catz mused. Her father and grandfather had both worn the

Royal Air Force blue and flown interceptors. She was glad her *Typhoon* currently carried the six *Meteors,* with their 300 km range; it was nice to be able to engage and still have 200 kilometres to play with before the *Flankers* could employ their AA-12 *Adders*. With four additional *ASRAAM* infrared-guided missiles and a 27mm Mauser cannon, theoretically the first two *Typhoons* could take down the entire raid before running out of missiles.

Oh, to live in a world without ECM and self-protective jammers, she thought, giving a quick scan of her aircraft's main Multi-Function Display. The Soviet raid was broken into two formations. One of four aircraft, probably the escort, flew a couple of miles ahead of the main formation of twelve aircraft.

Probably Fencers, *hopefully not* Fullbacks. The former aircraft, resembling the Americans' F-111, had only rudimentary air-to-air capability. The latter, roughly analogous to the F-15E *Strike Eagle*, had the ability to carry four AA-12s for self-protection. Catz had not been on the flight that had first found that out, but it had resulted in three dead *Tornadoes* and a badly damaged *Typhoon*. In any case, first priority would be the escort, with the hope that their destruction would cause the bombers to turn around. Although Catz had yet to see this happen since the war had begun, allegedly just such an event had occurred on the war's second day.

If intelligence is to be believed, that flight commander was executed. Evidently, Soviet authorities took a dim view of aircrew that turned back, even if continuing on meant certain destruction. She turned her head to port, seeing that the second pair of *Typhoons* were now in position.

Here we go. Catz turned up threat and went to full military power, Carr following. They kept their CAPTOR radars silent for the moment, waiting until they were well within range of their Meteors. At 250 kilometres, Catz illuminated the radar. The *Typhoon's* systems quickly sorted the targets, selecting those that it assessed were the greatest threat. She armed the aircraft's weapons and waited half a second.

"Select Target One, *Meteor* One," she told the *Typhoon's* weapon system.

"Target One, Meteor *One selected,"* the aircraft's computerised voice confirmed.

"Fox Three! Fox Three!" Catz announced, her first radio call of the sortie.

The *Meteor* missile dropped away from the belly of the aircraft, its solid rocket igniting once it was clear. She saw the weapon flash away, then become a streak as its ramjet took over and pushed it past Mach Four.

"*Target Two selected*," the *Typhoon*'s computer intoned. Catz pushed the pickle button for a second time, transmitting yet another warning. With four missiles in the air from her formation, Catz and Carr shut down their radars, reversed course and lost height to try to avoid any return fire.

The lead pilot of the Soviet formation had expected to come under attack at some point—the radar warning receiver (RWR) of his Su-27M had been warning him about several airborne and ground radars scanning his aircraft. Amongst the plethora of warnings, he initially missed the addition of the *Typhoons'* radars; he could not miss the strident warning of missile lock, however. The Soviet officer activated his aircraft's defensive systems and began to manoeuvre hard, but it was too late. The *Flanker* was well within the *Meteor*'s "no escape zone," and it blasted the Soviet fighter in half. The pilot managed to eject from his crippled aircraft, starting his descent towards the unforgiving North Sea below.

Catz could see that the four *Meteors* fired by her flight and the second pair of *Typhoons* had all found their targets. 'RAID BRAVO ONE THREE' had lost its escorts and was now vulnerable. To her surprise, the bombers did not attempt to evade; instead they broke into two formations and came at the British aircraft, missiles separating from under their wings.

"*Warning! Warning! Radar lock!*"

"Oh my God, it's a fighter sweep!" Catz radioed, even as she fired her own *Meteors*, then began to evade.

5

Sentry AEW.1 ZH107

Dammit!" Squadron Leader Gambon exclaimed, Catz's warning blaring across the speakers. He quickly checked the display; if the Soviet formation made it past the four *Typhoons*, there was only a pair of *Tornado F.3*s between them and ZH 107. As he watched two of the *Typhoons* and another three *Flankers* wink out, Gambon was well aware the Soviets would happily sacrifice sixteen aircraft in exchange for a *Sentry*. That didn't even account for the two additional raids starting to move out of the Baltic behind Bravo One Three.

"Captain, Tactical Director: I am designating 'RAID BRAVO ONE THREE' as a direct threat to this aircraft. I'm authorising you to take evasive action as necessary to safeguard us."

"Roger that," the Aircraft Captain replied from the cockpit.

"Fighter Controller, Tactical Director, tell those two Tonkas from CAP position Charlie Three Four to go after anything that gets past the Tiffies. We're not going to wait for reinforcements to save us."

"Roger that," the Fighter Controller acknowledged.

While the Aircraft Captain and Fighter Controller were carrying out their tasks, Gambon sent an urgent message to the ground. If his *Sentry* was at threat, it was likely that the second aircraft also was.

Delta Flight

Wing Commander Foster had been waiting to be ordered to intercept a formation of Tu-22M4 *Backfire* bombers when he received the message about the threat to the Sentry.

"It's turned into a real furball, boss," Squadron Wilkinson reported from the rear cockpit. He could see that the two remaining *Typhoons* were fighting for their lives against Bravo One Three's remnants. "Two bandits are heading our way."

"Right, George, got it. Time for us to earn our pay."

The pair of *Tornado F.3*s turned up threat and went to full military power. Like the *Typhoons* before them, they kept their Foxhunter radars silent; there being no point to alerting the enemy to their presence before they could engage. The *Tornadoes* had a much harder task, as their *AMRAAMs* had around the same range as the missiles carried by the *Flanker*s. The Soviet aircraft would have a small window of opportunity to return fire once the RAF aircraft had engaged.

"Coming up on ideal firing range, boss, in...three...two...one...lighting them up now."

"Fox Three! Fox Three!" Foster announced as soon as he had lock.

In normal circumstances, he would have launched a single missile at a target; after all, the *AIM-120C* had a kill probability (pK) of something like .95, at least in theory, anyway, against target drones. However, these were not normal circumstances and the enemy were certainly not target drones, so he fired a pair of missiles at each *Flanker*, knowing that his wingman would do the same.

"Hold on to your hat, George!" Foster told Wilkinson as he turned the *F.3* sharply away from the Soviet aircraft and put it into a dive, pushing the throttle through the gate and engaging reheat. The aircraft creaked and groaned alarmingly as he pushed it to its limit.

Whoops, forgot the drop tanks, he thought, levelling off. The two 2,250-liter Hinderburger drop tanks were not rated for supersonic flight, and he punched them both off the wings just in time. Trading altitude for speed, Foster finally pulled up around a hundred meters above the North Sea. As at this altitude, there were very few other aircraft out there that could keep up with a *Tornado F.3* and the Radar Warning Receiver was silent, the initial danger seemed to have passed.

Time to take stock of the situation, he thought, reducing to full military power.

6

Sentry AEW.1 ZH107

"Looks like we're got some Tiffie and Tonka mates to thank for saving our bacon," Gambon commented as he observed the end of the engagement.

The Soviet fighter sweep had been decisively defeated—four Su-27Ms were now fleeing east. On the negative side, three *Typhoons* had been lost; at least it appeared that their aircrew had survived. At least, they would if SAR hurried up.

"Well, they achieved something with that trick," Sergeant Harris observed. "We're going to have to dispatch the reserves."

Over the North Sea,
east of the Bass Rock.

Two sorties in one day is getting old, quickly, Flight Lieutenant Simon Darkshade, RAAF thought, stifling a yawn as he maintained formation off the port wing of a 43 (F) Squadron *Tornado F.3*.

"...Angels...incoming..."

Damn jammers, Darkshade thought. Soviet jamming was currently making radio conversation with his wingman, the *Tornado F.3s* the pair of

Hawks were flying with, or the ground impossible. Therefore, Darkshade was keeping one eye on the rear cockpit of the interceptor.

Glad we're not doing this at low level, he thought. A moment later, there was a flashing light coming from the navigator's torch. The Morse code gave an instruction to go to combat spread and where to expect the enemy to approach from.

Glad to put my arse on the line for Queen and Country, Darkshade thought sarcastically. *Just what I thought would happen when I agreed to be an instructor pilot over here*. Darkshade was an Australian exchange officer serving with No.79 (Reserve) Squadron. He had nominally come to the United Kingdom to help the No.1 Tactical Weapons Unit train pilots on weapons systems before they were assigned to a specific aircraft type. No.1 TWU's *Hawk T.2*s were similar to the RAAF's *Hawk 127s*, so learning the aircraft had not been a problem.

Kind of hard for the Tornado *to point me in the right direction if we can't talk*, Darkshade thought. There were two *Tornadoes* guiding four *Hawks*, and not for the first time, Darkshade wished a JTIDS terminal had been retrofitted to his aircraft.

Too expensive, my arse, he thought. He checked over his four *ASRAAM*, wishing he had two more rather than the fuel tanks underneath his wing. However, even with the T.2's fuel refuelling probe, the *Hawk* was too short-ranged to carry six missiles and the cannon for a military useful length of time.

Darkshade looked up from his weapons display just in time to see the *Tornados* engage unseen targets with *AMRAAMs*.

Well, I guess we're in it now, he thought, following the *Tornadoe*s as they descended rapidly and turned to attack the enemy formation from the rear. Darkshade stuck to his *Tornado F.3* like glue until distant puffballs of exploding Soviet aircraft oriented him towards the opponent. At this distance, they were little more than specks, but from their actions, he guessed they were Su-24 *Fencers*, rather than the more modern Su-34 *Fullbacks*. Lacking the *Tornadoes'* radar, he closed to visual range, ensured he had good tone as the *Fencer* remained unaware of his presence, then squeezed the trigger.

"Fox Two!" he announced to anyone that could hear his radio call.

The missile raced off the port wing-tip pylon, rapidly accelerating to Mach 3 as it tracked the *Fencer*. The Soviet aircraft jettisoned its weapons load, then began to radically manoeuvre as it spewed out decoy flares.

I'll take a jettison, Darkshade thought. A couple of second later, the

ASRAAM blew off the Su-24's tail, making it a total loss rather than just a mission kill. The crew ejected as their fighter began to disintegrate.

Time to find more trade, Darkshade thought as he looked around his aircraft to regain situational awareness. He spotted a *Tornado* chasing after a pair of Su-24s that were running towards the coast in the chaos of the Soviet-RAF merge.

Brave lads, Darkshade thought briefly. He punched off his two tanks and pushed the *Hawk*'s throttle forward to maximum. *We'll see if I can make them dead ones*.

"Annoying buggers aren't they, boss?" Squadron Leader Wilkinson said from the rear cockpit of the pursuing *Tornado F.3*.

"You can say that again, George," Wing Commander Foster replied, frustrated.

The two *Fencers* were jinking just enough to prevent him from getting a lock on.

Only one missile left, and I'd like to make sure it hits so I don't have to go to guns, Foster thought.

"Looks like we've got a *Hawk* trying to join us," Wilkinson observed.

"Optimistic sod," Foster commented. "Well, good luck to him."

The four aircraft raced down the Firth of Forth, causing alarm aboard the ships below. In a few minutes, both *Fencers* would be able to drop their weapons on the dockyard and naval base at Rosyth if they chose to. Finally, Foster got a tone and fired.

"Fox Two! Fox Two!"

"Go! Go! Go!" Wilkinson urged the missile.

The *Fencer* pilot had seen the flash from the pursuing *Tornado's* wing and turned sharply to try and defeat the missile, releasing flares as he did so. Since he was keeping his eye on the incoming *ASRAAM*, the pilot did not see the island of Inchcolm looming up in front of his aircraft. His navigator's screamed warning caused him to reverse his turn—right into the *ASRAAM*.

Well, looks like that's one, Darkshade thought, hurtling past the dark ball of smoke that had been two men and their attack aircraft. Seeing the second

Su-24 bank tightly and pass over the coast, Darkshade slammed his stick over to cut the corner.

Never would have caught him if he hadn't have turned. Focusing on his target, Darkshade was not paying particular attention to the ground below him.

"Fox Two!" he said on getting a good tone and firing.

As with most of its siblings the missile ran true, destroying its target. The burning wreckage, minus the crew who had ejected, slammed into the ground.

"Oh, shit!" Darkshade exclaimed as he finally noticed where his 'kill' had come down.

"They're not going to thank him for that!" Foster commented as he circled the crash site.

"You can say that again, boss!" Wilkinson agreed.

Below them, a column of smoke was rising from the crash site on the edge of the Mossmorran Petrochemical complex. Mossmorran was home to two plants: the Fife Natural Gas Liquid Plant, operated by Shell, and the Fife Ethylene Plant operated by ExxonMobil. The products that both plants worked with and produced were somewhat flammable, so it was unfortunate that the crashing *Fencer* had already set fire to one storage tank.

Foster and Wilkinson could already see blue flashing lights belonging to fire appliances hurrying along the nearby A92 dual carriageway towards the growing blaze.

"We're nearly at Bingo fuel, so I think it is time we made ourselves scarce," Foster decided, turning away from Mossmorran.

7

Durham Tees Valley Airport,
County Durham

Squadron Leader Gambon jerked awake as the Sentry touched down.

Good God, I cannot keep this up, he thought. *I can't fall asleep while we're flying back to the airfield.*

"Shame about Waddington," one of the controllers was saying to another.

"How many missiles did they say hit?" the second controller asked.

Enough, Gambon thought. *The answer you're looking for is* enough. *Sentry* ZH107 had diverted to Durham Tees Valley Airport due to the damage at RAF Waddington. Gambon was glad the RAF had seen fit to base its auxiliary flying squadrons at civilian airports near their recruiting areas, as otherwise, there'd have been no support at their destination.

Even though No. 607 is based on the RAF Middleton St. George side, there's a lot of difference between supporting a Tornado *squadron and* Sentries, Gambon thought. ZH 107 taxied to where ground crew were waiting to service the big jet. There was also a crew bus with the new crew waiting; once the swap-over was accomplished, it would take Gambon's crew to their local accommodation.

"All right, then, let's get off her quick," Gambon said. Leading by example, he scrambled through the exit door, taking a deep breath once he reached the bottom of the air-stair. The kerosene-filled atmosphere was the closest he could get to fresh air after being cooped up in a metal tube for nearly ten hours. After counting his crew off, he spotted his counterpart from B Flight, No. 8 Squadron and went across to say hello.

"Hi, Bruce, how are you?"

"Hi, Gambo," Squadron Leader Bruce Cameron replied. "I'm not bad, feeling a wee bit knackered, though. You?"

"Same, really, mate. Feeling lucky to be alive, too. The Russians tried to kill us today."

"What?" Cameron asked, concerned. Gambon relayed the details of the Frontal Aviation fighter sweep.

"Didn't feel personal until today, know what I mean?" Gambon concluded.

"Aye, they're just blips on a screen until they are trying to kill you," Cameron agreed with a nod. "They tried to kill some of our tankers today, as well. I hear we got lucky, although a few air bases were hit again."

Gambon saw the man look up the ladder.

"Anyway, time I was aboard. I'll catch you later. You get off and get some kip."

"I'll do that, Bruce," Gambon said. "See you when in a few hours."

RAF Leuchars,
Fife, Scotland

Wing Commander Foster did not realise that he had fallen asleep as his *Tornado* was being winched backwards into the Hardened Aircraft Shelter until the Flight Sergeant who served as Crew Chief tapped him on the shoulder.

"Wakey, wakey, boss," the NCO said softly.

"Oh, sorry, Flight," Foster replied with a start as he woke up.

"Don't worry about it, boss; Mr. Wilkinson was kipping, too," the Senior NCO replied cheerfully. "You need my boys to paint any more kills on your plane?"

"Err...yes, I think so, Flight," Foster said, yawning. "I think we got at least four today, but I'll need to get back to you. How was it here?"

"We got hit twice; the Rock Apes got quite a few of them, thankfully," the NCO replied, referring to the base defence force. "They hit our peacetime HQ, though...and the buggers killed our cockerels and chickens."

As No. 43 Squadron was known as "the Fighting Cocks" and had a cockerel on its crest, the squadron had long kept cockerels and chickens as mascots. The fresh eggs the chickens produced was a very welcome side benefit.

Foster felt a single tear run down his left cheek.

We've lost pilots and ground crew, and it's some damn birds that I'm feeling emotional about, he thought. Even with that thought, he didn't lose his anger.

"Bastards," he muttered as he climbed down from the cockpit.

8

Over the North Sea

Captain Dimitri Komissarov was somewhat surprised to be alive. As he had expected, during the transit to his target in the UK, NATO forces on the continent had thrown everything they could at him. So far, he had managed to escape by accelerating up to Mach. 2.8, the fastest he could go without damaging the airframe of his *Mi-25RBsh*, or risking having the four 500lb bombs he was carrying detonating.

This is insanity, Komissarov thought. *Reconnaissance missions are dangerous enough without also asking me to drop bombs on a radar station.* From his protective system's constant bleeping, Komissarov knew that his aircraft was being scanned by at least one airborne and several ground-based radars.

So much for surprise. He had not exactly expected to sneak up on the RAF, but it was clear the British were well and truly agitated. Glancing at his systems, he drew some comfort that the all of the electronic emissions were likely being recorded by the MiG-25RBF that had accompanied him for much of the flight.

Flight Lieutenant Catz shifted in her Martin-Baker ejection seat as she put her aircraft into yet another wide orbit. Catz was on her third sortie of the day, although this one was somewhat different to the last. Rather than the *FGR.2* model, she was flying one of only six *Typhoon FGR.4*s that the RAF had in service. This version had the electronically scanned version of the CAPTOR radar, known as CEASAR, the ability to carry conformal fuel tanks, 2-D thrust vectoring and, crucially for this mission, an extra fifteen percent more power in its EJ200 turbofans.

Someone is about to get a surprise today, she thought. *At least this one probably isn't a fighter sweep*.

The task of intercepting MiG-25s was, appropriately enough, referred to as 'Fox Hunting'. The *Typhoons* assigned to the task were only armed with a pair of *Meteor* missiles, carried no other external stores, and had been so thoroughly stripped that even the wings' hard points were blanked off.

Glad the Soviets obliged us by waiting a few hours to send this mission. Pairs of 'Fox hunters' would be launched only once it was certain that a '*Foxbat*' was on its way. Even then, success was not certain, as only a relatively small number of the Soviet recce birds had been shot down.

Catz's datalink blipped as the *Typhoon FGR.4* crept past Mach. 1.7.

Thank God for supercruise, she thought, seeing the vector from the *Sentry*. Catz and her wingman pushed their throttles to the stops, accelerating to the *Typhoons*' maximum speed. Catz energised the radar as she pulled back onto the stick. Just as the *Typhoon* was about to stall, she got a continuous tone in her ears.

"Fox Three! Fox Three!" she announced, firing both *Meteors*. A split second later, her wingman echoed the radio call, then both of them nosed their fighters over and retarded their throttles.

Now for the exhilarating task of finding a tanker before we run out of fuel, Catz thought, noting just how much avgas the ascent and launch had cost her. Setting up the rendezvous in the navigational computer, Catz turned to watch the intercept unfold.

The lead *Foxbat* turned away and began to accelerate, trying to escape. Four decoys separated from the big fighter, and for a moment Catz was certain that the *Meteor*s were going to lock onto them. However, on this occasion, the jettisoning and acceleration was just a bit too late. One of her missiles, just about to run out of fuel, got close enough to activate its proximity fuse.

You poor bastard, Catz thought, genuinely sympathetic. She could envision the blast-fragmentation warhead tearing chunks out of the airframe of the Soviet aircraft. At the speed the *Foxbat* was traveling, the effect was almost immediate. The contact bloomed briefly as the MiG-25 began to tumble and was torn to pieces in less than a second.

Too bad we missed the second one, she thought, seeing her wingman's missiles arc past the rushing *Foxbat*.

As she made contact with the *VC.10 K3* Catz felt somewhat pleased with herself. She was fairly sure she had killed the target.

Although the destruction of his aircraft had happened in the blink of an eye, the MiG-25RBF's pilot had still had enough time to scream. Captain Komissarov could still hear the man's final moments, broadcast over the Soviet command frequency, ringing in his ears.

Well, it looks like the people in Moscow who wanted electronic intelligence are not going to get what they so desperately needed, Komissarov thought. He armed his weapons and started his aircraft's cameras. There would only be a fraction of a second to drop the first pair of bombs at the right time.

They never should have modified these aircraft to allow supersonic strikes, he thought angrily. *Even with precision guid—*

His thoughts were interrupted by the incessant warning of a *Broadsword* SAM flight locking on. Quickly pickling his bombs as he entered the delivery envelope, Komissarov immediately activated his jammers and turned out to sea.

Unbeknownst to Komissarov, his flight computer had an error in its navigational routines. As a result, both bombs were already off target as soon as they dropped off his MiG, with their point of impact growing even further afield as they ran into shearing winds while crossing over the border into Norfolk. They passed over the radar station at RAF Neatishead, their intended target, then landed in the nearby Burnt Fen broad. Their twin explosions killed quite a lot of wildlife, but had no impact on the nearby RAF station other than causing a great deal of consternation.

It would not make the Commissar happy, but I have a feeling that someone Up There is looking out for me, Komissarov thought, seeing the sixth *Broadsword* SAM fall away behind his hurtling fighter. It seemed as if after the destruction of the other *Foxbat* that the RAF had 'shot its bolt' in terms of fighters that could threaten him. Just to be sure, he took his MiG-25 well out over the North Sea so that he could approach his second target, RAF Boulmer, from the north.

Let's hope that was the last Broadsword *battery up here*, he thought. Intelligence swore the British only had limited numbers of the system, but Komissarov had strong doubts. As he crossed back over land, he once more turned on the cameras and armed his bombs. With no strident warning, he waited patiently to close to optimal release range, pressed his button...and felt nothing. Quickly stabbing the button again, Komissarov began cursing as there was a second instance of absolutely nothing.

"Dammit to hell!" he muttered, pushing a few buttons to reset the computer and begin other troubleshooting procedures. He was halfway through the troubleshooting when the fighter lurched from first one, then the second, bomb dropping away.

"Fucking shit!" he exclaimed. Taking a look at his navigational system, he saw that there was no way the glide bombs could circle back towards his target.

Well, at least it would land somewhere in Britain, he thought. *Hopefully either a military target, or at worse, some fields.*

If he'd been able to see where his bombs headed to, Komissarov would have lost all of his briefly flickering faith in a higher power. Rather than an open field or even a distant military outpost, the unshakeable laws of ballistics took the two bombs to possibly one of the worse destinations that they could reach: the Freeman Hospital. Like all other NHS hospitals, the facility had thankfully been cleared of all non-essential patients in expectation of being needed for war casualties. Unfortunately, that still left a fair number of staff from the night shift, transplant patients, cancer sufferers and, of course, their visiting family members.

The effects of two bombs, each containing over 200-kilograms of high explosives, on the hospital were catastrophic.

Komissarov knew nothing of what had happened behind him as he finally turned his big fighter for home.

I have to run a gauntlet to the tanker, he thought, thinking of the SAMs and fighters between his current location and home base.

There was suddenly a cough from somewhere aft that caused the MiG-25RBsh to shudder violently. He urgently checked his heads down display;

to his horror, he could see that the temperature of the right-hand engine was rising rapidly. It had just reached the red band when the FIRE light came on, followed by the MASTER CAUTION warning, along with several urgent audible alarms.

Shit! Shit! Shit! Komissarov thought, shutting down the right-hand engine as he punched the fire extinguisher button. Fear ran through him as the engine's temperature continued to rise, despite the fact that the engine's RPM had dropped down to almost nothing. There was only one explanation: he had an uncontained fire in the aft fuselage.

I do not feel like going for a swim today, he thought angrily, banking his burning fighter back towards land. He had no desire to be taken prisoner, but bailing out over the North Sea would probably just lead to the question of whether he froze to death or drowned.

The MiG-25 was slowly losing both height and speed, making it vulnerable to interception. Although the 'MASTER CAUTION' and fire warning had now been stilled, they were quickly replaced by increasingly strident tones from the Radar Warning Receiver.

Well, looks like I'm about to get a Tornado *pilot a medal*, Komissarov thought angrily, noting he was being illuminated by a Foxhunter radar. Very soon, the *Tornado F3* it belonged to would be able to engage him, but likely not until after he had made a considerable distance inland.

The thirty seconds passed quickly. As the *Tornado* closed into the outer edges of its envelope, Komissarov tightened the straps on his harness, checked that there were no loose objects in the cockpit, and paused for a moment. It was often a difficult decision for a pilot to choose to leave the relative comfort and warmth of the cockpit.

It is time to go. With a sigh, he pulled the ejection sea handle.

Detective Sergeant Freddie Spicer stopped his car as he spotted the figure in the descending parachute. He had been driving to the Freeman Hospital to offer what help he could with crowd control. Like a lot of Northumbria Police's detectives, Spicer was also pulling uniform duty, something that most CID officers had a great deal of distaste for.

Well, time to figure out if this is a Russian or one of our chaps, Spicer thought, getting out of the car. He was keenly aware of being unarmed, but so far, no Russians had attempted to shoot it out after dropping into Great Britain.

Three hots and a cot will go far to making the other side come along peacefully, Spicer thought, placing on his peaked cap. He walked towards the pilot as the man stumbled to his feet, then began gathering up his parachute.

"You one of ours, or one of theirs, bonny lad?" Spicer asked.

"I am Captain Komissarov of the Soviet Air Force, officer. I wish to surrender," the pilot said, handing Spicer his pistol.

"Well, you'd better come wi' me then," Spicer said, gesturing back towards his car. The pilot dutifully got into the vehicle's rear seat.

"Control, I have a Soviet pilot in custody on Freeman Road by the tennis courts," Spicer reported. "I'm going to drive him back to the station. Can you let the military know please, over?"

What does this bloody lot want? the Detective Sergeant thought, looking at a crowd that was beginning to head his way. People had begun to congregate shortly after the hospital had been bombed and had continued to watch the fire. Rumours were already spreading as to how many people had been killed, and he'd heard the reports that the Maggie's Centre had been destroyed, along with its cancer patients. The mood of the local population was already very black.

"That's a bloody Russian!" someone shouted, pointing at Spicer's car.

Oh, shit.

"Control, I'm going to need back-up. I've a crowd turning nasty here, over," Spicer radioed urgently. He turned in the seat.

"You're not a bomber pilot are you, lad?"

The Russian hesitated, and Spicer sincerely hoped it was because he was processing the question.

"No, I fly, how you say, reconnaissance aircraft," the Soviet replied. "What you call the *Foxbat*."

The crowd, now a mob, was advancing on the Detective Sergeant and pilot. There was no sign as yet of the promised back-up. Spicer drew his baton and turned to Komissarov.

"I think you'd better run, lad," Spicer said firmly. "I'll hold them back as long as I can."

HQ RAF Strike Command,
RAF High Wycombe, Buckinghamshire.

Air Chief Marshal Johnson reviewed the events of the past twenty-four hours as he sat down to record his final log.

Another day of wastage that didn't seem to move the needle at all, he thought, scribbling. *The defences held up, but damned if we didn't take some damage to the bases*. He ran his hand over the stricken bases. Wick had been damaged badly enough that Air Vice Marshal Hazel had decided to temporarily relocate operations to Sumburgh Airport in Shetland. The Buncefield refinery, which produced aviation fuel, had been set on fire.

On the plus side, losses were relatively light for us, he thought. Three *Tornado F.3s*, two *Typhoons*, and a pair of *Hawks*. The last two had been caught on the ground, something he was amazed had not happened to several of his fighters. A *Tristar KC.1* had also been damaged on approach to Aberdeen Airport when it ran into a flock of seabirds. Although it had lost one of its RB211 engines, the tanker had landed safely.

More importantly, we're getting better at saving the crews that punch out, he thought. *Even the enemy ones. Well, the ones in the sea, anyway*. There were reports from Newcastle that a mob had hung a Soviet pilot from the nearest lamppost after blaming him for a local hospital's bombing. The same mob had also badly beaten a police officer who had tried to protect the pilot.

"Victoria, please ask Chief Constable of Northumberland Police if it'd be possible for me to visit the officer who was beaten today," Johnson called out after a moment's thought. "I'll make a statement to the press afterwards; don't want this sort of thing becoming a regular occurrence."

"Yes, sir," Victoria replied from the outer office.

CINCUKAIR looked over the reports on stocks of weapons, fuel and spare parts. They were not quite as healthy as he would have liked. Still, they were not at the stage yet of being a cause for concern. It did remind him that he was due to speak to the commander of RAF Support Command about his logistical needs in the morning.

"Sir, you should probably head for bed," Victoria stated from his office door. Johnson started. He looked towards his watch, only to recall taking it off in the gent's toilet.

"What time is it, Vicky?" Johnson asked, standing.

"Five to midnight, sir," she replied, having looked at the wall clock behind her boss. "You really need to get some sleep, sir," she pressed. "You'll not be any use to anyone if you don't get some rest."

"You should, too, Vicky."

"Oh, I'm young, sir," she replied, her voice belying her confidence. "I'll manage for a while yet."

The implied suggestion that he was old made Johnson smile for the first time in several hours. It felt good, and that was a bad sign.

"Okay, Vicky, I'll get away to bed," he said with a chuckle and a nod. "Wake me if something serious happens."

With that, Johnson took off his tie and shoes, and then climbed into the narrow cot. Within a few seconds, he was asleep.

AUTHOR'S NOTE

Readers of my ongoing online novel, *The Last War*, will notice that this story shares some characters and the general scenario from that work. However, it is not a TLW story. Rather, as the great Arthur C. Clarke said of his *Odyssey* novels, it is from a very close parallel universe.

ABOUT JAN NIEMCZYK

Jan Niemczyk was born and brought up in Scotland, where he currently lives. He has long had an interest in military history, aviation, naval warfare, cats and horses. He also has an interest in the Cold War.

Mr Niemczyk is the author of the web novel The Last War, an alternative history where the USSR has survived into the early 21st Century. He is currently employed in the public sector.

EXCERPT FROM ACTS OF WAR

James Young

Turn the page for an excerpt

1

CAREFUL WHAT YOU WISH FOR...

Follow me—You have the advantage of necessity, that last and most powerful of weapons.

— VETTIUS MESSIUS OF VOLSCIA

Thames River
0900 Local (0400 Eastern)
23 August 1942

London was burning.

Somehow I doubt that this is quite how anyone expected Adolf Hitler's death to turn out, Adam Haynes thought bitterly as he regarded the burning capital's skyline. The wind, thankfully, was blowing away from where he and his girlfriend stood at the bow of the *Accalon*. Adam had the awful feeling that if it had been blowing toward the 40-foot pleasure yacht, there would have been many, many smells he would have preferred to forget filtering their way.

Like Guernica, only...he started to think.

With a roar, a Junkers 52 swept low over the *Accalon*'s deck, its passage so close that the aircraft's slipstream fluttered the white flag hanging from the yacht's antennae mast. An intense, white-hot rage sprung from within him as he watched the canary yellow German transport.

I hope you crash, you bastard, Adam thought, blood rushing into his ears.

"Adam, *my hand*!" A woman's voice broke through his fury.

With a start, Adam realized that he was well on the way to breaking his companion's hand. Although such an act was always unconscionably bad form, it was doubly so when its possessor was the cousin, albeit distant, of England's king.

"God, Clarine, I'm..." Adam started, opening his hand as if suddenly realizing it held a hot brick. His face colored to the roots of his thinning brown hair, making his blue eyes all that more intense. At a shade under six feet, with shoulders broad enough to fit on a man six inches taller, Adam looked very much like a bear wearing an RAF uniform. Unfortunately, when enraged, he had the strength to match.

"That is quite alright," Clarine Windsor replied lightly, doing her best to smile as she worked her hand. A small, wiry woman who stood several inches shorter than Adam in the black flats that came with her Women's Auxiliary Air Force (WAAF) uniform, Clarine was far from weak. Still, her pale face was scrunched up in obvious pain.

Holy shit, I hope I didn't hurt her, Adam thought guiltily. Seeing his worry, Clarine brought up her left hand and brushed back a stray blonde hair, her brown eyes meeting Adam's as she smiled.

"You were just having the same thought I had: wishing you could shoot the bastard," she said simply. "It's understandable, given what has happened these last few days."

Still no reason to try and convert your hand to paste, Adam thought. *You didn't drop the bomb that killed Hitler.*

"Understandable, but most unfortunate," her father, Awarnach Windsor, stated as he joined them at the yacht's bow. "Especially as his escorts would probably blow the *Accalon* out of the water."

Looking up and back toward the vessel's stern, Adam mentally kicked himself for not noticing the eight Me-410s circling roughly four thousand feet above their heads. The gray fighters were hard to see in the haze of smoke roiling off London, but that was no excuse. Smoke had been a fact of life for Fighter Command over the last two weeks, and failing to see an opponent hiding in it was just as fatal as if the assault came from more naturally formed clouds.

"While I am sure you wish you had a *Spitfire* right now," Awarnach observed flatly, "I doubt your efforts would be any more successful than they were previously."

You bastard, Adam thought, fighting to keep his emotions off his face. The tone of Awarnach's voice had far too much "told you so" in it.

"Well father, at least someone was attempting to defend our nation," Clarine observed coolly. "Since many of those who were born to it could not raise themselves from their slumber."

Awarnach turned his baleful gaze from Adam to his daughter.

"Those of us who were 'slumbering', as you put it, merely believed we should have continued to enjoy the peace we had hammered out rather than meddle in affairs on the continent," Awarnach replied. "Instead, that idiot Churchill has now managed to make us forget his idiocy at Gallipoli."

"This is hardly the same as..."

"No?!" Awarnach snapped. He turned and pointed off their port bow, to where London's East End was starting to come into view. "Tell me *that* is not more terrible than some idiotic frontal assault on the Ottomans."

The "*that*" in question was the furious blaze that roared unchecked almost as far as the eye could see. The low rumble of the fire was a constant sound beating upon their senses, but Adam had managed to suppress it by concentrating on the river itself. Now, as if Awarnach had ripped open a shade, the magnitude of Fighter Command's defeat lay before them. It was like looking into a corner of Hell, and Adam was once more glad that the wind was blowing so strongly from their back.

Once you've smelled burning flesh, you have no desire to enjoy that particular sensation again, Adam thought.

"You can't negotiate with the Germans," Adam said lowly, feeling the rage starting to creep back again.

"Oh? Well then, I am certainly glad that you have pointed this out for me, my American friend. Unfortunately, it would appear that your President and Congress feel very, very differently."

"Father..."

"No, please, I would like to hear this fine young man explain to me why we should not negotiate with the Germans when his countrymen cannot be bothered to even help us," Awarnach raged, his own face starting to color to match Adam's.

"It wasn't our President that chose to accept the armistice with Himmler after Bomber Command killed Hitler," Adam snapped.

"Oh? And what would you have had us do? Were we somehow going to invade France by ourselves? Perhaps build a massive bomber fleet like that idiot Portal wanted to and bomb the Reich's cities into rubble? Would that have satisfied your need for bloodlust? There was nothing more that could be done!"

"Yes, well, *perhaps* the people in that," Adam said, gesturing toward the burning city in front of them, "would have preferred you not giving the Germans over a year to perfect their bombing techniques."

"Perhaps, gentlemen," Clarine said crisply, her hand pointing, "we should be more concerned about that patrol boat's intentions."

Adam followed the point and saw the craft she was speaking of. One of the Royal Navy's MTB-class boats, the vessel was moving away from where it had been standing off the docks and turning toward the *Accalon.* As they watched, the craft began accelerating, signal light blinking furiously.

"Conroy, come about!" Awarnach shouted back towards the wheel house. Adam felt the *Accalon*'s engines stop, the helmsman turning her broadside to the oncoming MTB.

Holy shit, Adam thought, translating the other vessel's Morse code. He was about to say something when Awarnach spoke first.

"My God," Awarnach said, his face paling. "Gas?!"

"Obviously you've never read Douhet," Adam observed dryly.

"Who?" Clarine asked.

"The Italian Trenchard," Adam continued smoothly. "He recommended using gas in addition to incendiaries on enemy population centers. Explains the no-confidence vote a little better, I think."

The patrol boat began slowing, its own helmsman swinging the vessel wide so that he could put it alongside the *Accalon*. Three men crowded the bow and, with a start, Adam realized they were wearing full hoods and rubber gloves. Seeing that no one aboard the *Accalon* was in the bulky protective suits, the man standing in the center reached up and pulled the hooded apparatus off of his head.

Well now, small world, isn't it? Adam thought, feeling a smile cross his face as he regarded Lieutenant Commander Reginald Slade, Royal Navy. Tall, almost gaunt, with a face whose left side was thoroughly scarred from the explosion of a German shell, Slade wore his blonde hair closely cropped.

"You seem to be a fair distance from the North Atlantic, Mr. Haynes," Slade shouted as the patrol boat drew smoothly alongside the *Accalon*, his face breaking in a wry grin that reached his eyes. Reaching up, the RN officer scratched the area around his left eyepatch. The motion drew attention to the damaged side of his face, and Adam heard Awarnach inhale sharply.

"Sorry, I have been wanting to do that for hours," Slade said, ignoring the man's gasp.

"Yeah, I can see how that might be the case," Adam replied with a small smile.

"I do hope you folks aren't planning on going any further down the Thames," Slade continued. "By King's decrees the East End is off limits to anyone not on official business."

"I'm trying to find one of my mate's wife, mother, and child. He's in the hospital or else he'd be down here himself," Adam said.

Slade grimaced at Adam's words.

"Where did he say they were living?" the naval officer asked, his tone brusque.

"His mum's apartment is in Poplar," Adam replied, raising an eyebrow at the other man's coldness.

Adam had seen the look that briefly crossed Slade's face enough times to know what was coming next. The man paused for a moment, obviously choosing his words carefully.

"Unless they were extraordinarily lucky, I wouldn't hold out much hope, I'm afraid. The Germans dropped some sort of gas that got all the way through the area, and then followed it up with incendiaries. Without anyone to put out the fires..."

The officer's trailing off said all that needed to be said. In the last couple of days, Adam had heard a word for the phenomenon that some were calling the Second Great London Fire: Firestorm. The East End had become one huge flame pit, and the *Luftwaffe* had returned for three solid days to help things spread.

"Thanks Commander Slade," Adam spoke after a few moments more of quiet. Sighing at the heavy burden that now lay upon him, he looked up again at the smoke-filled sky, hoping to catch a glimpse of the big Ju-52 again.

"Looking for that arse who came tearing through here about ten minutes ago?" Slade asked.

"Yes, actually," Adam replied ruefully.

"I think that was Himmler arriving to negotiate terms with Lord Halifax."

The disgust in Slade's tone at the latter name almost matched the venom reserved for the first.

"Who knew there was a bigger bastard than Hitler in the Nazi Party?" Adam observed grimly.

"Certainly not that bunch of flyboys who killed him," Slade shot back. "Stupid pilots, always mucking things up."

Clarine chuckled behind Adam. Looking at Slade, Adam was unable to tell if the man was serious or not.

"Heard the poor bombardier blew his brains out yesterday," Adam replied. "Not his fault any of this," he continued, gesturing towards the burning city, "happened."

Slade shrugged.

"No, it's not, but that's what happens when you drop your bombs over a capital city. Sometimes you hit things you don't intend to," Slade retorted bitterly.

Spoken like someone who's never had to jettison something in order to make the fuel equation work out, Adam thought. He'd been a pilot since his seventeenth birthday, and non-flyers' superiority complexes never ceased to amaze him.

"Still. Berlin's a big city," Adam allowed. "No way they could've known they'd drop a bomb that would kill ol' Adolf."

Slade uttered a sound that made his disagreement quite clear on that one.

"Yes, and a 500-lb. bomb makes a big mess. No matter, that bastard is dead now, Himmler took over, and our betters were dumb enough to believe that tripe the Germans were spouting about the *Fuhrer*'s loss making them recognize the error of their ways."

"Excuse me, Lieutenant Commander, but as one of those *betters*," Awarnach snapped, "maybe a better explanation was that we did not want to continue losing men such as yourself in a war that we quite clearly were not in position to win."

Slade turned and looked at Awarnach, the contempt in his gaze almost physically palpable.

"So, in order to save *my* life, you buggered the French, spat on the rest of the Continent, pissed off the Americans, and gave Himmler breathing room," Slade retorted, his voice cold as ice. "During which time he hanged Goering, blew some industrialists' heads out at a meeting, and thus apparently motivated them to build a bloody great lot of planes, bombs, gas, and submarines."

Adam watched as Awarnach's face began to color while Slade continued, obviously taking a great relish in venting his spleen.

"Of course, the bloody Krauts then proceeded to kill a whole lot more of my countrymen. Capital work, your Lordship, just capital, please do not go into anything of importance."

Awarnach's mouth worked in shock. Before he could reply, one of the sailors stuck his head out of the patrol boat's bridge.

"Lieutenant Commander, we have been ordered to a new location," the man called.

Slade continued locking his gaze with Awarnach. It was the older man whose stare broke.

"Would hate to keep you, Lieutenant Commander," Awarnach said, his voice strained. "I'll go back to the bridge and con us out of your path."

"Well, guess we will be about it then," Slade replied, watching the man walk stiffly away.

"So what's going to happen to you next?" Adam asked. "If that is Himmler negotiating the peace treaty."

Slade gave a sideways glance to Clarine.

"I do not share my father's views," Clarine muttered quietly. "Indeed, I think he and the rest of the House of Lords were, and remain, a bunch of fools."

"In that case, understand that this war will *not* end here," Slade said lowly. "As Churchill said before the no confidence vote, there is an entire Commonwealth that will sustain the candle attempting to hold the darkness at bay."

"You mean you're going to flee to Australia or somewhere?" Adam asked, genuinely curious.

Slade snorted.

"You'd best do the same," he replied. "Rumor has it that Himmler intends to ask for all foreign fighters to be turned over as part of the peace treaty."

"What?!"

"Well, can't have a bunch of Poles, Danes, Norwegians, and Frenchmen hanging around and possibly doing something subversive, can you? Especially not after they killed Milch while there was allegedly an armistice between Great Britain and Germany," Slade replied grimly.

With a cold feeling in his stomach, Adam could see the government being formed by Lord Halifax agreeing to such madness. Even worse, he knew what the Nazis would likely do with the men.

"I'm flying with a Polish squadron," Adam said quickly, his tone urgent. "How do I get them the hell out of here."

Again Slade gave Clarine a look, then held up his hand before Adam could say something.

"It is not that I mistrust her," Slade said. "However, you of all people know the Nazis as well as I do. Have you heard the stories of how their Gestapo broke several of the Resistance cells in France during the last year?"

Clarine paled, looking almost physically ill.

The thought of being strapped to a metal mattress and electrocuted for hours on end doesn't appeal to most people, Adam thought. *Especially given where those bastards were placing the electrodes.*

"I will go speak with my father," she said simply. "Please hurry—I do not think he would be opposed to making you swim for it."

Taking Adam's hand and squeezing it, Clarine turned and departed.

"Get the whole bloody lot of your men to Portsmouth," Slade said as soon as she was out of earshot. He pulled out a piece of paper and a grease pen from under his rubber top. Scribbling something quickly, he handed it over to Adam.

"You have less than twenty hours," Slade said, meeting Adam's eyes. "After that, you best leave that pretty lass without any idea how to find you and disappear, as I get the distinct feeling that some of my former countrymen will be quite happy to 'help' run down foreign mercenaries."

"Thanks Slade," Adam replied, extending his hand. The Lieutenant Commander took it with both of his.

"No, *thank you*," Slade said, his voice raw with emotion. "You and the others like you tried to save us, even when we have done little to deserve it. Now only you remain."

"I'm sorry we couldn't do more."

"Well, maybe you'll have more opportunity one of these days. Hopefully your President can make people see reason soon, or else it will be too late."

"I think this," Adam said, gesturing towards the burning docks behind Slade, "will help."

"Yes, yes it will. Now get out of here, and see to your men."

With that, Slade drew himself up to attention and saluted. Adam returned the salute, then watched as the man nimbly sprang back to the patrol boat. The small craft backed away under low power, then ponderously turned its bow around. Adam sighed as he heard Clarine's soft footsteps behind him.

"Father is furious," she said softly. "Strangely, I don't give a damn."

"You know that I have to go almost as soon as we get back," Adam said. Turning, he saw Clarine's eyes were moist already.

"Yes, yes I know," she said softly. "And there's no chance father will let me out of his sight until you do so."

Adam could hear the deep tone of bitterness in her voice.

"Life becomes very lonely when you hate your parents," he said chidingly.

"I have half a mind to come with you," Clarine replied fiercely. "That would bloody well serve him right."

"Well, wouldn't be the first scandal an American has caused in this country," he said musingly, rubbing his chin theatrically.

"I am serious, Adam," Clarine retorted.

"I may not even be alive in a fortnight, Clarine," Adam said somberly. "Think about that. Do you really want to throw away your future, inheritance, and family name for some vagabond American mercenary?"

Clarine searched his face.

"Is that really how you think I see you?"

"No, but it's how your father and the rest of your social circle see me. Yes, I come from the right circles and know which fork to start with at dinner, but at the end of the day I am like some exotic animal that is best petted and left alone."

"Adam, *I love you*."

"And I you," Adam said, fighting the urge to sweep Clarine into his arms. "So much that I will not let you ruin the rest of your life to flee with me."

"What about what I want?" Clarine asked as the *Accalon* came around. "Don't I get to decide the rest of my life, or is that solely the province of my male betters?"

Adam sighed.

Strong women will be the death of me, he thought with a deep sense of melancholy.

"Why don't you tell the truth, Adam?" Clarine continued. "You're scared of what will happen to me if I try to escape with you."

"Yes, the thought of you drowning or freezing to death in the Atlantic does strike me with some trepidation."

Clarine snarled in exasperation.

"Not every event in life ends the worst way possible, Adam!" she breathed lowly through clenched teeth.

Adam turned and looked behind him at the burning London, then back to Clarine.

"Perhaps now is not the time to try and convince me of this. More importantly, Clarine, I have to look after my men."

Clarine opened her mouth to argue, then stopped.

"Then when this boat docks will be the last time we see each other," she replied coolly.

Adam felt as if someone had stomach punched him. He started to reach for Clarine, but she held up her hand to stop him.

"You seem determined to leave Adam," she said. "You are even more determined to make sure I do not leave with you in some misguided attempt to 'save' me. Perhaps it is best then, that I acknowledge you have greater experience in dealing with disastrous circumstances such as these."

The words were delivered with cold precision, and they found their mark with the same brutal finality of a knife thrust.

"I do not want us to end this way, Clarine," Adam bit out, feeling his stomach sinking to his feet.

"If you had stopped after the seventh word of that sentence," Clarine said, her voice quavering, "I might have been inclined to reconsider. Instead, I believe that I am feeling rather nauseous from the smoke and will go below. Have a safe journey, Adam."

With that, Clarine turned and began walking back towards the deckway hatch, moving quickly as she wiped at her face. Adam watched her go, his stomach in knots.

Well, at least it's an improvement from last time I went through this, he thought. Fighting the urge to curse loudly, he slowly rotated back towards the *Accalon*'s bow, and then walked forward to where only the Thames could see his tears.

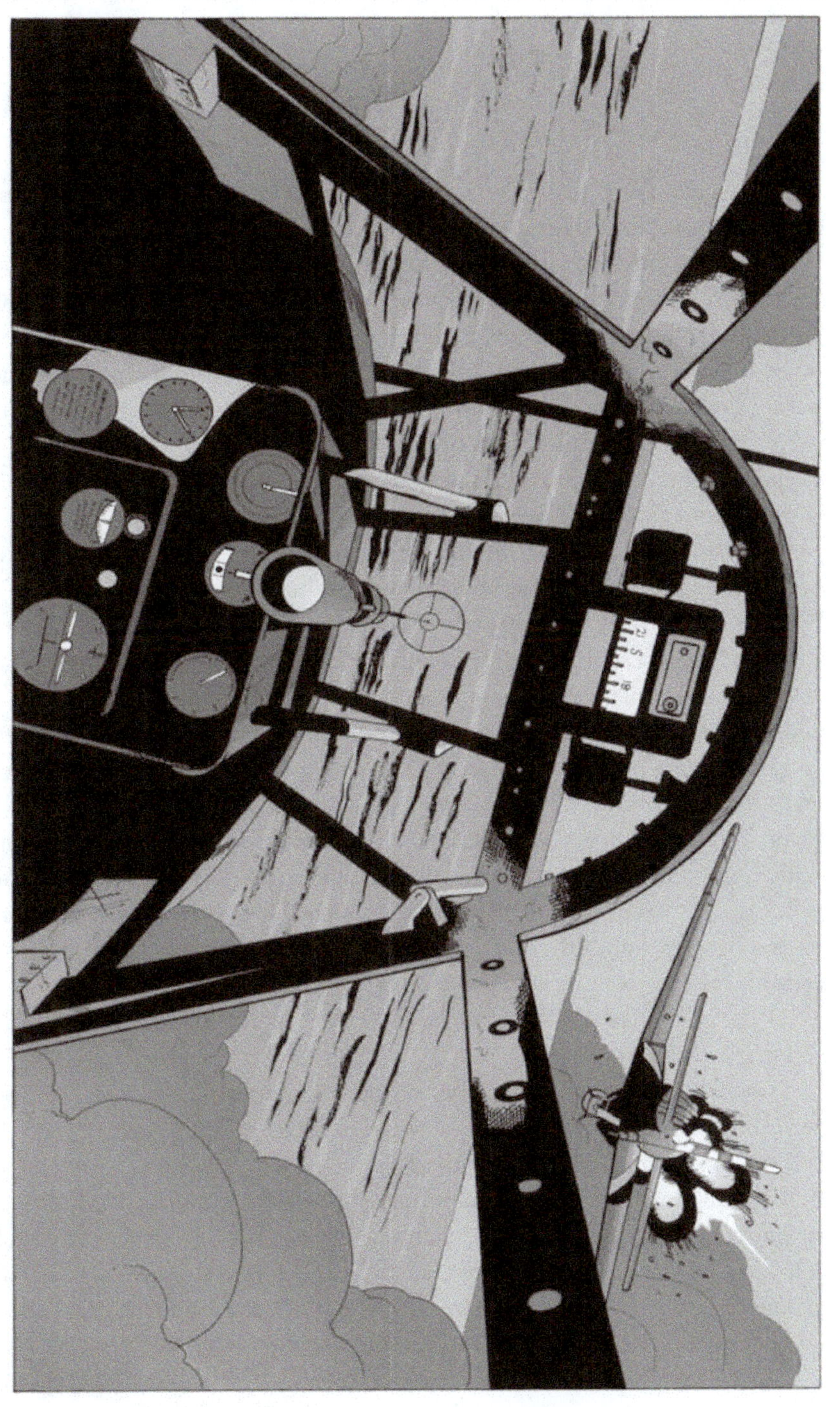

Red Two
North Atlantic
1000 Local (0700 Eastern)
12 September

Lieutenant (j.g.) Eric Cobb, like many aviators, did not lack for confidence. It took a very confident or very stupid man to step into a single-engined aircraft, then take off from a small postage stamp of a warship on a flight over hundreds of miles of featureless ocean. Some people, to include Eric's father, believed that repeatedly doing this was the height of idiocy. Eric, on the other hand, had developed a liking for the hours of solitude, sunlight, and beautiful ocean vistas that were only visible from several thousand feet of altitude.

Unfortunately for Eric, the 12th day of September in the year of our Lord nineteen forty-two had none of the above.

"Okay asshole, I think we're getting a little bit close to the Kraut fleet's estimated position," Eric muttered, his hands white knuckled on his SBD *Dauntless*'s stick and throttle. The "asshole" in question was VB-4's squadron leader, Lieutenant Commander Abe Cobleigh, and the soup that passed for a sky all around them made following Red One's plane a feat of concentration and skill. The conditions were making Eric's forward canopy fog and he had to fight the urge to take his feet off the rudder pedals and brace himself up to look over the top of the forward glass. At several inches over six feet Eric wouldn't have had to stretch far, but taking one's feet off the rudder in the current conditions was not a recipe for longevity. Even though the radial-engine "Slow But Deadly" was as beloved for its handling characteristics as its ruggedness, Eric had no desire to see how well he could pull out from a stupidity-induced spin.

"What was that, sir?" Radioman 2nd Class Henry Rawles asked from the tail gunner position.

"Nothing Rawles, nothing," Eric called back, keeping his voice level so the young gunner wouldn't think he was perturbed at him.

Not Rawles's fault our squadron leader is a...

Without warning, the *Dauntless* burst out of the cloud bank. Eric had just enough time to register the changing conditions, give a sigh of relief, then start looking around before all hell broke loose. The anti-aircraft barrage that burst around the two single-engine dive bombers was heavy and accurate. With a seeming endless cascade of *crack! crack! crack!*, heavy caliber shells exploded all around Eric's bomber, the blasts throwing it around like backhands from a giant.

Jesus Christ! Eric thought, stomping left on his rudder and pulling back on the stick to get back into the clouds.

"Sir, Lieutenant Commander Cobleigh's been hit!" Rawles shouted.

Before Eric could respond, another shell exploded on the bomber's right side with a deafening roar and flash. Eric felt a sharp sting and burning sensation across the back of his neck as the canopy shattered in a spray of glass, the *Dauntless* heeling over from the explosion. Stunned, Eric instinctively leveled the dive bomber off and found himself back in the cloud bank before he fully recovered his senses.

With full recovery came consciousness of just how screwed he was. First Eric realized that it was only by the grace of God that he hadn't been laid open like a slaughtered animal. His shredded life vest, damaged control stick and throttle, and a very large hole in the cockpit's side were all evidence that several fragments had blasted all around him. Fighting down the urge to vomit, Eric quickly checked both of his wings, noting that the surfaces were thoroughly peppered as he fought to keep the SBD level. Fuel streamed behind the bomber, starting to gradually slow as the self-sealing tanks proved their worth.

Oh we are in trouble now. The two SBDs had been near the limit of their search arc when fired upon. Even with the self-sealing tanks working as advertised, Eric was certain that the damage to the wing tanks had just guaranteed Rawles and he would not be landing back aboard *Ranger*. Swiveling his head, he attempted to find Red One's SBD *Dauntless* dive bomber through the murk.

"Rawles!" Eric called over the intercom.

"Yes, sir?" his gunner responded.

"You see what happened to One?" Eric began, then suddenly remembered Rawles' report. "I mean after he got hit."

"Sir, there was no after Lt. Commander Cobleigh got hit," Rawles replied, his voice breathless. "He just exploded!"

Eric felt the sick feeling return to his stomach. After a moment's temptation to just go ahead and vomit over the side, he fought the puke back down.

"What else did you get a chance to see?" Eric asked.

"It looked like there were at least two battleships, maybe three. Jesus they were close!"

"Okay, you need to get off a position report of those German bastards. Send it in the clear back to *Ranger*, keep repeating it until someone acknowledges, and I will try to figure out if we're going to make it back."

"Aye aye, sir," Rawles replied. A few moments later, Eric heard the Morse code starting to get tapped out. Pulling out his map, he suddenly realized he had no clue which direction he was flying. Looking down at the compass, he felt a sudden sigh of relief when he saw they were heading southwest, away from the Germans and generally towards their own fleet.

"Sir, I've got an acknowledgment from the *Augusta*. She's asking our status," Rawles said.

"Send this in code: Red One destroyed, Two unlikely to return to fleet. Will send crash location," Eric said tersely.

They broke out of the low clouds into an area of open sky, the sun beaming down on the battered *Dauntless*. Eric suddenly felt exposed and began scanning around the horizon. He heard and felt Rawles unlimber his twin .30-caliber machine guns and was glad to see that he wasn't the only one on edge.

Those bastards tried to kill us! he thought, then remembered how close the Germans had come to doing just that.

"Rawles, you all right?"

"I got nicked on my calf, but it's not serious. Are we actually about to crash, sir?" Rawles asked.

"It's about two hundred miles back to the fleet, and we don't have two hundred miles of fuel..."

"Smoke! Smoke to starboard!" Rawles shouted. Eric whipped his head around and saw the smudge that Rawles had sighted low on the horizon.

"Well, you just might have kept us from a day in the raft, Rawles," Eric said happily, grabbing the stick with his left hand. Reaching down the right side of his seat, he opened his binoculars' case and reached in. There was a sharp prick on his gloved finger, and he jerked his hand back. Reaching down more carefully, he realized that while the lid was still present on the case, the container itself was twisted metal.

"Rawles, you still have your binoculars?"

"Roger sir," Rawles came back.

"Let's see what you can see," Eric replied. "Mine are shot to hell."

There was a slight rustling in the backseat as Eric brought the SBD around to begin closing with the smoke. After a few moments, it was clear there was more than one column. About ten minutes later, it was very obvious that the *Dauntless* was closing with an entire group of ships.

"Sir, that looks like the Brits!" Rawles said. "I can't tell very well, but that looks like one of their heavy cruisers and a few destroyers heading away from us."

"Great," Eric muttered. "I get to be shot at by both sides today."

"What was that, sir?"

"Nevermind, just talking to myself. Send this location in code also, then get ready to start signaling with a lamp."

"Approaching aircraft, approaching aircraft, these are Royal Navy vessels," a clear, accented voice crackled into Eric's earpieces. "Do not continue to approach or you will be fired upon."

Eric turned the SBD away, banking to show his silhouette and national insignia. The dive bomber initially complied with the movement, then suddenly staggered and began to roll to the left. Eric fought the maneuver, but found that he was only able to hold the aircraft level with the stick pressed almost completely to the right. Looking out at his ailerons, he saw that both were in the down position.

Great, just great, Eric thought.

"Royal Navy vessel, this is a United States Navy aircraft in need of assistance," Eric said once he had control of his aircraft. "Request permission to ditch close aboard."

There was a pause of a sufficient length that Eric felt his arm starting to shake from the effort of maintaining level flight.

"American aircraft, you may ditch close aboard," came the response.

Eric heard Rawles wrestling around in the rear cockpit.

"Sir, I've got the code books in a sack with a box of ammo. Want me to throw it over the side?"

"Great plan, Rawles," Eric gritted. "Get rid of the guns too, don't want you getting brained when we get out."

A moment later, Eric heard the twin machine guns bang down against the fuselage on their way over the side. Shortly after, there was a similar noise as the code books and ammo followed suit the .30-caliber tail guns. Taking a little pressure off the stick, Eric brought the *Dauntless* around in a gradual left-hand turn to see the large cruiser coasting to a stop. The five destroyers accompanying the vessel circled like protective sheep dogs, smoke drifting up from their stacks.

I hope those tin cans don't find anything. Don't feel like adding "got torpedoed" to my list of bad things that have happened today. His right arm began twitching, warning of impending muscle failure, and he quickly grabbed the stick with his left hand for a couple of moments.

"All right Rawles, I've never done this before so I don't know how much time we have," Eric said, fighting to keep his voice calm. "Stand by to ditch."

As Rawles acknowledged his order, Eric had a chance to give the British cruiser a good look. A twin-stacked, three-turreted ship, the RN vessel was painted in three tones of gray, the pattern seemingly random from above. As the dive bomber circled downward from five thousand feet, Eric realized that the captain had placed the vessel athwart the wind, leaving a relatively calm area on her lee. Eric recognized the maneuver as one occasionally conducted by American cruisers in order to recover their seaplanes.

Glad to see things aren't totally different between our navies. The *Dauntless* shuddered, and Eric noted the engine starting to run slightly rougher. Giving a prayer of thanks that Rawles had sighted the vessels, Eric resolved to put the dive bomber down as quickly as possible. Clenching his teeth, his right arm starting to burn with muscle fatigue again, Eric finished the last turn of his gradual spiral down barely one hundred feet over the water and half a mile from the stopped ship. Fighting at the edge of a stall, he pulled the nose up slightly to start killing the SBD's forward momentum.

It was an almost perfect ditching. The dive bomber stalled, the wings losing their last bit of lift barely ten feet above the ocean. There was nothing Eric could do to prevent the nose starting to come down, with the result that the landing was not as smooth as he had hoped. The impact slammed him forward, his restraints failing to prevent his head from snapping against the instrument panel. Seeing stars, Eric slumped backward briefly into his seat and took a moment to gather himself. As he ran his tongue over his teeth to make sure they were all there, Eric felt the airplane lurch and start to settle towards starboard. The swirl of water into the bottom of the cockpit told him that he did not have long to get out of the crippled aircraft.

"Sir, you okay?!" Rawles asked, standing on the port wing by the aircraft. Eric turned and looked at him, the movement sluggish. Rawles didn't wait for an answer, reaching in and starting to help Eric unbuckle.

"Get the..." Eric started, fighting hard to get through the mental fog. "Get the life raft."

No sooner had he said that than water began pouring over the edge of his cockpit. The cold North Atlantic did wonders to clear the cobwebs, and he realized with a start that Rawles was already up to his chest in the water. Kicking his feet free of the rudder pedals and disconnecting his radio cord, Eric pulled off his shredded life vest and started to stand up. The movement didn't come off as planned as the *Dauntless* slid out from under him. In moments, he and Rawles were both swimming in the cold Atlantic, their plane a momentary dark shape underneath them before it slid into the depths.

"Guess we could've left the codebooks after all," Rawles muttered. "Damn sir, you look like someone hit your noggin' with a sledgehammer."

Eric kicked his legs to get out of the water while reaching up with his left arm. He winced as he touched the massive goose egg on this forehead.

That explains why I'm a little out of it, Eric thought, pleasantly surprised he was able to form a semi-coherent thought. *Although it would appear going for a swim in cold as hell water helps clear up getting knocked on the head.*

Worryingly, Eric could feel his arm cramps returning as he treaded water.

I'm not sure how long I'll make it without a life vest, he thought worriedly. The sound of a boat moter carrying across the waves was the sweetest sound he had ever heard. Turning, he saw that the cruiser's boat was almost upon them. Eric attempted to start swimming towards the whaleboat and realized with a start that his legs were going numb.

"Just stay there, gentlemen, we will be with you shortly!" a man in the boat's prow shouted.

Minutes later the Royal Navy lieutenant was proven as good as his word, with blankets being dropped over the Americans' shoulders and rum shoved into their hands. Rawles threw his shot back quickly, only starting to shiver once he got it down. Eric, hardly a drinker, took two swallows to get the rum into his stomach and had to fight against retching.

"My name is *Leftenant* Aldrich, medical office for the His Majesty's Ship *Exeter*," the man began as the whaleboat began returning to the cruiser. Eric saw that the man was tall and thin, his navy blue jacket hanging off him like he was a walking clothes hanger.

He must be older than he looks, Eric thought as he took in the man's youthful freckled face and dark red hair. While his voice was deep and firm, Aldrich looked like he hadn't been shaving for more than a week. After a moment's silence, Eric realized the man was awaiting similar information from him.

"Lieutenant junior grade Eric Cobb," Eric said. "This is my gunner, Rawles. Since you guys actually gave us some warning, I'll assume it's not your fleet that gunned us down."

If Aldrich was non-plussed that Eric didn't give him any more information the man did not show it.

"It would appear that you have met our erstwhile adversaries the *Kriegsmarine*," Aldrich replied. "I take it that you, then, are the aircraft who sent the position report in the clear?"

"That would be us," Eric replied. Aldrich smiled.

"Well thank you for not making my wife a widow," Aldrich said. At Eric's look, Aldrich just smiled.

"I am sure Captain Gordon will explain everything to you if he sees fit. Until then, please enjoy our hospitality. *Leftenant* Cobb, you appear to have taken a pretty good knock on the head. I'll need to check you out once we get aboard."

Eric started to nod, then realized that would be very foolish.

"That would probably be a good idea," he began, then belatedly added, "sir."

Ten minutes later, Eric stood watching Aldrich's finger as the young-looking officer moved his hand back and forth. The two men were standing in *Exeter*'s port dressing station, a space that was normally the petty officers' mess. When the heavy cruiser was getting ready to enter combat, the space was set aside for casualty treatment and stabilization before the unfortunate subjects were taken to sick bay below.

"You mentioned something about me saving your wife from becoming a widow?" Eric asked after a moment.

"Yes, I did," Aldrich replied.

"Sir, I can tell the ship is at Condition Two," Eric continued. "Obviously you guys are expecting a fight. I got sort of confused after getting shot up, but weren't the Germans a bit far away for you to be preparing for combat?"

"Very astute observation, *Leftenant*," another voice interjected. Eric saw the two ratings in the room jump to their feet, followed at a more leisurely pace by Rawles. Eric started to turn his head to see what they were looking at.

"I will not be able to tell if you have a concussion if you turn your head, *Leftenant* Cobb," Aldrich said, causing Eric to stop his movement. "Captain Gordon, sir," he said, nodding towards the door.

"*Leftenant* Aldrich," Captain Gordon replied. "I see you've been fishing again."

Aldrich smiled as he finished moving his finger back and forth.

"I think this one is a tad bit large to have thrown back, Captain," Aldrich said, stepping back. "We're done here, *Leftenant*."

Eric turned around, well aware of his sorry appearance in a borrowed pair of Royal Navy overalls. Rawles and he had both gladly handed over their waterlogged clothes in exchange for dry clothing, but now he felt vaguely self-conscious in meeting the *Exeter*'s master. Gordon was a man of slightly above average height, with piercing eyes and gray, thinning hair topping an aristocratic face.

"Well, I must agree," Gordon said, giving Eric a pensive look. "I suppose you play what you Americans call football?"

"I did, sir," Eric replied. "For the Naval Academy."

"Barbaric sport," Gordon said. "Can't see why anyone would enjoy watching roughly twenty men bash each other's brains out over some poor pig's hide."

Eric found himself starting to smile as he contemplated a comeback. Gordon continued without giving him a chance to defend American honor.

"But, that's not what you were talking about to *Leftenant* Aldrich, and time is short. Our mission, when you sighted us, was to gain contact with the German fleet so that we could ascertain its position."

Eric nodded, starting to get a glimmer of understanding.

"Since our own aviators believed that the weather was far too much of a dog's breakfast to fly, the task fell upon the Home Fleet's cruisers, or more correctly, what cruisers broke out of Scapa Flow with His Majesty."

"Broke out of Scapa Flow?" Eric asked, confused.

Gordon and Aldrich shared a look.

"You are aware of the armistice signed a fortnight ago, yes?"

"The one between you guys and the Krauts? Yes, sir, I'm aware."

"There was some fine print agreed to by Lord Halifax's negotiators that did not sit well with the King," Gordon continued simply. "Namely the part about turning over the occupied nations' governments-in-exile and all of their forces that had fought under our command."

"That part was not covered in our briefings," Eric replied.

Of course, we've been at sea ever since it looked like you guys were about to be knocked out of the war, he didn't add. Eric was certain the term "neutral country" would lose all meaning. if the full details of the USN's actions to facilitate Great Britain's war efforts ever came to light.

Which may explain why the Krauts turned two American aircraft into colanders.

"This breakout wasn't exactly long in the planning, *Leftenant*," Gordon replied with a tight smile. "However, this is of no matter. What is important is that the Home Fleet and a few fast liners did manage to break out. What we did not expect was for the Germans to have anticipated our decision and placed submarines in our path."

Eric fought to keep the astonishment off of his face.

The submarines were part of the reason you guys had to surrender! he thought, incredulous.

"The *Queen Mary*, carrying a large contingent of forces, was torpedoed last night," Gordon continued, either not reading Eric's brief change of expression or choosing to ignore it. "She did not sink, but her speed was greatly slowed. This morning, it was decided to offload her passengers and scuttle the vessel."

Eric looked at Aldrich and then Captain Gordon.

"I am coming to the reason behind *Leftenant* Aldrich's comment," Gordon said with a slight smile. "Before the fleet departed Scapa Flow, there were reports that the German fleet was expected to sortie in order to attempt to intercept the Royal Family and compel their return. They were believed to be another two hundred miles east of the position you radioed."

I am beginning to understand now, Eric thought.

"As I noted, our own pilots did not think the conditions were suitable for flying as dawn broke. Which is why this vessel is currently part of a picket line, and as *Leftenant* Aldrich alluded to, would have likely encountered Jerry much as you did—guns first."

Eric could hear the disdain in Gordon's voice and decided to intercede on behalf of his British counterparts.

"Sir, with all due respect, the weather *is* too bad to be flying," he said bitterly. "Our commander volunteered the most experienced pilots in our squadron, and even then he had to persuade Admiral No...our admiral to allow us to fly."

Gordon's small smile broadened.

"Lieutenant Cobb, I am well aware that you are off of the aircraft carrier *Ranger*, specifically from VB-4. I am also aware that your signal was picked up by the cruiser *Augusta* and that your commander, apparently, perished. Finally, I am aware that Rear Admiral Noyes is under strict orders not to engage in direct combat with the *Kriegsmarine* unless they cross the established neutrality line."

This time the surprise was far too great for Eric to maintain any hint of a poker face.

"Guess I could have passed on tossing the codebooks over the side," Rawles said coolly.

"Unfortunately, *Leftenant*, the manner by which I know all this information also means that your fleet realizes we have plucked you out of the Atlantic. That," Gordon continued, his smile disappearing, "places us in a bit of a quandary."

Gordon turned towards Rawles and the two ratings in the room.

"Gentlemen, if you could excuse us?" he asked, the tone of his voice belying the appearance of his question being a request. Eric was glad to see Rawles follow the two men out into the passageway.

"As I was saying, your presence here places us into a bit of a fix. You, *Leftenant*, are an officer of a neutral nation. More importantly a neutral nation with certain elements who would gladly seize upon your death or serious injury in order to support the agenda of keeping your nation from rendering His Majesty's government any aid. I am sure that you are familiar with the term 'impressment' as it applies to our nations' shared histories?"

Eric nodded, starting to see where Gordon was going.

We fought a minor debacle in 1812 over just that issue as I recall, Eric thought somberly.

"So, in order to avoid any discussions of that sort of thing, I have consulted with my superiors. We can hardly just stuff you in a whaleboat and leave you in the middle of the Atlantic. Therefore, I am here to offer you a choice to transfer to the H.M.S. *Punjabi*. This vessel will then be tasked with escorting the liners out of harm's way, and that is probably the safest thing we can provide at the moment."

Well, no, you could actually return me to American forces or put me on a neutral vessel, Eric thought sharply, but decided some things were best left unvoiced.

"What effect will this have on your force?" he asked instead.

Gordon paused for a few moments, and Eric could see the wheels turning in the British captain's head.

"The effects would not be positive," Gordon finally answered. The man then took a deep sigh, with the breaking of his mental dam almost perceptible.

"The division of destroyers with us is one of two that departed Scapa Flow with their actual assigned crews, full complement of torpedoes, and allotted depth charges," *Exeter*'s captain said, his voice clipped. "The size of the German force is unknown, but it is highly unlikely that our advantage is so great that we can afford to lose a destroyer before the action begins. The choice, however, is yours *Leftenant* Cobb."

The silence in the compartment after Gordon's explanation seemed to press in on Eric. At least thirty seconds passed, with Gordon growing perceptibly impatient, before the American replied.

"We were briefed before we departed Newport News that our forces were to make every effort to avoid giving the impression that we were aiding RN forces," he said, and watched Captain Gordon's face start to fall. "However, we were also instructed to respond to hostile acts in kind. Those bastards killed my squadron commander and nearly killed me. While I hesitate to give them another chance to finish the job, I'll be damned if I'll make their lives easier."

Gordon exhaled heavily.

"You do realize that when I transmit this news to Admiral Tovey your own forces are going to overhear it, correct?"

Eric shrugged.

"If I end up in Leavenworth it means no one else will be shooting at me," Eric replied grimly. "Seems to me that the situation is bad enough if I force you to take this ship out of the line, the. After what they did to London, I'm not sure I want them to catch the King or his family."

Eric saw several emotions flit across Gordon's face. The man was about to respond when the ship's loudspeaker crackled. Both men turned to look at the speaker mounted at the front of the compartment.

"Captain to the bridge," a calm, measured voice spoke. "I say again, Captain to the bridge."

"Last chance to back out, *Leftenant*," Captain Gordon said, heading for the companionway hatch.

"We'll stay, sir," Eric said, right before a thought struck him. "However, I do have one request."

"What would that be, *Leftenant*?"

"Do you think that His Majesty could consider asking President Roosevelt to give me a pardon? You know, just in case?"

Gordon stopped dead for a second, confusion on his face. Still looking befuddled, he shrugged.

"I'll be sure to pass along your request," the British officer allowed. "Even though I am unsure as to what you are referring to."

Eric smiled.

"I'm sure His Majesty will have someone who can advise him as to what I mean," Eric replied. Gordon shook his head and opened the hatch. There was a quick exchange of words with Aldrich that Eric couldn't quite hear, then the man was gone. A moment later, Lieutenant Aldrich stepped back through the door.

"What is your hat size, *Leftenant?*" Aldrich asked.

"Seven inches even," Eric said.

"I'll see what we can find in the way of a helmet for you."

Eric felt and heard the *Exeter*'s engines begin to accelerate. Aldrich's face clouded as the loudspeaker crackled again. A few moments later, the sound of a bugle call came over the device followed by the same clipped voice as before calling the crew to "Action Stations".

"Well now, it appears that our German friends have been sighted once more," Aldrich said grimly as he walked towards the speaking tube at the back of the compartment. "Either that or Jerry's bloody U-boats are at it again."

Eric suddenly thought about the implications of either of those events and didn't like what he was coming up with. Rawles and the two British seamen reentered the compartment as Aldrich began calling down to the ship's store for a helmet. Eric gave a wry smile as he saw that Rawles had already been given a helmet. The pie plate-shaped headgear looked slightly different than its American counterpart, but close enough that Eric was sure the gunner wouldn't have looked too out of place aboard *Ranger*.

"I see that our hosts have already seen to your comforts, Rawles," Eric teased his gunner.

"I'd be a lot more comfortable with a pair of guns in my hand aboard a *Dauntless*, sir," Rawles said, his voice tight. Eric could see the man was nervous, and he didn't blame him. He was about to make another comment when Aldrich's voice stopped him in his tracks.

"Right, understood, I will send *Leftenant* Cobb to the bridge with the runner while his gunner remains here," the medical officer said into the tube. "Aldrich out."

"Did I just hear what I think I did?" Eric asked, struggling to keep his tone neutral.

"The captain is afraid that one shell will kill you both," Aldrich replied simply. "That would be bad for a great many reasons."

I hate it when people have a point, Eric thought. *At least, I hate it when said point means I'm about to get a front row seat to people shooting guns at me.*

"Well it's hard to argue with that logic," Eric said, looking up as a man arrived in the hatchway with his helmet and flash gear. "Rawles, try to stay out of the rum."

"Aye aye, sir," Rawles replied, his expression still sour.

"Midshipman Radcliffe, you are in charge until I get back," Aldrich said, then turned to Eric. "Given what I've been told, there's enough time to give you a quick tour of the vessel before I drop you off at the bridge. That is, if you'd like a quick tour."

"Certainly, sir," Eric said. "I did a midsummer cruise on the U.S.S. *Salt Lake City*, so it will be interesting to see how differently your side does things."

U.S.S. Houston
Cavite Naval Base
2020 Local (0820 Eastern)
13 September (12 September)

Whereas most men would have felt butterflies in their stomach prior to meeting their boss, Commander Jacob T. Morton found himself hoping that the rage and bitterness he felt did not show on his lined face. He took a deep, steadying breath as the orderly returned from inside the captain's day cabin.

"Captain Wallace will see you now, sir," the marine said, coming to attention.

"Thank you, corporal," Jacob replied, his accent betraying his Maine roots. With that, he stepped through the hatchway. Stepping forward to three steps before the desk of *Houston*'s master, he saluted.

"Commander Jacob Morton reporting as ordered, sir," Jacob said crisply. Standing well over six feet, with a tall, gangly frame, Jacob forced the short, heavyset man standing behind the desk to slightly crane his head back as he returned the salute of the *Houston*'s newest XO.

"When I heard they called you 'The Stork,' I wondered how someone got a nickname like that," Captain Sean Wallace observed drily, his Texas twang quite evident. "Now I see a slight resemblance to you and a crane. Please, take a seat before I develop a crick in my neck."

Jacob's expression didn't change, his green eyes continuing to hold Wallace's brown ones as he followed orders.

"Why do they call you 'The Stork,' if I may ask?" Wallace continued.

Why do people always ask if a question is okay ***after*** *it's already been said?* Jacob thought.

"Plebe boxing class, sir," Jacob replied. "One of my opponents stated fighting me was like being attacked by an angry stork. It stuck."

Captain Wallace nodded, running a hand through his thinning brown hair.

"Horrible class, that," Wallace replied. "I think that's probably the worst experience I've ever had in my life. I take it that you did all right?"

"I boxed in the Brigade intramurals," Jacob replied evenly. "I placed second in the light heavyweight class."

Wallace smiled.

"Well, glad to see your aggressiveness won't be a problem," he said with a smile. "Its part of the reason you're here. But before we get started, would you like me to have the mess send up something? There should be sandwiches or something available, I realize you're probably famished after coming all the way out from Pearl."

"No thank you, sir, I actually ate before coming aboard," Jacob said. "I will, with your permission, have some of that water in the corner however."

"By all means," Wallace said, gesturing towards the pitcher and glasses. As Jacob stood, *Houston*'s captain began their discussion.

"I understand that you were somewhat surprised when BuPers cut your orders."

"It's rare that an officer is requested by name, much less by someone he has never met," Jacob replied cautiously. "Serving twice as an XO is lucky, but three times is unheard of."

Wallace grimaced.

"When Captain Rooks got cancer three months ago it was a shock to the entire wardroom," Wallace replied. "Admiral Hart offered every one of the officers the opportunity to transfer to other vessels, and most of the division chiefs were reassigned throughout the fleet or sent back to Pearl. I only requested that Admiral Hart give me the most experienced XO possible, and apparently your name was selected."

Well that explains it, Jacob thought, fighting the urge to curse aloud.

"I understand you had been slated to take a destroyer in about six months," Wallace continued. "I realize that an XO tour, much less one here in the Forgotten Fleet, is hardly an equal trade, but Admiral Hart has assured me that he will personally see to it that your career doesn't suffer."

Jacob was taken aback by Wallace's frankness. Usually mere commanders were not informed of admiral and captain's personnel machinations, much less apologized to for their careers being possibly set back.

"Thank you, sir," he said, feeling a great deal of tension leave his body. Wallace gave a slight smile.

"I think, were I in your position, I would be ready to punch my captain out at the first opportunity. Given that you apparently have some experience with that, I would much prefer to clear the air before we have to work together."

Jacob smiled in return at Wallace's slight joke.

Obviously not one of those men who believes that the captain must appear as a god before all mortals, he thought. As if reading his mind, Wallace continued.

"I'm not a man to stand on protocol between us in private, especially given your seniority. I also won't beat around the bush—I expect you to be my hatchet man. All six departments on this ship are good, but I need you to make them excellent," Wallace said simply. "Especially as I think we'll be in war within a month."

Jacob gave his captain a measured look.

"I'm not saying I disagree, but what is your reasoning, sir?"

"The damn Japs are probably going to take the news out of Europe as a blank check to start 'liberating' some colonies around here, and we need to make sure they don't think the Philippines are also on the foreclosure list."

"I was told before I left Pearl that there's talk of still making the Philippines independent at the end of the year," Jacob replied. "With Great Britain's surrender, is that still going to happen?"

"Apparently that idiot MacArthur thinks that the Philippines can defend themselves with Navy help," Wallace snorted. "So, yes, it will probably happen, but that won't change any of our war plans."

"So Admiral Hart still intends to retreat to the Dutch East Indies if the Japanese attack? That was the last plan I was privy to when I was on CINCPAC staff."

"Yes, we're not staying here to absorb shells for the Army," Wallace replied.

"Instead we're going to die defending some occupied countries' colonies," Jacob replied, his voice more bitter than he intended. Wallace fixed him with a hard look.

"I will forgive that outburst XO since we are alone. But I would caution you that I will have considerably less patience if you display one iota of that opinion in front of any of our junior officers. Do I make myself absolutely clear, commander?"

Jacob reined in his temper, surprised that he had grown so annoyed.

"Very clear, sir," Jacob said calmly. "I apologize."

"It happens that I agree with you," Wallace said with a wave of his hand. "However, neither of us are in charge and the hour grows late. I notice you don't wear a wedding ring, but your personnel jacket indicated that you were married."

"My wife passed away six years ago," Jacob replied evenly. "She had a massive coronary when I was in Norfolk."

Wallace's face clouded for a moment.

"My apologies," Wallace said. "It'd be nice if the damn personnel folks had let me know that before I made an ass of myself."

"For some reason BuPers is incapable of passing that information to any of my duty stations," Jacob replied, his voice with a hard edge. "I go through this every time I have a new assignment. Thankfully to date they have never messed up Jo's file."

"Jo? You have a son?" Captain Wallace asked.

"No, short for Josephine," Jacob said with a broad smile. "My wife started calling her Jo because she swears it was quite obvious to everyone that I had wanted a boy."

"I have three sons myself," Wallace said. "Trust me, in some ways daughters are easier. At least you don't have to worry about them being in harm's way."

"I wish that were absolutely true, sir," Jacob returned, his smile disappearing like morning fog.

Honolulu, Hawaii
0530 Local (1030 Eastern)
12 September

I am crazy. As in, "Welcome to the nuthouse, Josephine, we are so glad to see you" insane, Josephine Marie Morton thought for the fifth time that morning. Fighting back a yawn as she stood on the quay looking out into Honolulu's harbor, she turned to look at her three companions. Two of them loomed far above her own height even in the low heels she wore with her plain brown dress. The other was only a half foot taller than her with the athletic build of a long-distance runner. Giving a sideways glance at the trio, a thought came to her mind that nearly made her giggle.

"You're in somewhat good spirits," the smaller man said quietly. Turning to face him while simultaneously brushing back her shoulder-length brunette hair, Jo finally couldn't hold the light laugh in anymore.

"I'm sorry, Nick, but every time I see you three together I cannot help but wonder how your mother went from big, bigger, biggest to runt," Jo replied.

Nick Elrod Cobb, Lieutenant (j.g.), United States Navy, gave Jo a half smile.

You know, you could really be a lady killer if you tried, Jo thought wistfully. *However, you've made it very clear that you don't want to try with me—but a gal can dream.*

Nick, unlike his three brothers, had dark hair to go with his blue eyes. While none of the Cobbs were hard to look at, the youngest of the four sons had definitely gotten more than his fair share of handsome. Moreover, unlike the two blonde-haired grizzlies behind him, Nick wasn't so big that a woman felt she had to worry about being broken in half.

"I think our father figured he could get just as much manual labor for half the groceries," Nick replied, looking sideways at his two brothers.

"That's a theory..." Samuel Michael Cobb, Captain, United States Marine Corps began.

"...but probably not very valid," David Aaron Cobb, Captain, USMC and Sam's twin, finished.

Nick made a sound of frustration.

"You know, four years away from you two lugs and I'd forgotten just how fu...darn annoying that habit is!"

"You know, Nick, you really can swear around me," Jo said with a chuckle. "I promise, my father has said many, many worse things around the house, to include references to the act of copulation."

"It's not your opinion he's worried about," Sam observed, giving his younger brother a glower.

"No, it would be the fact that we wouldn't want him to ever give the impression that our mother didn't raise us to act like gentlemen around a lady."

Jo shook her head.

"Has anyone ever told you Southerners that the age of chivalry has long since passed?"

"Just because you Yankee women don't know how to demand proper behavior from your men doesn't mean that we have to stop giving it," David replied, looking out towards the harbor. "I do believe that is Patricia's vessel."

"Only half a day late," Nick observed. "Damn merchant..ow!"

Jo was amazed at how quickly Nick turned around, starting to raise his hands to punch one of his brothers then stopping to think better of it.

"Why do I get the feeling I'm witnessing a family story that has played out many, many times over the past twenty-four years?" Jo asked bemusedly.

"Because you're an astute observer of human behavior," Sam said lowly, not taking his eyes off Nick.

"In addition to being highly intelligent," David continued, also watching Nick like a hawk. "Oh, and very pretty."

Jo felt herself starting to blush and was glad for the olive tint of her skin.

Sorry boys, I own a mirror, she thought. While she didn't consider herself *fat* by any means, Jo knew she could stand to lose a few pounds. *Thankfully it seems to go to the right places, though*. Voluptuous was a fair word to describe her even if pretty wasn't.

"Yes, these two think it's funny to both pick on someone," Nick said lowly, his voice making it very clear that there'd be a fight if either brother touched him again.

"Mama raised you better than to curse in front of a lady," Sam replied simply.

The incoming vessel sounded its whistle, interrupting the brothers' discussion. A small liner, the *S.S. Hampton Roads* made a regular trip between Hawaii and the mainland. Usually it returned with mostly military dependents and those seeking to make their fortune working at Pearl Harbor or one of the various Army posts scattered around the islands. Ten minutes after sounding her whistle, the ship's crew was tossing ropes to the men gathered on the dock. Shortly after that, Jo got to see yet another member of the Cobb family.

"Will you look at the hams on that one," a man said a little too loudly to his companion as they walked by. Jo, focusing on the ship, whipped her head around to see that both men were likewise looking at the gangplank as a tall, beautiful brunette began to descend. The woman was wearing a yellow dress and a matching hat, with curly locks trailing all the way down past her shoulders.

I wonder if that's...

"Well that's a sight for sore eyes," the second man replied, "Looks like we're about to get some fresh round eye..."

The man never got to finish his sentence. One second Sam, David, and Nick were standing on opposite sides of her. The next, Nick had seemingly teleported the ten feet to the ogling duo's location. Looking at the two men, Jo could tell that they were soldiers. She couldn't have identified what clued her in about their manner or their walk, but upon a closer look it was blindingly obvious.

"Excuse me, mister," Nick said lightly, "but you wouldn't happen to be about to make a comment about that women in the yellow dress, would you?"

The two men looked at Nick, then looked at each other.

"She your wife or something, pal?" one of them asked belligerently. "Looks a little young to be married."

"As a matter of fact, no," Nick replied. "She's my sister."

The two men looked at one another, then looked at Nick.

"Okay, so even if my buddy and I here were about to say something, we were having a private conversation. We doubt your sister minds."

Not only soldiers, but stupid ones, Jo thought.

"Yes, but *I* mind, and I know exactly what someone means when they start talking about roundeye," Nick continued. "I would appreciate it if you talked quieter or maybe keep your comments to yourself."

The first man looked somewhat sheepish, but his companion apparently had been having a bad day.

"Well we'd *appreciate* it if you minded your own business," the man sneered. "You'd probably like it a lot more too."

Just like that, I'm standing by myself, Jo thought to herself, as Sam and David both ambled over behind their younger brother.

"You know, we're not quite as sensitive about what we may overhear," Sam said.

"After all, with the wind blowing in our direction, you may not have realized that your comments about our sister were audible to us," David continued.

"But Nick here asked you kindly enough to maybe take your comments elsewhere, and you have refused," Sam resumed, his voice dropping lower.

"So maybe it would help if we told you a bit more forcefully to *go somewhere else*," David finished. Jo felt the hair on the back of her neck rise at David's tone.

Never thought I'd see someone beat to death, she thought nervously. Fortunately the quieter of the two soldiers realized that his friend's mouth was about to put both of them in the hospital if they were lucky, morgue if not.

"Let's go, Matt," the man said. "I don't think that dame's going to give you the time of day if you're in traction."

"Matt" gave all three Cobbs a cold, hard look as he allowed his friend to tug him away. If he was trying for intimidation, he could have saved his breath and energy.

I think he'd have more luck scaring one of the volcanoes around here, Jo thought, fighting the urge to shiver from the adrenaline rushing through her. She was about to say something when she heard a very exasperated, feminine sigh behind her. Turning, Jo saw that the woman in yellow had made a beeline towards the three glowering men, her brow furrowed and mouth in a thin line. Looking at the other woman's features close up, Jo felt a sudden, insane pang of jealousy.

No wonder her brothers are protective of her, Jo thought bitterly. *Probably had plenty of practice*.

"Well, glad to see some things never change," the woman snapped, the ice in her voice freezing the honey of her drawl. "Let me guess? Did someone make an untoward comment about my attire and you three felt the need to defend my honor?"

Jo was in shock at the transformation of all three Cobbs. One moment the trio had been clearly ready to perform carefully choreographed mayhem. The next, Sam, David, and Nick wore almost identically sheepish looks.

Holy shit, I need to take lessons from her, Jo thought.

"I am once again reminded of why I will probably die a spinster," the woman continued, her delivery rapid and tone sharp.

"We figured fleeing Alabama like a wanted fugitive two weeks before your wedding to Beau might have had a bit more to do with that," Nick responded, his face hard. Both of his brothers stepped away from him, the move so quick that it was obviously unconscious. Jo didn't blame them, as if looks could kill Nick would have simply ceased to exist.

Her eyes turned into green death rays, Jo thought, remembering a line from some dime store novel she had read as a teenager.

"The only state I am a 'fugitive' from is matrimony, Nick," the woman observed. "Don't you stand here and judge me when it is *obvious* that you do not find it very palatable yourself—or is the issue more that I jilted your guys' childhood friend?"

Nick sighed exasperatedly at his sister.

"Yes, of course, because I have had so many opportunities to meet women in my line of work. Why, just the other day the *Nautilus* stopped off at this tropical refuge where there were all these doe-eyed maidens..."

"So I suppose we'll just forget all the wonderful young women that mother tried to set you up with? At least Eric was smart enough to finally ask Joyce to marry him."

"Well judging from the current situation, a 'yes' sure doesn't seem to mean..."

Jo stepped between Nick and his sister, the movement causing him to stop mid-sentence. She stuck out her hand, catching the rapidly reddening Patricia by surprise.

"Hello Patricia, my name is Josephine Morton, and I'm a friend of your brothers," Jo said calmly. "As I know Nick here likes to run his trap to excess sometimes, I thought I'd see if you were interested in seeing your room sometime before nightfall."

"My room?" Patricia asked, so shocked that her anger was forgotten. "I'm sorry, there must be some..."

"Mistake? No, not really," Jo continued. "I've known Sam, David, and Nick since they got on the island. Rather than have you live by yourself, or move in with David only to have to move out when he gets hitched to Sadie, your brothers thought it'd be nice if you had a more experienced roommate to show you around."

Patricia released Jo's hand, her expression going from angry to suspicious.

"They did, did they?" she asked, arching an eyebrow. "And what do you get out of this, Miss Morton?"

You mean, other than the chance to see your brothers more often? Jo thought, successfully keeping a smile off of her face.

"I'm living in a four bedroom house by myself," Jo replied. "My father just got sent to join the Asiatic Fleet, and it'd be nice to have someone to help with household chores."

"I have very little independent means," Patricia said. "I was hoping to find a job at the shipyard or someplace else suitable to my skills."

"What skills do you have for the shipyard?" Jo asked, befuddled.

"I worked for an architect for the past four years working on blueprints," Patricia replied. "I understand drafting ships' plans is similar work."

Jo shrugged.

"Got me, but I do know the library is looking for more staff. Seems that one of the girls up and ran off with a *Dauntless* pilot."

"I have never understood why some women are so fascinated with pilots," Patricia replied. "No offense to present company."

Sam and David both gave their little sister a hurt look.

"Yes, it's sort of like having a father in the Navy—I don't get impressed at the sight of men in summer whites, you probably don't find silk scarves anything other than a waste of cloth."

Patricia smiled at Jo's sarcastic tone.

"I think that your offer sounds quite nice, um, Jo," Patricia said. "Especially if you've managed to put up with my brothers this long without going mad."

"So why did we come to meet you at the dock, again?" Sam asked.

"Because you thought some random stranger might ravish me," Patricia replied simply. "Or that I'd fall in with villainous company due to a need for someone to help me with my luggage. Speaking of which, here are my chits."

Sam took the proffered claims forms, scanning them for a moment. Shaking his head, he turned to the other two.

"One would think Mom and Dad would have realized something was afoot when half their belongings disappeared. Nick, you go get the car—no need throwing our backs out."

Patricia sighed.

"If you look closer, oh dim-witted brother of mine, you will see that everything except for two chests of clothing and a container of housewares is due to arrive as a separate shipment. As to how I got everything out of the house, that will just remain my little secret."

"Like how you got the money to pull all of this off?" Nick asked *sotto voce* as he walked off. David and Sam moved off in the other direction, leaving Patricia and Jo standing alone at dockside.

"Have you always been able to get them to listen to you?" Jo asked.

Patricia smiled slightly.

"Only once I stopped being their tomboy shadow," she replied. "I think it's because I look so much like Mom now."

"Well, that and it's readily apparent they love their little sister," Jo observed.

Patricia's smile grew wider.

"Yes, that does help. Being the only girl does have its advantages."

"Like having your father wrapped around your finger so that he helps you escape Alabama?"

Patricia started, her smile immediately disappearing.

"How did you..?" she started, then stopped.

Jo grinned broadly.

"I'm an only child. I'm also Daddy's little girl. I know there's no way my father would let me marry an idiot or someone who was going to make me unhappy. From the way your brothers talk about your Dad, I think that applies for you also."

Patricia gave Jo an appraising glance.

"I think I understand why my brothers obviously like you," she said slowly.

"Yes, like the little sister they missed, not..." Jo started, then stopped with a blush.

That came out a little bit more bitter than I intended, Jo realized sheepishly.

"Not like you want them to?" Patricia finished for her.

"Well, Sam and Nick, yes," Jo replied, her face still heated. "I love Sadie."

"Ah, yes, the ever elusive Sadie. You know my mother is absolutely furious that David got engaged without her meeting his fiancée?"

"I heard that rumor somewhere," Jo allowed. "Might've been tied in with the Western Union lines melting down a couple weeks ago. I'm sure the telegram folks are going to get really, really familiar with your brothers as soon as your mother knows for sure you've turned up here."

"There are worse reasons to become familiar with the telegraph man," Patricia said, a flicker of worry crossing her face.

"Has there been any more word from Eric? The boys say all they know is that he's on the *Ranger* out in the Atlantic."

"No, none," Patricia replied. "I just hope he's all right."

"He's a Cobb," Jo replied. "Of course he's all right."

H.M.S. Exeter

North Atlantic

1330 Local (1030 Eastern)

12 September

Whether or not Eric was all right was likely a matter of opinion. He wasn't flying anymore, as the weather conditions had started to become much worse since he'd left *Ranger*'s deck that morning. The base of the clouds had once again descended, and he estimated that the ceiling was well under ten thousand feet. At sea level, visibility was under ten miles, and an approaching squall promised to make it less than that very soon.

I don't blame the Brit pilots for nixing the thought of flying reconnaissance in this, Eric thought. *Yet for some reason I'd still rather take my chances in that soup than be on this ship right now. She's definitely going into harm's way, and fast.*

The heavy cruiser's deck throbbed beneath his feet, and the smoke pouring from her stack and stiff wind blowing onto her bridge told him that *Exeter* had definitely picked up speed.

"Sir, I've brought *Leftenant* Cobb," Adlich said, causing Captain Gordon to turn around. *Exeter*'s master had obviously been mollified by the worsening conditions, as he gave Eric a wry grin when the American officer stepped up beside him.

Whoa, it's cold out here, Eric thought. As if reading his mind, a petty officer handed him a jacket.

"We remove the windows when we're getting ready to go into action," the man said. "Lesson learned after River Plate."

"Thank you," Eric said. "I guess the windows would be a bit problematic in a fight."

The petty officer gave a wan smile, pointing to a scar down his cheek.

"Glass splinters are a bit sharp, yes."

"Your squadron commander was either a very brave man or a much better pilot than anyone I know," Gordon said solemnly from behind the ship's wheel.

Or alternatively, Commander Cobleigh was an idiot who didn't check with the meteorologist before we took off.

Eric was about to reply when the talker at the rear of the bridge interrupted him.

"Sir, *Hood* should be coming into visual range off of our port bow," the rating reported. "Range fifteen thousand yards."

"Thank you," Gordon replied. The captain then strode to the front of the bridge, stopping at a device that reminded Eric of the sightseeing binoculars atop the Empire State Building. Bending slightly, Gordon wiped down the eyepieces, then swiveled the binoculars to look through them.

"Officer of the deck," Gordon said after a moment.

"Yes, sir?" a Royal Navy lieutenant answered from Eric's right. Roughly Eric's height, the broad-shouldered man looked like he could probably snap a good-sized tree in half with his bare hands.

"Confirm with gunnery that the director's tracking *Hood*'s bearing to be three one zero, estimated range fourteen thousand, seven hundred fifty yards."

"Aye aye, sir," the officer replied. Eric heard the RN officer repeating the information as Gordon stepped back from the sight and turned to look at him.

"Well, if you want to see how the other half lives, *Leftenant* Cobb, feel free to have a look."

Eric hoped he didn't look as eager as he felt walking forward towards the bridge windows. Bending a little further to look through the sight, he pressed his face up against the eyepieces. Swinging the glasses, he found himself looking at the H.M.S. *Hood*, flagship of the Royal Navy. With her square bridge, four turrets, and rakish lines, the battlecruiser was a large, beautiful vessel that displaced over four times the *Exeter*'s tonnage. Black smoke poured from her stack, and her massive bow wave told Eric that she was moving at good speed.

"You can change the magnification with the switch under your right hand," Gordon said, startling Eric slightly. He followed the British master's advice, continuing until he could see the entire approaching British force as it closed. Destroyers were roughly one thousand yards in front of and to either side of the *Hood*. Behind her at one-thousand-yard intervals were two large vessels, either battleships or battlecruisers, with another one starting to exit the mist like some sort of great beast stirring from its cave. After a moment, Eric recognized the distinctive silhouette as that of a *Nelson*-class battleship.

"That is the *King George V*, *Prince of Wales*, and *Nelson* behind her. *Warspite* should be next."

Eric nodded at Gordon's statement, continuing to watch as the final battleship made its appearance. A moment later, Gordon starting to give orders to the helmsman. *Exeter*'s bow began to swing around to port, causing Eric to step back from the sight with a puzzled expression.

"We'll be passing between the destroyer screen and the *Hood* to take our place in line," Gordon said. Eric turned back to the device, continuing to study the British battleline. A few moments later, there was the crackle of the loudspeaker.

"All hands, this is the captain speaking," Gordon began. "Shortly we will be passing by the *Hood*. All available hands are to turn out topside to give three cheers for His Majesty. That is all."

Eric stepped back from the sight, his face clearly radiating his shock. Gordon smiled as he came back up towards the front of the bridge with the officer of the deck.

"The *King* is going into battle?" he asked incredulously. "Isn't that a bit..."

"Dangerous?" Gordon finished for him. "Yes, but much like your situation, circumstances precluded His Majesty's transfer to another vessel."

"What? That doesn't make any..."

"His Majesty was apparently aboard the *Hood* receiving a briefing from the First Sea Lord when the *Queen Mary* was torpedoed," Gordon said, his voice cold. "We were not expecting the German surface units to be as close as they were, and it was considered imprudent to stop the *Hood* with at least two confirmed submarines close about. Is that sufficient explanation to you, or would you like to continue questioning our tactics?"

Eric could tell he was straining his host's civility, but the enormity of what was at risk made him feel he had to say something.

"I'm no expert at surface tactics..."

"That much is obvious," Gordon snapped.

"...but the *Hood* is a battlecruiser," Eric finished in a rush. "While I didn't get a great look at the Germans before they shot up me and my commander, Rawles saw at least two battleships."

"Your concern is noted, *Leftenant* Cobb, but I think that you will see the *Hood* is a bit hardier than a dive bomber."

Okay, I'm just going to shut up now, Eric said. *I may have slept through a lot of history, but I seem to recall the last time British battlecruisers met German heavy guns it didn't go so well. A quote about there being problems with your "bloody ships" or something similar comes to mind.* The Battle of Jutland hadn't been that long ago, as evidenced by the *Warspite* still being a front-line unit. Eric sincerely hoped Gordon's confidence was well-placed.

"Sir, we are almost on the *Hood*," the officer of the deck interrupted. Eric turned and realized that the lead destroyer was indeed almost abreast the *Exeter*, with the *Hood* now a looming presence just beyond.

"The *Hood*, after her refit, is the most powerful warship in the world," Gordon continued, his voice a little less frigid. "The *Bismark* and *Tirpitz* have only recently gone through refit, while the *Scharnhorst* and *Gneisenau* have not been in the open ocean for almost six months. There should not be any major danger."

If you're looking around the room and you can't find the mark, guess what? ***You're*** *the mark.* Eric's father's words, an admonishment to always be suspicious of any situation that seemed too good to be true, came back to him with a cold feeling in his stomach.

The Germans would ***not*** *be out here unless they had a plan*, Eric continued thinking. *Somehow I think that, much like the Royal Air Force, the Royal Navy is about to receive a rude shock.*

"All right lads, three cheers for His Majesty," The loudspeaker crackled. "Hip...hip..."

As the *Exeter*'s crew yelled at the top of their lungs, Eric studied the *Hood* in passing. The two vessels were close enough that he could see a party of men in white uniforms standing on the battlecruiser's bridge and the extraordinarily large flag streaming from the *Hood*'s yardarm. Picking up a pair of binoculars resting on a shelf near the bridge's front lip, he focused on the pennant.

"That's the Royal Standard," Gordon said after the last cheer rang out. The device consisted of four squares, two red with the other pair gold and blue, respectively. The two red were identical, forming the top left and bottom right portions of the flag. Looking closely, Eric could see elongated gold lions or griffins within the squares. The gold square had what looked like a standing red lion within a crimson square, while the blue had some sort of harp.

"What do the symbols mean, sir?" Eric asked. Gordon shook his head.

"*Leftenant*, I could probably remember if I thought hard enough about it, but I do not think that is very important right now."

Eric nodded, placing the binoculars back down as the *Exeter* continued to travel down the battleline. After *Warspite*, there were two more British heavy cruisers. At Gordon's command, the *Exeter* finished her turn, taking her place behind the other two CAs. Satisfied with his vessel's stationing, Gordon began dealing with the myriad tasks that a warship's captain was expected to perform before battle. Eric observed these with a sense of detachment, noting that the bridge crew operated like they had been there dozens of times. Mentally, he compared the men to those he had observed aboard the American heavy cruiser *Salt Lake City*.

Things are so similar, yet so different. You can tell these men have been at war for over three years, Eric thought, feeling strangely comforted by the obvious experience in front of him. The feeling was fleeting, however, as the talker at the rear of the bridge broke the routine.

"Sir, *Hood* reports multiple contacts, bearing oh three oh relative, range thirty thousand yards," the talker at the rear of the bridge said. It was if his words touched off a current of electricity around the entire compartment, as each man seemed to stiffen at his post.

"Well, glad to see that she's got better eyes than we do," Gordon muttered under his breath. "Pass the word to all stations."

Eric saw motion out of the corner of his eye and turned to see the *Exeter*'s two forward turrets training out and elevating.

"Flag is directing a change in course to one seven zero true," the talker continued. "Vessels will turn in sequence. Destroyers are to form up for torpedo attack to our stern."

Gordon nodded in acknowledgment, and Eric could see the man was obviously in pensive thought. After their earlier exchange, Eric had no desire to attempt to discern what he was thinking. Judging from the look on the man's face, it was probably nothing good. Looking to port, Eric could see the British destroyers starting to steam past for their rendezvous astern of *Exeter*, a scene that was repeated a moment later on the starboard side.

Is it my imagination, or is it getting a little bit easier to see again? Eric thought. *If so, is that a good or a bad thing?*

"Enemy force is turning with us," the talker said quietly.

*Now **that** is definitely a bad thing.*

Eric had a very passing familiarity with radar, as he had been the target dummy for *Ranger*'s fighter squadron to practice aerial intercepts. It was obvious, given the visibility, that the *Hood* hadn't sighted the enemy with the naked eye. Unless the Germans had a team of gypsies on their vessels, it appeared that they also had the ability to detect ships despite the murk.

Explains how they were able to shoot down Commander Cobleigh, Eric thought, feeling sick to his stomach. *My God, they probably knew we were there long before we came out of the cloudbank but wanted to make positive identification.*

The visibility was definitely starting to get better, at least at sea level. With only the distance of the British line to judge by, Eric guesstimated that visibility to the horizon was somewhere around twenty thousand yards.

Well within maximum range of everyone's guns, he thought. *I hope someone on this side knows what size force we're facing, as I doubt the Germans are idiots.*

"Sir, the *Hood* reports she is..."

With a roar and spout of black smoke from her side, the British flagship made the talker's report superfluous. The rest of the British battleline rapidly followed suit, the combined smoke from their guns floating backward like roiling, black thunderheads.

I can't see what in the hell they're shooting at, Eric thought, searching the horizon as he felt his stomach clench.

In truth, *Hood* and her counterparts had only a general idea of what they were engaging. Indeed, if the commander of the opposing force, Vice Admiral Erich Bey, had actually followed his orders to simply compel the Home Fleet to sail a relatively straight course while avoiding contact, there would have been no targets for them to engage. Instead, Bey had decided to close with the last known position of the Home Fleet in hopes of picking off the vessel or vessels the *Kriegsmarine*'s U-boats had allegedly crippled that morning. Regardless of his reasoning, Bey's aggressive nature had inadvertently led to his superiors' worst nightmare—the hastily organized Franco-German force being brought into contact with the far more experienced Royal Navy.

Admiral Bey, to his credit, played the hand he had dealt himself. Moments after *Hood*'s initial salvo landed short of his flagship, the KMS *Bismarck*, the German admiral began barking orders. The first was for the radar-equipped vessels in his fleet to return fire. The second was for the entire column to change course in order to sharpen the rate of closure and allow the Vichy French vessels, limited to visual acquisition, to also engage. The final directive was for a position report to be repeatedly sent without any encryption so that nearby U-boats could immediately set course in an attempt to pick off any stragglers.

"Well, looks like the other side is game," Captain Gordon drily observed as multiple waterspouts appeared amongst the British battleships. A moment later the distant sound of the explosions reached Eric's ears.

"Looks like they're over-concentrating on the front of the line though," Eric observed.

Gordon turned to look at the American pilot.

"Would you prefer they spread their fire more evenly so we can have a taste, *Leftenant*?"

"No sir, not with the shells that are being slung out there."

Gordon brought his binoculars back up.

"Still can't see the enemy yet, but that's why the boffins were aboard during our refit," Gordon said. The man turned to his talker, jaw clenched.

"Tell Guns they may fire when we have visual contact or the enemy reaches nineteen thousand yards, whichever comes first," Gordon said, his voice clipped. "Inform bridge of the eventual target's bearing so we may get a look."

"Aye aye, Captain."

Gordon turned back towards Eric and opened his mouth when he was interrupted by the sound of ripping canvas followed by the *smack!* of four shells landing between *Exeter* and the next British cruiser in front of her. A moment later, a bell began ringing at the rear of *Exeter*'s bridge. Eric was about to ask what the device signified when the heavy cruiser's forward turrets roared, the blast hitting him like a physical blow. The look of shock was obviously quite apparent, as Gordon gave Eric an apologetic smile.

"Sorry, guess I should have..."

Exeter's captain was again interrupted, except this time by two bright flashes aboard the cruiser forward of her the British battleline. The other vessel was visibly staggered by the blows, with a fire immediately starting astern.

"Looks like *Suffolk* has worse luck than we do," Gordon observed grimly. The British heavy cruiser's turrets replied back towards the enemy, but it was obvious, even to Eric, that their companion vessel was badly hit.

"Guns reports target is at bearing two nine zero, range twenty thousand yards..."

The bell ringing cut the rating off, as it was followed immediately by the *Exeter* unleashing a full broadside. Gordon had already begun to swing his sight around to the reported bearing, and bent to see what his guns were up to. Eric, looking past the captain, saw *Suffolk* receive another hit, this one causing debris to fly up from the vicinity of her bridge. He suddenly felt his mouth go dry.

Someone has the range, he thought grimly.

"Bloody good show Guns!" Gordon shouted into the voice tube near his sight. "Give that bastard another..."

The firing gong rang again, *Exeter*'s gunnery officer apparently already ahead of Gordon. Eric braced himself, the roar of the naval rifles starting to cause a slight ringing in his ears. He turned to look towards the horizon, following the direction of *Exeter*'s guns.

"These will help," the officer of the deck said from beside him, handing him a pair of binoculars.

"Thank you," Eric said, turning towards the officer only to see the man go pale.

"Oh bloody hell! Look at the *Hood*!"

Eric turned and looked down the British line, noting as he turned that the *Suffolk* was heeling to *Exeter*'s starboard with flames shooting from her amidships and rear turret. Ignoring the heavily damaged heavy cruiser, he brought up his binoculars as he looked towards the front of the British line. In an instant, he could see why the officer of the deck had made his exclamation. The battlecruiser's guns appeared frozen in place, and oil was visibly gushing from her amidships. As Eric watched, another salvo splashed around her, with a sudden flare and billow of smoke from her stern indicating something serious had been hit.

"Captain, the *Hood* is signaling a power failure!" the officer of the deck shouted. Eric turned to see the man had acquired another set of eyeglasses and was also studying the flagship.

Gordon nodded, stepping back from his captain's sight and brought his own set of binoculars up to study the battlecruiser. Eric quickly handed his over before the OOD could react.

"It would appear that our Teutonic friends can shoot a bit better than we expected," Gordon said grimly.

Admiral Bey would have agreed with Gordon's assessment had he heard it, as he too was pleasantly surprised at how well his scratch fleet was performing. Unfortunately for the Germans, however, the British could shoot almost as well, their guns seemed to be doing far more damage, and they had much better fire distribution. The only British capital ships with major damage were the *Hood*, set ablaze and rendered powerless by the *Tirpitz* and *Jean Bart*, and *Nelson* due to hits from the *Bismarck* and *Strasbourg*. Among the cruisers, only the *Suffolk* had been hit, being thoroughly mauled by the KMS *Hipper* and *Lutzow*. In exchange, only the *Jean Bart, Gneisenau,* and *Bismarck* remained relatively unscathed among his battleline. Of the rest of his vessels, the French battlecruiser *Strasbourg* had been thoroughly holed by the H.M.S. *Warspite*'s accurate shooting, *Tirpitz* was noticeably down by the bows, and *Scharnhorst* had received at least two hits from *Prince of Wales* in the first ten minutes of the fight.

Bey's escorts, consisting of the pocket battleship *Lutzow* and a force of

German and Vichy French cruisers, had arranged themselves in an *ad hoc* screen to starboard. The fact that they outnumbered their British counterparts had not spared them from damage, albeit not as heavy as that suffered by the Franco-German battleline. Moreover, while *Exeter*'s shooting had set the lead vessel, the French heavy cruiser *Colbert*, ablaze and slowed her, this was more than offset by the battering the *Suffolk* had received from the *Lutzow*, *Hipper*, and *Seydlitz*. As that vessel fell backward in the British formation, the remaining cruisers split their fire between the *Exeter*, *Norfolk*, and the destroyers beginning their attack approach.

Word of the British DDs' approach caused Bey some consternation. While it could be argued that his force was evenly matched with the British battleline, the approaching destroyers could swiftly change this equation if they got into torpedo range. Deciding that discretion was the better part of valor, Bey ordered all vessels to make smoke and disengage. It was just after the force began their simultaneous turn that disaster struck.

The KMS *Scharnhorst*, like the *Hood*, had begun life as a battlecruiser. While both she and her sister had been upgraded during the Armistice Period with 15-inch turrets, the *Kriegsmarine* had made the conscious decision not to upgrade her armor. The folly of this choice became readily apparent as the *Prince of Wales*' twentieth salvo placed a pair of 14-inch shells through her amidships belt. While neither shell fully detonated, their passage severed the steering controls between the light battleship's bridge and rudder.

The *Scharnhorst*'s helmsman barely had time to inform the captain of this before the second half of *PoW*'s staggered salvo arrived, clearing the battleship's bridge with one shell and and hitting *Scharnhorst* on the armored "turtle deck" right above her engineering spaces with a second. To many bystanders' horror, a visible gout of steam spewed from the vessel's side as all 38,000 tons of her staggered like a stunned bull. Only the fact that her 15-inch guns fired a ragged broadside back at the British line indicated that the vessel still had power, but it was obvious to all that she had been severely hurt.

One of those observers was the captain of the KMS *Gneisenau*, *Scharnhorst*'s sister ship and the next battleship in line. Confronted with the heavily wounded *Scharnhorst* drifting back towards him, the man ordered the helm brought back hard to starboard. In one of the horrible vagaries of warfare, the *Gneisenau* simultaneously masked her sister ship from the *Prince of Wales*' fire and corrected the aim of her own assailant, the H.M.S. *Nelson*.

No one would ever know how many 16-inch shells hit of the five that had been fired at the *Gneisenau*, as the only one that mattered was the one that found the German battleship's forward magazine. With a massive roar, bright flash, and volcanic outpouring of flame, the *Gneisenau*'s bow disappeared. *Scharnhorst* and *Jean Bart*'s horrified crews were subjected to the spectacle of the *Gneisenau*'s stern whipping upwards, propellers still turning. The structures only glistened for a moment, as the battleship's momentum carried her aft end into the roiling black cloud serving as a tombstone for a 40,000-ton man-of-war and the 1,700 men who manned her.

"Holy shit! Holy shit!" Eric exclaimed, his expletives lost in the general pandemonium that was *Exeter*'s bridge.

"Get yourselves together!" Gordon roared, waving his hands. As if to emphasize his point, there was the sound of ripping canvas, and a moment later, the *Exeter* found herself surrounded by large waterspouts.

"Port ten degrees!" Gordon barked, the bridge crew quickly returning to their tasks.

"Sir, *Nelson* is signaling that she is heaving to!"

"What in the bloody hell is the matter with her?!" Gordon muttered, a moment before *Exeter*'s guns roared again.

"Guns reports we are engaging and being engaged by a pocket battleship. He believes it is the..." the talker reported.

Once again there was the sound of ripping canvas, this time far louder. Eric instinctively ducked just before the *Exeter* shuddered simultaneously with the loud *bang!* just above their heads. Dimly, he saw something fall out of the corner of his eye even as there was a sound like several wasps all around him. Coming back to his feet, Eric smelled the strong aroma of explosives for the second time that day, except this time there was a man screaming like a shot rabbit to accompany it.

"Damage report!" Gordon shouted. "Someone shut that man up!"

Feeling something wet on his face, Eric reached up to touch it and came away with blood. He frantically reached up to feel if he had a wound, and only came away with more blood. Looking around in horror, he suddenly realized that the blood was not his, but that of a British rating who was now missing half of his head, neck, and upper chest. Eric barely had time to register this before a litter crew came bursting into the bridge. The four men headed to the aft portion of the structure, obviously there for the man who had been screaming before a gag had been shoved in his mouth. Eric followed the litter team's path, then immediately wished he hadn't as his stomach lurched. The casualty's abdomen was laid open, and Eric saw the red and grey of intestine on the deck before turning back forward.

Oh God, he thought, then had another as he thought about the injured man's likely destination. *I hope Rawles is okay.*

"Hard a starboard!" Gordon barked. Eric braced himself as the *Exeter* heeled over, the vessel chasing the previous salvo as her guns roared back at the German pocket battleship. He noticed that the guns were starting to bear even further aft as the cruiser maneuvered to keep up with the remainder of the British battleline. Looking to starboard, Eric saw the battleship *Nelson* drifting past them on her starboard side. The vessel's forward-mounted triple turrets, still elevated to port, fired off a full salvo once *Exeter* was past, but it was clear that the battleship had suffered severe damage.

"Sir, we took one glancing hit to the bridge roof," the OOD reported, pointing at the hit that had sprayed splinters into the structure. Eric was amazed at the man's calm. "We took another hit aft, but it detonated in the galley."

"*King George V* signals commence torpedo attack with destroyers," the talker interrupted. "All ships with tubes to attack enemy cripples."

Six waterspouts impacted approximately three hundred yards to port, and Eric found himself questioning the wisdom of staying aboard the heavy cruiser after all.

"Well, looks like this ship will continue her tradition of picking on women bigger than her," Gordon observed drily. "Flank speed, port thirty degrees. Get me the torpedo flat."

Eric looked once again at the hole in the bridge roof.

A step either way and I'd probably be dead, he thought wildly. *Or worse, if that shell had it full on we'd all be gone.* Shaking his head, he turned to look off to port as the throb of *Exeter*'s engines began to increase.

"You ever participate in a torpedo attack during your summer cruise, Mr. Cobb?" Gordon asked after barking several orders to the helm.

"No sir," Eric croaked, then swallowed to get a clearer voice. "Our cruisers don't have torpedoes. I'm familiar with how to do one theoretically..."

Exeter's guns banged out another salvo, even as the German pocket battleship's return fire landed where she would have been had the cruiser continued straight.

"Well, looks like you're about to get to apply some of that theoretical knowledge," Gordon said, bringing his binoculars up. The man scanned the opposing line.

"The three big battleships are turning away under cover of smoke along with the majority of the cruisers. That Frog battlecruiser looks about done for, and that pocket battleship and heavy cruiser will soon have more than enough to deal with when the destroyers catch up," Gordon said, pointing as he talked. *Exeter*'s master turned to give his orders.

"Tell Lieutenant Commander Gannon his target is the pocket battleship! Guns are to..."

The crescendo of incoming shells drowned Gordon out, this time ending with the *Exeter* leaping out of the water and shuddering as she was hit. Once again the bridge wing was alive with fragments, and for the second time Eric felt a splash of wetness across his side. Looking down, he saw his entire left side was covered in blood and flesh. For a moment he believed it was his, until he blissfully realized that he felt no pain.

"Damage report!" Gordon shouted again. "Litter party!"

"Sir, I believe I am hit," the OOD gasped. Eric turned to see the man's arm missing from just below the elbow, blood spraying from the severed stump.

"Corpsman!" Gordon shouted angrily, stepping towards the lieutenant. The captain never made, it, as the OOD toppled face forward, revealing jagged wounds in his back where splinters had blasted into his body.

"Helmsman! Zig zag pattern!" Gordon barked. "Someone get me a damage report! Midshipman Green, inform damage control that we need another talker and an OOD here!"

"Aye aye, Captain!"

"*Leftenant* Cobb!"

"Yes sir?" Eric asked, shaking himself out of stupor.

"It might be prudent for you to go to the conning tower," Gordon said.

"Sir, I'd prefer to be here than in some metal box," Eric said. "With the shells that bastard's tossing it won't make a lick of difference anyway."

"Too true," Gordon said. "Looks like the heavy cruisers and that pocket battleship are covering the bastards' retreat."

. . .

Gordon's supposition was only partially correct. In truth, the pocket battleship *Lutzow* had received damage from the *Exeter* and *Norfolk* that had somewhat reduced her maximum speed. This had prevented her from fleeing with the rest of the screen, their retirement encouraged by a few salvoes from the *Nelson*. Realizing that she could not escape the closing British destroyers, *Lutzow*'s captain had decided to turn and engage the smaller vessels in hopes of allowing *Scharnhorst* to open the distance between herself and the British. Unfortunately, *Lutzow* had failed to inform the heavy cruiser KMS *Hipper*, trailing in her wake, of her desire to self-sacrifice while ignoring Admiral Bey's signal to retire. Thus the latter vessel, her radio aerial knocked out by an over salvo from the *Nelson*'s secondary batteries, found herself committed to engaging the rapidly closing British destroyers along with the larger, crippled *Lutzow*.

The British destroyers, formed into two divisions under the experienced Commodore Philip Vian, first overtook the damaged French battlecruiser *Strasbourg*. Adrift, afire, and listing heavily to port, the *Strasbourg* wallowed helplessly as the British destroyers closed like hyenas on a paralyzed wildebeest. Just as Vian was beginning to order his group into their battle dispositions, flooding finally compromised the battlecruiser's stability. With a rumble and the scream of tortured metal, the *Strasbourg* rotated onto her starboard beam and slipped beneath the surface.

That left the crippled *Scharnhorst*, the *Lutzow*, and the hapless *Hipper*. Still receiving desultory fire from *Nelson* and *Warspite*, the trio of German vessels initially concentrated their fire on the charging *Exeter* and *Norfolk*. After five minutes of this, all three German captains realized Vian's approaching destroyers were a far greater threat. The *Lutzow* and *Hipper* turned to lay smoke across the retreating *Scharnhorst*'s stern, the maneuver also allowing both vessels to fire full broadsides at their smaller assailants. The *Hipper* had just gotten off her second salvo when she received a pair of 8-inch shells from the *Norfolk*. The first glanced off the heavy cruiser's armor belt and fell harmlessly into the sea. The second, however, impacted the main director, blowing the gunnery officer and most of the cruiser's gunnery department into disparate parts that splashed into the sea or onto the deck below. For two crucial minutes, the *Hipper*'s main battery remained silent even as her secondaries began to take the approaching British destroyers under fire.

. . .

The respite from *Lutzow*'s fire had arrived just in time for *Exeter*, as the pocket battleship had been consistently finding the range. Staggering to his feet after another exercise in throwing himself flat, Eric looked forward to see just where the heavy cruiser had been hit this time. His gaze fell upon the devastation that had been *Exeter*'s "B" turret, where a cloud of acrid yellow was smoke pouring back from the structure's opened roof to pass around the heavy cruiser's bridge. Damage control crews were rushing forward to spray hoses upon the burning guns, even as water began to crash over the cruiser's lowering bow.

"Very well then, flood the magazine!" Gordon was shouting into the speaking tube. "Tell the *Norfolk* we shall follow her in as best we can."

Looking to starboard, Eric could see the aforementioned heavy cruiser starting to surge ahead of *Exeter*, smoke pouring from her triple stacks and her forward turrets firing another salvo towards the *Hipper*.

"We are only making twenty-three knots, sir," the helmsman reported.

"Damage control reports heavy flooding in the bow," the talker stated. "Lieutenant Ramses states we must slow our speed or we may lose another bulkhead."

Gordon's face set in a grim line.

"Torpedoes reports a solution on the pocket battleship," the talker reported after pausing or a moment.

"Range?!" Gordon barked.

"Ten thousand yards and closing."

"Tell me when we're at four thousand..."

The seas around the *Exeter* suddenly leaped upwards, the waterspouts clearing her mainmast.

"Enemy battleship is taking us under fire!"

Looking over at *Norfolk*, Eric saw an identical series of waterspouts appear several hundred yards ahead of their companion.

"Two enemy battleships engaging, range twenty-two thousand yards."

"Where's our battleline?" Gordon asked bitterly. "Report the news to the *King George V*."

Another couple of minutes passed, the *Exeter* continuing to close with the turning *Lutzow*. Four more shells exploded around the *Exeter*.

"The *Nelson* is disengaging due to opening range," the talker replied. "The remaining ships are closing our position to take the enemy battleship under fire."

Again there was the sound of an incoming freight train, and the *Exeter* was straddled once more, splinters ringing off the opposite side of the bridge.

"Corpsman!" a lookout shouted from the crow's nest.

Okay, someone stop this ride, I want to get off, Eric thought, bile rising in his throat.

"Commodore Vian reports he is closing."

"Right then, continue to attack!" Gordon shouted. Eric winced, convinced he was going to die.

Unbeknownst to Eric, the *Bismarck* and *Tirpitz* had only returned to persuade the British battleline to not pursue the *Scharnhorst*. Finding the two British heavy cruisers attacking, Bey had decided some 15-inch fire was necessary to discourage their torpedo run as well. In the worsening seas the German battleships' gunnery left much to be desired, but still managed to force the *Exeter* and *Norfolk* to both intensify their zig zags.

Unfortunately for the Germans, the decision to concentrate on the heavy cruisers meant that Commodore Vian's destroyers had an almost undisturbed attack run. Vian, realizing that he would not be able to bypass the aggressively counterattacking *Hipper*, split his force into two parts. The lead division, led by himself in *Somali*, continued after the crippled *Scharnhorst*. The second, led by the destroyer *Echo*, he directed to attack the *Hipper* in hopes that the heavy cruiser would turn away.

The German heavy cruiser reacted as Vian had expected, switching all of her fire to the approaching *Echo* group. For their part, the British ships dodged as they closed, the *Echo*'s commander making the decision to close the range so that the destroyers could launch their torpedoes with a higher speed setting. Seeing the German cruiser starting to turn, *Echo*'s commander signaled for his own vessel, *Eclipse*, and *Encounter* to attempt to attack from her port side, while the *Faulknor* and *Electra* were to move up to attack from starboard.

Discerning the British destroyerman's plan, *Hipper*'s captain immediately laid on his maximum speed while continuing his turn towards port. Ignoring those vessels attempting to move in on her starboard side, the German vessel turned her guns wholly on the trio of British destroyers that was now at barely seven thousand yards. With a combined closing speed of almost seventy knots, there was less than a minute before the British destroyers were at their preferred range. In this time, *Hipper* managed to get off two salvoes with her main guns and several rounds from her secondary guns. Her efforts were rewarded, the *Echo* being hit and stopped by two 8-inch and four secondary shell hits before she could fire her torpedoes. That still left the *Eclipse* and *Encounter*, both which fired their torpedoes at 4,000 yards before starting to turn away. The latter vessel had just concluded putting her eighth torpedo into the water when the *Hipper*'s secondaries switched to her as a target, knocking out the destroyer's forward guns.

Pursuing the *Hipper* as the German cruiser continued to turn to port, the *Faulknor* and *Electra* initially had a far longer run than their compatriots. However, as the German cruiser came about to comb the *Echo* group's torpedoes, the opportunity arose for the two more nimble vessels to cut across her turn. Hitting the heavy cruiser with several 4.7-inch shells even as they zigzagged through the *Lutzow*'s supporting fire, the two destroyers unleashed their sixteen torpedoes from the *Hipper*'s port bow. Belatedly, the German captain realized that he had placed himself in a horrible position, as he could not turn to avoid the second group of torpedoes without presenting a perfect target to the first.

It was the *Eclipse* which administered the first blow. Coming in at a fine angle, one of the destroyer's torpedoes exploded just below the *Hipper*'s port bow. The heavy cruiser's hull whipsawed from the impact, the explosion peeling twenty feet of her skin back to act as a massive brake. The shock traveled down the vessel's length, throwing circuit breakers out of their mounts in her generator room and rendering the *Hipper* powerless. Looking to starboard, the vessel's bridge crew could only helplessly watch as the British torpedoes approached from that side. In a fluke of fate, the braking effect from *Eclipse*'s hit caused the heavy cruiser to lose so much headway the majority of the tin fish missed. The pair that impacted, however, could not have been better placed. With two roaring waterspouts in close succession, the *Hipper*'s engineering spaces were opened to the sea. Disemboweled, the cruiser continued to slow even as she rolled to starboard. Realizing instantly her wounds were fatal, the *Hipper*'s captain gave the order to abandon ship. The order came far too late for most of the crew, as the 12,000-ton man-o-war capsized and slid under the Atlantic in a matter of minutes.

"Well, the destroyers just put paid to that heavy cruiser! Let's see if we can get a kill of our own!" Gordon said, watching the drama unfolding roughly twelve thousand yards to his west. Another salvo of 15-inch shells landed to *Exeter*'s starboard, this broadside somewhat more ragged due to the heavy cruiser's zig zagging advance.

"Battleships are returning to aid us."

"About bloody time!" Gordon snapped.

When the *Warspite*'s first salvo landed just aft of *Jean Bart*, Admiral Bey had more than enough. Signaling rapidly, he ordered the *Scharnhorst* and *Lutzow* to cover the remainder of the force's retreat. Firing a few desultory broadsides, the Franco-German force reentered the mists.

Eric watched through his binoculars as *Lutzow* gamely attempted to follow Bey's orders, slowly coming about so she could continue to engage the destroyers closing with *Scharnhorst*. Barely making fifteen knots, the pocket battleship was listing slightly to port and down by the bows. Just as *Lutzow* finished her turn, several shells landed close astern of the German vessel.

"*King George V* is engaging the pocket battleship."

"Good. Maybe she can slow that witch down so we can catch her."

"*Warspite* and *Prince of Wales* are switching to the closest battleship."

Gordon nodded his ascent, continuing to watch as *Lutzow* attempted to begin a zig zag pattern.

"Destroyers are running the gauntlet," Gordon observed drily, pointing to where the *Lutzow* was engaging the five destroyers passing barely eight thousand yards in front of her. Eric nodded grimly, then brought his attention back to *Lutzow* just in time to see the *King George V*'s next salvo arrive. Two of the British 14-inch shells slashed into the pocket battleship's stern, while a third impacted on the vessel's aft turret with devastating effect. Eric was glad that *Exeter* was still far enough away that he could not identify the contents of the debris that flew upwards from the gunhouse in the gout of smoke and flame, as the young American was sure some of the dark spots were bodies.

"Looks like you got your wish, sir," Eric observed as the *Lutzow* began to continue a lazy circle to port. There was a sharp crack as the *Exeter*'s secondary batteries began to engage the pocket battleship, leading to a disgusted look from Gordon.

"Tell Guns we may need that ammunition later," he snapped. "I'm not sure those guns will do any damage, plus she's almost finished."

I was wondering what good 4-inch guns would do to a pocket battleship, Eric thought. *Especially when* ***Norfolk*** *is pounding away with her main battery and a battleship has her under fire.*

"*King George V* is inquiring if we can finish her with torpedoes?"

Gordon looked at the pocket battleship, now coming to a stop with fires clearly spreading.

"Report that yes, we will close and finish her with torpedoes, she may assist in bringing that battleship to bay," *Exeter*'s master stated.

"*Norfolk* is firing torpedoes," the talker reported.

Eric brought up his binoculars, focusing on the clearly crippled *Lutzow*. As he watched, one of the German's secondary turrets fired a defiant shot at *Norfolk*. Scanning the vessel from bow to stern, Eric wondered if the gun was the sole thing left operational, as the pocket battleship's upper decks were a complete shambles. Looking closely at the *Lutzow*'s forward turret, he could see two jagged holes in its rear where *Norfolk*'s broadsides had impacted. The bridge was similarly damaged, with wisps of smoke pouring from the shattered windows, and the German vessel's entire amidships was ablaze. The vessel's list appeared to have lessened, but she was clearly much lower in the water.

"Should be any time now," Gordon said, briefly looking at his watch. "Tell guns to belay my last, we're not wasting any more fish on her than necessary."

Eric turned back to watching the *Lutzow*, observing as *Norfolk* hit the vessel with another point blank salvo an instant before her torpedoes arrived. Given that the *Lutzow* was a stationary target, Eric was surprised to see *Norfolk*'s torpedo spread produce only a pair of hits. It was still enough, as with an audible groan the *Lutzow*'s already battered hull split just aft of her destroyed turret. Five minutes later, as *Exeter* drew within five hundred yards and Eric could see German sailors jumping into the sea, the *Lutzow* gave a final shuddering metallic rattle then slipped stern first into the depths.

"Stand by to rescue survivors," Gordon said, dropping his binoculars. "How are the destroyers doing with that battleship?"

The answer to Gordon's question could be summed up with two words: very well. The *Scharnhorst* had briefly managed to work up to sixteen knots, and had *Lutzow*'s fire been somewhat more accurate, may have managed to escape the pursuing destroyers. However, as with the *Hipper*,

Vian's destroyers split into two groups even as *Scharnhorst*'s secondaries increased their fire. Another pair of hits from *Prince of Wales* slowed the German light battleship even further, and at that point the handful of tin cans set upon her like a school of sharks on a lamed blue whale.

Like that large creature, however, even a crippled the *Scharnhorst* still had means to defend herself. As the *Punjabi* closed in from starboard, the battleship's Caesar turret scored with a single 15-inch shell. The effects were devastating, the destroyer being converted from man-of-war to charnel house forward of her bridge. Amazingly, *Punjabi*'s powerplant was undamaged by the blast, and the destroyer was able to continue closing the distance between herself and the larger German vessel. The timely arrival of a salvo from *Warspite* sufficiently distracted the *Scharnhorst*'s gunnery officer, preventing him from getting the range again until after both groups of destroyers were close enough to launch torpedoes.

Severely damaged, *Scharnhorst* still attempted to ruin the destroyers' fire control problem at the last moment. To Commodore Vian's intense frustration, the battleship's captain timed his maneuver perfectly, evading twelve British torpedoes simply by good seamanship. Had *Scharnhorst* had her full maneuvering ability, she may have then been able to pull off the maneuver *Hipper* had attempted by reversing course. Whereas geometry and numbers had failed the German heavy cruiser, simple physics served to put the waterlogged battleship in front of three torpedoes. Even then, her luck remained as the first hit, far forward, was a dud. Then, proving Fate was indeed fickle, two fish from the damaged *Punjabi* ran deep and hit the vessel just below her armored belt. Finishing the damage done by *Prince of Wales'* hits earlier, the torpedoes knocked out the German capital ship's remaining power and opened even more of her hull to the sea. Realizing she was doomed, her captain ordered the crew to set scuttling charges and abandon ship.

"*King George V* is inquiring if any vessels have torpedoes remaining."

Gordon gave the talker a questioning look.

"I thought Commodore Vian just reported that the enemy battleship appears to be sinking?" Gordon said, his voice weary. "No matter, inform *King George V* that we have all of our fish remaining."

Wonder what in the hell that is about? Eric thought. Looking down, he realized his hands were starting to shake. Taking a deep breath, he attempted to calm himself.

Well, this has been a rather...interesting day. I just wish someone would have told me I'd get shot down, see my squadron leader killed, and participate in a major sea battle when I got up at 0300 this morning.

"*Leftenant* Cobb, are you all right?" Gordon asked, concerned.

Eric choked back the urge to laugh at the question.

"I'm fine sir, just a little cold," he said, lying through his teeth. The talker saved him from further inquisition.

"*King George V* is ordering us to come about and close with her. She is also ordering Commodore Vian to rescue survivors from *Punjabi* then scuttle her if she is unable to get under way. *Norfolk* is being ordered to stand by to assist *Nelson*."

"What about the Germans?" Gordon asked.

"Flag has ordered that all other recovery operations are to cease."

There was dead silence on *Exeter*'s bridge.

"Very well then, guess the Germans will have to come back for their own. Let's go see what *King George V* has for us," Gordon said.

Eric was struck by just how far the running fight had ranged as the *Exeter* reversed course. From the first salvo to the current position, the vessels had covered at least thirty miles. The *King George V* was a distant dot to the south, with her sister ship and *Warspite* further behind.

No one is going to find any of those survivors, Eric thought. *Especially with this weather starting to get worse*. He could smell imminent rain on the wind, and even with *Exeter*'s considerable size he could feel the ocean's movement starting to change.

"I hope this isn't about to become too bad of a blow," Gordon observed, looking worriedly out at the lowering sky. "Not with the flooding we have forward."

"If you don't mind, sir, I'd like to avoid going swimming again today," Eric quipped.

"Wouldn't be a swim lad. If we catch a big wave wrong, she would plow right under," Gordon replied grimly. "What has got *King George V* in such a tussy? She's coming at us full speed."

Eric looked up and saw that the battleship was indeed closing as rapidly as possible. As she hove into visual range several minutes later, the *King George V*'s signaling searchlight began flashing rapidly.

DO YOU READ THIS MESSAGE? DO YOU READ THIS MESSAGE?

. . .

"Acknowledge," Gordon said. A few moments later Eric could hear the heavy cruiser's signal crew employing the bridge lamp to respond to the *King George V*.

YOU WILL PROCEED TO *HOOD*. ONCE ALL SURVIVORS ARE OFFBOARD, YOU ARE TO SCUTTLE.

"*What in the bloody hell is that idiot talking about?*" Gordon exploded. He did not have time to send a counter message, as the *King George V* continued after a short pause.

YOU HAVE TWENTY-FIVE MINUTES TO REJOIN. FORCE WILL PROCEED WITHOUT YOU IF NOT COMPLETE. TOVEY SENDS GOD SAVE THE QUEEN

"God save the...*oh my God*!" Gordon said.

Eric looked at the *Exeter*'s captain with some concern as the man staggered backward, his face looking as if he had been personally stricken.

"Ask," Gordon began, the word nearly coming out as a sob before he regained his composure. "Ask if I may inform the ship's company of our task?"

Three minutes later, the *King George V* replied.

AFFIRMATIVE. EXPEDITE. HER MAJESTY'S SAFETY IS THIS COMMAND'S PRIMARY GOAL.

"Acknowledge. Hand me the loudspeaker," Gordon said, his voice incredibly weary. Eric could see tears welling in the man's eyes.

This is not good, Eric thought. *This is not good at all.* Although he was far from an expert on British government, he dimly remembered seeing a newsreel when *Ranger* had been in port where the Royal Family had been discussed. He felt his stomach starting to drop as he began to process what the *King George V* had just stated.

"All hands, this is the captain speaking," Gordon began. "This vessel is proceeding to stand by the *Hood* to rescue survivors. It appears that His Majesty has been killed."

Holy shit, Eric thought. *Isn't Princess...no,* ***Queen*** *Elizabeth barely sixteen?*

Eric looked around the bridge as the captain broke the news to the *Exeter*'s crew. The reactions ranged from shock to, surprisingly, rage. As *Exeter*'s master finished, the young American had the feeling he was seeing the start of something very, very ugly for the Germans.

I would hate to be someone who got dragged out of the water today, he thought. *That is, if* ***any*** *Germans get saved*. Eric's father had fought as a Marine at Belleau Wood. In the weeks before Eric had left for the academy, his father had made sure that his son understood just what might be required of him in the Republic's service. One of the stories had involved what had befallen an unfortunate German machine gun crew when the men tried to surrender after killing several members of the elder Cobb's platoon. Realizing the parallels to his current situation given the news he had just heard, Eric fought the urge to scowl.

Looks like you don't need a rope for a lynch mob, Eric thought as he reflected on the "necessity" of leaving the German and French sailors to drown. He was suddenly shaken out of his reverie by the sound of singing coming from below the bridge.

"*Happy and glorious...long to reign over us...*"

The men on the bridge began taking up the song, their tone somber and remorseful.

"*GOD SAAAAVEEE THE QUEEEEENN*!!"

Almost a half hour later, the *Exeter* sat one thousand yards off of the *Hood*'s starboard side, the heavy cruiser's torpedo tubes trained on her larger consort. The *Hood*'s wounds were obvious, her bridge and conning tower a horribly twisted flower of shattered steel. Flames licked from the vessel's X turret, and it appeared that the structure had taken a heavy shell to its roof. Further casting a pall on the scene was the dense black smoke pouring from the *Hood*'s burning bunkerage, a dull glow at the base of the cloud indicating an out of control fire. The battlecruiser's stern looked almost awash, her bow almost coming out of the water with each swell, and as Eric watched there was an explosion of ready ammunition near her anti-aircraft guns.

Might be a waste of good torpedoes at this point, Eric thought. He realized he was starting to pass into mental shock from all the carnage he had seen that day.

"I'm the last man, sir," a dazed-looking commander with round features, black hair, and green eyes was saying to Captain Gordon. "At least, the last man we can get to."

"I understand, Commander Keir," Gordon said quietly. "I regret we do not have the time to try and free the men trapped in her engineering spaces."

"If we could have only had another hour, we might have saved her," Keir said, his voice breaking. It was obvious the man had been through hell, his uniform blackened by soot and other stains that Eric didn't care to look into too closely.

It's never a good day when you become commander of a vessel simply because no one else was left. From what he understood, Keir had started the day as chief of *Hood*'s Navigation Division. That had been before the vessel took at least three 15-inch shells to the bridge area, as well as two more that had wiped out her gunnery directory and the secondary bridge.

Captain Gordon was right—she was a very powerful warship. Unfortunately that tends to make you a target.

"Commander, you are *certain* that..." Gordon started, then collected himself. "You are *certain* His Majesty is dead."

"Yes sir," Keir said. "His Majesty was in the conning tower with Admiral Pound when it was hit. The Royal Surgeon positively identified His Majesty's body in the aid station before that was hit in turn. We cannot get to the aid station due to the spreading fire."

"Understood. His Majesty would not have wanted any of you to risk his life for his body," Gordon said.

"I just..." Keir started, then stopped, overcome with emotion.

"It is not your fault lad," Gordon said. "Her Majesty will understand."

Gordon turned and looked at the *Exeter*'s clock.

"Very well, we are out of time. Stand by to fire torpedoes."

"Torpedoes report they are ready."

"Sir, you may want to tell your torpedo officer to have his weapons set to run deep," Keir said. "She's drawing..."

There was a large explosion aboard *Hood* as the flames reached a secondary turret's ready ammunition. Eric saw a fiery object arc slowly across, descending towards the *Exeter* as hundreds of helpless eyes watched it. The flaming debris' lazy parabola terminated barely fifty yards off of *Exeter*'s side with a large, audible splash.

"I think we do not have time for that discussion," Gordon said grimly. "Fire torpedoes!"

The three weapons from *Exeter*'s starboard tubes sprang from their launchers into the water. Set as a narrow spread, the three tracks seemed to take forever to impact from Eric's perspective. *Exeter*'s torpedo officer, observing *Hood*'s state, had taken into account the battlecruiser's lower draught without having to be told. Indeed, he had almost set the weapons for too deep a run, but was saved by the flooding that had occurred in the previous few minutes. In addition to breaking the battlecruiser's keel, the triple blow opened the entire aft third of her port side to the ocean. With the audible sound of twisting metal, *Hood* started to roll onto her beam ends. She never completed the evolution before slipping beneath the waves.

2

AFTERMATH

We should never despair, our Situation before has been unpromising and has changed for the better; so I trust, it will again. If new difficulties arise, we must only put forth New Exertions and proportion our efforts to the exigency of the times.

— **GEORGE WASHINGTON**

Cape Town, South Africa
0700 Local (0100 Eastern)
26 September

"Well now I know things have gone to Hell," a familiar voice said from just behind Adam. "There are bloody Americans here, and Lord knows they always portend something very, very bad."

Adam whipped around from his breakfast so quickly he nearly fell out of his chair. Stumbling to his feet, he made sure the speaker was whom he thought it was, taking in the man's tall, lanky frame and sandy brown hair before wrapping him in a giant bearhug.

"Braddon Overgaard, how in the hell are you doing?!" he asked. "Pull up a chair. I was just finishing breakfast, courtesy of His...*Her* Majesty's government."

"Yes, it is a bit difficult to change that, isn't it? Although, if certain individuals get their way you may be reverting back to what you started to say," Overgaard replied.

Adam stopped, fork halfway to his mouth.

"What? I sort of thought that line of succession thing was pretty set," the American said.

Overgaard had a seat at the table across from Adam.

"You can tell that you have been stuck aboard some tub for the past two weeks," Overgaard said.

"Hell, we hadn't even heard about the Battle of the Regicide until we were a couple hours out from harbor yesterday," Adam said. "What the hell else has happened?"

"The Duke of Windsor has returned to London."

Adam recognized the title but was not immediately able to recall why that was important. Seeing his perplexed look, Overgaard saved him the trouble.

"The Duke of Windsor is also known as King Edward," the South African officer said quietly.

Adam raised an eyebrow.

"I must confess I do not completely understand the Royal Family despite spending the last nine months in its employ," Adam said carefully. "Didn't he abdicate the throne because he had a similar problem to King David?"

Overgaard gave a thin smile.

"While I am sure Ms. Simpson would be flattered by the comparison to Bathsheba, that wasn't exactly what happened," Overgaard replied.

"Close enough," Adam replied around a mouthful of eggs. "Basically the man got the chop, as you guys put it, for taking up with another man's wife."

A couple of South African men at the table to their left turned and gave Adam a glance that was hardly favorable. Feigning obliviousness, Adam continued.

"I mean, I seem to recall there being an Act that basically said he wasn't the King of England anymore, correct?"

Overgaard nodded.

"Yes, but in light of recent events the Halifax government is attempting to reverse the Abdication Act and restore King Edward to the throne," Overgaard said.

Adam shook his head in amazement.

"Is that legal?" he asked.

"Well therein lies the rub," Overgaard said bitterly. "When the current sovereign is in another country that sort of prevents many people from raising a fuss."

"You know, I thought things couldn't get much worse a couple weeks ago," Adam said grimly. "Now I realize that I suffered from a large dose of ignorance."

"Well, Her Majesty is only sixteen," Overgaard continued. "There is a push from Prime Minister King for all the Commonwealth nations to recognize Her Majesty as the current sovereign with Churchill as head of a reformed Commonwealth government. But..." Overgaard said, then stopped suddenly and shrugged as if to say he had no idea what would happen. Their conversation was interrupted by the waitress, a rather plain-looking brunette, interrupting to ask Overgaard if there was anything he'd like to eat.

"So how did you get back here?" Adam asked after the woman had left Overgaard water and gone to make him his eggs benedict.

"Caught a liner back," Overgaard said simply. "The Germans accorded us non-belligerent status."

"What?!"

"Prime Minister Halifax, for all his faults, negotiated a decent treaty. Between you and me, if you've read that bastard Hitler's book you'd realize that France and England were a sideshow to the Nazis," Overgaard said, taking a sip of his water. "Hitler only attacked us to clear his backside before he went east. Hell, he didn't even technically attack us—just went after Poland."

Adam made a face at that one.

"Sorry mate, but as much as I know you love those Polish blokes you flew with, it's not like either us or the French really kept their promises to them," Overgaard said. "I mean, between the Germans and that bloody bastard Stalin, I'm not so sure the men who got away should not just consider themselves lucky and call it a day. Realistically, there is probably nothing worth going back for, and even if the rest of your countrymen decide to grace this war with their presence, it is highly unlikely anyone will be prying Poland from the Germans and Soviets anytime soon."

"Would you leave someone like Himmler or Stalin in charge of your home?" Adam asked incredulously.

"There comes a point when you have to accept reality," Overgaard said. "My grandfather fought against the English during the Boer War. His commando swore they would fight until the death. Well, you notice the Boers aren't in charge and my grandfather is still out on my family farm."

"The English never compared to anything the Nazis or Soviets have done," Adam snapped.

"Really? Remind me again where the term concentration camp comes from?" Overgaard replied easily.

Adam felt his face warm.

"The English *never* did what the Nazis have just done," he seethed. "They didn't even do something as horrible as Guernica."

"But would they have if they'd had the capability?" Overgaard asked simply.

Adam opened his mouth to protest, then stopped.

He has a point. Unfortunately... Adam mentally conceded as the waitress returned with Overgaard's order.

"Now the difference is the English would not have gassed or burned about forty thousand people *today*," Overgaard continued after taking a bite of his eggs. "Well, at least they would not have until a couple of weeks ago. Which is part of the reason Himmler and Halifax were able to come to an agreement, albeit one that is probably going to make you Yanks a bit upset."

"I haven't even seen a newspaper talking about this treaty yet," Adam said. "So please, do tell."

"That's because Prime Minister Smuts is studiously avoiding starting any discussion of it in Parliament," Overgaard replied quietly. "You are probably not aware, but my government was split on whether or not we should enter the war. There are those among us who do not necessarily disagree with the Nazis' philosophy regarding a master race."

Adam put his fork down, suddenly feeling sick to his stomach.

"Thankfully the number of those who absolutely feel that way is relatively small, but I think that was part of the reason Himmler allowed for the immediate release of all Commonwealth forces," Overgaard said. "The man does not want to give Her Majesty's government any assistance by upsetting Australia, New Zealand, Canada, or South Africa."

"What about any forces from the Occupied countries he could lay his hands on?" Adam asked bitterly. "I suppose they were shot out of hand?"

"Strangely enough, no. Himmler offered them a choice—they could basically serve in the Nazi armed forces for three years or be imprisoned for six," Overgaard replied.

"What?!" Adam exclaimed.

"You'd be surprised how many takers the Germans had," Overgaard continued. "Not many Poles, of course...but there were a fair number of so called 'Free French' who seemed to be a whole lot less willing to spend the next six years in a German prison camp rather than three years someplace else."

"Can't blame them, really," Adam sighed. "His Highness and Halifax persuading Churchill to call for a truce sort of screwed the French. Add on shooting up their fleet back in 1940 and I would start to wonder just how good of allies the British were."

"There's only so much that one nation by herself can do. It's not like you Americans were giving any indications of coming into the war anytime soon."

"Too many people still think we did enough last time," Adam replied. "In their mind, we don't need dead Americans cleaning up Europe's mess again."

"If your country waits much longer, they will be facing all of bloody Europe," Overgaard said resignedly. "Or at least a large European coalition led by Germany. But I'm obviously preaching to the choir."

"Yes, and this particular singer is thinking it might be a good idea to keep moving along," Adam said.

"Well you're about nine months too late for China," Overgaard observed. "At least, not unless you want to be shooting up Warlord A so that Warlord B can take over his territory then proclaim his fealty for the Nationalists."

"Yes, well, no one saw the Japanese leaving. I wasn't following that close enough to know what in the hell happened there," Adam observed. "One minute it looks like we're getting ready to go to war with them last December, Churchill sends four more battleships to Singapore, and next thing you know they go and attack the Russians."

"In retrospect I think they would like to have that decision back," Overgaard observed wryly.

"Getting an entire army annihilated will do that," Adam observed. "What did the Russians say they were going to call Manchuria, Manchukuo, or whatever it was?"

"I don't remember," Overgaard said. "I just remember that one minute they were on the offensive against the Russians, then four months later that Soviet general's accepting their surrender in South Manchuria."

"Zhukov was his name," Adam said. "Looks like he studied *blitzkrieg* at the same school the Germans did."

"I don't care if he learned it from Mars himself, he sure used it to kick the Japanese right out of China. My father told me just the other day that there was some rumor their entire cabinet committed suicide over the loss of face," Overgaard replied, putting a fork of eggs in his mouth.

"Well, I lost track of the situation about the same time you did, and for the same reasons," Adam replied, his voice haunted. "Something about the *Luftwaffe* trying to kill us."

Overgaard nodded grimly as he chewed on his eggs.

"So where do you think you'll go then?" the South African asked after swallowing.

"According to the consulate here the isolationists are talking about stripping all of us of our citizenships," Adam replied. "There's even some poor bastard who the Germans shot down over the Atlantic that they're trying to have banned from ever reentering the country."

*H.M.S. **Prince of Wales***
Halifax Harbor, Canada
1000 Local (0900 Eastern)
26 September

So this is how an ant feels in a room full of elephants, Eric had time to think to himself as he walked into the admiral's day room of the H.M.S. *Prince of Wales*. Scanning the room, he saw more gold braid and stars than he had ever witnessed in his life in one place. That the civilian dignitaries present made the aforementioned constellation seem rather dim by comparison was more than enough to make a junior officer pray for invisibility.

"Speaking of *Leftenant* Cobb, here he is right now," Vice Admiral John Tovey, commander of Home Fleet, stated.

Oh look, the ant is now expected to play the trombone for everyone, Eric thought as all eyes turned towards him. There were five individuals in the large compartment besides Vice Admiral Tovey. Eric immediately recognized Secretary of the Navy Frank Knox and Admiral Ernest J. King from the pictures that *Ranger*'s captain had required every one of his officers to memorize prior to coming aboard. The other four star standing with them, on the other hand, Eric had no clue about. The tall, dark-haired man regarded Eric with a neutral expression, as if he was weighing and measuring the aviator. The other civilian in a dark blue suit similar to the one worn by Secretary Knox was standing beside the mystery full admiral. Lastly, sitting in a chair next to the four standing Americans was none other than Winston Churchill, the man puffing contentedly on one of his trademark cigars with one hand, the other clenching a tumbler of some amber liquid.

Okay, now I'm really starting to worry, Eric thought as he came to attention.

"Lieutenant Cobb reporting as ordered, sir," he said to Secretary Knox as the highest ranking man in the room. In actuality, it had been Tovey that had requested his presence from the officer's barracks ashore one hour previously. Eric had been rather surprised at the summons, as the American ambassador to Canada had conveyed, in no uncertain, terms that neither Rawles nor he was to set foot aboard another British vessel until further notice. As that particular missive had been delivered in the presence of Captain Gordon before *Exeter* had even pulled up to the dock to unload her wounded, Eric had a feeling Admiral Tovey was well aware of it.

Knox gave Admiral King and the mystery four star a bemused look, then turned back to Eric.

"At ease lieutenant, you're not here for a court-martial," Knox said easily. "We just want to hear what happened to you in your own words."

What the hell? Didn't anyone get my after action review? Eric thought to himself. His surprise must have showed because the unknown admiral spoke up.

"Son, we know you already prepared a report for Lieutenant Colonel Gypsum," the man said, referring to the American military attaché to Canada. "However it's important that Secretaries Knox and Hull hear your story for themselves."

"What Admiral Kimmel is actually saying, in polite terms, is that he bloody thinks we altered your report!" Winston Churchill thundered.

Okay, there's a little tension here, Eric thought. Tovey stood stonefaced as Churchill took a puff of his cigar, daring any of the Americans present to deny his accusation.

"*Mr.* Churchill is correct," King responded, bitterness in his voice. "There are those in Congress and elsewhere in the United States government who have come to wonder just how coincidental it would be that you and your squadron leader just happened to blunder into the German fleet at a time when the British had been forced to dispatch cruisers to make contact with it."

"Permission to speak freely, sir?" Eric asked quietly.

"Go ahead, Lieutenant Cobb," King snapped, glaring steadily at Churchill.

"The reason why we just *happened* to be there is Commander Cobleigh convinced Rear Admiral Noyes that the best *Dauntless* pilots could establish a search even in that weather."

King snorted, his nostrils flaring.

"Yes—and of the twelve of you who launched, only six recovered successfully," King snapped.

Eric fought to keep his face expressionless.

Some of those men are, or maybe ***were****, my friends*, he thought grimly.

"Lieutenant Cobb, why don't you tell us what happened?" Kimmel broke in. Admiral King pivoted as if he was about to snap a response when a stern look from Secretary Knox stopped him in his tracks. "Come on over here to the plot if that will help."

"We started the day at 0300..." Eric began. He spent the next thirty minutes recounting his role in the Battle of Regicide, or as the British fleet was calling it, the Battle of the Remnants. As he talked, Eric realized just how lucky both Rawles and he had been to have survived. By the time he had stopped, he realized that his hands were slightly shaking while he stood at parade rest.

"How long until the *Exeter* is back in action?" Admiral Kimmel asked thoughtfully. "From what Lieutenant Cobb described, she sounds almost a total wreck."

"Six months," Admiral Tovey replied. "She'll be sailing for Sydney within the fortnight."

"What? You don't have any facilities closer?" Secretary Knox asked, shock clear in his voice.

Churchill and Tovey shared a pained look. After a moment, the former Prime Minister spoke.

"There is some discussion among the Commonwealth nations as to whether they will agree to be bound by the Treaty of Kent," he said solemnly.

"It appears that the former king returning to claim the throne threw a monkey wrench in your plan to continue to fight if England fell," Admiral King observed.

Eric could tell from the shocked looks on every other American's face that he was not the only one horrified by King's bluntness.

"Another 'monkey wrench' was our belief that a certain nation's assistance would go beyond fine words and promises," Churchill said after a moment's pause.

"What Admiral King meant," Secretary Hull said, his tone making it quite clear that nothing good would come from King contradicting his next words, "is that it does not seem as if the possibility of England's fall was discussed among the Commonwealth during the truce period."

"Of course not," Churchill sneered. "No one wanted to consider the fact that the Germans might resume hostilities. Hell, I had a hard enough time persuading Parliament to continue producing the items already authorized. No one wanted to believe that bastard Himmler was just playing for time to strengthen the *Luftwaffe*."

"Having your agents attempt to kill Heydrich in Prague and a Free Frenchman blow up Alfred Rosenberg might have had something to do with the Nazis resuming the war," Admiral King observed, gaining him a rancorous look from Hull and Knox alike. Eric watched Churchill's face start to redden as the Prime Minster opened his mouth to speak only to be cut off by Tovey.

"Perhaps you would be more interested in the present situation than a discussion of the past, Admiral King?" Home Fleet's commander asked, his voice colder than the gusts blowing through Halifax Harbor.

"Actually, gentlemen, We would be very interested in hearing about the present situation as well," a calm woman's voice observed from the hatchway behind Eric. He turned to a slender, short brunette in a black mourning dress. Out of the corner of his eye Eric saw Churchill and Tovey both whirl away from the map, then come immediately to attention.

"Your Majesty, we were not expecting you for another three hours," Churchill said evenly as the woman strode into the compartment followed by two very large men in the bright red tunics and bearskin caps of the British Army's Guard Regiments. Eric was somewhat shocked to see that both men carried Thompson submachine guns. Judging from Admiral Tovey's face going pale, he was not the only one. While both men ensured their weapons were not pointed at anybody in particular, Eric could feel the tension rise in the room.

I'm guessing, given that she's currently the Queen, just had her father assassinated by the Germans, and has no issue, these men would kill everyone in the room if they thought it necessary, Eric thought. *I don't blame them one bit.*

"My...*Our* apologies, Lord Churchill," Queen Elizabeth replied, her voice genuine. "The meeting with the new Air Minister took far less time than expected. Admiral Tovey, for your information Captain Leach was given direction from me not to interrupt your meeting. We are the ones off schedule, not you gentlemen."

"Your Majesty, all of us appreciate that you made time in your busy schedule for us," Secretary Hull began. "It is a difficult time for both our nations." Behind him, Eric saw Secretary Knox give Admiral King a look that could have blistered paint.

I'm not sure I want to be in the same room with men who can silence a full admiral just with a look, Eric thought quietly. *I'm reasonably certain that Secretary Knox will relieve him on the spot if there is another outburst.*

"Thank you, Secretary Hull," Her Majesty replied. "My father considered the United States to be our strongest friend even if not strictly an ally."

Pointed comment there, Eric thought, seeing Admiral King starting to color somewhat.

"There are those in our nation, even now, who do not realize that the Nazis intend to conquer the entire world," Hull replied.

"Well, let us discuss how we will stop them from doing that, shall we?" Queen Elizabeth stated firmly.

"Your Majesty, I want to be perfectly clear—I do not have the power to negotiate a treaty and, to be frank, President Roosevelt does not anywhere close to the votes in Congress for a declaration of war."

Queen Elizabeth II regarded Secretary Hull with a gaze that radiated determination.

"I am certain that, sooner or later, Nazi Germany will provide you with no other choice than to go to war. At that time, the Commonwealth will stand with you even if England proper does not."

"That is part of the reason we are here, Your Majesty," Secretary Knox interjected smoothly. "There has been no public information regarding just what is involved in the Treaty of Kent. All we have in Washington is rumor, and some of them are so wild as to hardly be believable."

"You may find that some of the agreements Lord Halifax and my uncle have made are as terrible as you imagined," Queen Elizabeth remarked.

Is it just me, or does it seem like the teenager in the room is dealing better with the world turned upside down than all the men? Eric thought, stunned at the Queen's composure. *I'd be a wreck if Dad died, nevermind was* ***killed****.*

"Naturally I am sure the United States' primary concern is the disposition of our fleet units," Queen Elizabeth continued. "I believe your isolationists have been roaring with full throat about President Roosevelt's folly in lending us aid when the 'bulwark of the Atlantic remained even if England did not,' correct?"

Eric had to struggle not to wince at the cold politeness in Queen Elizabeth's tone. Looking over at Secretaries Hull and Knox he could see that the young sovereign's words had stricken home.

"President Roosevelt intends to lend whatever aid he can..." Secretary Hull began.

"Yes, of course," Queen Elizabeth snapped, her reserve slipping for the first time. "That is precisely what he told Lord Churchill aboard this very vessel in August of last year."

Eric, looking at Admiral King's face, realized the man was turning an unpleasant shade of red.

"Strange then, is it not, how my nation lies prostrate and *my father slain* yet your 'political exigencies' still seem to prevent action," the Queen finished.

I didn't think that shade was possible on a person, Eric thought. *Admiral King is almost purple*.

"Admiral King, why don't we go get some fresh air?" Secretary Knox said. King whipped around and was about to respond, then belatedly realized suddenly realized that his superior was not actually making a request.

When the Secretary of the Navy asks you to step outside, you ***step*** *outside*.

With a slight neck bow to the Queen, Secretary Knox gestured for Admiral King to lead the way out of the compartment. Eric noted that Admiral King pointedly did not render any honors to the Queen on his way out of the hatch.

"Perhaps it would be best if *Leftenant* Cobb and the other two gentlemen left as well," Admiral Tovey stated.

"Those two gentlemen have been given direct orders to go with Her Majesty everywhere she goes," Churchill snapped. "While I trust we have nothing to worry about from anyone in this room, it would be best if we not set the precedent now."

"*Leftenant* Cobb may stay," Her Majesty said, favoring Eric with a small smile. "Given his luck so far, this will probably be yet another thing he can tell his grandchildren about."

Assuming I survive the next six months, nevermind long enough to marry Joyce, Eric thought. *That is, if she got my letter. Hell, I don't even know if* ***Mom*** *knows*

I'm still alive. I think I'm going to end up missing Patricia's wedding next month at this rate.

"Please proceed Admiral Tovey," Queen Elizabeth continued.

"Your Majesty, Secretary Hull, at this moment the Commonwealth controls the majority of our ships. The only exceptions are four battleships, two carriers, a dozen cruisers, and twenty destroyers," Admiral Tovey said.

"What do you mean by 'control'? There are hardly that many ships here in Halifax," Admiral Kimmel asked.

Tovey and Churchill shared a look, then the latter answered.

"By 'control,' we mean ships that are not currently answering the orders of the Halifax Government or pledging allegiance to the Duke of Windsor."

Queen Elizabeth's nostrils flared at the last.

"My uncle renounced all of his titles the minute he set foot in London to usurp my throne and authority," she snapped.

"Your Majesty..." Churchill began.

"Lord Churchill, that topic is not open for discussion," Queen Elizabeth continued, even more forcefully

Eric saw several emotions flitter across Churchill's face, but there was no mistaking the steel in Queen Elizabeth's voice.

I would not want to cross this woman, he thought.

"Your Majesty, I for one would like to know what he should be called then," Secretary Hull said quietly. "If you allow our newspapers to come up with a name, they may choose something which gives the Halifax government the very legitimacy you seek to deny them."

Queen Elizabeth turned her gaze from Churchill to Secretary Hull.

"The Commonwealth government will refer to my uncle as The Usurper," Elizabeth said coolly. A look of surprise briefly flitted across Churchill's face so quickly that Eric was fairly certain no one else noticed it due to their focus on the Queen.

"Back to your original statement, Admiral Tovey—how did these vessels end up outside of your control?" Admiral Kimmel asked.

"*Anson*, *Howe*, and *Lion* are just completed," Tovey responded, his tone somber. "The remaining vessels either are not Home Fleet, were recently damaged, or were en route to Great Britain and could not divert due to their fuel state."

"Why didn't the crews scuttle their vessels?" Kimmel asked, his voice disgusted.

"Because the Germans threatened to resume hostilities if there were any more incidents," Churchill snapped. "To be more specific, that bastard Himmler threatened to rip up the Treaty of Kent and lay scourge to every city within Southern England."

"So what will be the vessels' ultimate disposition?" Hull asked, his voice conveying that he was already resigned to what the answer would be.

"The Germans expect to face you sooner or later and intend to use the vessels until their three new battleships are complete. *Anson* and *Howe* have apparently already been dispatched to Wilhelmshaven along with several of the destroyers. *Lion* will be sent within thirty days. It is expected that they will take six months to be in German service."

"So you're saying the Germans just got three modern battleships gift wrapped and dropped off at their door?" Kimmel asked, his tone one of disbelief.

"Are you familiar with the effect of nerve gas on unprotected civilians, Admiral Kimmel?" Queen Elizabeth asked quietly. "I can place you in touch with several officers who can tell you exactly just how agonizing a death it appears to be."

"No one is suggesting that your government should have called Mr. Himmler's bluff," Secretary Hull said smoothly, giving Admiral Kimmel a hard look. "Admiral Kimmel is understandably upset, as this will affect our own strategic calculus."

"We understand your concerns, Secretary Hull," Queen Elizabeth said. "However, given your upcoming construction we do not see cause for quite that level of alarm."

"Do not understand the reason for that level of alarm?" Admiral Kimmel asked unbelievingly, his Kentucky drawl getting more pronounced due to his anger. "How about those are three modern battleships that we will now have to account for in order to maintain open supply lines to Iceland? Or that we will have to destroy in order to return you to your throne?"

"Again, *Anson* and *Howe* will take at least six months to be worked up with German crews, *Lion* even longer." Admiral Tovey snapped. "I doubt that they will be anywhere near as experienced as your own."

"You're making the assumption they will have *German* crews," Kimmel said seethingly. "Our intelligence indicates that the Halifax government has not necessarily ruled out supplying 'volunteers' in exchange for concessions."

"That is a ploy to ensure that we continue grain shipments from Canada," Churchill observed, nostrils flaring slightly.

There was a moment when Kimmel and Hull both looked at him in shock.

"From your response you make it appear that you are thinking about continuing to do so," Hull said after a moment, his voice heavy.

"We will not starve our subjects," Queen Elizabeth said flatly.

"Perhaps you do not understand the gravity..." Secretary Hull started to say.

"I will *not* be lectured like I am some ignorant child, Secretary Hull," Queen Elizabeth snapped, her icy demeanor finally cracking. "You have the *audacity* to tell any one of us that we do not *understand* the *gravity* of the situation? Tell me, Mr. Secretary, when was the last time your home was bombed? Your capital burned? Your father *murdered*?"

Hull bit back a response, taking a deep breath.

I know a thing or two about willful women, Eric thought. *I'm pretty sure all of you underestimate this woman at your peril.*

"The American people will find it hard to understand how on one hand you can consider your uncle a...*usurper* yet you continue to supply grain to the people who follow him. There will be those who wonder if you are prepared to do what is necessary to regain your throne."

*If looks could kill...*Eric thought as Queen Elizabeth stared venomously at Secretary Hull for a brief moment before regaining her composure.

"Our government has done what is necessary throughout this conflict, Secretary Hull. We do not think the same can be said of yours," the monarch replied, her tone almost making Eric shiver from the intensity it contained.

The proverbial pin drop would have echoed like thunder in the compartment.

"Perhaps, Your Majesty, a break is in order," Churchill suggested after a moment, his voice neutral.

"That sounds like a wonderful idea, Lord Churchill," Queen Elizabeth replied, her lips pursed.

"Gentlemen, let us return in fifteen minutes," Churchill said briskly, looking at the clock on the far bulkhead.

"I will have a steward bring some coffee for our guests," Admiral Tovey said, heading for the watertight door.

"Lieutenant Cobb, we should probably get you ashore," Admiral Kimmel spoke from behind Eric. "A detachment should already be at your guest quarters collecting your gunner, and they should have transportation for you to return to the *South Dakota*."

I recognize an order wrapped in a suggestion when I hear it, Eric thought. *Not that I mind—an ant does not need to be standing around when elephants are dancing.*

"Yes sir," Eric replied, turning for the hatch.

"*Leftenant* Cobb," Queen Elizabeth called after him, causing Eric to stop dead in his tracks.

"Yes Ma'a...Your Majesty?" Eric said, tripping over himself.

"Thank you," Queen Elizabeth said simply.

"You are welcome, Your Majesty," Eric said, giving a slight neck bow. He stopped to wait for Admiral Kimmel to go out the hatchway, but the senior officer gestured for him to lead the way. Five minutes later, Eric found himself standing with Secretary Knox along with Admirals Kimmel and King next to the *Prince of Wales*'s gangway. The fleet's service launch approached the battleship, bobbing in the choppy harbor water from the stiff wind.

"Lieutenant Cobb, I think it goes without saying you are to not to speak about anything you saw or heard today," Admiral Kimmel said quietly.

"Yes sir," Eric replied.

"Especially anything having to do with your senior's behavior," Secretary Hull snapped, staring directly at Admiral King.

"I will not be lectured by some teenaged skirt with delusions of grandeur," Admiral King snapped as he took a heavy draw on his cigarette. Eric watched Secretary Knox's face start to color as he looked to make sure no one was in ear shot.

"The British lost," King continued. "They left the Germans a pretty sizeable portion of their fleet and we don't have the necessary power to go smash up Scapa Flow like they did the frogs when France fell. So pardon me if I don't get all wrapped up in protocol when I'm thinking about all the American boys who are about to die because some overwrought girl wants to avenge her daddy."

King looked out over the side as he flicked away his cigarette, and suddenly Eric could have swore the admiral aged five years right before his eyes.

"I've got six girls of my own, and I don't think anyone's going to ask several thousand boys like Lieutenant Cobb here to die if I end up on the wrong end of some German shell."

"Your personal opinions aside, I need to know if you can control yourself, Admiral King," Secretary Knox seethed.

"Gentlemen, I'm not sure now is the time..." Kimmel attempted to interject soothingly, only to be cut off by King.

"Mr. Secretary, if you think I'm incapable of fighting this war perhaps you need to go ahead and send me back to the General Board," Admiral King said lowly. "Especially if that job requires treating the people in there as equal allies who are bringing as much to the table as they're taking off of it. I took an oath to uphold and defend the Constitution, not cater to the Queen of England."

Secretary Knox took a visibly deep breath.

"We will discuss this further when we return to Washington," he said, his voice heavy with emotion. "For now, I think Lieutenant Cobb has a boat to catch."

Eric came to attention at the top of the gangway, saluting his seniors.

"Good luck, Lieutenant Cobb," Secretary Knox replied, returning Eric's salute.

"Thank you, sir," Eric replied, then started making his way down to the launch.

I have a feeling I just saw something that's not going to end well, he thought as he stepped into the small boat. The coxswain let him sit down, then began the small launch's journey back towards shore.

Ewa Air Station, Hawaii
1800 Local (0000 Eastern)
30 September (1 October 1)

"So I hear the new admiral's a real nutcracker," Sam said as he worked the ratchet in his hand.

"Is this why you stay late, Sam?" his brother asked disgustedly. "So you can gossip while you're helping to service a freakin' engine?"

There was a muted guffaw as one of VMF-14's enlisted mechanics struggled not to laugh. Master Sergeant Schwarz, VMF-14's chief mechanic, looked up from the other side of the engine to fix the offender with a baleful glare. While Sam and David had been strenuous in their declarations that they were just there as handymen and observers, Schwarz was not about to let one of his young Marines abuse their hospitality. Sam had developed the distinct impression that the tall, wiry gray-haired master sergeant sometimes enforced discipline with a bit more than his sharp tongue and gaze that would make a gorgon proud. While he hadn't brought the topic up with David in the three months the twins had been with the squadron, he doubted his brother had seen anything that would contradict that impression.

He reminds me of ol' Deputy Guston who used to oversee the chain gang back home, Sam thought grimly. *Nice man, polite to his peers and betters, but hell on wheels to those under him.*

"No, I stay late so I learn how my airplane works," Sam replied to David. "I'm just trying to make conversation."

"Well, whether the man's a nutcracker or not, he's already got Colonel Benson hopping," David said lowly, referring to Marine Aircraft Group Twenty-one's commander. "It's not like the man was a bump on the log in the first place."

Sam double checked his handiwork then went on to the radial engine's next cylinder head. Examining it closely, he raised an eyebrow and gestured for Master Sergeant Schwarz to take a look.

"This looked cracked to you, Master Sergeant?" he asked, reaching up to angle the shop light so the enlisted man could have a look. Schwarz leaned in close, squinting, then cursed.

"Yes, sir, it does. Guess we know why this aircraft was such a dog yesterday," Schwarz said, his annoyance clear.

"Better to find the fault now rather than end up going for a swim later," Sam replied.

"Attention on deck!" someone shouted, causing a rustling inside the hangar bay. Sam released the light as he stepped out from behind the engine to face the door, David close behind. Seeing the visitor, he felt the blood drain from his face as he snapped to attention.

Okay, Mom always used to say if you speak the devil's name he shall appear, but this is absolutely ridiculous, Sam thought.

Striding into the hangar was a man who looked, to quote one of their squadronmates, "older than Moses." Tall and broad shouldered, with an erect gait that made his stature seem even larger, Admiral Hank William Jensen was the newly minted Commander in Chief Pacific Fleet (CINCPACFLT), having been assigned when Admiral Kimmel had been tapped for CINCATLFLT. The senior officer's wizened features and wispy hair made him look a full decade older than his sixty years, but looking into his dark brown, almost black eyes was enough to show that age had not affected the man's mental abilities one bit. His dark, bushy eyebrows showed what color the few wisps of combed over white hair on his head had once been.

Standing beside Jensen was a rear admiral that Sam immediately recognized.

Holy shit, that bastard Bowles really does look just like his old man, Sam thought, thinking of one of his squadron mates.

Vice Admiral Jacob Bowles Sr. was a man that looked like an older Clark Gable, but with green eyes and a full head of brown hair. As he stepped away from the *Wildcat*, Sam noted the submariner's dolphins on the right side of the man's uniform shortly before Admiral Jensen started to speak. Three more men, two captains and a full commander, accompanied the admiral.

"Who is the senior man here?" Jensen thundered.

There was a moment's pause as all of the enlisted men looked at Sam and David, who in turn looked at each other.

"Sir, I am," David said, stepping around Sam to stand beside him. "Captain David Cobb, VMF-14."

"Why are you out of uniform, captain?" Jensen snapped, showing no sign of surprise at being presented with twin Marines.

"Begging the Admiral's pardon, Marine regulations clearly stipulate that when conducting services personnel are allowed to wear coveralls as their duty uniform," Sam replied evenly.

"That regulation only applies to enlisted personnel!" Admiral Bowles snapped. "Do not correct Admiral Jensen ever again."

I see being an asshole is a family trait, Sam thought quietly.

"Yes , sir," Sam replied. "Then, begging the admiral's pardon, the regulation in question is not rank specific."

Sam heard David's sharp intake of breath and watched as Bowles face started to color. Before the admiral could unleash a tirade, the hangar door opened again.

"Captains Cobb, two ea..." Major Max Bowden started to bellow, then stopped as soon as he realized that the squadron had company. A short, stocky man with thinning blonde hair and blue eyes, Bowden had so far proven to be quite capable as a squadron leader. He was also the third commander VMF-14 had had since Vice Admiral Bowles had arrived in Hawaii.

Someone is trying to do his damndest to get their son a squadron commander slot early, Sam thought bitterly.

"Good evening Admiral Jensen!" he said loudly, immediately

recognizing CINPACFLT. The reason for his extra volume was apparent a moment later as Colonel Benson walked in followed by a man in civilian clothes.

"Good evening, sir," Benson said solemnly, coming to attention as he removed his cover. "Welcome to Ewa Air Station. I would have prepared a tour if I had known you were coming."

He looks tired, Sam thought as he looked at the group commander. An older man with a shock of gray hair and blue eyes, Benson had been a Marine aviator long enough to have seen action in several of the Banana Wars throughout the Caribbean. At just a shade under six foot normally, Benson seemed to be bowing under the weight of command that had descended upon his narrow shoulders.

"That's quite all right, Colonel," Admiral Jensen said. "Captain Cobb was just informing me of the finer points of Marine regulations."

There was a moment when both Benson and Bowden gave the Cobb brothers looks which clearly signified they doubted the junior officers' sanity. Before either man could speak, the chaplain politely cleared his throat.

"Admiral Jensen, I hate to interrupt, but I have some urgent news for both Captains Cobb."

"And you are?" Bowles thundered.

"Rear Admiral Bowles, I am Chaplain McHenry," the man replied evenly. "Specifically, I am *your* staff chaplain. We met six weeks ago when you took over as Chief of Staff. I understand if you do not recognize me—while I saw your son at church last week, I had not seen you recently. It is a large congregation, of course."

Whoa. Talk about soft answer turneth away wrath, Sam thought, watching as Bowles' mouth worked a couple of times in shock. McHenry turned away from the man and backed to Admiral Jensen.

"I apologize Admiral, but I am covering for MAG-21's chaplain," McHenry continued. "I just received a telegram that I need to deliver to Captain Cobb. Both of them."

*Oh no...*Sam thought.

"I think that the message..." Bowles began.

"Go ahead, chaplain," Admiral Jensen said, cutting his chief of staff off. "As a matter of fact, why don't you step outside with the two captains for a moment?"

"If you gentlemen will follow me?" McHenry said.

Feeling numb, Sam began following the chaplain out the door. There was never a good reason for a chaplain to come deliver a message.

"Who is it?" David asked as soon as they were standing outside the hangar.

"Your brother Eric is fine," McHenry replied quickly. "However, he was shot down by the Germans on September 12."

"*What?!*" Sam and David asked simultaneously. McHenry held up his hands.

"Easy, easy, let me finish then I will answer what questions I can," McHenry said. He quickly told both Cobb twins what their brother had been up to for just a little more than a fortnight.

"That's all the information I, or for that matter, anyone else here in Hawaii has," McHenry finished. "I'm sure there is additional information, but the communiqué mentioned your brother hasn't been fully debriefed and that the other information was classified."

"Holy shit," Sam breathed, then caught himself. "Sorry chaplain."

"Captain Cobb, I think if I just found out my brother had been in Canada for a fortnight after nearly getting killed by the Germans I'd probably be using some blue language as well."

"Has anyone informed our brother, Nick?" David asked.

"Rabbi Howe, the Submarine Force chaplain, was hoping to make arrangements after I informed him of the telegram. I received the news courtesy of a friend of mine who is on Admiral King's staff," McHenry replied. "He indicated that the Navy had only informed your mother your brother was 'missing' yesterday."

"Oh Jesus," David breathed. "Mom is going to be *pissed* at Eric."

"In your brother's defense, I suspect that he was either ordered not to contact your family or that someone held his mail," McHenry replied evenly. "The poor young man is already more famous than he is probably going to like."

"What do you mean, Chaplain?"

McHenry looked at both men.

"Neither one of you read the newspapers, do you?"

Sam and David both looked sheepish.

"No Chaplain," Sam replied.

"The Germans are rather incensed and are demanding Lieutenant Cobb's incarceration upon his return to the United States," McHenry replied evenly. "Secretary Hull has pointed out that the German Navy did open fire on a neutral aircraft so they are hardly the wronged party."

"You know, he always had a knack for finding trouble," Sam muttered.

"This is a bit different than stealing peaches from Widow Fitzsimmons," David drawled. Turning to look at his brother, Sam could see that David was obviously more upset than he was.

"Well he's safe now, and he's headed home," Sam replied evenly. "I'm pretty sure he'll have one hell of a story to tell Mom."

Singapore
1700 Local (0500 Eastern)
4 October

I almost feel sorry for the man, Rear Admiral Tamon Yamaguchi thought as he stoically regarded the fuming Englishman in front of him. Of average height, with close set, almost catlike features and a stocky build, Yamaguchi had once been likened to a gregarious catamount by one of his Princeton classmates. Like that predator, he remained almost perfectly still except for his almond eyes that tracked the tall, lanky, and clearly agitated British officer in front of him. Almost casually, he dropped his hand to the officer's sword on his left hip. He could see his superior, Vice Admiral Chuichi Nagumo, similarly tensing in front of him.

There are only three of them in this room, Yamaguchi thought. *I would not think they were so foolish as to cause an incident, but I know what path I would take in this situation.*

"I will tell you what is *reasonable*, Admiral Ciliax," Lieutenant General Arthur Percival hissed through his two protruding front teeth. "*Reasonable* is that I be advised that your nation had no intention of taking possession of this colony, but rather intended to turn it over to this bunch of barb... *gentlemen*. *Reasonable*..."

"I demand that you would not speak of the Reich's allies as if they are not standing here, General," Admiral Otto Ciliax thundered, both his hands on Percival's desk. "We are not, in any way, *negotiating* terms. The Treaty of Kent is clear, and the fact that you or your staff remain here is merely a formality and courtesy."

Percival glowered at his German opposite number, his face reddening around his clipped moustache.

"I have three divisions of troops under my command..." the Englishman began, only to be cut off again by Ciliax.

"Field Marshal Kesselring has over three *thousand* aircraft poised like a dagger at England," Ciliax said coldly, his accent growing thicker with emotion even as he casually waved. "How many women and children are you willing to kill with your pride?"

Percival opened his mouth then shut it again. Taking a deep, shuddering breath the man turned and looked at Vice Admiral Nagumo, then back at Ciliax.

"Then I will be damned if me or my staff will stay here to help some *Jap*," Percival spat. "For men who talk of the white race's superiority you seem to be awfully willing to do the slant eyes' dirty work."

Yamaguchi felt a rush of blood to his face even as he tried to keep his features impassive.

"Perhaps now would be a good time to tell you that Vice Admiral Nagumo will be the *Kriegsmarine*'s outside representative for inspecting the Royal Navy's indemnity payments for the loss of the *Scharnhorst*, *Gneisenau*, and damage to the *Bismarck* and *Tirpitz*?"

Percival's eyes narrowed.

"What the devil are you talking about?" he snapped.

"I am sure you will find out soon enough," Ciliax replied icily. "I believe you were taking your leave?"

Yamaguchi was as perplexed as General Percival. Even as he watched the British officer and his staff storm out of Singapore's command post, he found his mind alive with questions.

What outside representative? How is Nagumo-san going to inspect warships in Europe? Yamaguchi thought, confused.

"Gentlemen, I am sorry that you had to deal with...that," Ciliax said stiffly.

"His attitude is typical," Vice Admiral Nagumo replied, his English somewhat slow and stilting. "All of the West has long considered us inferior."

Ciliax gave a thin grimace at that.

"Despite that idiot's claims, the Fuhrer does not share that view," Ciliax replied, as a gradually building hum could be heard. "Indeed...who is flying those aircraft?"

The headquarters windows were vibrating with the roar of piston engines by the time that Ciliax finished his question.

"Admiral Yamamoto thought it best if we prepared some additional persuasion," Yamaguchi replied, his face still blank other than a slight narrowing of the eyes. "Just in case General Percival misunderstood our relative positions."

. . .

Ten thousand feet over Rear Admiral Yamaguchi's head, Sub-Lieutenant Isoro Honda gave his *Zero* some gentle right rudder to follow the maneuvers of Lieutenant Commander Shigeru Itaya, *Akagi*'s fighter squadron commander. Looking back at the two other aircraft in his *chutai,* the IJN's typical three-plane formation, Isoro allowed himself to feel a small degree of pride. Their configuration was perfect, Warrant Officers Watanabe and Yoshida moving as if they were extensions of his own aircraft. The nimble, responsive *Zero*es were weaving four thousand feet over the assembled strike aircraft of the *Kido Butai*, the Imperial Japanese Navy's strike force of six heavy carriers.

I only hope the British are stupid enough to start a fight, Isoro thought with grim satisfaction. *It will be nice to face worthy opponents again after three years of killing Chinese*. The Chinese had been like schoolchildren armed with rocks set upon by a horde of samurai, and the eight kills he had scored felt almost shameful given the *Zero*'s superiority.

Not that the Russians were much better, Isoro thought bitterly. *Perhaps if the Army had actually managed to slow the Russians down then we might have gotten to test our mettle against them some more. Or maybe if we had been given a chance to fight those foreign mercenaries down in the south...*

Shaking himself out of his reverie, Isoro sighed as he continued to scan the skies around his aircraft. Several wingmen had often made fun of him for his tendency to always move his body in the cockpit, nicknaming him "Sea Snake" due to the undulations of his long, gangly frame. His nickname had taken on a decidedly different connotation when he started being the first to spot, then kill hostile aircraft. He turned back forward just in time to see a red and green flare arcing out from the lead torpedo bomber below.

No trade for us today, Isoro thought, shaking his head in disappointment. *It would appear that the British are going to accept the Germans giving us Singapore after all*. There had been rumors in the ready room that the Germans had not only ceded Japan Singapore but Malaya as well. If so, it was a gesture of goodwill that had Isoro reconsidering his view of Japan's alliances.

"*Akagi* fighters will land ashore," his headphones crackled with Lieutenant Commander Itaya's voice. "All others will return to carriers."

Well, well, looks like Lieutenant Commander Itaya wants to be the first to see Japan's latest colony, Isoro thought. *Hopefully the women will be friendlier than the Chinese were...or at least the Army dogs won't have time to make them hate us.*

U.S.S. ***Houston***
Manila Bay
1434 Local Time (0134 Eastern)
6 October

Jacob looked thoughtfully at the chart spread out on the table before him, then back across at the captain of the U.S.S. *Houston*.

"So, Admiral Hart has decided that we are going to ally with the Dutch and attempt to keep the Japanese from the East Indies?" Jacob asked incredulously.

"Yes, XO," Captain Wallace replied. "I take it you do not approve."

"The damn Japs have Singapore," Jacob said, incredulous. "That's like trying to close off a flooded compartment when the overhead's been blown away.

Captain Wallace regarded him calmly for several seconds, then replied.

"How much oil is there in the Philippines?"

"None, sir," Jacob replied, instantly seeing the light.

"Exactly. Just as there is none in Japan, which is why it is widely believed the East Indies is one of her primary objectives if war breaks out. I don't see the Germans trying to maintain convoys from Iraq during open hostilities, do you?"

I still can't believe we're just letting the Krauts sail tankers right by us, Jacob thought. *What's the good of having a navy if we're afraid to use it?*

"But that's not what our war plan states we are to do," Jacob replied. Captain Wallace smiled benignly.

"War Plan Orange is somewhat vague on what we're supposed to do, actually," Captain Wallace replied evenly. "Other than die bravely, and if I'm going to do that I want it to be for some other reason than General MacArthur's pride."

"I'm not sure I follow, Captain," Jacob replied.

"The fate of the Philippines is directly linked to that Army bastard's reputation, his 'place in history' as he's always telling Admiral Hart," Captain Wallace said, the disgust veritably dripping off his words. The man paused to take a drink from the coffee mug at his left elbow.

"Should the Philippines fall, General MacArthur would be disgraced.

Especially since he has been spending so much to train the Filipinos over the last year."

Captain Wallace jabbed his finger at Lingayen Gulf.

"MacArthur sees our fleet as something to hurl against the Japanese transports to disrupt them when they land here," Wallace sneered. "He doesn't comprehend that the Japs will probably bring up battleships to blow this vessel out of the water."

Jacob nodded at that statement.

Trying to explain to an Army officer that 8-inch guns aren't all that heavy is like trying to explain to a toddler that the bath water isn't all that hot, he thought bitterly. *It's all a matter of scale and experience.*

"The Commonwealth commander, Admiral Phillips, just spent the last two days guaranteeing Admiral Hart that Her Majesty's Navy will fight for the Dutch East Indies," Captain Wallace continued.

"Be nice if he'd had some of that fighting spirit for Singapore or Malaya then," Jacob observed, doing his best to keep his voice matter-of-fact. Captain Wallace's glare told him that he'd succeeded only enough not to be immediately relieved.

"Rumor has it that admiral the Krauts sent out here basically told the Brits they'd gas London again if they tried to put up a fight. Given that Percival still answered to King Edward, he really didn't have a choice. Phillips, on the other hand, answers to the rightful Queen."

Jacob nearly laughed at that, but stopped himself.

Rightful** Queen?! He says that as if she's **ours, he thought as Captain Wallace continued.

"Admiral Phillips, per previous agreement with the Dutch, will set out from Sydney for Java if hostilities appear imminent. There he, and we, will combine with the Dutch East Indies fleet and deny the oil fields to the Japanese."

"Sir, that's suicide with the little bastards owning Singapore," Jacob replied in disbelief. "Hell, they can row small craft from there to Sumatra, never mind bring any fleet units they station in the harbor! How will we fight under enemy air cover?"

"We won't," Captain Wallace snapped. "With the amount of air power the Dutch and Commonwealth will have concentrated in the Dutch East Indies, intelligence estimates that the Dutch and Brits have the Japanese air force outnumbered two to one. Factor in their advantage in quality, and it's probably going to be a rout. Air superiority is a two-way street."

Looking at the charts in front of him, Jacob found himself slightly mollified.

Yet the Japanese aren't stupid, he thought. *I have to imagine some little yellow son-of-a-bitch is staring at his own charts right now.*

"You seem unconvinced, Commander," Captain Wallace observed.

"Sir, I can't help but think that the Japanese have to have figured this out as well," Jacob said slowly. "They picked a fight with the Russians and got their heads, hands, and feet handed to them before they slunk back to Tokyo to lick their wounds. A thorough beating tends to make a man introspective."

"Commander, there's a natural order of things," Captain Wallace replied. "A bunch of people who were in the Dark Ages less than eighty years ago aren't going to beat us, the Brits, and the Dutch. That's why they backed down back in '41, and if they don't remember what's good for them we'll give them a beating that will make the Russian fight seem like a love tap."

"What about the Philippines?" Jacob asked.

"If the Japanese don't take the East Indies, they can hold this place until Judgment Day—they won't be getting any oil through to their Home Islands, German or otherwise. Six months to a year of that and we'll be able to sail right into Tokyo Bay."

Captain Wallace stepped back from the map.

"But enough talk of fighting in the Dutch Indies," the man said, looking at the clock. "What's our status?"

"Well, when it comes to a fight, I think we're as ready as we can be," Jacob stated firmly. He pulled out a small notebook in which he had written notes to himself.

"All departments completed their last checks early yesterday, and we finished taking on ammunition about an hour ago," he said. "I still think our damage control is shaky, but it's getting better and I've drilled as much as possible without asking for the *Boise* to shoot us with a live shell."

"I don't think having his cruisers shoot one another is what Admiral Hart intended when he stated we needed to conduct realistic training," Captain Wallace replied sardonically. "Admiral Hart is conducting a captain's call at his quarters in about an hour and a half. Set a skeleton watch and get the men some liberty—I get the feeling we're about to start training with our new allies."

"Aye aye, sir," Jacob replied.

"Oh, and Commander—not a word of our discussion to any other officers," Wallace warned. "We don't need talk getting around about what our plans are. General MacArthur has many connections. I don't want some fat, dumb, and happy senator in Washington deciding this vessel is expendable after all, just as long as precious Dougie doesn't get hurt."

"Understood, Captain," Jacob acknowledged.

"Until then, I'm going to my cabin to get cleaned up." With that, Captain Wallace turned from the chart table and headed for the hatch leading from his day cabin to his quarters. After he left, Jacob took another look at the map.

It's going to be one hell of a fight if it comes to that, he thought. *It's almost as if everyone is just waiting for a reason to go to war.*

3

CATALYSTS AND DIABOLISM

Changes in military systems come about only through the pressure of public opinion or disaster in war.

— **BRIGADIER GENERAL BILLY MITCHELL**

Mobile, Alabama
1000 Local (1100 Eastern)
1 November 1942

"Maybe if we just pretend the calendar's not there, your leave won't be almost over," Joyce Cotner said quietly, her breath moving the hair on Eric's chest. The couple were laying in her bed, a large king size with mahogany posts, dark red drapes, and a similarly colored bedskirt that hid the box spring underneath.

Eric chuckled as he looked down at the petite blonde, stroking her back.

"I've still got two weeks. That is, if I don't decide to go over the hill," he replied.

"Why Mr. Cobb, whatever would make you want to do that?" Joyce asked sarcastically as she ran her hand down his stomach. He gasped as she gently gripped him underneath the sheets.

"I don't know, Miss Cotner," he replied evenly. "Maybe getting to lay with you like this more often than just when your parents conspicuously decide to go to the Gulf Coast for vacation?"

"Well if you'll recall, they were planning on hosting a certain married couple along with them," Joyce said, her voice getting a bit of an edge.

So is it generally a bad idea to have your manhood in your fiancée's hand when she's thinking about strangling your sister? Eric thought with a slight edge of dismay.

"Penny for your thoughts?" Joyce asked, looking at him with her blue eyes.

"Just hoping that you remember it's not my sister's neck you're holding," Eric said worriedly. Joyce's mouth dropped in shock, then she started laughing.

"I love you, Eric Cobb," she said as she lay her head back down on his chest. "And I wouldn't be doing *this*," she replied, giving him a few strokes, "with your sister's neck."

"I would hope not," he snorted, his hips moving involuntarily to meet her touch. "But how about we stop talking about relatives..." he started, then stopped as Joyce slid her lower body over onto his.

"Good plan," she replied lightly, then slid herself onto him. "Or stop talking period."

"Okay, I think you're trying to kill me," he said later as they both sat down for lunch.

"Eric, you've known me almost my entire life: Would *that* really be how I tried to kill you?" Joyce asked sarcastically as she spread some salad dressing on homemade bread. Eric felt a slight smile cross his face.

"The fact it would be so unexpected would more than make up for the unpleasantness I had to suffer," Eric retorted, then whipped his head out of the way as Joyce flung some salad dressing at him.

Even in that white sundress she throws better than some men I know, he thought. *Must be the only daughter thing.*

"It'd be hard to explain to mom how I got salad dressing on this shirt," he replied, checking to make sure no errant dressing had ended up on his collar or shoulder. "It will definitely show up with this blue."

"Gee, maybe you should have thought about that before you were such a smarty pants."

"I think my exertions may be causing me to have a delirious stretch," Eric replied. "Being ridden like a stallion does that to a man."

Joyce blushed deeply under her tan.

"You know, some women firmly believe in waiting until they're married to do what we just did," Joyce said archly. "Do not convert me to that way of thinking by your complaints."

"I don't think you'd be able to resist my dashing good looks that long," Eric said. "Besides, I've said many times we should just go to the Justice of the Peace..."

Joyce gave him a look that would have combusted a gorgon.

"Right, Buck Rogers, because you've got a space ship for us to escape both of our mothers parked out in your barn. Or were you planning on sailing to Berlin for our honeymoon so someone could collect on that alleged bounty on your head?" Joyce continued, then switched to a mock German accent. "Ja, Herr Cobb, vee will make your death quick and painless."

Eric searched Joyce's face to see if she was joking, then realized that there was more than a little edge in her voice.

"It's just...I want to start the rest of our life together *now*, not on our mothers' schedules."

"Then why don't you take Secretary Knox up on his offer to let you out of your commitment then?" Joyce asked hopefully. "Father could probably find you a job at one of the steel mills, or you could go back to school to be a lawyer..."

"Yes, I could," Eric replied. "But what kind of man would I be to cheat my country like that?"

"A sane one?" Joyce replied incredulously. "You can't tell me or anyone else what happened, but father says if the Germans ever catch you, they will *shoot you*."

"Your brother just volunteered for flight training!" Eric snapped back, then instantly regretted it Joyce's face went pale with rage.

"Yes, and do you think just *maybe* he's finding a spectacular way to commit suicide thanks to a certain person *fleeing to Hawaii*?" Joyce screamed. "Which you seem to just want to ignore every time it comes up!"

Why does she keep mentioning that? Eric thought as he took a deep breath.

"I will *not* have you screeching at me, Joyce," Eric said slowly. "That's not acceptable."

Joyce opened her mouth, then stopped as she saw the look on Eric's face.

"Well, I see that having things your own way remains a Cobb family trait," she observed icily. "What if I think screeching at you is perfectly, as you say, *acceptable*?"

"Then I would wonder if the woman I loved was driven away by my sister hurting her brother or me disappearing for two weeks," Eric said flatly.

Joyce's face fell, her eyes starting to well with tears.

"Get out," she sobbed.

"You can't just..."

"I said, *get out*!" Joyce said, pushing back from the table. Turning from him, she stalked back towards her bedroom, her shoulders shaking with sobs as she went. A few moments later Eric heard the door slam from upstairs.

Well that could have gone better, he thought to himself. After cleaning up the kitchen, he followed Joyce's orders.

Twenty dusty minutes later found him standing in front of the Cobb family's home. A gleaming white two-story, the house was at the end of a long double lane of cedar and maple trees. A squirrel ran up one of the latter and chattered at him from one of the lower branches. Eric favored the animal with a glare.

"You know, I can shoot *you*," he said hotly. "I'll even wear you like a hat as a warning to the others."

"Your mother would never forgive you," his father said from behind him, causing Eric to jump and the elder Cobb to start laughing.

"So what has you so distracted your old man was able to sneak up on you like a ghost while you were threatening your mother's squirrels with haberdashery?" Samuel Cobb asked. The Cobb family patriarch looked like a slightly older and heavier version of his eldest sons, from the bear-like physique to the mischievous blue eyes. While a pair of wire-rimmed glasses and worry lines made telling the three men apart quite easy up close, they were easily confused from a distance.

"Nothing," Eric replied uneasily, unable to meet his father's eyes as he fibbed.

Samuel shrugged.

"Well I hope you're better at cleaning up than you are at lying, because unless my nose deceives me Joyce was really happy to see you."

Eric looked at his father, feeling a warm blush rise to his cheeks.

"What? The eyesight goes as you get older so something has to make up for it," Samuel replied, holding his hands up in innocence. "Now you'd better hope your mother isn't outside because the wind's blowing from behind us, and if there's one smell a woman can detect from five miles away it's another woman's perfume."

Eric sniffed himself.

"Does it really smell that strong?!" he asked, horrified.

Samuel looked at his son and shook his head.

"Actually, no, I can't smell a thing—but you sure do look guilty now."

"Dad!" Eric replied, aghast.

"You must be a joy to play cards with, son," Samuel said, shaking his head.

"There's a reason I stopped playing with Nick, Sam, and David," Eric replied heatedly.

"So why the long face? I know it's not because Joyce is pregnant...yet."

"You know, you're enjoying us all being grown up a little too much," Eric said, shaking his head.

"Well I thought once I got your sister out of the house..." Samuel said wistfully.

Eric felt his face scowl before he caught himself.

"Ah. I take it the lovely Miss Cotner is a bit upset with Toots?"

"You could say that," Eric replied quietly.

"Tell me, son, do you really think Beau would have been able to handle Toots?" Samuel asked.

"What?"

"Seriously. Beau's a good man, may possibly even be a great one—but I think he wanted to marry Toots more out of a sense of that's what his mother told him to do than actually loving your sister. She ran circles around him in more ways than one," Samuel observed.

Eric looked askance at his father.

"I thought you liked Beau, Dad?" Eric said, shocked.

"I think of Beau like another son, Eric, you know that," Samuel replied with a heavy voice. "I now Toots hurt him desperately, and I worry about him going off to flight school with that pain."

"But?"

"Your sister is a strong woman just like her mother," Samuel continued.

"Your mother's a handful and despite twenty-eight years I've never been under any illusions as to which one of us was smarter, law degree or no."

The depth of emotion in Samuel's voice made Eric smile, which in turn made Samuel get a sheepish look on his face.

"So, father, what do you think of Joyce and I?" Eric asked with raised eyebrow. Samuel's smile only dimmed a slight amount.

"That you guys love each other enough that you shouldn't have to rush into marriage because there's a baby on the way?"

"Oh no, that's never happened in this family before," Eric observed.

"Yes, and your grandfather never forgave me until he died. You want to give Theodore and Elma more reasons to hate us?"

"You're avoiding answering the larger question, Dad."

Samuel took off his glasses and pulled out a handkerchief to wipe them down.

Uh oh, Eric thought. *I may not have a poker face, but Dad has a couple of hellacious tells.*

"There is no question that you love Joyce with the fury of a thousand suns," Samuel said slowly. "I do believe that she *thinks* she loves you that same way, but I'm not sure she does."

Eric felt as if he had just been punched in his chest.

"Well Dad, don't hold back," he said quietly.

"Believe me, son, that *is* holding back," Samuel replied. "You pushed, son. I raised you kids well enough o know you shouldn't push unless you're prepared to face the truth."

"She asked me to take Secretary Knox up on his offer," Eric replied hotly. "I think that says something, doesn't it?"

Samuel turned and regarded his son with a pained look.

"That she truly doesn't know you at all," Samuel replied. "That she's certainly fond of you, more fond of you than a brother, but not that she loves you."

"How could you say that?" Eric snapped.

"Experience, son, experience," Samuel replied.

The front door to the house slammed open.

"Eric Thaddeus Cobb, is there a *reason* you left your fiancée looking at her lunch while you sit here gabbing with your father?" Alma Cobb shouted from the front porch, a jar of olives in her hands. Standing on the front porch in a blue gingham dress with matching flats, the Cobb family matriarch had her brunette hair up in a bun behind her head. Tall, with an aristocratic face and piercing blue eyes, Alma still looked almost exactly the same as she had on her wedding day.

"I guess that I must have misunderstood what she sent me over here for," Eric called to his mother.

"Oh no, that doesn't sound suspicious at all son," Samuel muttered.

"How hard is it to understand *olives*?" Alma asked sardonically.

"You know, Alma, you could act like you're still overjoyed to see your son," Samuel observed. "I mean, it's not like he's just had a near death experience or anything."

Alma turned to look at her husband, and Eric suddenly found himself glad that he was not in direct line of sight.

"Gee, maybe someone should not have talked him into being an aviator rather than a normal sailor or a marine?"

"What, so he could be sitting on some godforsaken island waiting for the Japs to show up or going swimming in the Atlantic?"

"Funny, I thought he ended up in the Atlantic anyway?" Alma observed archly. "Then he was so busy hobnobbing with royalty he couldn't be bothered to send a telegram."

"More like they wouldn't *let me*," Eric breathed.

"You know, I can *see* you sassing me, young man, even if I can't necessarily *hear* it." Alma continued. "Now are you going to get these olives or do I have to take them to the Cotner's to have lunch with Joyce myself?"

Eric shook his head as he fought not to smile. Walking up to the porch, he took the jar from his mother, sweeping her into a hug.

"Love you, Mom," he said in her ear.

"Love you too, son," Alma replied tenderly. "You guys should come here for dinner, but only after you wash up. You smell like a bordello."

Rose of Amsterdam
Tjilatjap, Dutch East Indies (DEI)
1100 Local (2300 Eastern)
4 November (3 November)

"Excuse me, sir, I'm looking for a Mr. Adam Haynes. Do you know where I might find him?" a man asked in heavily accented English.

That accent sounds suspiciously German, Adam thought without turning around. *Guess I should have stayed up in Surabaya with Petr and the boys*. Much to his surprise, five of his Poles had decided to accompany him to China from South Africa. Adam was fairly certain that the American Volunteer Group wouldn't mind some additional veterans even if their English wasn't the greatest.

"Do I need to be worried?" Adam asked lowly of the black-haired woman sharing the table with him. A short, slightly overweight woman whose caramel skin and blue eyes bespoke of mixed heritage, Marta and he had met the day before in the local market. Now she looked at him with a raised eyebrow, watching the bartender and the stranger interact behind him.

"How should I know?" she responded in her lilting voice. "Are you a wanted man?"

"Let's just say that depends on whom you ask," Adam replied.

"Well if memory serves, that man works at the local constabulary office," Marta replied. "But I don't get down here all that often, and I certainly don't tend to get involved with the *politie*."

Adam gave her a slight smile.

"Well I generally don't either, but thanks for making me a little more comfortable," he said, standing up. The stranger saw the movement out of the corner of his eye and turned towards Adam, raising his hand in greeting. The balding man's tan jacket, black shirt, and slacks plus his demeanor reminded Adam more of a pastor than a police officer.

"I assume you are Mr. Haynes, yes?" the man asked in barely understandable English. "Mr. Worcasaw told Wing Commander Collins we could probably find you somewhere down here."

"Okay, you found me," Adam replied. "Mind telling me who you are?"

"Oh, sorry...I am, how you English say...um...oh yes, *Officer* Stille with the Tjilatjap Constabulary. Mr. Worcasaw told me to tell you, first of all, that the 'sun always shines in Krakow'."

Adam had to fight not to laugh at Stille's pronunciation and diction.

"Okay, I'm somewhat mystified as to what could be so important that a policeman would come and find me, but I'm sure it must be critical given Worcasaw gave you a code. What is the message?"

"That you need to return to Surabaya as soon as possible," Stille said. "I do not know why, I just know that my chief normally does not usually use me as an errand boy."

Shit, Adam thought.

"Okay, when is the next train to Batavia?"

"In twenty minutes," Stille said.

Adam sighed.

"Could you give me a couple of minutes to meet you outside?"

"Certainly," Stille replied.

Adam went back to his table, giving Marta an apologetic smile.

"I'm not sure if I am a wanted man, but I must be a stupid one to leave a beautiful woman for parts unknown," Adam said sorrowfully. "I've had a good three days."

"So have I, Adam," Marta replied. She pulled a piece of paper from her purse and quickly scribbled down some information.

"If you are ever in Surabaya, please look me up. I work at the governor's office in the mailroom if you're unable to ring me here."

Adam nodded, placing the paper in his pocket. Marta stood up and wrapped him in an embrace. After a moment's surprise, Adam embraced her back.

Okay, apparently I was much more charming than I thought over the last couple of days, he thought to himself as he inhaled her perfume.

"Now off with you," she said with a smile, kissing him on the cheek. With a last wave, Adam turned to join Stille outside.

Perhaps I should have stayed in Tjilatjap, Adam thought to himself four hours later. He and the five Poles were sitting on thatch chairs along a grass runway, cold drinks in hand as they watched ground crews swarming over a group of *Spitfire* fighters. The elliptical-winged, elegant aircraft were painted in the dark green tropical colors of the Dutch East Indies Air Force.

"Did I just hear you right, Wing Leader Collins? You're wanting us to fly *Spitfires* and commit an act of war against Imperial Japan?" Adam asked slowly.

If Adam had been standing, the wing commander would have been a couple of inches shorter than he was, with a runner's build. The Australian ran a hand nervously through his parted blonde hair.

"I'm not sure I would have put it quite like that, Mr. Haynes," Collins replied.

"No, because then we'd all justifiably look at you and wonder why the Australian government is asking a bunch of Poles and one American to do this when, correct me if I'm wrong, your pilots flew those planes in."

Collins pressed his lips together.

"Due to the Ottawa Compact, all Commonwealth forces are restricted from..."

"Wait, the Ottawa what?" Adam asked. His question got him a bewildered look from Collins before there was a flash of cognition.

"Of course you wouldn't know. Apparently your Secretary of State and Prime Minister King forced Her Majesty to agree not to engage in any offensive operations against the Axis powers," Collins explained, obviously agitated. "Therefore, none of my men can fly north of Java."

"That doesn't explain why the Dutch can't fly them, given that they're all nice and painted now."

"He was not here," Petr Worcasaw reminded the Australian officer. Tall, with a shock of dark hair and brown, almost black eyes, Petr looked positively emaciated. Thankfully, the look was just his normal one as opposed to a sign he had caught some tropical disease.

"Well, let me catch you up to speed, Mr. Haynes," Collins said after a moment. "The reason why 'the Dutch can't fly them' is that they're not qualified. Oh, and that slight matter of having several of their best pilots killed yesterday."

"*What*?" Adam asked.

"It was an ambush," Petr said. "The Japanese come over every morning at 0800, then every afternoon at 1400. Yesterday the Dutch tried to catch the morning flight with their *Hurricanes*. It ended poorly."

"I thought the Japanese flew pieces of crap?!" Adam observed. "That was the rumor."

Petr shrugged.

"Apparently the Japanese 'crap' should scare plumbers everywhere," Petr observed grimly. "The Dutch took off with twelve fighters, came back with four. Another three crash landed elsewhere."

Adam whistled.

"Given that disaster we did not think it was a good idea to send pilots up again in aircraft they had just received," Wing Commander Collins observed drily.

"Instead you're going to have six men who haven't touched a *Spitfire* in literally months do so?" Adam snapped.

"Mr. Haynes, you are a double ace who, if rumors are to be believed, was currently heading to China to seek further employment flying P-40s against warlords," Collins responded. "Perhaps I missed something, but when have you ever flown the *Tomahawk*? Because I know none of your companions have."

"Funny, I missed the part where His Majesty was still paying me," Adam observed drily.

"*Her* Majesty," Collins corrected, his voice stiff.

"Either way, I believe last time I flew *Spitfires* was for a certain government that proved willing to turn me over to its former enemies," Adam observed.

"No Americans were turned over to the Nazis..." Collins started to say.

"No, just some more of those stupid Poles," Petr interrupted darkly. "But I guess we should be used to Englishmen abandoning us by now."

Collins pursed his lips again, giving Petr a disapproving glare.

You know, I think Petr just might hurt you, Adam thought with a slight grin that broadened as the Australian looked away.

"Your hosts may not look kindly on your refusal to help," Collins said with an edge to his voice.

"If our 'hosts' want our help, they can pay for it. Otherwise I'll be happy to inform the U.S. consulate that we're being detained for refusal to partake in a military act. I'm sure *that* will go over swimmingly."

Collins looked positively apoplectic.

"Are you that much of a mercenary, Mr. Haynes?" he asked.

Adam laughed outright at him.

"How many Fascists have *you* killed, Wing Commander?" he asked pointedly, noting the lack of decorations on Collins' uniform.

"Excuse me?" Collins asked.

"I'm just thinking that for someone who is questioning my ethics, you seem to be rather bereft of combat experience yourself," Adam observed conversationally.

"You bastard!" Collins shouted, taking a step towards him. The man didn't get to complete the maneuver before Petr was already out of his chair and stepping between the Australian and Adam, the Pole's face split by an ear-to-ear grin. Adam didn't even move, instead noting that a couple of the ground crew had stopped working on the *Spitfires* and were watching the festivities.

"Now Wing Commander, there's no need to get yourself grievously injured," Adam continued, his tone condescending. "It'd be a shame to sit out an entire war only to have some crazy Polack break your jaw in five places."

Collins went pale with anger but wisely didn't take another step towards Adam.

"Her Majesty's government is willing to offer you one hundred pounds..."

Adam guffawed.

"...apiece. The Dutch government will offer you three hundred gulden as well."

Well now that's more like it, Adam thought.

"How much per kill?" Petr asked speculatively.

Collins looked at him, then back at Adam.

"I am sure we can come to some arrangement," the Australian gritted through clenched teeth.

"Those *Spitfires* don't look like the Mark Vs we flew," Adam replied. "We'll take them for a test flight, then come back and see what you come up with as far as payment goes."

A little over sixteen hours later, Adam was glad that he had insisted on the test flight. Even after a taking a second hop to familiarize themselves and a good night's sleep, he still felt only slightly better about his ability to fight in the new *Spitfire*.

The kite may look similar but it sure as hell doesn't handle like a Mark V, Adam thought as he led the Poles north from Sumatra. Thirty thousand feet below him, the blue-green waters of the Strait of Malacca glistened from the early morning sun. He took a deep breath and looked at his watch.

I really hope the Aussies weren't wrong about the general vector and timing the last flight took, Adam thought. *I'd hate to be short fuel because some newbie radar boffin messed up his intercept data*. It had been somewhat of a surprise to find out that the Australians had placed three of the radar sets along Sumatra's north coast in the past two weeks.

It's almost like they really do plan on helping the Dutch hold this place if the Japanese come south, Adam thought. *Folks in their government must be sweating buckets*.

The glint of sunlight off glass below and to his port side stopped his thoughts. A moment later, the reflection became a single aircraft heading south on an opposite heading just at the edge of his vision.

Well at least these guys are as punctual as the Germans, Adam thought. He gave the *Spitfire* left rudder to swing wide of the reconnaissance aircraft, pulling back on the stick to give himself more height.

Now let's just hope the Japanese are much, much less observant...and don't have radar, he thought. *Of course, if all you're expecting is Hurricanes, you're probably not looking up at this point.*

Continuing north, Adam continued to search the sky ahead. Five minutes after the reconnaissance aircraft had passed, a swarm of dots followed along the same general path appeared to his port side below him.

Well, well, well, sometimes it's nice when your opponent is predictable, Adam thought. *Looks like the guests of honor are falling into the trap, but let's just keep flying to make sure there are not any party crashers coming up from behind.*

Five minutes later, Adam was sufficiently satisfied there were no additional Japanese fighters behind the eighteen or so they'd sighted. Waggling his wings, he brought the *Sptifire* around in a gentle turn so as not to cause any vapor trails from his wing, then advanced his throttle. With a gentle shudder and black smoke from its nose, the *Spitfire* leapt ahead.

Even though the Dutch do only have Hurricanes, if I'm that Japanese commander then I'd still expect them at altitude. Easy does it, Adam thought, looking at his altimeter.

A few minutes later, Adam was glad to see that the new *Spitfire* appeared to have a significant speed advantage over the Japanese fighters. As he closed, the American could see the single-engined craft were painted dark olive green and arranged in groups of three flying in a V of Vs.

Odds could be better, but it looks like we're calling the tune here, Adam thought, his pulse increasing. *Hope everyone remembers the plan and doesn't get buck fever, we* ***cannot*** *stay here*. Making one last check of his guns, he pushed the spade control panel forward and shoved his throttle to war emergency power.

Choosing the rearmost V, he aimed for the leader as he came down from the sun. The aircraft swelled in his sight as he skidded to add slight deflection, watching as he could pick out more and more detail. Just as Adam was pressing his trigger, the Japanese pilot apparently saw Death plunging at him from above. Smoke was pouring from the fighter's exhaust and its wings starting to come up in a snap roll when the twin cannons and machine guns in the *Spitfire*'s wings began shaking the gunsight. Before Adam had a chance to register any hits, the Japanese aircraft exploded, debris flying towards him and causing him to flinch upwards.

Dammit, he thought, then quickly reacted by bringing his nose around to line up an aircraft in the lead trio as he hurtled over the Japanese formation. Smoke poured from the enemy fighter's radial engine as the pilot added throttle and started to reef his aircraft around. Unfortunately for the Japanese airman, his maneuver put the dark green fighter directly in front of Adam's second quick burst, his cannon and heavy machine guns slicing the aircraft's port wing from its fuselage. The shattered plane started to spin crazily as Adam hurtled past while bringing his nose up as he headed south. He glanced briefly to make sure Flight Officer Kantor, his wingman, was still with him then continued to haul ass away from the bedlam behind him.

Well that went better than expected, Adam thought, fighting the temptation to turn back around and have another go at the chaos he had left behind him. Then a thought occurred.

I wonder if that reconnaissance plane is still in front of us? he thought with a slight smile. He continued to scan the horizon as he ran like a thief from a bank robbery, adrenaline making his hand jittery on the stick. A couple of minutes later, his persistence was rewarded, as he sighted the reconnaissance aircraft for the second time that day, headed on a reciprocal course to his starboard front. Turning, he glanced back to see empty sky.

Well this ought to be interesting, he thought, skidding to bring his nose around in a pursuit curve. The reconnaissance aircraft saw him and put its nose down, trying to add speed. Despite the pilot's best efforts, Adam was quickly able to close within range, the twin engines swelling in his reticle. The aircraft's tail gunner opened fire on him, the tracers arcing back behind the *Spitfire* just as Adam squeezed his own trigger. White flashes all along the fuselage, exploding glass, and sudden cessation of return fire told Adam he had hit the tail gunner, while white smoke that quickly became black from the port engine told him that the reconnaissance aircraft had been severely damaged. Adam pulled up to avoid running into the back of the aircraft, turning to look behind his wingman...where he saw a single olive green aircraft closing rapidly from behind.

"Break Kantor! Break!" Adam shouted in Polish as he brought his own nose around. Flight Officer Kantor didn't question his order, whipping his own *Spitfire* into a tight turn just as the closing Japanese opened fire. Adam's sense of relief turned to horror as the olive green fighter managed to cut inside of the *Spitfire*'s turn, gaining enough lead to open fire again even as Adam was closing from the Japanese pilot's port side. Firing a snapshot, Adam saw his burst knock pieces off his target's tail just before the two fighters crossed paths.

He just fucking outturned a ***Spit***, Adam thought with a moment's panic, pulling up into a loop. Looking through the top of his canopy, he watched the enemy fighter continuing to turn after the now diving Kantor. Rolling through the loop into an Immelman, Adam followed the two other aircraft down.

Dammit, dammit, dammit, Adam thought, angry at himself for getting greedy. Slipping side to side, he checked his rearview mirror to make sure there were no other enemy fighters behind him, then poured on the coal. The enemy pilot never realized that Adam had a speed advantage, presenting an easy target as he focused on trying to catch Kantor. Lining up the reticle, Adam fired and this time was rewarded with a brilliant streamer of fire that engulfed the enemy fighter's fuselage. Before Adam's horrified eyes the Japanese fighter's canopy came hurtling back, followed a moment later by a burning comet with writhing limbs.

Ignoring the falling fighter, Adam rejoined with Kantor. Turning, he looked the other *Spitfire* over, noting several bullet holes just behind the cockpit and down the fuselage.

"You all right Two?" he asked in French.

"Yes, yes," the shaken Pole answered. "But next time, I think we let the extra kill go."

Adam laughed in relief.

"Follow me, I think we've done enough for today," Adam said. Even as they winged back towards Java, he kept a sharp lookout behind them, expecting more Japanese to make an appearance.

Well we can outrun and outdive them, but I'll be damned if I try to outturn one of those bastards if we do this again, he thought as his hands shook on the controls as he came down from the rush of adrenaline and fear, and he took several deep breaths to calm himself. Unbidden, the image of the burning Japanese pilot came back to his mind, and he found his mouth suddenly thick with saliva as he had the urge to vomit. He swallowed forcefully, hating his reaction.

Then again, the point where burning another man alive becomes blasé might be the point where I need to eat a bullet, he mused to himself. It wasn't the first time he had set a man afire, and he had the sinking suspicion it was not going to be the last.

Batavia was upon him before he knew it. As Adam passed over the airfield while Kantor landed, he noticed a group of twenty or so people gathered at the front of the four *Spitfire*s that had already landed.

I'm always worried when there's a welcoming committee. Turning into his own final approach and lowering his landing gear, he wondered who the gathered people were. Shrugging, he plopped down in a perfect landing and then taxied over to the end of the line of *Spitfires*.

You know, it might be a good idea to start staggering these aircraft, Adam thought as he opened the *Spitfire*'s canopy and was hit by Batavia's tropical heat. He quickly shrugged out of his flight jacket, just as a flashbulb burst at the edge of his vision. As if that had been a starting gun, he was suddenly beset by a horde of questions shouted at him in Dutch. Adam stepped out on the wing, then took off his Mae West, oxygen mask, and flight helmet. Placing the items on his seat, he shrugged out of his flight tunic and immediately felt cooler as the cacophony died down around him.

"Mr. Haynes! Mr. Adam Haynes!" someone shouted. Adam snapped around, recognizing the speaker's Midwest twang. He saw that the individual calling to him was a slightly rotund, brown-haired man in a tan suit. Two of the local constabulary were making a hole for the man as he got closer to the *Spitfire*. Stepping to the ground, he turned to face the man as the latter was furiously mopping at his face.

"Adam Haynes, you are a hard man to find," the stranger said.

"I'm sorry, have we met before?" Adam asked, casually crossing his arms so that his right hand was closer to his still holstered revolver. The Dutch policeman standing to the man's right noticed the movement and tensed.

"My name is Harold Parks, and I'm with Standard Oil," the man continued, extending his hand. Moving his hand away from his holster, Adam extended his own hand as the hubbub around the two of them died down.

"Is there someplace private we can talk?" Parks asked, looking at the reporters pressing all around them.

"Clear the way!" someone shouted, then repeated their statement again in what Adam could only assume was Dutch. The two policemen, hearing the voice, immediately started gesturing for the gathered press to get out of the way. Adam recognized Wing Commander Collins walking behind four more Dutch police, but did not recognize the man walking beside him in the uniform of a Dutch East Indies officer.

"Well Mr. Haynes, glad to see that you made it back in one piece," Wing Commander Collins said stiffly.

Why does your tone make me doubt your sincerity? Adam thought.

"That makes two of us," Adam replied wryly as the Poles joined him.

Collins gave him a slight smile, his face softening. He turned to the officer beside him.

"This is Wing Commander Wevers of the Dutch East Indies Air Force," Collins continued.

Commander Wevers shot out his hand, and Adam took it. The Dutchman shook vigorously then, giving a sound of joy, dragged the American in for an immense bear hug.

"Thank you! Thank you!" the man said in heavily accented English as he let Adam go, then turned to the gathered group. "Thank you all for... how you say...*avenging* my men."

Ah, that explains it, Adam thought, slightly bemused.

"Our pleasure," Petr returned. Adam could see the Pole was almost overcome with emotion himself.

Kindred spirits, these men, Adam thought. *Which is unsurprising given that their home countries are still occupied.*

"Mr. Haynes, I really do need to give you my information as soon as possible," Parks said, getting a strange look from Collins.

"Wing Commander Wevers, is there someplace we can go in private?" Adam asked. Getting a puzzled look, Adam was about to ask Collins for help when Parks rapidly translated. Nodding emphatically, Wevers began barking at the gathered reporters and the police, gesturing towards a cluster of buildings at the north end of the airfield. There was a low murmuring among the crowd but the press throng began to grudgingly move away from the group of pilots.

"I'll be along in a moment, Wing Commander," Adam said, gesturing for Parks to follow him. Once they were out of earshot, Adam turned to find his companion reaching inside of his suit jacket to pull out an envelope.

"I have a message from your father," Parks said flatly.

*Oh you can go fuck...*Adam thought, his expression turning into an ugly scowl.

"Please Mr. Haynes, I think you need to read this," Parks pressed. "It's urgent, and he's had a hell of a time finding you."

"Funny thing about that," Adam snapped. "I seem to recall last time he saw me he considered me a disgrace and that I could consider myself disinherited for being a 'paid assassin'."

Parks handed the message over without saying anything further. Adam snatched the envelope from his hands then put it in his pants pocket. Parks shook his head.

"I was given clear instructions to make sure you *read* the message," Parks said sharply.

Adam shook his head in disgust as he took the envelope back out of his pocket.

"Well can't have one of father's minions go back without..." Adam started, recognizing the handwriting as that of his father's personal assistant, Cassandra.

Oh my god...

"When was this letter written?!" he snapped.

"It was given to me two days ago. I understand it first arrived in England in mid-August."

"Fat lot of good it would have done me there," Adam muttered, then said louder, "I assume you have a way for us to get out of here?"

"Yes," Parks replied. "I have an itinerary, but only if you can leave in the next three hours. Otherwise you will have to wait until tomorrow morning."

"Give me a few moments to make my goodbyes," Adam said, his voice thick as the enormity of the letter's contents began to register.

"Understood. I'll get my driver to come around to the flight line," Parks said.

Adam headed back to the clump of officers, fighting the burning in his eyes. Seeing the look on his face, the Poles took a couple of steps towards him.

"Adam, what is wrong?" Kantor asked in heavily accented English.

"My mother..." Adam began, his voice cracking. "My mother has cancer. She may already be dead. I am sorry, my friends, but I must leave you."

Sea of Japan
1000 Local (2000 Eastern)
7 November (6 November) 1942

With a muttered curse, Isoro shoved the throttle forward, waited for the engine to respond with a spew of black exhaust smoke, then pulled back gently on his stick while applying left rudder pedal. The round nose of his *Shiden* fighter skidded back online with the carrier *Akagi*'s gently pitching deck, and he felt the fighter begin to lift slowly back from just above the waves. Sweat beading all over his face, Isoro watched as the carrier's landing lights indicated that the *Shiden* was back on the correct path for touching down on the carrier's deck.

I am glad we do not use an officer for this as the Americans do, Isoro thought grimly. *I would be so ashamed that another pilot saw how I am handling this aircraft.* Even as an experienced pilot, Isoro had found the *Shiden* to be a handful during familiarization flights the previous week. Biting his tongue in concentration, Isoro tried to avoid thinking about the two men whom had died because their skills had been found wanting.

Almost there...almost there...now! Isoro thought, feeling the fighter thump down hard and immediately pulling his throttle backward. A moment later he was jerked forward as the arresting hook stopped his forward movement. Exhaling in relief, he allowed himself a moment of giddiness before shutting down the engine. As the prop finished whirring, the *Akagi*'s deck crew sprinted out to shove the fighter forward. Isoro unbuckled, jumped out of the cockpit, and then almost ran towards the *Akagi*'s island while the deck crew manhandled the *Shiden* forward.

"Honda!" Commander Mitsuo Fuchida shouted, causing Isoro to whip his head around. He saw the older man standing with Lieutenant Commander Itaya and a couple of other officers.

Nothing good comes from being called over, he thought, steeling himself as he made his face impassive.

"What do you think?" Fuchida asked amicably, gesturing towards the *Shiden*.

It is a farm girl to the **Zero***'s geisha...* Isoro thought internally.

"It is much faster and it rolls quicker," Isoro said tentatively.

"Oh come on, we are not your sister asking how her kimono looks," Itaya sneered derisively. "What is your honest opinion?"

Isoro turned and looked as the next *Shiden* made its approach. He could tell the pilot was struggling with the controls, the fighter getting further and further out of the best glide path. Finally, with what he imagined was probably a scream of frustration in the cockpit, the pilot applied throttle and brought the fighter around to attempt another pass.

"It is hard to learn," Isoro said simply. "I enjoy the additional power and the way it rolls, but I miss flicking my wrist and changing directions like a bird."

Fuchida nodded, smiling slightly.

"I can understand that," the senior officer replied. "Still, if Captain Genda's reports from Germany are to be believed, the *Zero* is close to being eclipsed by both the British and German fighters which battled over Britain last summer."

"Which means those American bastards will probably have something almost as good by the time we fight them," Itaya said grimly. His response drew a sharp look from Fuchida, to which the *Akagi* fighter commander shrugged.

"The man is not an idiot, Fuchida-san," Itaya continued with a shrug. "It is easy to see that the Germans will be fighting the Americans before a year is out. When that happens, the oil flow stops and we are right back to late 1941 when we attacked the Communists."

We all know how well that went, Isoro thought.

The roar of the next *Shiden* landing ended the conversation before Itaya could reveal more. The pilot hit the deck heavily, but still managed to catch the last arrester wire on the *Akagi*'s deck. Itaya shook his head in disgust.

"We are going to break these fighters before we even get a chance to use them," the man muttered.

"Everyone is having a difficult time with their new aircraft," Fuchida said stiffly. "We will do what we must for the Empire."

"Of course," Itaya said. "I just do not look forward to the next few weeks."

IJNS Musashi
1030 Local (2030 Eastern)

Fifty miles to the Akagi's southwest, Rear Admiral Yamaguchi found himself echoing Itaya's sentiment. The *Musashi*'s flag plot was relatively empty, the cavernous space currently holding less than two dozen men gathered around a large scale map of the Pacific. The air passing through the vessel's open portholes carried the normal sounds of a man of war at sea, from the sound of petty officers bawling out an unfortunate sailor to the low, steady rumble as the massive warship cruised at the head of the battleline stretched out behind her.

"With the support of the aircraft from Singapore, I do not think that I need the carriers," Vice Admiral Nobutake Kondo was stating. The stocky man with a broad, open face continued in a firmer tone as he gestured towards the Dutch East Indies. "I would rather have more escorts for the transports than have destroyers and cruisers tied to the *Hiyo*, *Junyo*, and *Ryujo*."

Across the table, a bald man in gleaming whites that contrasted with the other officers' dark blue uniforms placed both hands on the table and pressed himself to his feet. The maneuver drew all eyes briefly to the missing index and middle fingers on his left hand, shortly before the taller, older man spoke.

"Yamaguchi-san, can the *Kido Butai* fit the additional planes on their carriers?" Admiral Isoroku Yamamoto asked simply.

This is why I wish Vice Admiral Nagumo had not been chosen to do the inspection, Yamaguchi thought to himself.

"It will drastically lengthen the time it takes to launch and recover strike waves, sir," Yamaguchi replied evenly. "We will hit harder, but only at the cost of having a second wave that has completely lost surprise. Losses will be heavy given the shore based fighters."

Yamamoto regarded the map.

"What if we no longer planned to strike the Americans in Pearl Harbor?" Yamamoto asked, his eyes meeting Yamaguchi's.

There was a sharp intake of breath from one of the other conference participants. Yamaguchi kept his own face impassive even as he felt a current of shock course through him.

For Yamamoto to argue that we will no longer attempt surprise means that a great deal has changed in the talks with the Germans, Yamaguchi thought to himself. *I wonder what they have offered us in concessions to so change our war plan. No matter, I am a sword for the Emperor*.

"According to our consulate Admiral Jensen, the new American commander, has begun rotating capital vessels on a three, rather than six, day schedule. He has also directed all vessels will be prepared to steam within four hours notice," Yamamoto replied, his voice solemn. "For this reason, I believe it unlikely that we will catch most of the American fleet in harbor."

"It would be preferable to let the Americans come towards us in that case," Vice Admiral Kondo said stiffly. "We would be able to attrit them as they steamed towards the Marshalls."

Kondo-san is always one for caution, Yamaguchi thought.

"Rear Admiral Yamaguchi, do you think you can find the Americans at sea?" Yamamoto asked.

"Yes, sir, I can," Yamaguchi replied, his tone puzzled. "However, I would think Vice Admiral Nagumo..."

"Vice Admiral Nagumo will be remaining in Germany for the near future," Yamamoto replied, his tone pleasant despite having cut Yamaguchi off. "You are now in command of the *Kido Butai*, *Vice* Admiral Yamaguchi."

Yamaguchi felt a sense of shock as Vice Admiral Ugaki, Yamamoto's Chief of Staff, stood with an ornate box in his hand. Opening it, the Chief of Staff revealed a Vice Admiral's epaulettes as the gathered men began applauding.

"Sir, I am honored," Yamaguchi said, feeling his chest tighten as the shock wore off.

"You have earned it, Yamaguchi-san," Admiral Yamamoto replied formally. "I am sorry that our current exigencies have prevented us from having a formal ceremony. Nagumo-san indicated that you have always sought to conduct operations in the most aggressive manner with your division. When I asked him who should undertake this task if he were unavailable, you were his first choice."

Today is just full of surprises, Tamon thought to himself, feeling numb even as Kondo and Ugaki began to replace his epaulettes. Looking across the compartment, he saw that not everyone was as enthusiastic as the Combined Fleet's senior officers. Indeed, Rear Admiral Ryunosuke Kusaka, the *Kido Butai*'s chief of staff, looked as if he had just had a full lemon shoved into his mouth.

I may need to think about staff changes, Yamaguchi thought grimly. *Kusaka has always been far too cautious, and I am sure he has some belief that this job should be his*. He had no more time to consider things as the compartment's occupants came one by one to congratulate the Imperial Japanese Navy's newest Vice Admiral.

"Now, let us continue," Admiral Yamamoto said once everyone had shaken Yamaguchi's hand.

"With the six carriers reinforced by *Hiyo* and *Junyo*'s air groups, I will likely sink three battleships if I face them at sea..." Yamaguchi began.

"That is a very optimistic estimate," Kondo interrupted him. "This will be much different than attacking these same vessels in harbor!"

"I will launch over three hundred aircraft," Yamaguchi replied simply. "Since I no longer have to worry about attempting to destroy battleships with level attacks, all of my torpedo bombers will be available to attack."

"Yes, and they will likely cause grave *damage*. But to sink three battleships?" Kondo replied. Yamaguchi was about to respond when Admiral Yamamoto cleared his throat.

"Captain Sugiura, now would be as good a time as any to give your briefing," Admiral Yamamoto said, gesturing towards a tall, slender officer standing in the back of the room. Yamaguchi had never met the man, but was familiar with his work as one of the IJN's foremost torpedo experts. The officer bowed slightly towards Admiral Yamamoto, clearly nervous.

"Honored superiors," Sugiura began, his voice trembling "superior," "I was sent to Germany along with Vice Admiral Nagumo. As per the Treaty of Kent, the Royal Navy was forced to share technical data with the *Kriegsmarine*. One of the projects that the British was working on was a new explosive substance for their torpedoes which was far superior to anything either the Germans or our mission had seen."

There was the noise of chairs moving along the deck as most of the Japanese officers shifted. The IJN, as a force that expected to be outnumbered in any war it fought, had long believed itself the foremost experts in all aspects of torpedo warfare.

"The British called this experimental warhead material TORPEX in all of their documents," Sugiura continued. "Our navy has determined to call it *Sandaburo*, and it is roughly one and a half times as powerful as the compound we currently use."

"How soon can we begin producing this material?" Vice Admiral Kondo asked. "Can you fit it to our destroyer and cruiser torpedoes?"

"The explosive is complicated," Admiral Yamamoto answered for the junior officer. "In our initial experiments, we have discovered that if the production is not conducted with the proper materials the results are not favorable."

That explains why there have been several torpedo bomber crashes as of late, Yamaguchi thought to himself. *There had been rumors of possible sabotage or shoddy production.*

"The Ordnance Bureau, at Admiral Yamamoto's direction, have focused our production on aerial warheads until we were confident in our ability to produce safe weapons," Sugiura continued. "The loss of a torpedo bomber, while unfortunate, is nothing compared with damage to a cruiser or destroyer."

"How many warheads?" Yamaguchi asked.

"We expect to have three hundred and fifty aerial torpedo warheads available by March," Sugiura replied.

A collective gasp rippled across the compartment.

"Even with the new warheads, things will be extremely difficult for my operation," Yamaguchi stated. "Have the Germans given us a date they intend to attack?"

"March 26th," Yamamoto replied.

So we have a date for war, Yamaguchi thought. His stomach clenched like an angry man's fist as he turned to the map.

"The *Kido Butai* will be ready by then," Yamaguchi said tersely. "We will do our part to preserve the Empire."

Pearl Harbor
0600 Local (1100 Eastern)
9 November

Captain William Greenman, USN had a major problem. Tall, with narrow features, and aristocratic bearing, slightly graying brown hair, and dark brown eyes, the new Pacific Fleet G-2 had the sinking suspicion that his predecessor had been handed a blessing in disguise.

Whether Captain Layton was fired or simply reassigned, Fortune certainly gave him a golden ticket, Greenman thought, feeling acid starting to rise in his throat.

"What do you mean, the Japanese changed their code, Lieutenant Commander Crewe?" Greenman asked archly, looking at the lieutenant commander standing in front of him. The short, overweight officer gave him an unimpressed look that bordered on belligerency, and Greenman fought the urge to scream at the man.

I may have to see about getting Commander Rochefort back here, no matter what our new chief of staff's opinion of him was, Greenman thought angrily. *His replacement is an idiot.*

"Around 0100 hours there was a transmission that read 'a tiger slinks silently through the grass.' It was repeated three times, then next thing we know, we're looking at gibberish," Crewe said with a shrug. "There were a couple of out stations that asked for a repeat of the signal, but they were ignored."

Admiral Jensen is going to hit the fucking roof when I tell him this, Greenman thought, suddenly feeling as if his collar was two sizes too small. One of the reasons that Layton and Rochefort had been transferred was CINCPACFLT felt the two men were far too confident in their abilities. The lesson Greenman had taken from that experience was to add some shadow of doubt in his statements, but still rely on the information coming from the broken Japanese codes.

"Do we still have the ability to tell what operators are signaling?" Greenman asked. "I mean, if we have the same signal techniques, that's at least something."

"Still trying to determine that, sir," Crewe replied, running a hand through his thinning brown hair.

"I suggest you try *harder*, Lieutenant Commander," Greenman snapped. "Admiral Jensen has requested a briefing at 0900 on what the Japanese are up to now that they have Singapore and Burma."

Crewe looked as if he wanted to say something, then thought better of it.

I need to get in touch with ONI, Greenman thought. *Maybe the boys in Washington have some idea on what in the hell the Japanese are doing, as I certainly don't*. The captain glanced up at the clock.

"This is going to be an utter disaster," Greenman muttered to himself.

Five and a half hours later, there was concrete proof that Greenman at least understood his own navy's chain of command even if his window into the IJN's had just become opaque.

"Sir, we don't know why the Japanese changed their..." he began again, before once more being cut off by Admiral Jensen slamming his hand on the desk.

"It is readily apparent, *Captain*, that you would not know where your feet were if they weren't attached," CINCPACFLT said. The man's volume had barely raised above normal, but there was no doubt as to the intense anger the four-star admiral was feeling.

"Perhaps we should have General Short's intelligence officer come and brief us," Vice Admiral Bowles observed airily. "Even if it's wrong, it will be nice to have someone actually give us information and stand by it."

I have spent the last hour and a half giving you information, Greenman thought. *The fact you are more concerned with stabbing your son's squadron commanders in the back than reading the packets I give you...*

"Sir, I only give you the information I can verify," Greenman replied, a little heat coming into his voice. "It is a fact that the Japanese have moved three battleships and two light carriers south to Singapore. It is a fact that their air groups have begun flying shuttle missions between Formosa to Singapore and Vichy French bases in Indochina."

"So what does all that mean, Captain? A bunch of slant eyes burning fuel doesn't tell me anything about what the threats *here* may be," Jensen barked.

"Sir, it tells me that the Japanese are practicing reinforcing Singapore in preparation to seize the East Indies," Greenman stated, fighting to keep his voice calm. "They know President Roosevelt will reenact sanctions if they formally occupy Indochina again, so they are making sure pilots know the way from Taiwan to their new bases."

"So are you telling me that the Japanese are not going to try and strike here?" Admiral Jensen asked.

"Sir, with all due respect, I don't think *we* could sail all the way across the Pacific in one go and successfully strike a fleet at sea," Greenman replied evenly. "There is no reason to believe that the Japanese are able to do so."

"Layton and Rochefort believed that this 'First Air Fleet' was formed for just that reason," Vice Admiral Bowles retorted. "Are you saying that they were wrong?"

"Sir, everyone looks at data differently," Greenman said. "Captain Layton..."

"That was a yes or no question, Captain," Bowles interrupted.

"Yes, sir," Greenman bit out sharply. "I think that the First Air Fleet has been formed for strictly administrative purposes. Given what we know of the IJN's structure and customs, the placement of a junior admiral such as Yamaguchi in charge of it would be indicative of it being a minor command."

"Nagumo was in command of it before Yamaguchi, according to your packets," Bowles challenged.

Well maybe he did read what we put out, Greenman thought.

"Sir, Vice Admiral Nagumo was sent to Germany," he replied evenly. "I don't think admirals in good esteem are sent several thousand miles away from any available fleet."

Admiral Jensen's eyes narrowed at that, and Greenman remembered the man had been assigned to Great Lakes Training Command before his ascension to CINCPACFLT.

"Sir, the men are getting tired of our alert schedule," Vice Admiral Bowles noted. "I've also got Secretary Knox asking very pointed questions about our fuel and parts expenses."

"So in your opinion, Captain Greenman, are the Japanese going to attack soon?" Admiral Jensen asked directly.

"Sir, I don't think the Japanese will be attacking in the next sixty days," Greenman replied.

"Based on what?!" Bowles asked derisively. "Your crystal ball?!"

"No sir, based on the *calendar*," Greenman snapped back. "Japan is not going to go to war with us without Germany, and the Krauts aren't going to attack the Russians in November."

Admiral Jensen held up his hand before Bowles could respond.

"Vice Admiral Bowles, we will reduce our readiness for the next month," Jensen said. "Furthermore, we will send Pye's division and escorts back to the West Coast for refit, effective next week."

Greenman was sure the burning sensation he felt as Jensen's gaze swiveled back to him was all in his head.

"You had better be correct, Captain Greenman," Jensen said ominously. "A lot of men are going to die if you are not."

OTHER BOOKS BY JAMES

First in Series or Standalone Books

Usurper's War

Has Audiobook

Alternate History Collection

Available in ebook and print

Available in ebook, paperback and hardback

Cavalry Stories

Raconteur Press

Mecha Stories

Raconteur Press

Standalone

(Vergassy Universe)

Has Audiobook

The Spartan Trilogy

(Vergassy Universe)

Has Audiobook

Works Previously Published

in *To Slip the Surly Bonds* (2019)

by Chris Kennedy Press

"In Darkening Storms" by Rob Howell

"Friends in High Places" by Joelle Presby and Patrick Doyle

"Perchance to Dream" by Sarah Hoyt

"Red Tailed Tigers" by Justin Watson

"Zero Dark 30" by J.L. Curtis

"Per Ardua Ad Astra" by Jan Niemczyk

www.ingramcontent.com/pod-product-compliance
Lightning Source LLC
Chambersburg PA
CBHW072331020726
47503CB00012B/271

* 9 7 8 1 9 6 3 8 3 0 0 6 4 *